ALL BECAUSE OF YOU

ALL BECAUSE OF YOU

A NOVEL

LISSA LOVIK

This is a work of fiction. Names, characters, organizations, places, events, and incidents are either products of the author's imagination or are used fictitiously. Otherwise, any resemblance to actual persons, living or dead, is purely coincidental.

Text copyright © 2025 by Lissa Lovik
All rights reserved.

No part of this book may be reproduced, or stored in a retrieval system, or transmitted in any form or by any means, electronic, mechanical, photocopying, recording, or otherwise, without express written permission of the publisher.

Published by Thomas & Mercer, Seattle

www.apub.com

Amazon, the Amazon logo, and Thomas & Mercer are trademarks of Amazon.com, Inc., or its affiliates.

EU product safety contact:
Amazon Media EU S. à r.l.
38, avenue John F. Kennedy, L-1855 Luxembourg
amazonpublishing-gpsr@amazon.com

ISBN-13: 9781662530067 (paperback)
ISBN-13: 9781662530074 (digital)

Cover design by Caroline Teagle Johnson
Cover image: © GlobalP, © Reuben Demanuele / 500px, © Marcus Padovani / 500px / Getty

Printed in the United States of America

Deb, I'd never have finished this without your prodding.

1

I'm not particularly fond of grocery stores. Long lines, slow movers. People standing precisely in front of the item you need, forcing you to stand there and clear your throat, wait for them to get the hint. I *hate* grocery stores, so you can understand my surprise when I look up from the peanut butter I'm reaching for and feel my pants grow uncomfortably tight.

Her fingers are small and skinny, dwarfed by mine beneath the Jif logo. She's wearing a pink Spice Girls shirt, black leggings, combat boots with spikes jutting from the heel, and I think I'm in love.

Her dark-brown ponytail bounces as she looks up, startled, but she gives me a smile over the jar we're both holding. "Are you going to make me fight you for it?"

"I yield." I smile, looking down on her. I must be a foot taller, and I like it. Her eyes are blue, her skin is smooth, her lips the perfect balance between plump and Angelina Jolie, and the more I drink her in, the faster my heart pounds.

"What a gentleman." She dumps the jar into her cart. "Your mother did a good job on you."

I laugh and agree, but it wasn't my mother who did that. "Most people like smooth peanut butter," I say, even though most people are wrong. Crunchy is the only acceptable kind.

She cocks her head so the ponytail I want to touch swings over one shoulder. "Most people are wrong," she says, and I don't just *think*

I'm in love now. She bestows another smile on me, flashing wet, white teeth. "Thanks again."

She angles her cart around me, and I don't want her to leave, but it's hard to get too upset when the view from behind is this nice. I turn my back when she disappears into the next aisle, give her a few seconds' head start, and then follow.

I'm glad for the leggings. They mold against her, fit like a tattoo. The buckles on her boots clink with every quick step, and, Jesus, she moves fast. I hadn't expected such long strides on a girl that small.

She screeches to a stop. Her cart judders forward without her, but she snakes out a hand and tugs it back, her eyes on the Gatorade. So many options, and they seem to have stymied her. She consults her list, glances at the Gatorade, then back at the list as though it's telling her lies.

I'm watching, transfixed, from the end of the aisle as she slaps her phone to her ear.

"Hey, babe," she says, and my stomach sinks to my ankles. Babe. She's not single. "I'm at the store. Remind me what kind of Gatorade?" Her left foot twists back and forth on the tip of the combat boot, and her ponytail sways suggestively, like it's flirting with me.

She tilts her head back, squinting at the shelves. Fluorescent lights are generally unflattering, but the way they pour over her upturned face makes her look ethereal. Some Gatorade goddess sent to this Winn-Dixie to taunt me, when all I wanted to do was buy something for dinner.

"I don't think they've got that kind. What's your backup flavor?" Her eyebrows crash together. "You can cancel that shit right now, dude. I don't stock the fucking shelves."

Trouble in paradise. Good.

"What other color do you deign passable?" Her tone is heavy with sarcasm as she grabs the cart with both hands, her phone stuck between her shoulder and her ear. "Well, maybe you should do your own grocery shopping next time." Her nostrils flare. "I don't know. Walk. Take a bus, a bike. You have a bike, I bought you one three years ago, you just *had* to have it, but you only rode it like six times."

Maybe not a boyfriend? She's slight, with breasts that strain the *SPICE* emblazoned on her chest and a small waist above the curve of her hips. She doesn't look like she's gone through childbirth, and certainly not however many years ago it would take to make it acceptable to drop the f-bomb on a kid. I had her pegged for midtwenties.

She hangs up, shaking her head, slipping the phone back into her purse, muttering under her breath all the while. But she gets an assortment of Gatorade anyway, dumping the bottles unceremoniously into her cart.

I duck my head and pretend I'm having the same issue, deciding what kind of Gatorade will suffice, but she doesn't notice my plight. Keeps walking, her movements so quick they blur as she flashes around the corner, but something flutters to the ground as she disappears. Her grocery list. I consider handing it back for the excuse it would give me to talk to her again, but I don't. You can learn a lot through someone's grocery list, I'm guessing.

I pick it up as though it's some ancient relic and shove it into my pocket. I'll read it later. I don't have time now because I'd lose track of her.

In produce, she stands before a pyramid of apples that have been buffed to high shine. She plucks one up, palming it, and I don't think I've ever been jealous of an apple before.

The apple doesn't pass her muster. She replaces it, but it tumbles off the pyramid, bouncing onto the floor with the squishy sound of a nasty bruise. She's quick, crouches down to retrieve it, gives it an apologetic little pat and a whispered "Sorry!" as she returns it to its fellows.

I have no idea what else I came to the store for; I didn't make a list like she did, and she's driven all thoughts of Folgers and 2 percent milk from my mind. She stops again in the junk food aisle, lingering near the hard candy, but she's a good girl, says no, moves along. I wouldn't mind watching her suck on hard candy.

And she's off, walking as though a zombie horde is after her, steering her cart into lane two, the only checkout counter available at this early hour.

I let an old woman get in line between us, keeping my distance. I'm not creepy. Cross my heart.

"How's it going?" the checkout guy—an apt title; I can see his eyes darting all over her—asks.

"It's going," she says, singsong. I want to knock Granny out of the way and pay for this girl's order. "How are you?"

I hope she's only asking him that to be polite.

"Tired." It annoys me that he'd say that when the only appropriate response to such a question is "Fine."

I suspect he's ringing her up so slowly because he wants to prolong their exposure to one another. Can I blame him? I'd do the same thing.

"Have a nice day," he says as she heads out.

"You too," she calls over her shoulder.

What about my day? I want to shout after her. *Don't you want mine to be nice too?*

But she doesn't look back. Granny has three items and isn't sexy; Checkout Guy rings her up quickly.

"How's it going?" he asks when it's my turn.

I grunt out an "Okay," wait for my total, stuff my card into the machine. "Have a good day," he says, handing me my receipt.

I'm out the doors in a second, but she isn't in the parking lot, which is glowing beneath the freshly minted mid-October sun. Of course she isn't still there. The woman moves like a fire is chasing her. I sigh, pulling her list out of my pocket as I head to my car.

I smooth it out once I'm behind the wheel, and now I know her name.

◆ ◆ ◆

Serena. It's sibilant, sexy in all syllables. My tongue tickles the roof of my mouth when I frame the word, and if you could physically fuck a name, wouldn't that be the one?

She'd written her list out on the back of a packing receipt from Etsy that suggests she is Serena Archer of 12 River Street.

Serena, you forgot to buy your hair dye, and I had no idea you weren't a natural brunette. The color suits you, but I have a feeling you'd look good no matter what color your hair.

Even her writing is erotic, harsh and jagged, but someone else has added on to this list too. The writing isn't childlike, so her kid can't be too young. It's a boy, this child of hers, or at least it writes like it's male, and he'd tacked *Dr. Pepper* onto the list in blue pen, but she'd scratched it out in black. *Canned salmon?* she'd written. I didn't know salmon came in cans, that's disgusting. I'll forgive her this bout of poor taste.

How old can she be, with a kid whose penmanship looks like a high schooler's? Older than me? She doesn't look like it, and I saw her up close, her wrinkle-free skin and bright, clear eyes, her lips *kiss me* full when she shot me that smile that turned my heart in my chest.

Serena Archer is thirty-one, I find, when I look her up on TruePeopleSearch.com. Four years younger than me. The website lists her phone number and confirms her address, which is helpful, but what kinds of crazy people could use this information for nefarious purposes? This site should be illegal.

I pull up her Instagram on my phone, and good God, no, childbirth did not ruin her body. The picture doesn't look as though it was meant to be sexy, but it is. She's standing at a grill, a metal spatula in hand, wearing a pair of shorts and a bikini top, her phony brown hair loose around her shoulders. There's a boy in the frame, dark haired, long and lanky with the slightly sick look of a kid who has recently gone through a growth spurt. If that's her son, he's at least thirteen. You had him when you were eighteen, Serena, maybe that's why your flesh bounced right back to your prepregnancy body.

She doesn't wear a wedding ring; there's no guy tagged in any of her pictures—no men at all but for an older one I assume is her father, and her son. But then she doesn't seem overly concerned with Instagram. She's had this account for two years, but there are fewer than twenty pictures.

I download all the images and tap *Serena Archer Facebook* into Google. More than a dozen hits; none of them her. No Facebook page. I find that a little strange until I remember I don't have one either. I've never been interested in what people are having for dinner or how many awesome naps they've taken.

So I tab back to Google, searching just her name, scrolling through Serena Archers until I arrive at the right one. She's a real estate agent. You don't look like you're in real estate, Serena. I thought they all had blond bobs and names like Carrie. That sounds like an unsafe job, meeting strangers alone in empty houses. I can't help but imagine all sorts of horrible things that could befall a pretty girl at the mercy of some pervert in a vacant condo. A *Rape/Murder of Young Real Estate Agent* headline unfurls across my mind's eye as I scrape my keys into the ignition and start up my car.

Google Maps says 12 River Street is eleven minutes away.

2

Her house, what Realtors would deem a "Florida cottage," is in the middle of nowhere, no neighbors for miles, and I doubt it cracks a thousand square feet. It's got a huge yard, though, at least an acre, and the brush behind the fence surrounding her property is a decent spot from which to watch her sipping coffee on her back deck.

She pecks at a laptop one handed, taking another pull from her coffee mug, and then there's a rattling *hiss*, and a cloud of smoke rises into the air. She vapes. A device to quit smoking? I'm thinking yes.

When she stretches, her back curves like an archer's bow, her dark hair all over the place. I don't think I've ever seen something so sexy before in real life. It's almost painful to watch, like staring into the sun for long stretches.

I shudder, on the brink of convincing myself it's not perverted to masturbate here because it's not like it's public, when a hulking black mass rises out of the weeds in Serena's yard. It's breathing deep and slow, whatever it is, and its footfalls pad closer until I can make out a pair of yellow eyes and a set of teeth.

The dog doesn't look like a dog, it looks like a jet-black wolf, its only coloring from its jaw and irises. Even the lips rimming its fangs are black.

It's not growling, though, and in fact it seems to have ceased breathing completely as it sits before me. Probably because it wants to hear my movements and it wouldn't be able to over its own pants.

It calmly considers me with what I hope is friendly curiosity. When I inch backward, it springs up on all fours again, head bowed, gaze boring holes through the chain-link fence.

"Serious?" Serena shouts. Her deck is a soundstage, raised six feet off the ground, making her voice bright and loud. She's appeared at the railing, leaning over it, and I wish I could give her the attention she deserves, but I can't when this thing is looking at me like it would love nothing more than to pounce. It could steamroll right through that chain-link, which suddenly doesn't look so sturdy.

"Serious!" she yells again, and what in the fuck does that even mean? If that's the dog's name, it's fitting; this thing doesn't look like it's ever had fun in its life.

Serena's in the yard now, bare feet tramping through long grass. "Serious, get your ass over here." She stops ten feet away, her hands on her hips, and it's very hard to keep an eye on "Serious" and the gap between her thighs at the same time.

The dog gives me one last look, a parting blink, and grudgingly turns tail, heading back for its mistress, who stoops to give it a hug and me a look at her cleavage.

"What were you doing over there?" She squints in my direction. My pulse spikes, but she can't possibly see me. She can't. It's dark in here; the brush is covering me. "Did you find another dead thing?" She gives a delicate little shudder, which makes me want to wrap my arms around her, and kisses her dog on top of its massive blocky head.

"Mom?" someone yells from the distance, and I can't believe this creature is a mother. It's inconceivable, like imagining a stupid Stephen Hawking or a nice Kim Jong Un.

"Out here!" she calls back, slapping her thighs to get her dog to follow, but it sends me one more suspicious look over its undulating black shoulder before following her up the stairs to the deck.

The kid steps out to meet her. "I couldn't find the Pop-Tarts."

She brushes past him, the dog on her heels. "I'd be willing to bet they were right in front of your face."

He scowls.

"If the box is right out there in the open, I'm gonna make you mow the lawn."

I'd mow her lawn for free, no price tags, no bribes necessary.

"I hate mowing the lawn."

"And I hate this thing called *working*," she says, in that same singsong tone she used on Checkout Guy, "but unless you know some rich dude who wants to marry me, I have to suffer it all the same."

Well, I'm not exactly rich, but I'd definitely be willing to make that dream come true.

The kid follows her inside, shutting the sliding door with a little too much force, but I can still hear her voice floating through the screen.

"Found it," she crows, and I wish I could see her victory smile. "After school you've got a date with the lawn mower."

She pops back into view at her kitchen island, standing before a backdrop of light-gray paint on the walls and spotlighted like the angel she is by the ceiling lights. The dog rears on its hind legs, propping its front paws next to her hands, its head almost level with hers. This thing is massive, a fucking monster, 120 pounds, easy. I feel better for her safety, knowing she lives with this beast in the middle of nowhere.

She cracks a smile, looking down at it. "Too bad you can't make yourself useful—scrub the floors, bring in the mail." The smile suddenly vanishes as she tilts her head back to stare at the ceiling. "Keep stomping like that and I'll make you edge the lawn too!"

Headlights round the corner and into the circular driveway, and she twitches back the lace curtains on the side door.

"Dre's here!" she shouts at the ceiling again.

The kid swishes back into the kitchen and permits his mother to kiss his cheek, swiping the foil pouches of Pop-Tarts she holds out for him.

"One for you, one for Dre. Have a good practice, babe."

He grunts something inaudible before the side door slams shut.

"Well, at least you love me, huh?" she says to the dog, who sneezes in agreement.

She disappears for a while, and when she returns, she's in a green dress with fat pink rosebuds, carrying a pair of heels in her hand. I'm pretty sure I've seen the same dress on old ladies in my grandfather's home, but it's erotic on her, matronly camouflage.

Her hair is a mass of thick brown curls that she throws over her shoulder, her purse dangling from the inside of her elbow. She balances awkwardly, her hand on the kitchen island, working her right foot into a heel.

Do you have a house showing, Serena? This is the polar opposite of how you looked at the grocery store. I like the way your style flip-flops. It's exciting, leaves me breathless, wondering what you'll look like tomorrow.

She locks up, checking the windows (Good girl, I can tell someone watches *Dateline*), sliding the glass door over the screen, and says goodbye to the dog, who sits by the side door until it hears the engine of her Land Rover turn over.

I leave after she does, doubling back through the brush and into the woods behind her house, walking the half mile to my car.

"Today's not one of his best," a nurse in the facility my grandfather lives in says when she sees me signing the visitors' log that afternoon. "You might want to try again tomorrow."

"I'm already here." I shrug. And he's still my grandfather; I won't hold it against him if he throws his water jug at my head like he did last time.

She gives me a *suit yourself* look, and I follow her into his room. It's immediately evident that she hadn't been lying about his bad day. She'd been sugarcoating.

My grandfather is sitting atop his naked mattress, surrounded by a swathe of mussed sheets he's torn off the bed for reasons best known to himself. The elastic band on his underwear flaps loose, his white cotton candy hair stands on end, and he's glaring at the watercolor on the far wall as though it's just insulted his mother. His lunch sits on a bedside table, completely untouched, the pudding forming a flimsy skin.

I slide onto the bed, trying to catch his eye, but he doesn't stop glaring at the wall. "What's with the sheets?"

"They itch. Too much bleach. Do I know you?"

"For thirty-five years now," I say. "I can let the nurses know, maybe they can go easy on the detergent for you."

And it's like the light flips on in his brain. Even his eyes get clearer when he abruptly says, "Why are you here? Don't you have work?"

"Lunch break."

"Oh." He squints. "You look like shit."

I could say the same about him. At least I'm dressed. But I just laugh. "Thanks for noticing."

"Your mom might have been more tactful."

He means my grandmother, and yes, yes she would have. She'd always been the diplomatic one, her voice like a flatline, her expressions colorless.

"I miss her," he says, heaving a sigh.

Of course he misses her. They were never apart, not for longer than my grandfather's eight-hour workday. She'd never even leave the house without him, apart from the weekly grocery run. She made all his meals and listened to his stories and dedicated her entire life to him. I thought he'd throw himself into her casket at the funeral.

"Let me help you with those sheets."

I pull him to his feet, but his legs are like pale, hairy gelatin, white and wobbly. He steadies himself on my arm, and once I'm sure he won't keel over, I retrieve the sheets and get them back onto the bed.

"I wish you had someone like your grandmother," he says, watching me fight with the fitted sheet.

"You want me to find another grandma?"

"No," he snaps, like I'm being deliberately stupid. "Like someone your grandmother was for me."

"A wife?"

"I'd settle for a girlfriend. Unless you're gay. Are you gay?"

"I'm not gay, Dad." I help him under the covers, tuck the blankets beneath his chin. "I met someone this morning. In the grocery store."

"What's her name?"

"Serena."

"That's pretty." He groans, adjusting himself. "When are you going out with her?"

"I haven't actually asked her yet."

"You'd better get cracking." He coughs and hacks, turns away so he doesn't spray me with spit. "Something tells me I won't be around for long. I want to meet her before I croak."

"You're not going to croak," I lie, pouring him a glass of water, which he ignores.

He gives me the best deadpan look an eighty-nine-year-old man can muster. "This place is full of walking corpses. Doubt I'm any different."

My house feels thoroughly secondhand when I make it back. I suppose because it *is* secondhand. I moved back after my grandfather moved into the old-age home. I broke the lease on my apartment, packed up what little I owned. The place is horrible, but I know it well, having grown up here.

The same dusty art on the walls, lighter square patches on the paint where photos used to hang before my grandmother couldn't stand looking at them anymore and packed them away. Old mauve ceramic in the bathrooms, rust creeping into the grout. Chipped tile floors in the kitchen, switching abruptly to hardwood that long ago lost its luster. The living room is more like a living closet; I can't imagine how all four of us once fit in there.

Nothing's changed. But maybe it's time it did.

3

"Southern Realty," a voice chirps down the line, and is that you, Serena? It sounds like you, your singsong tone.

The old spine of my swivel chair lets out a deafening creak as I lean back. "Hi, I've been looking through listings online and was hoping to set up a viewing at one of your properties, 32 Camelia?"

"Sure," she says. "What time were you thinking? My availability is pretty open this afternoon."

I don't want afternoon, Serena. How exciting is it when the sun is at full roiling boil, humidity hanging thick, the heat turning the air into steam? Night is more romantic; it has an enchantment you can't find in daylight. It's got mystery and magic, flattering shadows and stars. If you ask a woman out to lunch, it isn't a date, not the way a dinner is.

"I'm working against a deadline right now, won't be able to call it quits until this evening. Is eight p.m. okay?"

She pauses. Wondering if I'm an axe murderer, probably, or some scary creep. "And it would only be you at the showing?"

"Just me, yes."

Another long pause. "Are you prequalified?"

Not yet, but give me thirty seconds. The side effect of having next to no life but a good job is that I have a lot of liquid assets and could potentially buy the house for cash, but that isn't what she wants to hear. She wants to know if I'm serious in my home-buying pursuits.

If I tell her I'm planning to pay cash, she won't have my information on any paperwork. I could give her any made-up name, and she'd never know the difference. I could get her in this empty house under the dark of night and kill her, and there wouldn't be any record of me.

I could do that in broad daylight, too, but I chose this house for a reason, Serena. It's in a busy, populated cul-de-sac. I want you to be comfortable.

"Of course."

"Would you mind emailing that information to me?"

"Absolutely. The second we hang up."

She's silent for a few seconds until a sigh crackles through the line. "I'm going to have to bring pepper spray, you know. Nunchucks. Maybe even a gun. I hope you don't have any evil designs, luring me into an empty house at night. I don't usually take such late appointments."

I feel a smile unfurl across my face. "Totally understandable. Bring your boyfriend, if it makes you feel better."

"Ha," she says, and what does that mean, Serena, are you not single? "All right, Mr.—I'm sorry, what was your name?"

"Chris. Fox."

"All right, Mr. Fox, I'll be there. With my nunchucks."

"I will be an absolute gentleman, I promise."

"I'll need to see that email beforehand: serena.archer@SouthernRealty.com. If I don't get it within the hour, I'll have to cancel."

"I'll make sure you get it."

"See you tonight, then."

She hangs up first, and I launch my bank's website on my desktop to fill out the prequalification forms. She doesn't take late appointments, but she broke her own rule for me. That has to mean something.

◆ ◆ ◆

It's 8:05, and my blood pumps hard, shunting through muscles. I can't remember ever being this nervous as I see the Land Rover swing into the driveway of 32 Camelia.

The dome light goes on over her head, and a leg slides out of her car, hovering over the brick drive, her hair hiding her face through the windshield.

The heel hits the ground, there's a *slam* as the light disappears and the steady *click-click-click* and the rustling of fabric as Serena walks closer. I slide out from behind the wheel of my Audi at the curb, hoping my voice won't crack. It feels like some mischievous cherub has drenched me in love potion, peppered me with arrows, hung me out to dry in front of this three-bedroom, two-story brick house.

"Chris?" she calls through the shadows in a voice made of rose petals and moonlight, that pretty dress whispering against her thighs in the breeze.

My movement up the drive sets off the motion-detecting lights above the garage, an accusing flood of white that makes us both flinch. "Hi. Thanks again for meeting me so late."

Her gaze is averted from the security light, one of her eyes clenched shut as she roots through her purse. "No problem."

Look at me, Serena. You know me, we've met, however briefly. I want to see the moment she recognizes me. "Looking for your pepper spray?"

She laughs, her face still buried in her purse as she heads for the front door. "You caught me. Let's get in there, this light is making me feel like a criminal." There's a jingling of keys, and after what feels like an eternity, the lock tumbles, and I follow her inside as she flicks on the lights.

Serena is a chameleon, can go from adorable to sexy in a heartbeat, and right now she's beautiful in a way that deeply disturbs me. She must not have been wearing makeup in the grocery store. She's wearing it now, and I'm finding it difficult to keep my heart in my chest. The whites of her eyes glow against her lightly tanned skin, and have her eyes gotten bigger and bluer in the fourteen hours it's been since I've seen her up close? Her lips are light pink, her eye makeup warm brown, and she's got six holes marching along the ridges of her ears but only wearing two diamond studs.

God must take requests or something; she is exactly what I've always wanted in a woman. She's holding my heart captive in floral.

She looks up into my eyes with her great big ice-blue ones and shuts the door. She recognizes me. I can see the wheels turning as *grocery store* clunks into place.

She points like she's picking me out of a lineup, her eyebrow arching as she presses a thick binder to her chest. "From the grocery store, right?"

I pretend to be just as surprised, and I do it very well. "Oh, wow, that's right."

"What a coincidence." Her gaze roams my face as she smiles, drinking me in. "Well, let's have a look around, okay?"

I agree. I think I'd agree with her on anything.

There's the merest suggestion of cleavage swelling beneath the neckline of that pale-green dress. It's hard not to look at it, but I don't want to henceforth be known as *that weird guy who wouldn't stop staring at my tits during a showing*.

"There's all new windows throughout the property," she says over her shoulder.

"Oh, great," I say, forcing myself to look at the windows when all I want to look at is her.

She knocks on the walls, a wry little smile playing across her lips. "Try not to get bogged down by the cosmetics. This color is awful, but the room would be gorgeous if it were painted in a . . . more toned-down palette."

"Burnt orange." I rock back on my heels. "Definitely not my first choice."

I love the laugh she gives me, and I love even more the hand she presses to my bicep. I feel myself flex automatically and promptly feel idiotic as she guides me toward the hallway.

"Brand-new crown molding." She walks backward into the kitchen, throwing the light switch. "All new appliances, and the granite countertops were installed about a year ago."

The granite is smooth and cold beneath my fingertips, white with gold flecks. "It's beautiful. I wish I had more time to cook, but it's mostly chicken wings in the oven or sandwich kind of stuff."

She crosses the room and turns on the gaudy chandelier above where I'm assuming a dinette set would go. "What do you do?"

"Software development. I work from home."

"Lucky," she says wistfully, turning to face me, the skirt of her dress swishing around her knees. "I'd love to work from home in my pajamas."

"That's definitely a perk."

Serena brushes past me, opens a cabinet. "These are five years old. They're self-closing, impossible to slam. I'd love some at my house—my fourteen-year-old has got to be the loudest kid on earth when he's digging around in the kitchen."

"You don't look old enough to have a teenager."

"I've heard that before." When she steps beneath the pool of light from the single fixture above our heads, I reach out a hand but stop myself from touching her just in time.

She blinks, confused, falls back a step.

"Sorry, you've got an eyelash on your cheek."

"Really?" She swipes blindly. "Did I get it?"

"Nope."

She tries again. "Still there?"

"Yep."

She blows out a sigh, tilting her cheek toward me. "Can you get it for me?"

So I do, and I hope my fingers don't tremble as I hold the eyelash out to show her. "I think you're supposed to make a wish now."

"I think it's your wish, actually." She gives me another smile, and I want to peel it off her face and carry it around in my pocket. "You found it."

I don't have to think hard about my wish. I wish she'd fall madly in love with me, right now, immediately.

"Let's go upstairs," she says, and it sounds so suggestive as she gestures for me to follow.

I smell her perfume and a whiff of deodorant as she lingers at the top of the staircase.

"The master's through here. It's oversized with a full bath. Brand-new tub with a backsplash." She turns on the light as she steps inside. "His and hers sinks."

I want to ask her to pick out which sink she wants, but I don't. We look good together, I think as I catch our reflections in the mirror. I put on my forest green button-down before heading over so we'd complement each other but not so much that it'd look matchy matchy, like those strange older couples who wear the same outfits on booze cruises. I should have shaved, but I was too keyed up to handle a razor. I hope she doesn't mind stubble.

I imagine if people saw us together, they'd think we looked like a good couple. She's slender, fragile, and I'm big enough to protect her. Broad shoulders, square(ish) jaw. Not overly muscled but not scrawny. My hair is a couple of shades lighter than the color she buys from a bottle. I have strange eyes, gifted to me by my father, apparently, which is why, on his bad days, my grandfather can't help but scowl at them. I'm no George Clooney, but I'm not ugly either.

She smiles at me in the mirror, and her glacial eyes have me thinking of those calm icy lakes in Norway. "It's nice, right? I could get used to this bathroom."

You can move in with me when I buy this place, Serena.

She's my tour guide throughout the rest of the top floor, and my heart sinks as she heads back for the staircase. "Do you want me to give you a minute alone so you can call your wife or girlfriend, talk it over?"

Are you asking me that to figure out if I'm single? "No, it's just me. No wife, no girlfriend."

"Oh," she says breezily, clacking down the stairs. "This is a lot of house for a single guy."

"Why waste money on rent?"

"True. Well, it's three hundred twenty-five thousand dollars, but you could probably beat the owner down a little bit—he's pretty anxious to sell." She pauses at the front door, juggling her purse and the binder.

"Here." I take the binder from her, freeing up one of her hands.

"Thanks." She smiles, looking up at me through her lashes and fishing a card out of her purse. "Here's my contact information. My cell number is on there, too, in case I don't answer my office line. I'm only part time."

I already know her cell number, but I thank her anyway and wait on the stoop while she locks the house up. "Thanks for coming out here so late. The place is great."

"Oh, it's my pleasure." She accepts the binder from me and holds out her hand. I'd rather kiss her, not shake her hand, but I do anyway. The security lights blast into life again as I follow her down to the drive.

"You didn't wind up needing your nunchucks," I say, a desperate bid to get her to linger.

She laughs, pausing by the hood of her car. "And I was so looking forward to using them."

"Do you want another opportunity? I should keep my options open and look at more properties, right?"

She takes a few backward steps to her driver's side door, and I'm not sure what to think, watching her back away but smile as though she wants to continue the conversation. "I might be able to make another exception. Call me."

"I will."

"Have a good night, Chris. I hope I hear from you soon," she says before she gets into her Land Rover and drives off with my heart in her passenger seat.

♦ ♦ ♦

I must drive faster than Serena because she isn't home by the time I get to her place. Someone else is there, a vision of a woman who looks Hispanic and at least ten years older than Serena, with a halo of wild, dark curls and with eyebrows that look perfectly sculpted by some ancient Greek artist. The dog knows her. It's lying beside her feet as she sits on the deck, pecking at her phone. The dog looked up, wary, when it heard me rustling around in the brush, but it seemed to assume I was some sort of scurrying small animal and hasn't come over to investigate. Yet.

One window has a vein of light worming around the edges. The pulsing quality makes me think it's a TV. The kid must be home. Is this woman his babysitter? Serena, I don't think a fourteen-year-old boy needs one of those.

A distant rumbling erupts from down the street. The dog is up in an instant. The woman opens the screen slider, and the dog rushes into the house, up on its hind legs, nose pressed against the window in time to see a set of headlights turning into the driveway. It knows when Mommy is home. That's sweet. I'd probably act the same if I lived with Serena.

"Hey, babe!" Serena shouts at the woman on the deck. "Sorry I'm late!"

Why is everyone *babe*? I want to be *babe* in the worst way.

"No problem, get in here!"

The dog doesn't bark or act like a fool, the way other dogs do when their owners come clattering through the door. It's perfectly silent, patient, lets Serena through without tripping her. She drops to one knee, nuzzles the dog's enormous face, and flings her jacket onto the kitchen table.

"Where are the boys?" Serena hangs her purse on the hook behind her, working her feet out of her heels. I'd rub those for you, Serena. You wouldn't even have to ask.

"Upstairs. My mother-in-law got Dre, like, fifty-nine new Switch games for his birthday. They've been at it for hours."

"Remind me to give Dre gas money. I forgot this morning, and then I felt like an ass." Serena pads out, barefoot, onto the deck.

"How'd it go?" The woman props one foot on the table next to a pitcher of something that looks toxic—neon pink with wheels of limes bobbing around. It screams *HANGOVER TOMORROW*. I'd shudder if I could do so without alerting the dog to my presence.

Serena pulls out her vape, takes a rattling drag, and emerges from the cloud of smoke to say, "It was fine, didn't take very long."

"Which house?"

Serena throws her hand out to the left. This must mean something to the woman, because she says, "Oh, on Camelia?"

"Yeah. What's this?" She prods the pitcher.

"Strawberry daiquiri."

"Oh God." Serena groans, sinking into a seat. "That shit screams *Hangover!*"

We're so in sync, Serena. It's kismet; our stars have aligned.

"So, Camelia? Think you'll finally unload it?"

She pours a fountain of daiquiri into a glass. "I don't know. Client seemed to like it well enough."

Client. That's me. It's incredible to hear her reference me, however peripherally.

"What kinda client? Old lady? Married couple?"

"Younger guy. Maybe my age. Ish. I didn't ask how old he was."

"What was he like?"

Serena takes a sip and almost chokes. "Oh God. How much strawberry syrup did you put in here, a gallon?"

Get back to the question, Serena. What was I like?

The friend waves a hand vaguely. "I don't know, a cup? So, your client?"

I like this woman.

"He was nice."

That's it?

"Was he hot?"

Even from here, I can feel Serena rolling those pretty blue eyes. "You're a nut, Rosa." She takes another sip, grimaces. "But . . ." I don't like that long pause. "Yeah. He was cute. Nice eyes. Brown, but one of them's green at the bottom."

I am thrilled to pieces that she examined me enough to notice. One quick glance wouldn't make anybody do a double take.

"Really? I always thought that was sexy."

"I hope he buys something—December will be here before I know it, and I'm sure Cole's got a list longer than my arm of shit he wants for Christmas." She puffs out a little sigh and looks down at her dog. "Serious get into anything that you noticed?"

Rosa leans over and pats the dog. "Nope. He's a good boy. Was a little too interested in something over there"—she swats her hand toward the spot where I'm hiding—"but I checked about an hour ago, and there wasn't anything around."

"He was doing that this morning too." Serena frowns at the brush swaying before me. "Maybe a rabbit's nest. I'll have to keep him away. I don't want him rooting out a bunch of poor little baby bunnies."

Something tells me my hiding spot won't be quite so hidden any longer, which is an unfortunate eventuality I planned for.

Just after 9 a.m. the next morning, I turn on my out-of-office autoresponder, grab my tools, and head over to Serena's place. The kid should be gone, and I'm hoping she will be, too, though a nagging doubt is still present—she'd told me her hours were only part time. This will be a risk, but one I'm willing to take.

But fate has smiled upon me once again. Her Land Rover is conspicuously absent.

I grab the tools, leave the engine running, and heave myself out of my car, then jog for her side door. The kitchen is my preference; she seems to spend most of her time at the table or on the deck, and this device can pick up sound within eight hundred square feet.

I've already decided where I'll drill the hole, just beneath the mint green vinyl siding right under the kitchen window.

The whir of the electric drill must be what draws the dog out, a colossal black specter lurking through the dark hallway. Through the window, I see him padding over the tile, his giant head bowed low, his yellow predator eyes locked on mine. And now he's so still he could be carved out of stone. No blinking, no panting, no nothing except staring raptly at me; it feels as though he's x-raying my soul, rooting it out, asking it what the fuck I think I'm doing back at his house uninvited and without permission.

There is something very strange about this dog. Why doesn't he bark, bound over to the glass, do the Lassie routine when he spies an unwelcome stranger in his midst?

I come in peace, I think loudly, practicing my telepathy. *You love your mother, and so do I, and by that reckoning, shouldn't that make us friends?*

I insert the device, cover the tiny hole with pale-green putty, and back away from the window. The dog advances, disappears briefly beneath the ledge, then pops up in the frame, his paws on the inside windowsill.

I'm glad dogs can't talk. I have a feeling this one would rat me out if he had a voice.

His eyes are simultaneously hollow and intelligent, blank with suspicion. *You don't know me yet, but you will,* I think. *You're a good boy, protecting your mother. Thank you for taking your job so seriously. Is that why she gave you such an odd name?*

He doesn't answer, so I wrestle with the tool case, snapping the plastic clasps together, and fling myself back into my car.

I wonder how long he stays at the window after I've hooked a left out onto the main road, the woods flashing past on either side then thinning gradually until I enter civilization. I fumble with my cell phone to pull up the device's app, and the only sound issuing from it is that of deep, slowly controlled breathing, as though he's still watching, waiting, wondering.

◆ ◆ ◆

The walls of my mother's old bedroom, now my home office, press in around me like a cave as I set up the admin for the mic on my laptop. I crack open a window, let it gasp in the humidity, the sun straining through the grime on the glass.

She'd been in here when she chose to die, I'm pretty sure. The decision must have been made within these walls. I can't imagine it was a spur-of-the-moment thing. *Right here,* I think, propping my feet on the desk. *Right here is where she decided I wasn't worth sticking around for.* I'm not sure if I've made my camp in here to be close to her or to spite her.

Jasper yawns as he stretches, claws extending like knives, and minces over from his perch on the far corner of my desk. He used to be solid black. Now he's silver at the edges. The weak light makes him glitter.

His paws cleave clean prints in the layer of dust on the desk, and he leaps into my lap. I kiss his furry head, stroke his cheeks the way he likes, feeling like a villain in my lair, petting my cat, except that I'm not. A villain, I mean. I love her.

4

Who the hell *is* this guy, Serena, and why is he in your house when you're not?

He's speaking to Cole as though they're old friends. I haven't heard the dog ripping out any throats, so I'm assuming this man is a regular fixture, and I'm trying very hard not to feel hoodwinked. I've ruled out the man who looks like her father from Instagram; this guy sounds much younger, and Cole hasn't called him any variation of *grandpa*. I suppose he could be Cole's father, but I'm not sure that's the impression I'm getting.

"Wow," this nameless intruder proclaims, slamming something as he barges into Serena's kitchen. "Your mom needs to go to the store."

"She went yesterday," Cole answers dryly. "She hardly buys anything edible."

"What the fuck is this?" There's a small pop and a gasp. "That's the most rancid thing I've ever smelled in my life."

Cole laughs, and those must be his footsteps thudding around. "She babies Serious. She makes his dog food herself."

"With what, roadkill?"

"Canned salmon and stuff like that. She thinks normal kibble is full of too many fillers or something."

There's the screech of a chair, then another.

"How was your game, kid?"

"I got a few minutes of playtime. More than at the last game, but still not much."

"Second string on varsity is still a win for a fourteen-year-old. Hell, I doubt I could have made it into a peewee league when I was your age."

"Do alternative high schools even *have* football teams?" Cole asks slyly.

The guy makes one of those drumstick-meets-cymbal sounds. What are they called? Rim shots? "Wow, cheap shot. I'm gonna tell your mom you were shitting on our alma mater."

You had to go to alternative high school, Serena? Why? Because you got knocked up so young? I bet your parents weren't happy with you, poor thing.

So this is some degenerate you met at a school for troubled youths? I doubt that's the best place to make friends, and do people make it a habit of strolling in and out of your house on their whims?

"How is she?" he asks. "We keep playing phone tag, constantly seem to miss each other. I always have to leave town when she gets a free night."

"She's fine, I guess."

"That's a ringing endorsement if I've ever heard one." He groans. Another screech of a chair. "I should get going, kid. I've got a rehearsal. Tell your mom I said she's it."

"She's it?"

"She's it in our phone tag game. Serious!" he bellows. "Come say bye to me! No? God, he's prissy sometimes, isn't he?"

"Mom says he's just very *selective*."

"Right. She's a spin doctor. I'll see ya later, bud."

"Thanks for the ride," Cole calls.

And then there's silence but for faint breathing, and I slam my laptop shut, eyeing the time on my phone. If she's not home, the most obvious place she'd be is work.

◆ ◆ ◆

And there it is, the white Land Rover, parked in front of her real estate office. It's humid as hell, all of Florida swimming in what feels like muggy shower fog, the sky heavy with bloated gray clouds, and I wonder what she's wearing today to combat the heat. Probably not the miniskirt I'm hoping for.

I don't have to wonder for long. The second I open the door, a swivel chair coasts into view from behind a desk. Do you smile this widely for just anybody, Serena?

I can actually breathe in here. This light and airy place is the opposite of my home office / dead mother's bedroom, sun drenched, with a sprawl of white birch floors blotched here and there with shaggy gray rugs.

"Hi, Chris," she says as she stands, closing the distance between us. She looks almost bridal in a short white dress with loose, lacy sleeves, and the frilly hemline ruffles provocatively around her thighs. I like how feminine she is. Florals, frills, finesse. "How are you?"

Better now that I'm next to her. "Great, you?"

"Well, I could do without this humidity, to be honest." She bites into her bottom lip, her eyes flickering between both of mine. "What can I do for you?"

"I finished up work early today and was hoping you were free for more viewings."

"Of course." She crooks a finger and heads back for her desk. "Come sit, you can look through the listings and tell me which ones you want to visit."

She hands me a binder. A little thrill goes through me when our fingers brush together, but I pretend I can't feel the electricity sizzling in the air all around us and open the binder at random.

I act like I'm mulling it over, flipping a few pages. "What do you think about this one?"

She creeps closer in her swivel chair, inclining her head so her hair tumbles off her shoulder, puddling on the pages. I catch a hint of something floral woven through the dark strands before she flips it over her back.

"That's a very nice place." She taps the photograph with a shiny nail. "But I ought to warn you that the backyard is like a postage stamp. Do you have a dog? I doubt a dog would be happy with a plot that small."

"No dog. I wish. Have you got one?"

"Yeah." She cracks a crooked little smile. "And don't ask me about him unless you want to sit through a slideshow of a thousand pictures."

"I've got time."

She stares at me for a moment as if she's waiting for the punch line, then pulls out her phone, taps in her code, and scrolls through her photos. "From this morning. He was pouting because I didn't have time for tug-of-war, but I just had to take a picture of that scowl on his face."

I cannot imagine her dog playing tug-of-war. He looks to be far above such buffoonery.

"What's his name?" I ask, innocently curious.

"Serious."

I raise my eyebrows. "As in the Joker? 'Why so serious?'"

"No, S-i-r-i-u-s. Sirius."

"Is that a . . . family name or something?"

"No, more like a *Harry Potter* thing. Sirius Black. He's an Animagus, a guy who can turn into a big black dog at will, he's Harry's godfather . . . and now I feel like the biggest nerd on the planet . . ." She trails off, actually blushing, color creeping up the delicate skin on her lovely throat, staining it pink. I love her. I love that blush and that dress and the way her throat bobs when she swallows hard. "Anyway. How about you make a note of the houses you want to walk through? I'll let my boss know I'll be out of the office with you."

I want her to wear that dress in the event of our wedding, I think, watching her slide through the cracked door of an office at the back, the *click-click-click* of her princess-pink heels tap-dancing on my newly reanimated heart.

Serena wants me to think deep, long, and hard about the houses she's shown me. It's a big decision, buying a house, probably the biggest decision of my life, in case I didn't know.

She's sitting beside me at a rickety card table in the dining room of the final house (a truly terrible McMansion monstrosity that's been foreclosed on and is on the market for half price), spreading out all the brochures from properties she's shown me.

"What's your gut telling you?" A tiny wrinkle crops up between her eyebrows as she cups her chin in her dainty little hand. "I feel like the one you really liked best is Camelia."

"It was. Hands down." She loved that master bathroom, she said. I could get used to seeing her soaking in that big tub.

"Sounds like you've got your answer then, huh?"

I look at her, and she looks at me, her small smile slowly widening into a chasm, and I find myself pushing the brochures away, twisting my chair so I'm gazing at her head-on.

"I actually wanted to ask you something."

"Yeah?"

"Would you want to have dinner with me sometime?"

She's suddenly shy, and I can tell she's only shuffling those brochures to keep her hands occupied; she's just pretending to read them. She wants to look businesslike to mask her nerves. I seem to have caught her hideously off guard.

Oh God, she's going to say no.

"Like a date?"

"Exactly like a date."

She very carefully pushes the brochures to the side, folding her hands in her lap. She won't look up at me when she says, in a would-be casual voice that fools neither of us, "I don't know if I've ever been on a real date."

"I find that extremely hard to believe."

"Well, a date as in some guy picks me up, takes me somewhere to eat for an hour, and then drives me back home."

So what exactly does that mean she's done on all her quasi dates before? I don't think I want to know. I just hope they didn't involve hotel rooms or parking the car on some far-flung, lonely side road.

"Well, I'd hope it would be for longer than an hour, but that's basically what I'm asking."

She presses her plump lips together and stares at her hands as if she's never seen such things before. My intestines seem to have turned into writhing snakes as she stares at everything else in the room but me. "What night were you thinking?"

Any night, any time, so long as it's soon.

My throat loosens with relief. "Whenever works best for you."

She tries on a smile, size extra small. "Is Wednesday night okay?"

"Wednesday night is perfect." Any night would be perfect. I'll make it perfect if it kills me.

"So, where did you have in mind?"

"I'll think about it and get back to you. I've got your cell phone number."

"Okay. I'll give you my address once you've figured the rest out." She stands, twisting her tiny Cinderella foot back into the heels she discarded a half hour before. "Chris?"

"Yeah?"

"You didn't . . . you didn't have me take you on all these showings today just to ask me out, right? Am I being a narcissist?"

"No. And you're not a narcissist. Has that happened before?"

"No."

"That's surprising."

She makes a face and tells me to shut up.

But I need to make her believe me, so I tell the best story of all—the truth. "I'm currently living in the house I grew up in. My grandfather moved into a facility a few months back. It's just me, an elderly cat, and all those bad memories."

"I'm so sorry, that's terrible. Now I feel like an asshole. That was stupid of me." *You're beautiful, Serena, and I think your heart is just as lovely as the rest of you.*

It's not stupid, it's wily. I hope she keeps that suspicious mind. Just not when it comes to me.

5

Night presses against my black window, flexing its muscles, wanting in. A hot wind growls, its breath steaming up the glass. My swivel chair creaks like an old floorboard when I recline in front of my laptop.

I want out of this place and into 32 Camelia. Dark night, dark walls, ghosts haunting the hallways. My mother lived and grew and died here, and I think most of my grandmother died with her. How do you get over that kind of thing, the loss of a child? I wouldn't know, and I guess she didn't either.

This house is decomposing, and it's caught me in its death grip. I wonder, as I tune in to Serena's kitchen, if she'll give me a few rescue breaths, bring me back to life.

She's not making any excited, girlish phone calls, gushing about our date. All I hear is typing, but I know it's her, not Cole, because every so often she speaks softly to Sirius—nonsensical sweet nothings and occasionally a sharp "Ugh, no licking."

I sit at my desk, my face in my hands, wishing something will finally happen when three hard raps reverberate through the speaker on my laptop.

"Hey," Serena says. "Just stick it all on the counter. How's it going?"

"Marlon's an idiot," the woman I assume is Rosa announces. "I asked him for *butter*, not I Can't Believe It's Not Butter! or this stupid-ass vegetable oil spread. I had to go to the store again to get the right shit."

Serena laughs sympathetically. She's such a good friend. "Men aren't much for details, I guess."

I like details. I remember every detail from every moment I've spent around you, Serena, and I would have bought the right stuff the first time, no problem.

"We should probably let it soften for a while, right?"

"It doesn't need to be room temperature, but we've got time before we have to get started. Want a drink?"

"Mojitos? You make the best mojitos."

"Can you see if I've got white rum?"

Cabinets bang, and then there's Rosa's triumphant whooping. "Found it."

"Grab some mint from the deck? I've got limes in the fridge."

There's chopping, the rapid-fire kind you hear on the Food Network when Bobby Flay's impressing the audience. Confident, precise, no hesitation or stilted bangs.

"How'd Cole get home? Dre needed to get that cavity filled—he's been complaining for months but refused to see a dentist until I had to put my foot down."

"He told me Derek picked him up."

Derek. I make a mental note to research him later, to find all the Dereks following Serena on Instagram.

"Has he moved back for good, then?"

"Yeah, but he's turning right back around and leaving for a few days. He has a show coming up in Nashville." The unmistakable sound of clinking ice rockets through Serena's kitchen, and both women start laughing.

"He always does that when I bust out the shaker," Serena says. "It's so cute when they cock their heads."

Frankly, I'm surprised that Sirius does anything even remotely doglike, that he's not the quiet, malevolent creature I've been vaguely introduced to.

"So I have some news," Serena says, and I sit up straighter at my desk, every pressure point in my body thrumming.

"Yeah?"

"Camelia Guy asked me out."

Camelia Guy is what I've been reduced to?

"No way. For real?"

"I know, I was surprised too."

"Well, what's so surprising about it?"

"I don't know. Nobody's asked me out in years."

"If you went out more, there'd be plenty of men hitting on you. What about that bartender over at Jack's?"

"Uh, that's a hard no on the bartender. I hate goatees." There's a moment of silence, until she adds as an afterthought, "Except maybe on Duff Goldman."

Who the fuck is that?

"The *Kids Baking Championship* guy?"

I type his name into Google and am utterly gobsmacked at what I find. *This* is her type?

"Yeah. I've always thought he was kinda hot."

Rosa laughs, full and throaty. "You're on crack. So what did you say?"

"What?"

"To Camelia Guy."

"I said yes."

Rosa's squeal makes me smile. "So you like him, you think it'll turn into something? Or just be a one-off type thing to get yourself back out there?"

Good God, is that a thing?

"I wouldn't have said yes if I didn't like him, what would be the point?" she says, and my panic drains away.

Rosa snorts. "I went out with people who didn't have a chance in hell just to get out of the house back when I was in my twenties."

"It's going to be so awkward," Serena says in dismay. "I'm not good at dating. I get nervous and always wind up saying something stupid.

I don't even know why he asked in the first place, he looks like he's got his shit together."

"Probably thinks you're hot."

She's not something as trivial as what the word *hot* implies. She's perfect.

"Maybe. I'm such a mess, it seems insane someone would want to be a part of that."

"You're not a mess."

Serena makes one of those derisive coughing noises. "I'm thirty-one with a fourteen-year-old boy who's gotten a pretty smart mouth recently. I'm not exactly a smashing success at my job. My house is nine hundred and fifty square feet. I haven't had sex in . . . what, eight years?"

Jesus. I'd love to help her break that dry spell.

"All teenagers have smart mouths—half the time I don't know if I want to hug Dre or kill him. And you just started in real estate, it'll take time. You love this house. And you can do the sex thing on your own for the most part, right?"

Serena laughs. "Yeah, basically."

God. The image of her masturbating is too much for me to handle. It makes me start throbbing again, little white stars crackling in my peripherals.

"You know where he's taking you?"

"No, I don't think he's decided yet."

"I hope it's not some overly fancy restaurant," Rosa says. "That puts a lot of pressure on the first date."

"I know, I'd die of embarrassment if he showed up with roses and had us go to some overpriced French place."

Duly noted. I don't want you dying on me, Serena.

"So you don't know what you want to wear yet? Please no floral, you don't want to look matronly."

"I like floral," she says, stung.

"Yeah, I'm aware. It doesn't exactly scream *sexy*. It's only ever my old-lady clients who want flowers on their couches or stenciled on their walls."

I think floral is sexy on you. Wear floral if you want, Serena. Don't listen to her.

"I'll keep that in mind."

"What's Cole think about it?"

"I haven't told him yet. I don't know how he'll take it."

"You think he'll be upset?"

"I don't know that either," Serena says after a pregnant pause. "I guess I'll find out soon enough." She sighs. "Shall we let the baking commence?"

I close my laptop when the speaker explodes with clattering dishes and the revving of the electric mixer, my thoughts not on Serena for once, but on Cole. Surely he wouldn't be too angry about his mother going on a date after eight years of celibacy. What reason would he have to be upset?

Derek Gallagher has black hair, blue eyes, pale skin, I find out later from Instagram. He's thirty-two, the lead guitarist in some modestly well-known local rock band, so I assume he has plenty of women to choose from. Why Serena?

She's in some pictures on his timeline, though she hadn't been tagged, which is why I hadn't known anything about their connection. The pictures had been uploaded long before Serena had made her own account.

There's a candid one captioned *North Florida Music Festival*; they're sitting in a grassy field, her head on his shoulder, and he's looking down at her, leaning back on his palms. The intimacy worries me slightly; he looks about three seconds away from kissing her. There's one of her from behind; she's in cutoffs and a T-shirt, her hand shielding the bloody setting sun from her eyes as a football practice rages out on a field. *Cole's first practice! Time flies*, it's been labeled.

Another picture—and this one makes my blood turn arctic—scares the shit out of me. She's wearing a *just get on with it, take the fucking picture* kind of look and sitting on top of what is clearly a hospital bed, bandages wrapped thickly around her forearm, purple patches of bruising ruining the exquisite skin on her throat, and Sirius is lying across her legs. He looks slightly smaller and younger, and the date this photo was shared is three years ago. *Don't fuck with his mommy*, Derek, clever soul that he is, had captioned it.

Jesus Christ, that's a story I'll have to persuade her to tell me. That dog is her hero; no wonder she feeds him salmon. What's the other guy look like? Serena walked away with a necklace of bruises and a gashed arm, Sirius looks unharmed in the image . . . did this person even walk away, or did he leave in a body bag?

I sit back in my swivel chair, wondering what to make of Derek. It doesn't look as though there's been any prior relationship between them, but come on, he had to have wanted more. What man wouldn't? Men and women can't be just friends. One party always winds up wanting more.

But I don't have time to wonder for too long. My grandfather's expecting me to meet him for a subpar dinner of meat loaf and mashed potatoes made from a packet over at his old folks' home.

◆ ◆ ◆

The first thing my grandfather says when I walk through his door is "What are you doing here?"

Nancy, the night nurse, gives me a *happens all the time* look and an apologetic smile as she shuts the door behind herself.

"You asked me to come."

He looks even battier than normal, like he's styled his hair with an eggbeater. "Don't you have school?"

"I haven't been in school for over ten years," I say, trying not to sigh too loudly.

He squints like I'm trying to pull one over on him. "Are you sure?"

"I'm positive." I drag the visitor's chair over to the bed, then sit, balancing the tray I'd gotten from the cafeteria on my knees. "How was your day?"

"Same shit as usual. All sorts of PMS going on with the nurses. Someone died this morning. I don't know who, but the medics made a hell of a racket." He spoons gluey mashed potatoes into his mouth, and I don't know how on earth he can make that much noise eating something that doesn't need any chewing. "How was yours?"

I fiddle with the mashed potatoes on my own plate. The gravy's collected into a murky well in the center, and I think I'd rather eat a possum, to be honest. "I asked Serena out. Do you remember I told you about her?"

"Good," he says gruffly. "That's good. Want some advice?"

Not even a little. But I say, "Yeah, sure," because he's an old man with little to live for and he loves to advise.

"Don't take her anywhere casual. First dates are for pulling out the big guns. All romance and flowers."

That's the exact opposite of what I heard Serena say earlier. I still haven't decided where I'll take her. Her Instagram isn't exactly a treasure trove of inspiration.

"Did I ever tell you about my first date with your grandmother?"

"No," I say, even though he has, repeatedly, throughout my whole life. I know that story by heart, front to back; it almost feels as if I were there too.

"I had to ask her father first," he says, this time through a mouthful of soggy meat loaf. *Because that's how it was back then*, I say silently, filling in the gaps. "Because that's how it was back then."

I try to look interested during what's got to be my millionth time hearing this story. "Oh yeah?"

"Oh yeah. I brought her a dozen red roses. It took her a while to find a vase, arrange them just right. You should have seen her smile." It looks like he's seeing her smile right now, the way he gazes off into space, somewhere far from this old-age home that smells like mashed carrots and antiseptic. "I took her to the most expensive Italian restaurant in town, cost me fifteen dollars. Not a lot of money to you, but back then it was an awful lot."

"I bet."

"She ordered a salad. So demure. I could tell she wanted some spaghetti, though, so I insisted she eat some of mine. She got sauce on her cheek, I had to help her wipe it off."

And then she blushed with embarrassment. "Spaghetti's messy."

"You should have seen the blush, looked like her head was a teapot. I thought steam would pour out of her ears any second."

I give him a weak laugh, which I know he's expecting before he barrels on.

"Brought her home at nine thirty on the dot. That's what time her father wanted her back." He focuses on me again with what seems like a lot of effort, blinking so rapidly his sparse lashes blur. "Make sure you bring her flowers, okay? Serena probably deserves them. Nice flowers. Roses. Not carnations."

Not a chance, I think.

"You should order for her at the restaurant, make her feel ladylike. Make sure it's a nice restaurant, not a Joe's Crab Shack or something. You don't want her to think you're a cheapskate."

Ordering for her would likely turn our first date into our last date, but I thank my grandfather for his wise counsel.

"Don't talk about yourself too much."

"There's nothing interesting to say about myself anyway."

"And don't use your phone. I know you kids are glued to those things, but put it away, for once."

"I'd worked that much out on my own, actually."

"When are you taking her out?"

"Wednesday."

He sighs, long and loud, like I've made some crucial mistake from which I can never return. "A date isn't a date if it's not on a Saturday night."

I shrug and stick my tray on his bedside table, tired of pretending to eat. "Maybe in 1930."

"And don't swear. Women don't like that. Good way to leave a bad taste in their mouth."

Serena swears just as much as—if not more than—I do, so I think it's safe to disregard this as well.

"You always have to pick up the bill too. You can't have a woman pay for your dinner."

"That's what I'd planned."

"Oh." He stabs his fork in my direction, bits of mashed potato falling onto his blankets. "Don't kiss her good night, it's not gentlemanly. I think I'd have scared your mom off if I kissed her on our first date."

"Don't worry, I won't," I lie, patting his knee.

I have time to kill before my 8 a.m. conference call with product management and the design team the next morning, so I indulge in my latest hobby. Serena may be long gone by now, headed to work, but I back up the recordings until just after six.

There's nothing interesting for a while, well over an hour with just her rhythmic typing, her talking to Sirius. Then footsteps pound into the kitchen, and that must be Cole's good morning grunt.

"Hi, babe," she says. "I wanted to talk to you before you head out."

"What?" he says suspiciously. "I didn't do anything."

"Can you sit?"

"Mom, I gotta get ready, I didn't know I'd have to listen to a sermon before I even took a shower—"

Her voice snaps taut. "I asked you nicely. Sit."

And he must, because there's an almighty thud.

"I wanted to let you know that someone's asked me out, and I'm going on a date tonight—"

"Gross."

"Thanks a lot."

"Who is it?"

"Nobody you know."

"But like, what's his name?"

"Chris."

"Chris what?"

"Fox. Chris Fox. He's a client."

"And you think it's smart to go out with a client? Your boss is gonna think you're a—"

"You'd better watch your mouth if you like it the shape it is, Cole."

"I'm just saying, you don't even know the dude."

"That's the point of dating. To get to know *the dude*."

Cole mumbles something inaudible.

"You want to say that again, louder for the slow ones in back?" Serena snaps. I wonder what she looks like when she's mad. Probably sexy.

"Dating didn't work out too well for you last time," he says slowly, deliberately.

Which is followed by a rather tense silence. I'm imagining epic stare-offs and glares. I never had balls like that when I was fourteen.

"I don't know if you've realized this, kid, but I'm your mother. I've got the fucking C-section scar to prove it, and all things considered, I think I've done a pretty okay job at being your mom, regardless of getting knocked up in high school. You have all your limbs. Ten fingers, ten toes. You've never been seriously injured or homeless or beaten, though your mouth lately has been making me rethink that last one. You have friends, you do okay in school, you're on the football team—you seem pretty well adjusted, if I do say so myself. And I raised you without any input from *you*, or anyone else, for that matter. I was willing to listen to your thoughts, but now I feel more like taking your phone for the next few days."

"You can't take my phone, how am I gonna contact Dre for rides and about practice—"

"The next time I hear you say anything even *slightly* rude, that iPhone's going in the safe." She blows out a long sigh. "Go get ready for school."

And with footsteps quite a bit heavier than seems necessary, he does.

"Well that went fucking gloriously," Serena mutters darkly to herself, but I think I know how to cheer her up.

$325,000 for Camelia? I text at 7:59, and I can tell the exact second she gets my message by the sharp intake of breath I hear through the mic.

Oh my God, Chris, she answers. Full price?

The promise of a fat commission check should lighten her mood.

I know what I want, I peck out one handed, sweeping Jasper into my arm for a celebratory hug. And I don't like to haggle.

6

I'd been planning to walk to Serena's front door, but she asked me to text her when I arrived, so I open our message thread as I pull up to her house.

Just got here, I say, the pumping of my heart feeling like a drumroll until I see the side door crack open. I drop my gaze to my lap and pretend to be busy on my phone. I don't want to gawk at her as she walks down her long driveway; *creepy* is not the look I want to wear tonight.

When she's five feet away, I pretend to have just noticed her presence and hit the unlock button.

"Hey." She arranges her purse on her lap as she climbs in. "Did you find it okay?"

The standard first line of any conversation with someone whom you don't know very well. We'll get past these awkward first encounters, Serena, don't worry.

She's wearing a strapless white blouse, a short denim skirt, and, I note, smiling slightly, a pair of floral sandals.

"Yeah, it was no trouble. You look beautiful."

"Thanks," she says, a faint blush on her cheeks, and I can almost taste her stress as she shifts in the passenger seat, fumbling with the seat belt. The slight scent of vodka lingers on her tongue. She wasn't kidding about dates making her nervous; she must have taken a shot before coming out to greet me. I like that I'm capable of inspiring nervousness. It means she likes me.

"You must hate neighbors," I offer, shifting the gear into drive and pulling away from her front lawn. "Living out in the middle of nowhere."

"Yeah, that's partly the reason. I liked the neighbors on the street of the house I rented before I bought this one, but I would have liked them a whole lot better if they lived at least a half mile away. And Sirius needs a big yard to romp around. He isn't really a *neighborhood* dog."

What the hell does that mean?

I nod, hooking a left out of the winding dirt paths and onto the main road. "What breed is he? I wondered when you showed me his picture, but I forgot to ask."

"He's a mix."

Why so reticent? "A mix of what?"

"He's mostly gray wolf with a mix of other arctic breeds. I don't usually tell people that right off the bat. I don't want them to judge him. He's a good boy. Just . . . very shy."

Shy would not be the word I'd use. *Terrifying*, that would fit. "Shy?"

"Maybe *wary of strangers* is more accurate."

That sounds ominous.

"He'd never attack anyone without cause," Serena says, seeing the look on my face. "I worked with him the minute I brought him home as a baby, hired a trainer with an outrageous hourly price tag. He needed a firm hand in the beginning, but he learned quickly—he's really smart. He's only territorial when people he doesn't know are inside the house. So long as he's properly introduced to someone, he's fine."

"Did you want him to be a guard dog?"

"No. I found him when I was up in Tennessee for a show my friend had about four years ago. It was a pretty bad breeding situation—most of the puppies died—but I couldn't leave Sirius there. He was the last man standing."

"So he's never had to defend his mistress?" I say lightheartedly, testing the waters. Will you lie to me, Serena? Sugarcoat the truth?

"Once." She looks at me sideways. "There was a robber in my old house. We'd surprised him. I'd just got back from a walk with Sirius when he was about a year old. The guy was hiding in the closet, I guess, burst out when I went into my bedroom. Sirius heard me shriek when the asshole grabbed me. I was fine, just bumps and bruises. Sirius tore off a huge chunk on his leg to get him to let me go. He was going for his throat by the time I caught my breath and called him off." She looks like she's puzzling over whether she wants to smile or frown. "He would have killed him if I'd let him."

"Christ. Make sure you introduce me properly if I ever meet him."

She laughs as I angle the car into the parking lot of the restaurant. "There really isn't anything to worry about. He just looks scary." She blinks up at the sign on the restaurant's doors, her eyebrows contracting. She wasn't even paying attention to where we were headed, she was so engrossed in our conversation. "This is one of my favorite places—how did you know?"

"Is it?" I say idly, unbuckling myself.

Serena may not be overly active on Instagram, but @TheRosaRobbins is. It only took a few minutes of poking around to figure out that Jack's is the place they frequent most often.

"Not that this is going to come as much of a surprise," Serena says through a smile, her fingers at her own seat belt, "but your offer on Camelia was accepted. The seller's Realtor called me this afternoon, but I wanted to surprise you with the news tonight."

"That's great." I want to kiss her in celebration, but I can't. Too soon.

My grandfather would stress that I run around the back of the car and open the door for a lady, but Serena would think that was pushy and strange, so I wait for her on the sidewalk instead, wishing I could grab her hand as we head inside.

You're the most beautiful thing in this shithole, Serena. I can't say I understand the appeal of Jack's. Cobwebs glitter from every corner, peanut shells blanket the floor like some kind of crunchy carpet, and I can hardly see you in the light from the naked bulb above our heads.

She orders a salad, but she's not really eating it. She's busy questioning me, which has caught me flat footed. She's not supposed to ask me anything; she's supposed to talk about herself. She's pushing the spotlight back on me, and I'm equal parts flattered and bemused.

"What's your family like?" She spears a strip of grilled chicken with the tines of her fork, but she doesn't take a bite.

"Mostly dead," I say, playing with a french fry. "Just my grandfather and me, now."

"Did you live with your grandparents growing up?"

"My mother lived with us too. I don't know my dad. She had me when she was sixteen but died when I was five."

"I'm sorry," she says, her hand flying to the hollow spot at her throat. "How did it happen?"

"Overdose." I want to leave it at that, but honesty is supposed to be important in relationships. "She'd slit her wrists too. Either one would have killed her, the coroner said."

I don't remember the coroner saying that, though. All I remember is her blood marbling the water inside that tub I found her in, the way her eyes stared at nothing when I shook her, called her. And then my grandmother stumbled in, shook her and called her just like I had with the exact same results. Enter my grandfather, same shit. Then we just stood there staring at one another until my grandmother crushed my face into her stomach, hugging me tighter than anyone ever had before, and got me out of that bathroom.

"Oh my God, I'm so sorry," Serena says, and now I'm glad I told her because she slips her hand over mine across the table. "That must have been so hard for you."

It was. I could tell her about it. I could tell her about my triple abandonment: father, mother, grandmother, the last one jumping ship at the exact second I'd needed her most. My grandfather had eventually bounced back from my mom's death, but my grandmother had acted like she had nothing left to live for, as if my mother had been the tenuous cord holding all of us together. She'd gone from sweet and docile to completely vacant.

I could tell her how my grandfather hardly even noticed how blank my grandmother's eyes were as she went through the motions. He'd only groused about her lack of affection.

Why do you have to be the center of my entire world, Bill? It was the only thing she'd said with any emotion, and I'd heard her shout it after he'd bitched about receiving such a perfunctory kiss of greeting one night when he'd gotten off work. *Why is it always,* always *about you?*

"I made it out all right." I turn my hand palm up and wrap my fingers around hers. She doesn't shrink away, just squeezes me tighter. "My grandmother died not too long ago, and pretty soon after that, my grandfather's health started to decline, so he's living in a facility. I visit him most days."

She takes a long sip from her drink, vodka soda with extra lime. "How's he doing?"

"Good days and bad. Sometimes he doesn't know who I am. Some days he thinks I'm still a teenager, asks me why I'm not in class. And then sometimes he understands everything perfectly and bitches about his accommodations."

"I can't imagine what that's like."

Don't imagine it, Serena; just let me lead the interrogation now. "What about your family?"

"Well, there's my mom, my stepdad, and Cole," she says simply. "No siblings."

"Is Cole's father around?"

"Nope. Never has been. I like it that way."

"He's not a charmer, then?"

"He was only a charmer when I was an idiot sixteen-year-old girl," she says dryly, rolling her eyes. "He stopped being charming the second

I found out I was pregnant. But I'm not sorry he's not around. I mean, it's sad for Cole—I know what it's like to not have a father—but we're all miles better off this way. Ray wouldn't have done anything but blow into Cole's life every once in a while and cause a disturbance."

"What about your friends?"

"There's pretty much just Rosa—I've known her for almost a year and a half—and Derek, who I've known for about fifteen years."

"You knew him in high school?" I prod, my tone light.

"Yeah." She watches my thumb running against the fingers she's got clenched around mine. "Well, yes, it was a high school, but an alternative high school. I had to go there when I found out I was pregnant. I met Derek the first day. He's like an uncle to Cole, was there in the hospital with me when I had him. I went into premature labor in homeroom, and he blew off the rest of his classes to drive me."

They're a hell of a lot closer than I thought if he was there for Cole's birth. "Well, it's nice that Cole has a male role model in his life," I say, for lack of anything better.

She withdraws her hand to drain the rest of her drink, and I mourn the loss of her touch for a moment before copying her, drinking my own. "What about your friends?"

"I never made them a priority. I was so busy with school, then with work, then with ailing grandparents, so I never really had time for friends. I regret it sometimes, but I wouldn't have done anything differently. My family needed me."

Don't be sad for me, Serena; wipe that little frown off your face. I have you now, right?

"Well, you won't have any problems making friends," she says, rallying her spirits. "You're great—they'll be lining up to hang out with you."

The only person I want to hang out with is her. "Do you want another one?" I gesture to her empty glass. "I was going to have one."

"Yeah." She gives me one long, blinkless stare as she chews the inside of her bottom lip. "Sure."

She's making rather a business of fastening the catch on her purse after I pull up to her house two hours later. I would have preferred to stay at the restaurant longer, but the waitress had gotten pissier and pissier with each extra minute we loitered.

I know why she's letting her hair swing forward like a curtain, obscuring her face. She's nervous; this is yet another awkward first-date moment. If she pretends to be busy, I won't notice her unease.

"Thanks for taking me," she tells the inside of her purse, fumbling with the clasps. "It was fun."

"Yeah, of course." I hook a finger beneath the hair she's hiding behind and smooth it over her back. Moonlight slanting through the trees and the windshield tiger-stripes her face. She looks like a deer right before a predator pounces. The wide, fearful way their eyes pop when they hear the snap of a twig, the rustle of brush behind them.

You don't need to be so jumpy, Serena, I would never hurt you.

"We should do it again sometime soon," I offer, and this time she makes eye contact.

"Yeah?"

"Yeah. Unless you don't want to."

"No, I do." There's a timid little smile on her lips, and I have no idea why she would be so surprised any guy would want to go out with her again.

I think the way her nerves ratchet lessens my own, and I slide my finger under her chin and lean closer. She surprises me by meeting me halfway.

She could land a commercial deal for ChapStick, lips as soft as hers are, and a hint of the Starlight mint she'd swiped from the hostess station at the restaurant still lingers on her tongue, mingling with the vodka. It's one of those kisses that makes your chest tight and your stomach roll over, and I'm surprised it's going on as long as it is, even more surprised when she works her fingers into my hair, nails grazing my scalp.

And then she pulls away, groping for the door handle. "I should go."

"Okay."

She runs her index finger under her bottom lip to make sure her lipstick hasn't smudged. "You'll call me?"

"Yeah. And I won't wait three days either."

She smiles as I lean in to kiss her again, and round two goes much the same as round one until she wrenches herself out of my grip and scrabbles for the door handle again. "I should really go inside."

"Let me walk you up."

"You don't have to do that. I know the way."

"But you've never been on a real date before now, you said. You're supposed to be walked to the door."

"If you say so," she relents, and yes, I do say so.

I grab her hand as we walk—I've already kissed her, it shouldn't be too out of the question, but she still looks surprised at my tenacity.

"Long driveway," I say, after a few beats of silence.

"I like it that way, being set far back from the street."

"Dark without streetlights. You never get scared, being out in the wilderness?"

"Nope. I have Sirius and a Smith & Wesson. Everyone asks me that when they hear where I live. *You better get a gun and a dog, and a gun for your dog.* But I've never been worried, never been scared."

"You're just scared of men trying to kiss you."

"Shut up."

I do shut up, stopping in the middle of the driveway to kiss her again, for as long as she'll let me, until she pulls back with a groan. "I really should get in there."

The walk to her side door could take forever as far as I'm concerned, but all good things have to come to an end, and we arrive in the little puddle of weak light from the lamp above the side door.

She takes out her ring of keys, finds the right one, and says again, "Thanks for taking me."

"You already thanked me." I like seeing her blush. I had no idea people were capable of blushing this much. She's a medical marvel. "One more."

She gives me the sternest look a blushing woman can muster and lets me kiss her again, her hand in my hair, and I brace my palm against the wall behind her, my fingers wandering up the back of her thigh. Then the light gets brighter as the side door flings open, and Cole stands there with Sirius behind the storm door, a revolted look on his face.

"What the fuck!" His hand flies to his face as he staggers back a pace. "Jesus Christ, Mom!"

Her hand at her heart, she snaps back, "Well, why did you fling the door open like that?"

"The doorbell rang," he says, as though she's dense.

"Oh." She looks behind herself, and doorbell, indeed. Her back must have hit it when I pressed her against the wall. "Sorry."

Cole stands there glaring, his chest heaving, and Sirius, too, has a pretty forbidding look in his yellow eyes. *Oh, you're back. I wonder what your flesh tastes like.* I can fill in the blanks of his glower.

Serena's eyes have gone harsh and slitty. "Cole, go away; don't you have something better to do? I'll be in in a minute. Christ."

After a parting look to me of deepest disgust, he turns and stomps away. Sirius, however, does not. He rears up on his hind legs, his huge hairy paws on the glass.

Serena raps her knuckles on the door. "Down."

He falls to the floor, sitting back on his haunches.

She closes her eyes for a second, gives me a forced smile. "Sorry. My Mother of the Year trophy should be arriving any day now."

I run my fingers through the lock of hair falling into her face and push it behind her ear. "No, it's my fault."

"I really should go in," she says, looking reserved and resolved. "I'll talk to you later." She waves behind the pane of glass before shutting the inside door, and Sirius's vulturine eyes are the last thing I see before I head back for my car.

It would be damn near impossible to stop that smile from spreading across my face on the drive home, so I don't bother trying to contain it. She kissed me like she really meant it. I like the way she looks when I've finished kissing her. Flustered and flushed, swollen lips, the tip of her nose glowing pink, her hair mussed around her face. It makes her look like she's mine. I saw my future the first time I looked at her, and it's finally beginning to take shape.

With one hand on the steering wheel, I fumble for my phone. It blinks to life in the dark cabin of my car, and I pull up the mic's app, expecting to hear a gushing call to Rosa, but the exact opposite has happened.

"What the hell was that!" Cole yells. "Do you really think I wanted to see my mother out there getting mauled by some random guy?"

"I was hardly being *mauled*," Serena says calmly, and I picture her passing a palm over her hair to conceal the evidence of my hands running through it. "And he's not a random guy."

"He was groping you right in front of the house where your kid lives. I can't believe you think that's okay—"

"You know," Serena says, firing up, her voice as loud as Cole's, "I'm pretty surprised you're having such a strong reaction to what was comparatively tame, up against the shit I've seen in your internet search history."

Cole splutters something that doesn't sound like English and then shouts about his utter lack of fucking privacy in this hellhole.

"Yeah, *I'd* love some fucking privacy, too, you know."

"Well why don't you keep your groping confined to his car from now on? How hard would that be?"

"Fine, you know what? I promise I will confine my 'groping' to the car if you promise to wash all those crusty socks I keep finding in your laundry basket yourself. Don't think I'm an idiot, Cole; I know exactly what you're doing with those socks, and I'd very much prefer to assume that you're not hiding in your bedroom, constantly jerking off. If I have to bury my head in the sand about that bullshit, you can pay me the same courtesy."

Jesus Christ, I think, navigating the long and winding dirt trail out of the deep, dark wooded middle of nowhere Serena's house is nestled within.

Cole doesn't answer, and after a while, it becomes clear he's left the room.

The street opens up as I drive beneath a vaulted ceiling of branches. Streetlamps in the distance begin to filter through the gaps between leaves, and I wonder how many parent-child spats there will be in the coming weeks.

Change can be rough, Cole. You'll get used to me.

7

At 5 a.m. I'm still riding that high from our date, so I get started on work early, reviewing the bugs in the code that failed in the night. I flag them all for the development engineers, schedule meetings for the afternoon, and now I can't put it off anymore. Serena is a physical pull that can't be ignored, the biggest distraction I've ever met. She has my heart in her hands, and she's squeezing. It'll burst if I put it off any longer.

I text her as early as common courtesy allows. **Thanks for last night**, at 7:03 a.m.

And I wait.

I'm really trying not to clock watch, but my eyes can't help flickering to my phone every fifteen seconds, and my throat gets drier and drier the longer I go unacknowledged.

I access the speaker to the mic, listen to what sounds like a coffee maker percolating. She's awake; surely she's seen that I've reached out.

Slip slip. Bare feet across the kitchen tiles. Her feet, I'm sure of it, because the sound is perfect and her feet are perfect; I know this because I commented on them last night. The nails candy coated a luscious pink, a perfect slope from big toe to small.

There goes her vape, hissing like a cat.

The screen slider opens, shuts.

Panic flocks through me like a murder, and *why are you ignoring me, Serena? You meant it when you kissed me, I felt it.*

Are you free Friday? I ask at 7:45.

And then: I don't think so. I'm not sure, at 8:02.

◆ ◆ ◆

Her kitchen is piercingly silent until eight thirty, when footsteps clomp and cabinets clatter, and now she's saying, "Have a good day," but the only response is the slamming of the side door.

Oh Jesus. Seriously?

This is why you're being so clipped with me, Serena? You're going to let your happiness be held hostage by a fickle teen? It's outrageous that a fourteen-year-old boy's hissy fit could bring all that chemistry to its knees.

When you know, you know. That's what my grandfather says, what he's always said when regaling me with stories of when he first saw my grandmother. *Chris, when you know, you know, and that's all there is to it.*

Well, I know. And a silly fight with her son won't ruin us. I can give her some space for now. I'll focus on work; I do still have to make a living. Especially now that I'm buying a fucking house.

◆ ◆ ◆

I said I'd give her space, not that I wouldn't check in on her, and after I've ended a conference call with my team that evening, I tune in to my new favorite radio station.

"Remind me what nonpareils even are?" Rosa asks, and those thumps must be her depositing grocery bags on the counter. "Is it French?"

"It certainly is." Serena's back to her singsong voice; she can't be feeling too terrible. "It means 'without equal,' but I don't know who decided to call sprinkles that. They're not *that* great."

Why are you two baking enough shit to feed North Korea?

"Why do we need them, again?"

"For the confetti cake pops."

Rosa, I am very glad you're here, but aren't you supposed to ask leading questions about Serena's date, like a good girlfriend would?

I don't get my wish for a while, long after the beat of the electric mixer has died down, once the talk of baking times and temperatures has ended and both women sit down with beers that will apparently bloat them for the rest of the night.

"Aren't you going to tell me about your date?" Rosa finally, thankfully, asks. "I was expecting you to tell me about it right away. Did it go badly?"

"No, it went great." Then why do you sound so sad? "I like him a lot."

"Then what's with your face?"

"Cole saw him kissing me and lost his fucking mind."

Rosa gives a very long *hmmm*. "It's been just you and him for so long. He doesn't remember much of Tom, does he?"

Great. Tom?

"Well, when I told him I was going out with someone, he very snidely said, 'What about the last time you tried dating?' so I think it's safe to say he remembers enough."

"Kids are assholes. Have you spoken to him yet today? Chris? That's his name?"

"Yeah, Chris. He texted me a few times."

And yet you remained mostly mum.

"What's he like?"

"He's very . . . forward."

Well, you're so shy, Serena. If I weren't driving things, we'd never go anywhere.

"Aggressive?" Rosa says sharply.

What? My mouth gapes, and my blood stutters in my veins. How the fuck is a kiss aggressive?

"No, just . . . like he wants to make sure I know how much he likes me."

"Demonstrative?"

"That's a good thing, right? It feels like a good thing. It's good that he's making his intentions clear."

Yes, it's a good thing. I'd never make you wonder how I feel about you.

"Sure. As long as you like him back, I guess, then sure."

"I just feel guilty at the thought of going out with him again after the way Cole blew up. I could never date someone Cole hated."

It sounds like Rosa's choking on her beer. "Cole doesn't hate him. Cole doesn't even know him. He was just surprised as hell to see his mother kissing someone. I'm guessing it wasn't some chaste peck, right?" There's a long pause before she laughs. "I'm gonna say no. Your face is bright red."

I love you, Rosa, and I've never met you. You're the best friend Serena could have.

"So, Cole will get over it. Do you have any idea how many times Dre has walked in on me and Marlon having sex? At some point it's hard to pull off the *We're just wrestling* line. He doesn't hate us because of it, he just finds us repulsive."

Serena sighs. "Yeah, I guess."

"It'll be fine. You deserve to be happy."

Yes, though I'd prefer she were happy with *me*, specifically.

I may be desperate, but at least I have a reason for stopping by the realty office without warning the next afternoon. My offer on Camelia was accepted, after all, and I've got to drop off the earnest money.

The office is quiet but for a flurry of fingers clacking against a keyboard, though the sudden influx of wind makes Serena push back from her desk and look around.

"Oh. Hi." The late-afternoon sun shifting through the bank of windows turns her gold at the edges as she gets to her feet. The floor is a bright, burning white and she's gilded like an angel, and I can't quite believe that she's going to be mine, this creature who makes my heartbeats slur and my chest simmer.

I hold up the check like a flag of surrender. "Sorry I stopped by without calling, but I've got the earnest money for you."

"No, that's fine, you don't need to call." She accepts the check and gives me one of those through-the-eyelashes glances, like she's afraid to look directly at me.

We're the only ones here, but it feels like we're the only people alive, and I want to fold her in my arms in the empty center of this fire-white office, but she's feeling shy, that much is obvious, and I can't risk being too *aggressive* and killing our relationship in its cradle.

Her dress is light blue and printed with songbirds. She's swept her hair into a messy bun at the back of her neck, but it somehow still looks sophisticated, even with a pen shoved in it. A necklace of dusty-pink roses circles her throat, and she fiddles with the big one in the center as she seats herself in the swivel chair.

I sit where she directs me. "How've you been?"

"Oh, fine," she says, but she doesn't seem to believe it.

I duck my head to meet her eyes. "Was Cole really upset?"

She leans back in her chair, crossing one leg over the other. "Well, he wasn't very happy, but he's not silent treatment-ing me anymore."

"You haven't dated anyone in a while, I'm assuming?"

"It's been eight years."

I'm gazing at her, and she's gazing right back, one corner of her lip slowly pulling back into the dawn of a smile, and my hesitation ebbs away.

I slide my hand onto her bony kneecap and drag her chair marginally closer. "Am I misreading things? I don't know if you've been trying to give me some *get away from me* signals that I keep missing," I say, though I already know the answer; I just want her to tell me I'm wrong. I'm buying a fucking house for you, Serena. Just throw me a bone.

"No," she says, surprise forcing her eyebrows up. "It's just hard to manage this kind of thing with a bratty teenager in the mix."

"So you really are busy tonight? That wasn't just some line you give all your loser suitors?"

She rolls her eyes, and I roll her chair closer, so our knees touch. "I really do have a thing tonight."

"A thing?"

"Football Booster Club meeting."

"What is that, like the football PTA?"

"Pretty much."

I run my gaze from the white heels on her feet to the (unfortunately) high neckline of her dress. She looks like she's been spliced into real life from an old-fashioned movie; I can't imagine her sitting in an assembly room, taking notes on bake sales and blood drives. "You don't look like a PTA mom."

"Yeah, they're all about fifteen years older than me and exchange these uppity looks behind my back. It's high school all over again, some bitch whispering 'Slut' when I walk down the hallway. I don't even know why I joined. It's full of a bunch of women named Karen with blond bobs who all have those god-awful *live, laugh, love* stickers on their living room walls."

"I thought all real estate agents had blond bobs and names like Carrie before I met you."

She laughs, kneading the back of her neck with a fingertip. "It's how I met Rosa; she was another *Why the fuck did I sign up?* mother. We've been making stuff to sell at the bake sale this Saturday. There's a meeting tonight. I have to show up with two hundred cake pops, three buckets of caramel, four dozen cupcakes, and about a million truffles."

"You made all that?"

She holds up her palm, twisting it this way and that. "Can't you tell? I've got workingman's hands."

She has the furthest thing from workingman's hands, but I snatch her palm out of the air and kiss her knuckles. "I think I'm in love."

I *know* I am, Serena, but I don't want to scare you off by saying so just yet.

"Shut up."

I don't think I've ever loved being told to shut up before I met her. "When's the booster thing end?"

"I don't know." She shrugs one slight shoulder. "Maybe around nine."

"Party animal."

"I wish they served alcohol there," she says somberly. "But something tells me the Karens will revolt if I sneak in a flask."

"I'd risk a Karen revolt to bring you some booze."

She rolls her eyes, getting to her feet. "They'd tear you apart."

I stand, too, though I don't know why or where she's going. I just got here, Serena. Are you leaving already? "Is it closing time?"

She flaps my check in the air, slipping her purse over her shoulder. "I'm going to have to lock up a little early and get this to the bank."

I follow her to the door, where she fiddles with a set of keys, looking up at me. "I'll see you later, then?"

Sooner than you might think. "Of course."

8

You're not being creepy, you're just making your intentions clear, I repeat to myself like a mantra. *She won't think you're some scary stalker, she'll think you're sweet.*

I mean, sure, Serena didn't actually tell me which high school her son attends, but how hard could that be to figure out? Freeport's not exactly huge. There's precisely one elementary school, one middle school, and one high school.

The clock on my dashboard ticks over to 8:47 as I shift in the driver's seat, gaze fastened on the gym doors of Freeport High School. Her car isn't here, which stymies me, but I'd been listening in when Rosa went over to pack up all the shit they've baked. She hadn't been lying about the meeting. She wouldn't lie to me; she likes me.

The red numbers say 8:52 by the time light begins spilling out the doors, and in twos or threes, women and the odd browbeaten-looking husband come trudging out into the parking lot, their voices carrying on the breeze. The husbands look thrilled to be leaving. I wouldn't drag my feet going to one of these things, Serena; I'd go willingly, happily, as long as you'd be there with me.

I get out, grabbing the flask, and park myself on the hood of my car.

The grumbling of engines erupts from all around me, tires crunching over dead leaves, when I catch sight of her.

Serena's headed my way with Rosa. In jeans and a leather jacket, ponytail and white sneakers, she looks like a student, some spectator leaving a football game, with her hands in her pockets. I love the way she walks, always one foot directly in front of the other.

She stops when she sees me, tugging on Rosa's jacket. They pause, both staring, and now I'm wondering if I've made a very big mistake.

"Chris?"

I hold up the flask. I'm not creepy, I just like you. "Hey."

She walks closer, Rosa in tow; thankfully she's smiling, and it doesn't look forced. "What are you doing here?"

"I told you I'd risk a Karen rebellion to bring you booze."

I get up from the hood in time for Serena to circle her arms around my waist, her upturned face bathed in yellow from the glare of the streetlights. "You're so sweet. I can't believe you did that." Thank God. I'm sweet, not creepy. "This is my friend Rosa. I've told you about her, remember?"

"Of course." I hold out my hand, which Rosa accepts, and her strong grip takes me somewhat by surprise. She's giving me an outright appraising look, which I suppose I should have expected.

"You must have it bad, braving a Football Booster's meeting," Rosa says dryly, finally letting my hand go.

"Rosa," Serena hisses, swatting at her.

"What?"

"I won't deny the allegation." I screw the lid off the flask and hand it to Serena.

She grimaces after a long pull and hands it off to Rosa, who does the same thing and passes it back to me. I've never been partial to vodka, but Serena is, so I drink it all the same.

"I feel like the principal is going to come out and expel us." Serena glances over her shoulder, ponytail whipping in the wind, and zips up her jacket.

She's cold, poor thing. I could warm her up.

Rosa zips up, too, taking her keys out of her purse. "I gotta get back to Marlon. Are you still going to need a ride home?"

Serena hesitates, looking at me, then at Rosa. They seem to be having a wholly nonverbal conversation. Rosa's beautiful eyebrows raise almost imperceptibly as the makings of a smile twist one corner of her mouth; Serena bites back her lip, her pupils whizzing between Rosa's.

Then she turns her wide blue eyes, made glassy by the streetlamps, on me. "You can take me home, right?"

"Of course." Yes. Ask me anything, anytime, and my answer will always be yes.

"All right," Rosa says, wearing a megawatt smile this time, dragging out the syllables as she walks backward toward a Mercedes SUV. "Don't stay out too late, young lady."

"You wouldn't keep me out too late, would you?" Serena asks, tugging at the hem of my shirt after Rosa waves and packs herself into her car.

"I'll keep you as late as you'll let me." I hand her the flask again and watch her take another slug. She shivers slightly as she swallows, her throat undulating in a way that makes me shiver too.

"Come inside where it's warm," I tell her, opening the passenger door for her. Once she's settled herself inside, purse at her feet, jacket unzipped, I lean in and kiss her like I've wanted to since the second she walked out the doors of the school.

"You're pretty slick," she says when I pull back. "Who taught you your moves?"

Who taught me about women? TV, I guess. My grandfather. My grandmother's battered old romance novels I'd read when there was nothing else to read or anything better to do. An old diary of my teenage mother's that I'd found beneath a loose floorboard, my father's name written over and over and over, embellished with hearts and artful squiggles. Desperate, frantic cursive: *Love me, see me, want me.* And yet he never had.

"It's born skill, not moves."

"Uh-huh," Serena says, crossing her arms over her chest, trying to look haughty, but her smile ruins the effect.

Fifteen minutes later, most of the cars have disappeared and she's crept over the center console, straddling my lap, with her arms around my neck and her tongue against mine. The windows are beginning to fog, and the whole cabin is stuffy, humid with hormones. She strips off her jacket and flings it away, her lips still mashed against mine all the while.

My fingers are under her T-shirt, hot against her skin, and her lips have migrated to my ear. Her breath is making the hair on my arms stand on end, my erection strain against my pants, and she yanks herself back as though she's experienced an electric shock.

"What's wrong?"

"I think things may be getting a little too heated," she says, smiling down at my crotch.

"I can't help it, you're all pressed against me and shifting on my lap."

"Sorry." She very deliberately and slowly kisses me again before climbing off and clambering into the passenger seat, and I lean back against the headrest, running my hand roughly over my face.

She strokes the thigh of my jeans, leaning against her own headrest. "I shouldn't get carried away like that. It never works out if you move too quickly."

I pick up her hand, lace her warm fingers through mine. "Why have you been single for eight years?"

"I don't have a great track record at dating. It just didn't seem like I was any good at it. And then I got busier as Cole got older, and all thoughts of it sort of fell by the wayside." She bites back her bottom lip and lets it out slowly from between her teeth. It's practically pornographic. "How long have you been on your own?"

"About three years."

"Why'd it end?"

"I didn't have much time to devote to a relationship back then. I think she resented all the time I had to spend with my family. What about you?"

"I was with someone for two years, ended it when Cole was about six. It was a trainwreck."

"How so?" Tell me how awful Tom was, Serena. Tell me everything.

"Well, we just *wanted different things*," she chirps sarcastically. "He was into some shit that I wanted nothing to do with. It ended badly."

"What kind of shit?"

"Kinky shit."

"Well, like what?" Spit it out, sweetheart, you can't leave me hanging like this. What if I'm into the same kinky shit? I don't want to make the same fatal mistake.

"Essentially he wanted to watch me having sex with other men," she says, and her lip curls at the memory. "And I didn't want a boyfriend who wanted to pass me around."

"God." I don't think I've ever used the word *aghast* in a sentence, but, Serena, I'm fucking aghast. I would lose my mind if I saw something like that. Over my cold, dead body would I share you with anyone.

"Anyway, so it was about a year into dating when he made that known, and right before we broke up, I found out he'd been distributing my nudes on the internet to other men, asking them what they'd like to do to his girlfriend, and I completely flipped my shit and reported him to the police. Derek was pissed. He had to be there when I told Tom it was over; I wouldn't have been able to do much physically if Tom had gotten violent. Lots of screaming and yelling and cursing, and Cole saw a bit of it, even though I tried shielding him from the worst."

Look, I get that Derek is her oldest friend and all, but I'm really not into his whole white knight thing. Thanks for getting rid of the perv, but I'll take it from here.

"Jesus." And just to put her mind at ease, I say, "Well, you wouldn't have to worry about me wanting to share you. I could never do that."

"Aren't you sweet." She breathes in long and slow while I press my thumb into her palm, massaging it, loving the way my touch makes a smile slither across her lips.

"Should I get you home now?" It's the last thing I want, but I'm assuming she won't want to be too late because of Cole, and then there's the whole *let's take this slow* thing.

"Trying to get rid of me?"

"I'd take you home with me if I thought you'd let me." But the thought of her stepping inside my grandparents' dank, depressing house, where misery paints the walls, is unthinkable. I'd never take her there. She'd suck up some of its gloom.

"Yeah. I should probably get back."

We look at each other for a long time in perfect silence. The moonlight makes her skin incandescent, makes it sparkle like she's from some other planet, and she reaches up to kiss me one more time before I start the car.

9

Serena wants me to meet her family today, a formal introduction, and it must mean she sees a future with me because I heard her tell Rosa she wouldn't introduce me to anyone until she was sure about us. It's been three months, and she knows I love her, I think; I've never actually said it aloud, but she's got to have some idea.

She's laying out the ground rules for Cole right now; they're in the kitchen, and Cole is acting pretty sassy for a boy whose iPhone hangs in the balance.

"Do you seriously expect me to *like* the guy I found groping my mom?"

"No, I don't." Really? "But I expect you to be polite. Maybe even friendly. Fake it if you have to, Cole; he's never done anything to you."

"Why does he have to go with us? You're going to make it awkward."

"*I* don't plan on making anything awkward. Grandma wants to meet him. This is what you do when you're dating someone. You meet the parents eventually. You're going to have to do the same shit when you start dating."

There's a long pause. I'm betting they're exchanging hard glares, Serena's hands on her hips, Cole's arms knotted over his chest.

"You need to get ready. You're not wearing those ratty old gym shorts. Grandma will turn it into my fault if you show up looking like a bum. God knows she's already got enough material, always despairing over my hair." Footsteps pound through the speaker, getting fainter every second. "And wear a shirt with a collar!" she shouts.

I look down at myself. My shirt doesn't have a collar. I should probably change before heading over.

◆ ◆ ◆

Sirius does not look especially glad to see me when Serena opens her side door, her hand clenched around his collar.

"Hey," she says, and her voice is how I'd describe a rainbow to a blind person. "Come on in, I've got him."

Oh, Sirius. You're even more alarming up close.

Now I can see the gold veins spliced through his wary yellow eyes, the way his lips have pulled back into what could be either a smile or a grimace of utter rage. His ears stand at attention, his limbs are rigid, and I'm not sure if that's the beginnings of a growl I hear, curdling at the back of his throat.

"Can you hold your hand out for him?" Serena asks, above the petrifying face of her guard beast. "He won't bite you, but he'll want to smell you."

"Sure."

Sirius's cold, quivering nose inches along my wrist, and he doesn't break eye contact throughout his inspection. Serena lets him go, but he doesn't seem to have noticed, because he's only got eyes for me.

Then he blinks, his tongue snaking up to lick his nose, and he turns and slinks away through the hallway, his tail whipping around the corner.

Serena straightens up, her hands on her hips. "That's about as much as we can hope for during a first meeting. He'll warm up."

I'm not sure if I'm buying that. "I get it; I didn't expect any different. His job is protecting you guys. It's good that he's not exactly welcoming to strangers."

Cole is trying very hard to arrange his face into a weak smile, but he's not succeeding when he holds out a hand for me to shake.

Serena perches on her kitchen table, wearing an apologetic expression and a ruffled skirt that I want to rip off her right now.

"Cole, this is Chris."

"Nice to meet you," he says, though his eyes broadcast otherwise.

But Cole doesn't know that it's not only Serena I listen to when I play back the recordings. There are plenty of conversations he has in this very kitchen, and I think I might know enough about him to win him over.

"I'm sorry I'm late." I slip an arm around her shoulder, giving her a kiss on the cheek. "I was playing video games and lost track of time."

Cole shoots me a sharp, covert glance that I pretend not to notice.

"It wouldn't be the first time I got thrown over for a video game," she says, her hand on the side of my neck, returning the cheek kiss.

"My grandfather always told me not to show up somewhere empty handed, so there's a case of beer and some FUNYUNS in the car."

Cole loves FUNYUNS. I doubt anybody else at this barbecue does, but it doesn't matter. I bought them with him in mind.

"Babe, why don't you grab Sirius's leash and hook him up for me?" She swings her purse onto her shoulder, sliding off the table. "I'm going to help Chris get his stuff into our car."

"You're bringing Sirius?" I ask once Cole has left.

"He loves my mom's place."

"Doesn't she have three little dogs?"

She smiles, wriggling her feet into a pair of sandals by the side door. "He loves them too. He's known them since he was a baby. They climb all over him like he's a big hairy jungle gym."

◆ ◆ ◆

It's very unsettling to spend a thirty-minute car ride with a dog that would love nothing more than to kill you panting its hot, wet breath on the back of your neck. Sirius is sitting directly behind me; I catch his wicked gaze in the side mirror every so often. Maybe I should bring him raw steak next time I see him. Buy him off with treats. But he looks to be quite high above bribery. This is principle. You can't buy the high ground with something as trivial as a steak.

If I had to describe Serena's mother's backyard in a word, it would be *Eden*. Greenery, beds of rich soil bursting in a riot of flowers, a white stone birdbath that blue jays are swimming in, a stone patio enclosed by a screen, twinkle lights twined around the pillars. When I think barbecues, I don't generally expect chafing dishes and tablecloths with gold piping, mountains of fruit cut into fancy shapes, and a literal chocolate fountain. I assume this display is supposed to come off as a grand show of welcome, but it just makes me feel like I've walked into a production I haven't necessarily been invited to.

Serena unclips Sirius from his leash when we make it through the backyard gate, and he tears off in pursuit of a fuzzy dog that probably weighs the same as the bag of FUNYUNS Cole is rooting through.

"Mom?" Serena calls, her skirt swaying around her thighs as she tramps through the grass.

"Over here," a voice answers, carrying on a gust of air that smells like scorched meat.

Serena's mother looks like one of those aging soap stars who have to be at least sixty but look no more than forty. She has the same eye color and chin as her daughter, but the similarities end there. Her hair is pale blond and shoulder length, she's dressed like she should be at a country club, and now she's got eyes for me, watching as I trail Serena over to the patio table.

"You brought Cole?"

"Of course I brought him. Mom, this is Chris," Serena says, and I sense a slight hint of nerves in her voice as she stands there, hands clasped in front of her.

Serena's mother's voice is warm, but her eyes have a cold film of evaluation as she holds out her hand. For a moment I wonder if she's expecting me to kiss it, like she's the reigning queen of this kingdom and I'm some visiting dignitary, but I grasp it in mine and hope my hands aren't sweating too much.

"Katherine," she says. "It's nice to meet you."

"You too. You've got a beautiful yard."

"Thank you." She surveys the place with a sharp gaze. "That's my husband, Vince, by the grill. Ignore the apron. It's hideous, but he loves it."

"Where do you want the beer, Mom?"

"The cooler is fine. What sort of outfit would you call the one Cole's got on?"

Serena gives me a look as her mother strides out into the yard after Cole. "It's always something. Just dump all the bottles in here, I'll grab the ice."

I watch her walking off, her flouncing skirt making the blood in my temples thrum, and when I finally break the spell and arrange the beer in the cooler, I can see, from the corner of my eye, Serena's mother standing twenty feet away in the yard, staring at me with an unfathomable expression.

Serena's back with a sweaty bag of ice, slitting into it with sharp nails.

"I don't think your mother likes me very much," I say under my breath.

She glances over at her mom, then back at me. "You met her thirty seconds ago."

"Just the impression I'm getting."

I suppress a sigh, wondering how long an appearance we'll be required to put in. The things I do for love, Serena.

"She takes time to warm up." Serena plants a wet kiss on my lips, and I'm glad she does it right here, right out in the open for her family to see.

Once all the adults are settled on the couches off to the side of the patio, Serena's mother begins her smooth line of questioning that feels like a police interrogation but sounds like general small talk.

"What do you do for a living, Chris?" She smiles. It's an inviting smile, but it still feels tinged with ice, like something she's been trained to do while in the company of cretins.

"Software development. It's great, I love the work. Serena told me you were a paralegal when you worked. My grandmother did the same before she became a stay-at-home mom."

Serena slips her arm into the crook of my elbow, giving me a light squeeze. "He gets to work from home. I'm jealous."

Katherine's eyes linger on Serena's hand, then flick back to me. "What about your family? Any brothers, sisters?"

"No, I'm an only child," I say after a swig of beer. "My grandparents raised me after my mother died. It's just my grandfather now. His health has been getting worse, so he's living in a facility." I make sure to set my beer down on a coaster; Serena's mother will appreciate that. "I visit him most days."

Katherine lifts a delicate brow. "Friends?"

I hate this question, I really do. The truth makes me sound like some weirdo loner on an incel website. The truth is that when I wasn't in school, I was taking care of an ailing grandmother and looking after the house as best as I was able since she couldn't anymore. How could I hit up keggers when there was cleaning to get on with, bills to pay, an old lady to feed with a spoon like an infant? We hadn't had the money to hire round-the-clock in-home care, and she may have stopped loving me after my mother died, but I still loved her, didn't I? Love meant doing the hard things.

"My grandmother was very sick all through my time in college," I say carefully, unable to stop myself from reaching for Serena's hand for comfort, solidarity, because she knows this is my soft spot. "My grandfather didn't make it a few years past her death before he got sick too. It's difficult to make friends as an adult. I haven't had the time to even consider trying until my grandfather moved into the facility."

"Do you like sports?" Vince barks out, manspreading his legs to Katherine's disgust; she shoots him a filthy look and moves over a few inches. I assume Vince is talking to me, even though his gaze is on his phone.

"Yeah, mostly football and hockey."

"I hate the Patriots," he offers.

Katherine's gaze is back on me as she unnecessarily stirs her drink, rattling ice around. "I'm sorry to hear that. Serena tells me your mother had you around the same age Serena was when she had Cole?"

"Yes, she did." Will she think that makes me white trash, fruit of the rotten tree? Serena told me her mother's fury had been quite the sight to behold when she'd told her about her pregnancy.

I don't know what she's searching for in my face. If I knew, I'd give it to her, no problem. Anything to get her to stop looking at me like she wants to crack my head open, dissect my brains to find out. All I can do is smile harder and hope she learns to love me.

Thankfully, Serena takes the wheel, leaning forward. "Chris is buying Camelia, did I tell you? Escrow's been slow—we've been waiting on the owners to make the appropriate repairs—but he'll be able to move in next week."

"That's a beautiful house," Katherine says, and I want to sigh with relief at her approval. "Except for that horrendous orange paint in the living room."

Apparently we need more ice, and I know the perfect driving companion to pick as I swipe Serena's keys and set off across the yard. Cole's throwing a tennis ball for the dogs; a cloud of frantic hairy legs and lolling wet tongues races off in the direction the ball is headed. The victor pops up, its maw wrapped around the tennis ball, with a wild look in its eye, and then the other three dogs chase after the winner.

"I need to get some more ice," I call over. "You want to come with me and grab more FUNYUNS?"

He's waffling with his decision, I can tell; I can decode the thoughts bubbling in his eyes. He's vowed to hate me to infinity and beyond, but then I did buy him FUNYUNS, and I do like *Red Dead Redemption 2*, so how awful can I truly be?

"Yeah, okay."

"We'll be back," I call to Serena, and Cole and I set off for the Land Rover.

"That's a nice house your grandparents have," I say, once we're buckled in and headed for the nearest grocery store.

"Yeah. We used to live there, Mom and me."

"When did you two start living on your own?"

He shrugs, running a hand through his hair as though intentionally messing it up. I never thought I'd be a man who thinks, *Kids these days*, but all the same. I don't know what to make of their hairstyles. "I think when I was about three. I don't really remember."

"I was close to my grandparents too. I lived with them growing up. My grandmother's gone now, but my grandfather's still around."

He nods disinterestedly. I'm going to have to try harder.

"Your mom says you're in football?"

"Yeah."

"You must be good at it, varsity at your age."

"I'm okay," he says modestly, staring through the window.

"What about—"

He turns to look at me, his eyes—replicas of his mother's—zeroed in on mine. "Do you love her?"

I balk, tightening my grip on the steering wheel. I thought we'd start at video games and work our way up to his mother. "Your mom?"

He doesn't dignify that with an answer.

"Well," I say, switching lanes, "I haven't told her that yet."

"But you do?" he presses, and suddenly I see the resemblance to his grandmother.

I give him a quick sideways glance. His jaw is set, his chin juts out, and his eyes look like boarded-up shutters on a condemned house.

"I'm crazy about her. I'm lucky she ever gave me the time of day."

He nods mutely, back to looking out the window.

"You're not going to rat me out, are you?" I say, making a right into the shopping plaza.

He considers that for a long time, staring down at his hands. "She thinks I just like being an asshole, but things always go wrong when she starts dating someone. She gets upset for weeks afterward and thinks I don't notice."

Now I feel bad for him. He's just some sad, scrawny kid trying to look out for his mother. I understand that, probably better than most people can. I couldn't have done a damn thing to help my mother, but it hadn't stopped me from trying.

"I get it. I get it probably more than most people would."

That snort of his strikes me as a noise of dissent, so I plow on. "My mom was sixteen when she had me too. My father was a little older, someone she'd known in high school. He was in boot camp when she found out she was pregnant. She was in love with him; he was her first everything, but I don't think she mattered much to him. I guess he promised to marry her when he came back, but he was stationed overseas and then kept reenlisting. When he sent her a pretty curt letter telling her he'd married someone else, she killed herself. I found her. It's not something you can forget in a hurry."

His eyes widen just like his mom's did when I told her the same story. "I'm sorry."

"I'm not trying to play on your sympathy; I'm only saying I get why you're apprehensive. You've got good reason. The last thing I want to do is hurt your mother. I'm sure she'll be the one breaking my heart if and when it happens." Hell, she breaks my heart every time she smiles at me.

Cole sucks in a quivering breath. "Okay."

"Are we good?" I ask, pulling into a free slot in the parking lot.

"Yeah."

"Think we should get some FUNYUNS for your grandma? She looks like the FUNYUNS type."

He gives me a big horselaugh, ripping off his seat belt and vaulting out of the car. "She says only truck drivers like them."

◆ ◆ ◆

Four hours later, Cole has decided to sleep over at his grandparents' and Sirius has settled onto the kitchen floor back at home, keeping his blazing eyes locked on me. I've got Serena (mostly) all to myself, up on the island, her lacy top slipping off one shoulder.

She stops kissing me with the enthusiasm of five minutes ago and pulls away, pressing her hand to her face.

"What's the matter?"

She shakes her head, holds one palm out in front of her. "It's just—I'm—this just makes me very nervous, scared."

"What does?" I love how shy she can be; it makes me feel like more of a man, for some reason.

She flaps her arms around the room. "*This*. You, what you're doing. I know what you want, and it scares me."

She's not kidding. She's shaking, and it's not a little quiver of anticipation like Nora Roberts writes about; it's a full-body tremble, an electrical current that hums under her skin, setting her teeth on edge. Her eyes are darting everywhere, sizing up exits, round with anxiety.

"What about all those times in the car?" A hard penis hadn't scared her then. Not that she'd done anything with it, but she could *feel* it. It had made its existence well known.

She leans back on her hands, rolling her eyes. "Jesus, Chris. I was never going to fuck you in a car, okay; I'm not fifteen."

I hadn't realized car sex was never going to be an option. She'd said she wasn't comfortable having me in her house because I hadn't met Cole, and I'd never entertained the idea of bringing her back to my grandparents' house; the car had seemed the most reasonable option.

But I'm here now, and Cole's not. It's as good a time as any.

"You don't have any reason to be scared of me," I say, pressing my forehead against hers, rubbing her back. I'd never do anything to hurt her, frighten her.

She mumbles something against my neck.

"We don't have to do anything," I say, wrapping my arms around her, even though we really do. "Just take a breath."

"I think I forgot how. I'll feel like an idiot. I won't know what the fuck I'm doing."

"I can teach you." I brush my lips against her temple. "It's not that hard."

She sucks in a long, ratcheting breath, and I think she's going to order me away until she says, so softly I can barely hear her, "Okay."

I'm a good teacher, it transpires. Patient, thorough, always willing to go over the trickier material more than once, and thirty minutes later, she pulls herself up on my chest from under the blankets, wiping the sweat pearling at my hairline off with her fingertips.

"You want me to get you some water, babe?"

I'm exhausted but victorious, because I am finally *babe*.

"I'll get it," I say, tracing the curve of her face with my thumb. "You're not my waitress."

"No, you stay here." She shrugs into her short robe, ties it around her waist, and opens her bedroom door. Sirius, who has apparently been leaning against it, tips over onto his back, half inside the room.

"Oh, you silly boy." She steps over him. He looks the furthest thing from *silly* that I've ever seen. "Eavesdropping?"

Sirius gives me an upside-down look of pure loathing and heaves himself to his paws to follow her. Serena pads back a minute later and closes the door in Sirius's face, ignoring his sad little whines and scratches. She hands me a water bottle as she sits on the edge of the bed, runs her fingers through the hair above my ear the way my mother used to, and kisses my forehead. A sheen of perspiration shimmers on her lips when she pulls away.

I tug her onto my chest. "Take that off and get back in here."

She does, propping herself up on her elbow, a curtain of snarled hair falling in her face. "Ugh. My hair's a fucking mess."

Yes, but it's a mess because *we* made it a mess, doing what we were doing. I love it. It's perfect. It makes me hard just looking at it. Her lips are swollen, her cheeks flushed, and, though I try not to notice, she must be cold if the way her nipples harden is any indication.

I never understood cannibalism before now. I almost feel like I want to eat her, consume her, keep her safe in my body.

I set the water bottle on her bedside table and turn to face her, tugging the sheets back over us.

"I love you," I say, even though I probably shouldn't. I can't help it. She's perfect and I love her and I want her to know. I love her more than those two idiots who were lucky enough to come before me ever did.

She doesn't say anything, doesn't even blink, but her eyes have gotten marginally wider.

"I've wanted to tell you for a while," I say, slipping my arm around her waist, "but I thought it'd be too soon."

Her eyelids dip low as she drops her gaze to the sheets, drawing patterns into them with her finger. I've rendered her speechless. I don't think that's a good thing.

"Does that freak you out? It's too soon, isn't it?"

"Well, the only two men I've dated told me they loved me within a month, and those relationships crashed and burned. You've got two months on them."

That isn't exactly what I'd been hoping for, but it's better than being ordered out of her bed, having Sirius sicced on me, and having the door slammed in my face.

"I love you too," she says shyly, her voice hardly above a whisper.

And now my heart is dancing the Macarena in my chest; fireworks flare behind my eyes when she leans in to kiss me, and I feel like going over our study syllabus again. There's plenty of material I wasn't able to cover the first time around.

10

I have been banished back to my grandparents' house. Cole will be returning home soon, and Serena has to clean up the evidence of my sleeping over, so I while away the time until I can see her again by sitting at my desk, listening to her bustle around her house in real time, until there's a loud creak and the kitchen is full of voices.

"Hey," she says. "How did it go?"

"Fine," Cole answers.

"*Fine*," Serena's mother echoes acidly. "It wasn't *fine*, it was great."

"Dirty clothes in your hamper, not on the floor!" Serena shouts, and I assume Cole has trudged out of the room. "Thanks for having him, Mom."

"We love having him."

"Well, thanks all the same."

"Did you get my email?"

What email? Her phone had chimed with a notification while I was there, but all she'd done was stare at the screen for a few seconds and slip the phone back into the pocket of her robe.

"I did," Serena says carefully, warily, and now I have a very bad feeling.

"You didn't respond, so I wasn't sure if you'd read it."

"I read it as soon as you sent it, I just hadn't had time to answer."

"Oh?"

"I think you're letting past mistakes on my part cloud your judgment, Mom. You're not giving him a fair shot because of it."

My heart plummets as my blood runs cold. It's me they're talking about.

"I don't think so. I don't think he's anything like Ray and Tom. I never said that—I said there was something off about him."

"Off like *what*?" Serena says, with definite coolness in her tone now.

"Trying too hard, for one."

"Mom, everyone gets nervous when they have to meet the parents."

I hadn't tried too hard. I want to reach through the speaker of my laptop, grab Katherine by the throat, and shout, *I wasn't trying too hard.*

"It just makes me uneasy. I didn't like the way he stared at you. Everywhere you went. To the bathroom, inside the house to grab something, walking across the yard to the dogs. Everywhere you went, he stared at you."

"Well, he thinks I'm hot."

"You brought him around Cole much too quickly."

"You introduced Vince to me on, what, your third date? It's been three months."

"That's not how I remember it."

"Of course it isn't," Serena mutters. "Look, you said you wanted to meet him, you asked me to bring him to your place—what, did you think Cole wouldn't be there?"

"Yes. I thought you'd leave him home and that it would be just the four of us."

"Well, I'm sorry that didn't work out to your satisfaction. You never said not to bring Cole."

"You don't need to get defensive."

"How can I *not* get defensive when you're attacking my boyfriend?"

Butterflies of hope flap in my stomach. I'm her *boyfriend*. She's never actually called me that before.

"I'd hardly call this an attack," Katherine says delicately, and I honestly think I want to smack her.

"Feels an awful lot like one to me," Serena says, and I feel myself nodding in solidarity.

"You've always been so defensive. I'm just discussing my misgivings with my daughter."

Serena scoffs loudly, and now she's making a great deal of noise, closing cabinets harder than necessary. "You're saying that because he was nervous to meet you and the fact that he looked at me is cause for alarm. I'm sorry, but that's categorically bullshit."

Yes, it is. Categorically. I cannot believe this is what her mother thinks of me. It's fucking appalling.

"Serena, he doesn't have any friends. He's lived here his whole life—it's not like he moved into town two months ago and hasn't met anybody yet."

"He has no friends because he had to take care of his sick grandparents morning, noon, and night for years on end!" she says. "He worked all the time, and when he wasn't, he was changing adult diapers and spoon-feeding his dying grandmother."

"You have friends and you've been quite busy with Cole and your career."

"I have exactly *two* friends. It's not like I'm swimming in them. Does that mean there's something wrong with me too? Are you going to go home and look up personality disorders on the internet to diagnose me with?"

I like how fervently she defends me, though I do wish it wasn't necessary.

"Well," Katherine huffs stiffly. "I can see that my concerns are getting us nowhere."

"Yes, thank you *very* much for your concern," Serena says in a tone that's anything but thankful, and they don't say goodbye to one another when Katherine leaves.

◆ ◆ ◆

Serena is such a sweetheart, insisting on helping me box up my possessions for the movers. I didn't—and still don't—want her in this depressing old place, but it'll all be for the best in the long run.

Her beautiful face is sad when she steps through the door. "I see what you mean. It just feels *morbid*, you know?"

This place and my grandparents have aged together, waned together. It's faded like an old Polaroid, steeped in sepia, suffocating in peeling wallpaper. I hate this house, and I think Serena can read it in my expression, because she takes my hand in hers as we head deeper inside.

She runs her fingers against the walls as we walk. "Was it always like this?"

"After my mother died, things went downhill fast."

She stops at a blank stretch of wall between two of those Thomas Kinkade monstrosities my grandmother loved. "There were pictures up here?"

"Yeah. Of my mother, her school pictures, pictures of her with me."

"They came off the walls after she died?"

"Pretty much immediately. My grandmother packed them all away."

"That must have made you so sad as a kid, not even able to see a picture of her after she'd gone."

It had made me sad. Or maybe a word bigger than sad.

I draw Serena into my arms and hold her flat against me, my chin resting on her head. "I stole one back. I kept it in my desk drawer."

"I'm sorry, babe."

I don't want to see that frown on her face, so I kiss it away. "That's just the way it was."

She's already peering down the hallway, her eyes lit with interest. "Can you give me the grand tour before we get started?"

I'm not sure how to make this tour anything other than morose as I lead her through the house. This is the kitchen, where a robot posing as my grandmother made all our meals. When I was five, she promised she'd teach me how to crack an egg but then my mom died and my grandmother forgot about me almost entirely, so I had to figure it out on my own. Here's the bathroom where my mother bled out, sweetheart. I was too afraid to use it for months afterward, would sneak into my grandparents' en suite until my grandfather learned of it and told me to "be a man." Oh, you want to see *my* room, where I spent virtually my entire childhood wishing I could leave?

"I've never had a girl in here before," I say, leaning into the doorjamb, with my hands tucked under my armpits.

"Never?" There's a wicked smile on her divine face when she pulls me inside and down onto the bed. She's featherlight when she climbs onto my chest, her hair cascading around my face as she flattens my lips with hers.

"Do I look scary from this close up?" she asks, her forehead against mine, the antithesis of *scary*.

"I don't think there's anything you could do to make yourself look scary," I say, my hand at the back of her neck. "You're perfect."

"And you say that with such a straight face."

"I meant it."

She burrows into the crook of my neck. "You really don't like this house, do you?"

"It was a weird place to grow up," is all I eventually offer.

Her hand drifts through the hair around my ear. "What was it like?" She pauses, waiting for me to fill the void, which I don't, because I can't think of a single thing to say. "You don't have to talk about it if you can't. I know you don't like to. But I'm here if you want to."

I don't want you to think I'm some weirdo, I want to say. *I need you to love me, not pity me.* But she wants something from me, and I've never been good at telling her no.

"My mom lived in the bedroom next door," I finally say, reaching over to knock on the wall we shared. "Sometimes I'd knock on the wall in the night to see if she was still awake too."

"She'd knock back?"

"Most of the time." The only time I remember her not answering was the night she died. "Things were mostly okay when she was alive.

And then my grandmother went catatonic after my mom died, and my grandfather didn't seem to mind very much unless she forgot to iron his pants or something, and I wondered what I'd done in my previous life to be stuck with these oddballs."

"Catatonic?"

My grandmother's face, lively as a cadaver, floats up to the surface of my mind. "She went through the motions, but there was something stiff about it. Like she didn't care about anything anymore. She'd ask about my day, but I could tell it didn't matter, she was only asking out of habit. It was like she wished she were anywhere else. I don't think she was as happy with my grandfather as he always claimed." Like he was color blind to her needs so long as his own were met.

"Anyway," I say, with a determined sort of cheer, "I think I turned out okay, despite it all."

She agrees that I turned out splendidly and becomes suddenly businesslike, sitting up on the mattress. "Okay. Where do we start?"

Back in the living room, I make a show of emptying my pockets, arranging everything on a side table in the living room. "Why don't you leave all your stuff here and we'll head to the garage first."

While I set her the task of sorting my grandfather's tools into boxes in the garage, I make an excuse to come back upstairs. I haven't dared attempt this at her house, where there are no guarantees how long she'll be out of the room. I couldn't risk it when she could catch me at any moment, her phone in my hand and me with a lot of explaining to do.

I need to know what people are thinking about me, texting about me, what sort of ideas they're planting in her head. It's not right that they can say such inflammatory things without my knowledge and with impunity. If I know what they're saying, I can at least be prepared.

She's not an idiot; it's protected by a PIN, but during one of the recordings I listened to, she shouted the numbers out to Cole so he could google something for her while his phone was upstairs.

The only difficult part of installing a spyware app is waiting around for the right moment. I trigger the download and run the program, listening for her footsteps pounding up the back stairs, but I keep confusing the thumps of my heart with the sound of her walking up.

With the download complete, I enter my access code, assign myself as the admin, and choose the "hide app" option when prompted.

But now she's headed up the stairs; it's definitely her, not my heartbeats. I can hear her coming closer, and any second she'll round the corner into the living room.

Hiding the app only does so much; it wouldn't erase all evidence from the vigilant eye, so I pull up her recent-download settings, get the two files I've downloaded deleted, and press the button on the side of her phone. The screen blinks off just before she appears on the threshold of the living room.

Her phone is exactly where she left it, innocently black, and oh, here's the Phillips head I've been looking for!

"Found it?" she says, scraping a sweaty strand of hair that's escaped from her ponytail out of her face.

"It's always the last place you look," I tell her, waving the screwdriver.

"Of course it is. You don't keep looking after you've found it, right?"

You're right, sweetheart. Of course you are.

I check up on things after Serena gave me a thoroughly nonverbal, prolonged goodbye and went back to her house. She's been texting Rosa, and the conversation plays out in real time as I sit at my desk.

Just got home, Serena texts at 8:46. I feel so bad for Chris, that house is so depressing

He'll be out of there soon enough, Rosa responds. You ever gonna give me the blow-by-blow, pun completely intended?

You are a complete and utter perv

At least tell me if it was good or bad! You can spare me that, come on, I haven't fucked a new person since 1875, I need details to remind me what it's like

                                            Yes, it was good

Camelia Guy has moves, huh?

                                            Jesus Christ

This is the kinda shit girls talk about, hun, get used to it

                                        He told me he loves me

When did he say that, in the middle of a BJ, that's when they all say stuff like that

                          It was not in the middle of a BJ for fucks sake

Was it afterward, did he take your chin all tenderly in his big manly hand and tell you he couldn't imagine life without you

                                            Not quite

Did you say it back?

                        Yeah, I did. I really do love him, he's perfect

    I'm perfect. That line warms me up from head to toe, like sinking into a hot bath.

    Well I'm happy for you, babe, it's about time you find a nice guy

About time you found a nice guy to bang, I should say

You are way too much, Rosa

I gotta go, I have to go find something for Marlon that's probably sitting there right in front of his stupid face, it never fails, love you!

Haha, call me tomorrow, love you more

I love you guys, too, I want to tell them.

Things between us are going so well, Serena, so much better than I could have ever hoped for. You haven't gotten any more mean messages from your mom, Cole is on board with us being a couple, Rosa has nothing but gushing praise for me, and I'm all moved into the house I bought for you. You're so happy; you've never been this happy before, and I know this because you are texting it to everyone. I can't believe I'm so happy, you say. I never thought it would happen! Work is going so well, Cole is doing great in school, and Chris is the best guy I've ever dated.

Derek is happy that you're happy, and he also wants to meet me. I gotta vet him, Mary, he texts. I don't like that he uses pet names for you, even if this is only the sarcastic name you received your first day of alternative high school when everyone found out you were pregnant. Virgin Mary is not something I want you calling my girlfriend, Derek.

But when I ask her to move in, she gives me a look that quite plainly says I've made a very bad mistake.

"Chris," she says, though she says it with a loving caress in her words and a soft smile, "I can't do that. That's moving way too fast."

It's been six months. My grandparents were engaged after a month, and my grandfather always said they were sure about each other from the start. I'm sure about Serena, she's sure about me—what is the point of waiting, stagnating for another six months, when we already know what we want, which is each other?

"It's just, you're always saying how small your place is. There's so much space here, space for both you and Cole."

"I wouldn't move in with anyone unless . . ." She shakes her head, wearing an expression I can't pinpoint. "I don't know, unless I get married or something. I can't uproot Cole's life on a whim. That's not fair to him."

It wouldn't be a whim, Serena; you love me. Love isn't a whim. It's not flighty, it's not something you wake up one day and change your mind about. Love is endless; it's something that endures, something you can't get rid of. I won't be sitting in front of the Xbox in the house I only bought because of you some afternoon and randomly think, *You know what, I don't think I love Serena anymore*; that will never happen, not ever. You love me, that's what you said, isn't it; and that means you're mine and I'm yours, just like Ygritte said to that fucking Jon Snow you adore. I only know that because you watch the damn show on repeat, which is pretty annoying, but I never tell you that because you love it and I love you, so I suffer in silence. I never say, "Down with George R. R. Martin, he must be a crazy incestuous freak, no more *Game of Thrones* for you, Serena." I never say that. I would never.

Why are you telling me no when I never do that to you?

"Don't get upset, babe," she says. "I'm not saying I don't want to be with you; I'm just saying I can't move in with you. Not yet. We just need more time."

I nod like I understand. That's what she needs to see, and I always give her what she needs.

But it would be nice if she paid me the same courtesy now and then.

11

Serena's hair is thick, fat with curls that hang loose down her back as she clacks down the sidewalk beside me, her hand tucked in mine. Her dress is emerald green, lacy, and off the shoulder, and she's wearing much more makeup than she's ever applied on one of our dates. I don't know how she gets more beautiful every day, but I am really not happy with that phenomenon right now; I'll be meeting Derek for the first time tonight, and I'd rather not have any distractions.

This place is some sort of speakeasy-type joint, the entrance nothing more than a black unmarked door down an alleyway in one of those quaint little towns the tourists love to walk aimlessly around. It requires a password for entrance; the one Derek has given Serena—*apres toi*, how fucking pompous—means we are able to enter without paying the cover charge.

The dark hallway, lined with quilted velvet walls, reeks of something like incense, and Serena grabs my hand, towing me around the corner into a small dim room stuffed with little tables and booths lined with more velvet, lit by fancy little electric candelabras on each flat surface. The gleaming dark wood of the bar lines the far wall, set behind fussy, fancy stools upholstered with even more velvet.

Someone calls her name, and she drops my hand, *clickclickclicking* across the room as fast as she can in heels that high, and has she ever attempted to run toward me in heels?

All Because of You

The man who must be Derek sweeps her into a hug that literally lifts her off her feet. When her heels are finally back on solid ground, Serena throws her hair out of her face and calls, "Chris, get over here!"

I plaster on my Friendly Guy smile and head toward them, weaving through the clustered tables.

Derek is holding Serena's hand but drops it to shake mine. "I've heard so much about you."

Everything about him makes me nervous, from his perfect black hair to his pale-green eyes. I thought they were blue when I looked through his Instagram, but I was wrong. Everyone knows girls are suckers for green eyes.

He matches her better than I do. Their dark hair, their light eyes—they complement each other in a way I can't. They look like they belong in *Twilight* or some shit, a frighteningly attractive vampire couple. Are people going to think they're together and I'm their weird, dateless friend?

"I've heard a lot about you too," I say, smiling so hard my eyes start to water. "I'm Chris."

"Derek. I'm glad Serena found you," he says, shooting a sideways look at my girlfriend. "It's about time she started dating."

"Shut up," she tells him. "I wasn't interested in anybody before Chris came around."

And suddenly I feel much better.

Derek slides back into the booth. "I ordered your vodka soda, extra lime," he says to her and then looks at me. "I wasn't sure what you'd want, so I got you an old-fashioned, same as me."

"Thanks," I say, while Serena sneezes out a chorus of thank-yous.

"I haven't seen you in so long!" she says, and it's like lights beneath her skin have brightened. "How've you been? How's your mom?"

"On her sixth marriage," he says dryly. "I've been good, busy. Too busy." Derek looks at me now, removing his jacket. "What do you do for a living? Serena said something with computers?"

"Software development." I play with the stirrer in my drink. "I oversee a team of engineers. You?"

"I'm in a band and give music lessons on the side. It keeps me busy. Moved back recently, though I'm still on the road a lot. Makes it hard to keep in contact with friends."

"I bet."

He gives me what feels like a dismissive smile and turns to Serena. "How's Sirius doing? I was in Tennessee not long ago and thought of him, passed by that house he was born in."

"He's good. Does his laps around the perimeter of the house every morning, hangs out on the window seat all day until he hears Cole or me come home, scarfs down his breakfast and dinner in about thirty seconds."

"That food you make him is fucking rank."

"It's not that bad," she says, her hand on my thigh beneath the table. "I don't know, maybe I'm used to it? Cole and Chris hate it too."

"Hard-boiled eggs and canned salmon smell terrible separately," I say, glad I seem to have something in common with this guy. "Add them together, and it's like knockout gas." I inhale a slug of my drink. "Serena says you guys were in alternative high school together?"

"Yeah." Derek laughs and adds sarcastically, "Best years of my life."

"What happened to get you sent there, if you don't mind me asking?"

"I was kind of the asshole class clown who sat in the back of the classrooms interrupting the teachers, and then I was caught smoking weed on campus a few times. I'd been there since the middle of tenth grade, and then junior year we get a new student who looks like a homecoming queen, and none of us could figure out why she was there," he says, his eyes on Serena. "Until we found out she was pregnant. Some smart-ass started calling her Virgin Mary, and the name kinda stuck."

She rolls her eyes. "Takes a real genius to come up with that nickname."

"What was his name, the guy who called you that your first day?" Derek rolls up his sleeves, exposing the blue veins on the inside of his elbows.

"Alden."

"I heard he's been in jail for a few years, some arson-type charge."

I don't like the way he looks at you, Serena. I don't like how his eyes hunt your face as if searching for something you can't give him because you're with me now; I don't like how he obviously loves seeing you laugh and making it happen. If you knew what to look for, you'd see what I see. You smile, and it makes his own increase in wattage. You laugh, and he can't help but laugh too.

He isn't your friend, Serena; he just wants to fuck you.

Serena finally stops giggling at one of Derek's unfunny jokes and pats my leg under the table. "I'm gonna go outside for a bit, babe," she says, waving her vape. "I'll just be a minute."

I really hate that she vapes. Not because of the health repercussions but because she goes outside alone, where scores of men will see her standing there in her high heels and pretty dress, being gorgeous, and they will somehow think this means it is okay to speak to her. It isn't okay, not with me, and it shouldn't be to her either, but I'm rapidly learning she doesn't see potential problems as acutely as I do.

Derek and I watch her leave, an awkward silence settling over us. It gives me lots of time to examine his perfect straight nose and his perfect hollowed cheeks. His eyelashes are so thick and black it looks like he's wearing eyeliner. I wonder briefly if he's wearing makeup (he's a musician, after all) but then he rubs his eyes vigorously, and there are no black smears when he blinks and looks over at me.

"I really am glad she found you, you know. She hasn't had much luck with men."

"That's what I've heard."

"I never met Ray, Cole's father, but Tom, her ex, was a real piece of work. I couldn't have been happier when she finally broke up with him."

"Yes, she told me he did some pretty disgusting things."

"*Disgusting* doesn't quite capture it, but yes." He takes a sip of his drink, his eyes on mine over the rim of his glass. "How do you and Cole get along?"

Is this a subtle barb? Is he trying to let me know, coyly and indirectly, that he's the only man in Cole's life? *I was here first, buddy?*

"I don't think he was thrilled with the idea of me at first, but he's warmed up a lot."

"And Sirius?"

"The same but switch out *warmed up* with *lukewarm*."

He laughs, and I see a flash of his perfect white teeth, which match his perfect lips. "I believe it. He's über-protective. You know about the robber?"

Of course she told me, I'm her boyfriend. "Yeah, she told me. I'm glad Sirius was there for her." I glance over my shoulder, looking for Serena because she's been gone for an awfully long time and I don't like it.

"She's quicker now that she's quit smoking."

I turn back to Derek, confused.

"When she smoked cigarettes, she was always outside longer," he elaborates. "But now that she's vaping, she's usually in and out." He leans back to get a better view of the mouth of the hallway. "There she is."

There she is, beautiful as usual, tucking her vape back inside her purse.

I get to my feet, let her slide into the booth, and reach for her thigh once I'm back behind the table. Gooseflesh sprouts in the wake of my fingers, but she jerks away like I've stabbed her, and the dismissal hits me like a gut punch. We're here with her "best friend" and I'm not allowed to touch her, but *he* can wrap his arms around her and hold unnecessarily long eye contact and her fucking hand, and is she moving closer to *him* in this stupidly designed circular booth? "Sorry, you tickled me," she says with a smile. "What did I miss? Someone out there was talking to me."

"Someone out there?" I ask.

"Oh, you know, just some drunk tourist." She waves her hand vaguely. "I think he was a tourist, anyway; no local I've seen has ever worn a DayGlo-orange Destin T-shirt. Apparently I'm gorgeous and they don't make them like me back in Ohio. Or something. He was slurring." She grabs her drink and knocks it back for the dregs.

"Well, he's right about gorgeous."

You see, Serena? *I* knew this would happen; why didn't you? I don't like you having to entertain horny drunks when you go outside to satiate your habit. I never thought I'd think this, but I am suddenly wishing you were ugly, average, even just a little plain—I wouldn't feel threatened every time you leave your house. I wouldn't have this overwhelming anxiety that someone will be out there, planning to take you from me.

We spend another two hours in this stupid speakeasy before Serena finally says we should call it a night. I take her home, where she cheerfully rejects me because Cole is there and kisses me goodbye at her side door, Sirius snuffling at her shoes.

"Sleep well, babe," she says, her arms around my neck. "Get home safe."

I tell her I will, but I'm not going home. Not yet.

A DayGlo-orange Destin shirt should not be hard to find. This area is popular with the tourists, packed with restaurants and shops that sell shit like sea glass and seashells, or petrified starfish enrobed in a bar of translucent soap with a price tag of $15.99. There are plenty of bars along the street, their doors flung open, loud laughter and music spilling out into the humidity, but it's not as packed as it would be during summer; it's not peak tourist season quite yet.

I'm not having any luck in my drive-by, so I feed three quarters into a parking meter and head out on foot, pretending to be engrossed in whatever my phone is telling me but using my peripherals to scan the streets. I've been at it for ten minutes, walking in a loop, sidestepping a tipsy older couple and a staggering horde of drunk women who will probably end the night with broken ankles—stumbling around the cracked pavement in heels that high—when I catch sight of something orange in an alley.

I stop beside a junk shop with a quaint and cutesy handwritten **CLOSED** sign on the door and glance around. The drunk women have made some progress; they're twenty feet away, with their backs turned, and the older couple seems to be hailing an Uber.

Backtracking to the alley, I find the wide, garishly orange back of an XXL T-shirt facing me, a plume of smoke ribboning to the night sky from the cigarette clamped in the man's fingers.

"Excuse me," I call, taking a few steps toward him, wedging my car keys between my knuckles.

He whirls around, unsteady and red faced, and the stench of alcohol permeating from him is pungent, streaming out of his pores. He must have been drinking for hours; maybe that's why he thinks it's okay to spout disgusting bullshit to other people's girlfriends.

"Yeah?"

The word has barely tumbled out of his mouth before I strike, the ends of the keys tunneling into his cheek. He doesn't have time to shout in surprise or pain or both. One second he's standing, and the next he's knocked out cold, spread-eagled on the ground, that orange shirt riding up to showcase a truly spectacular roll of fat.

And I feel much better on the walk back to my car.

12

Derek texts Serena the following morning, and I don't think I've ever read something more menacing than his terse **We need to talk**.

Why do you *need to*, Derek? What could possibly be so urgent that you need to pester my girlfriend at 5:59 a.m.? Have you finally noticed she hasn't sat around waiting for you to finally make your move? I can so easily imagine him knocking over a chair in his haste to stand up during the *speak now or forever hold your peace* portion of our wedding.

Serena doesn't respond to his text—she calls him, which is worse. She must be in her bedroom with the door shut because I hear nothing but vague, unintelligible murmuring from the kitchen bug.

I don't think Serena is stupid, but I do think she is very naive. She doesn't realize Derek wants to fuck her because she doesn't think the way men think; she doesn't know how easily a male mind can wander into the dark, that they all measure her by what they can take from her. I am a man, I know these things; I know perfectly well what happens every time she crosses paths with one. Maybe some women—and even then, I very much doubt it—can have strictly platonic male friends, but not her, by virtue of the way she looks and her approachable (a little too much so, if you ask me) personality.

She speaks to him for eight minutes and thirty-two seconds, and there is no activity on her cell phone for another two hours, until **Is Dre's car still in the shop?** to Rosa at 8:09 a.m.

> Yeah
>
> > I'll pick them up after school, you can come get Dre after work
>
> Sounds good

The high school's final bell rings at 2:45 p.m., so I suppose I should get some work done before then.

◆ ◆ ◆

But it is exceedingly difficult to get any work done when you get a call from an old-age facility stating that your grandfather has, to put it in clinical terms, gone off his rocker.

"We may have to sedate him, Chris," Maya, the midmorning aide, tells me. She's trying to keep her voice calm, but I can hear that thread of worry in her tone. She's one of the new ones, bless her. She hasn't yet become accustomed to the general insanity of a place like this. The old hands would sound irked, like their minds are on their dinner, when relaying such a message. You'd hear their nails tapping the counter in the background, the way they'd try to bite back long-suffering sighs. "He keeps asking for you; he thinks you're in high school again, he's demanding that I pull you out of class. If you can just stop by, maybe that'll put him at ease—"

I've already gotten up, and I'm stuffing my wallet into my back pocket. "Let me cancel my conference call, and I'll be right there."

◆ ◆ ◆

Upon my entrance through the double doors of the lobby, I can hear the dulcet tones of my grandfather's shouts echoing down the hallway. I don't stop at the front desk to sign in, and Maya runs around the counter to meet me, her eyes huge with concern.

All Because of You

"Thanks for coming in, Chris, I couldn't think what to do—"

"It's fine."

She keeps pace with my strides, knotting her arms around herself as we turn into my grandfather's room, which looks as though Axl Rose has just left. Overturned bedside table, trash spread across the stained linoleum, the bedding torn off once again and strewn across the floor.

"Grandpa," I call, and he looks up from the corner he's barricaded himself into with the pair of visitors' chairs.

His sweaty face shines through the forest of chair legs, his mouth falling open to reveal a set of dentures that look like piano keys. He must have fallen asleep wearing them; he's in no state to have put them in on his own. "Chris?"

"Why don't you come on out."

He pushes one chair aside and sticks his head out from behind it, a deep wrinkle carving a canyon into his forehead.

"When did you get so old?" he asks, milky eyes roaming my face.

I suppose he hadn't managed to look into the mirror over his dresser in his haste to fuck up his room. If he thought *I* looked old, he wouldn't want to catch his own reflection. "I heard you were asking for me?"

"Yes, I was," he says gruffly, heaving himself to his feet, kicking the chair aside. "I wanted to ask what the hell I'm doing in this place, if this was your idea of a bad joke. Where's your grandmother? I need a goddamn sandwich."

I never know what to tell him when he forgets why he's here, when he wakes up to the unfamiliar faces of young CNAs—bored nurses with stethoscopes slung around their necks like wilting halos. It must be terrifying, like he'd been abducted by aliens in the night, woken only to be poked and probed by these creatures in cartoon-character scrubs in primary colors.

He shuffles over, sinking next to me on the bed, shredding a piece of paper he must have found after he upended the trash can.

"A lot's happened while you were sleeping, Grandpa."

He squints, trying to focus, and when he does, he glares at me with the venom of a thousand cobras. "I hate your eyes."

"I know."

"They look like your father's."

I know that too. If I let him carry on, build up a head of steam, his rant will be epic, raging for hours. It can be difficult to distract the senile mind, but I've had a lot of practice. I know when to trot out the subject he loves most of all. The answer is easy; it's in the question—he loves love most of all. He's a big, soft romantic under that scary Albert Einstein hair and scowl.

"Do you remember when I told you about Serena?"

I can almost hear the gears in his head shifting. He looks at me as though suspicious I'm setting a trap, but he can't help but fall into it. And then he blinks, shakes his head, and it's like the real him climbs up into his cloudy eyes and gazes out at me.

"Your new girlfriend?"

"Not so new anymore, but yes."

"Of course I remember, I'm not stupid," he snaps.

"I thought I'd ask her if she wanted to come with me to visit you sometime soon," I say, in my best soothing therapist tone. "Do you think you'd be up for it?"

And it's worked. His face is transported, alive and incandescent. It almost seems like his wrinkles are receding, his eyes shedding their brooding menace.

"That's all I wanted since the first time you mentioned her."

"I'm sure she'd love to meet you." I cup his hand with mine. "I'll ask her next time I see her, okay?"

Nothing noteworthy occurs when Serena bangs into her kitchen through her side door with the two boys in tow later that afternoon, not unless you count her exclamations on how tall Dre has become, which I do not. She doesn't seem particularly distressed by anything. She's responded to my texts, but her answers have been short, stilted, to the point, which has given me a very bad feeling and painted my mood black. It wasn't that sunny to begin with after my grandfather's latest episode. Her clipped responses will probably wind up being the cherry on top of another lovely fucking day.

It's comforting to listen to her move about, making dinner, while I lean back in my chair at my desk. Almost like she's with me right now, a sweet little swearing housewife ("Jesus fuck, that's hot!") getting supper together while her husband works in the next room over.

It must be Rosa who invades my fantasy, bursting in through Serena's side door.

"What's up, Betty Cracker?" she says as the door clicks shut.

"I think it's actually *Crocker*."

"Not if you're that white."

"Betty Crocker *was* white, Rosa."

"Whatever. Where are the boys?"

"They finished homework. They're watching TV in Cole's room."

"Dre watches enough TV to turn his brain into Swiss cheese. He better pray he gets a football scholarship, with grades like that. I'm not spending an arm and a leg on college tuition if he's just going to dick around and flunk out." There's a screech, which I know is a chair leg being dragged out from under the table as Rosa settles herself at it. "How'd it go with Derek last night?"

"I . . . I thought it went pretty well, everybody got along. Not that I'd assumed they wouldn't; they're both friendly guys and everything . . ."

You don't sound too sure of yourself, Serena. You sound very much like a woman with state secrets on the tip of her satin tongue.

"Okay?"

A small clatter, four footsteps, a chair screech, and I surmise that Serena has joined Rosa at the table, her voice small and hushed.

"Derek wanted to talk to me this morning. I called him right away, it sounded so urgent."

Rosa's voice drops, too, and I picture them sitting there, heads bent together, Serena's dark hair wavy and wild, a contrast to Rosa's beautiful, bouncy curls. "What happened?"

"I don't . . . I don't even know."

"Well, what did he want?"

Serena sucks in a shuddering breath and blurts out, "He thinks he saw Chris do something last night. Something awful. After we left the bar, after Chris had taken me home."

Fucking Derek.

My nerves are barbed wire as Rosa's voice drops still lower. "Like what?"

"There . . ." She trails off distractedly. "There was this guy when I went outside to vape?"

"As usual. What about it?"

What, had Derek skulked around the streets on the off chance I'd go back for some reason, waiting for me? What had *he* been doing there?

"I don't know, he was this kind of drunk tourist, wandering around. I spoke to him for a bit; he told me I was hot or whatever, and I laughed it off and went back inside."

There's a pause, until Rosa breaks it with a confused "I'm not following."

"Derek stayed at the bar for a little bit, after Chris took me home. He says he was in his truck talking to his drummer on the phone, parked on the street, and he thinks Chris came back downtown . . . thinks he recognized him and his car. Says he watched him walk around for a few minutes until he went down some alley Derek couldn't see into, come back out really soon after, get in his car, and drive off." She seems to be attempting to marshal her thoughts. "He says when he saw Chris leave, he got out of his truck. Went into the alley. Saw that guy who was talking to me outside while I vaped. His face was mangled—someone had beat the shit out of him."

"Oh my God," Rosa breathes. "Are you serious?"

"He's not sure if it was actually Chris—he couldn't be positive. Obviously he's concerned about me dating someone who would do that."

Concerned. That's rich. Concerned that I don't like men saying disgusting things about my girlfriend. I doubt very much Derek would appreciate it if he were in my place. What would Derek have done? Shake the guy's hand?

That drone must be Rosa drumming her long, phony fingernails on the table. "Lots of people drive Audis. That doesn't mean it was Chris."

That is perfectly true. Serena, listen to Rosa, the bleeding heart of reason.

"Yeah," Serena says, but she doesn't sound particularly convinced.

"It just doesn't make any sense for Chris to do something so wild for no reason at all."

"Derek says he looked kind of anxious? Like jumpy? That he was acting weird when I went outside. That he kept looking over his shoulder, waiting for me to come back."

Rosa snorts. "So what? I'm sure he felt awkward, alone with your best friend of a hundred years, trying to make small talk."

"That's true. And he didn't seem flustered or angry when I came back in and mentioned that tourist. He just laughed. He was perfectly fine on the drive home, wasn't mad at all."

"So what did Derek do after he saw this drunk guy?"

"Took him to the hospital."

"And did this guy describe Chris when the doctors asked him who the fuck rearranged his face?" Serena must have shaken her head, because Rosa barrels on. "So there you go. It wasn't him. Chris has a memorable face—who wouldn't immediately say 'The guy has brown eyes, but one's got a patch of green at the bottom' when asked who punched him? That's not something you forget, is it?"

You're right, Rosa. You're totally right. And it helps that the guy was way too inebriated to even remember his own name, let alone my strange eyes from an encounter in a dark alley.

"Would someone that drunk even notice his eyes?"

"I don't know." She pauses. "Look, do you trust Chris? Do you trust that you know what kind of person he is? Is this something you can picture him doing?"

"Not at all." Serena heaves a sigh—a big one this time, the kind that makes me want to crush her against my chest and drizzle the top of her head with kisses.

"Did you ask him if he did it?"

"No. That's a huge, insulting accusation to make. Can you imagine how offended he'd be? I'd never ask unless I had cold, hard evidence."

"Are there security cameras on that street? Did Derek see a plate on the car this guy drove off in?"

"I don't know about cameras. He said he had half his mind on the conversation with his drummer, didn't really pay attention until the guy had left the alley to get in his car and drive off."

"Okay, then just forget about it. There's no proof, and you *know* Chris. You *know* he wouldn't do something like that. You love this guy; you know who he is."

"Yeah. Yeah, okay."

"Everything'll be fine, babe."

Just say *okay*, Serena.

"Yeah. Okay."

That's my girl.

◆ ◆ ◆

It warms the cockles of my heart to read the text she taps out after Rosa leaves.

> I gave it some thought, and it couldn't be him, Derek. I'm not angry or anything, I'm glad you're looking out for me and Cole, but I know it wasn't Chris.

As long as you're sure, he responds. I'll always look out for you two. She already *said* she was sure, asshole.

13

Serena perks up considerably after her talk with Rosa. She asks me to stop by her house that night, and I agree immediately because I am a gentleman, and when she answers the door, I almost want to call Derek to thank him.

All she's got on is a sheer robe, her pink nipples twin magnets for my eyes. I thought women only answered the door like that in porn movies.

"Hi." I don't bother trying not to stare. She wouldn't have turned up looking like this if she didn't want me to. "I'm guessing Cole isn't here?"

"He's sleeping over at Dre's." She shuts the door behind me, the breeze ruffling her robe around her thighs. She's not wearing underwear, and it's making blood pound behind my eyeballs.

"What's all this for?" I pull her flat against me. "Is this because I've been an extra-good boy or something?"

"Or something." She leans back, the better to look up into my face, tracing the contour of my jaw. "Have I ever told you you've got sexy eyes?"

"My grandfather just told me the opposite, that he hates them." I run my hand through the dark hair waving around her throat.

"Why would he tell you that?"

"Because he had a bad day."

Why did I mention my grandfather? Now she's pulling away, roughly securing the transparent sash in her robe, a pretty dent of confusion on her forehead. "So . . . when he's having a bad day, he insults your appearance?"

"Not usually. But he never was a big fan of my father, and I'm told I've got his eyes."

"You can't help that," she says, indignant on my behalf.

"He wasn't himself." I'm very much regretting mentioning it because she's crossed her arms over her chest, obstructing my view. "I was going to ask if you'd be willing to meet him sometime soon. On a good day, I mean."

She can't refuse, not when she'd thought so ill of me just this morning, when she'd even for a second entertained the notion that I wasn't everything she knew me to be—perfect. Her perfect boyfriend Chris, who wouldn't hurt a fly. The guy who'd suffered through many sexless months just for her, who bought a house just for her, the man who always says *yes, sure, anything you need, darling*.

"Of course," she says, after a moment's hesitation. "Anytime."

"Thanks. Can you get back over here now?"

Her face splits into a smile as bright as a sunrise, and she takes a step backward, playing hard to get. That's one of her favorite games. Probably because I take the bait every time. "Oh? You want me?"

I always want you. I've never wanted anything in my life more than I want you, but I think you already know that, sweetheart.

My mother's eyes are an opaline, crystal blue, faceted with craggy patches of icy white, navy, a color on the border of violet. So intense is the pigment that they almost look enameled, the perfect advertising image for colored contact lenses. They're also wide and blank with a clear *NOBODY'S HOME* look about them, which makes it very disturbing when her crusted, cracked lips part and she starts speaking.

She says my name, and she's the only person who has ever called me Christopher. My grandparents never called me Christopher, not even during scoldings. She named me, so I suppose she likes the longer version. It makes sense she'd want to use it.

It does not make sense that she's here, though, talking to me, when she hasn't for thirty years. I remember the last words she spoke to me—*Make sure you brush your teeth, Christopher.* Which I had done. I'd always been an obedient child.

"I missed you, Christopher," she says, the deep fissures in the corners of her lips filling with blood.

I wish I could say the same, but I haven't missed her in a long time. You can't much miss what you never really had. She'd signed her own death warrant and hadn't even bothered to say goodbye, just pointed me toward the bathroom and shut the door. That's the one thing I remember most about her, the door she shut in my face. I suppose I miss the idea of her being my mother, the fact that I'd never gotten to know her myself—instead of through the lens of other people's misty memories, battered and dented with time, embroidered to suit different moods.

She reminds me of Serena, in a way. I don't know what that means. Freudian logic would probably tell me it's an oedipal complex, but Freud was debunked a long time ago. Freud can kiss my ass.

If you missed me—if you'd loved me—you wouldn't have done what you did, Mom. You wouldn't have left me hanging out to dry. You would have controlled your depression, battened down the hatches. Maybe you're right, maybe you did love me in your way, but you didn't love me nearly enough. Weave that sob story to someone else. Take your razor blades with you.

I don't think she wants to take them with her, though, because she keeps holding one out beneath my nose. It's caked with old black blood, and it would seem that she scratched a heart in the corner, her macabre romantic touch before she punched her own ticket.

I don't want that razor, and I want even less to be this close to her because she's decaying right in front of me, growing deader by the second, her eyes withering in the sockets, her lips turning black and pulling back from her teeth so they're bared in the grin of some Grimm fairy-tale monster.

My heart pumps into overdrive, spilling adrenaline into my veins, and I turn to break into a run and promptly fall out of Serena's bed, disoriented in the dark. A shadow looms inside her closet, and for one wild moment, I wonder if my mother's followed me from the dream.

I'm back in bed just as Serena rolls over. "Are you okay?"

"I'm fine," I croak. "I had a nightmare about my mother."

"Oh, babe." She pulls me closer, and I lay my head against her heart. Her fingers twine through my hair, my pulse decelerating into nearly a flatline.

She uses her magic fingers on me until my body becomes all too aware of her own, that she's not wearing anything at all beneath that sheer robe, that the side of my face is pressed against her breasts. I could snake my tongue out and taste her nipple if I wanted.

I'm much stronger than her, and I think she likes it when I pin her against the mattress, crushing my lips on hers.

"Really?" She pulls back, a small and disbelieving smile materializing on her face through the semidarkness. "Right after you've had a horrible dream?"

"That's the best time," I say, my mouth on her throat, where her pulse flutters. "You make me forget about the bad things."

She jerks away when my breath tickles her neck, and when I tell her I love her, she responds in kind, stripping off her robe and letting it drift to the floor.

It seems ridiculous now that a stupid nightmare would scare me.

Why is Marlon in your kitchen, Serena? You didn't mention it this morning when you were naked in your bed with me. You didn't mention it when you kissed me goodbye at your side door, your hands in my hair that was still wet from our shower.

Should I be concerned that you're hosting your best friend's husband alone in your house? I'm going to have to cancel back-to-back meetings just to see what this is about.

I thought I loved that singsong thing Serena does, but when she graces Marlon with it, I realize I only like it when she uses it on me. Me, her boyfriend, or has she forgotten I exist? She knew who I was at the crack of dawn this morning when she comforted me with her flesh.

Marlon is a disturbingly handsome and tall Black man with skin like rich espresso and a strong, deep voice, which I've heard in video clips on Rosa's Instagram. Marlon has that *I can definitely fuck your girlfriend* look about him; it's tangible in his athletic movements, in his wide, easy smile.

He played basketball in college, got a full-ride scholarship, our dear Marlon. He was with Orlando Magic for a few years after he graduated, but Marlon must have decided that he simply wasn't perfect enough and left his basketball career behind, traded it all in for a respectable banking job, found a beautiful, perfect match in Rosa, and married her less than a year later. From the way Rosa had described him, talking in Serena's kitchen, I'd expected him to be some kind of bumbling Steve Urkel character, but when I looked him up on Instagram out of casual curiosity a few weeks after I'd first heard his name, I found that nothing could be further from the truth.

But who was Marlon, when you really thought about it? Some random side character with no lines to recite, no real screen time or backstory. Just the doofus husband of her pretty best friend. I do not like improvisations in my scripts. This was not how our story was supposed to play out, Serena. I was not supposed to have to contend with your best friend from high school and your other best friend's annoyingly attractive husband, who is quite a few inches taller than me.

"Hey!" she says, the way women text it to a potential hookup: *heyyy*. Insert slutty winky face here.

"How are you?"

"I'm great. Did you bring everything?"

"Yeah, it's all here. Oh, hey, buddy. I didn't hear you come over."

"I clipped his nails; he's always quieter when I do that. I was tired of him shredding my legs up with his claws."

Anytime I hear someone call Sirius *buddy*, I want to ask them what the hell is their problem. He does not remotely look like a *buddy*. He perpetually looks as though he's contemplating murder.

"She's a size ten?" Serena asks, and I have zero idea what this could mean. "I would have thought she was a bit smaller than that, her waist is so tiny. But you can't really ask a woman what size they are without it sounding rude. I'd kill for an ass like hers. You've got it made."

"I think that every day." I can hear the smile in his voice when he says, "But it said 'ten' on all her jeans."

"She may wear a different size in dresses, but I'll do my best. Did you buy the earrings?"

"I did. It's exhausting trying to figure out what to get her. I never know what to look for. I always get so worried about buying the wrong thing, and then I wind up getting a food processor."

Serena laughs even though it isn't funny. What kind of idiot would buy their wife a food processor as a gift?

"She saw the earrings last time I went shopping with her. I practically had to drag her away from the shop window. She'll love them."

"Thank God," Marlon says, as though he's Atlas and someone has finally lifted the weight of the world off his shoulders.

Well, this is a load off. You're obviously colluding with Rosa's husband for something to do with her birthday or whatever. I slump back in my new noncreaky swivel chair, wondering why she never saw fit to mention this birthday thing to me. I want to hear about her life. I want to know everything. I love her; she's my girlfriend. She's supposed to tell me everything.

Papers rustle. "I found a couple venues for you to look through that have open availability on such short notice. This one here is pretty new, but I've heard good things. The owners purchased the building from my boss, actually, and it's gorgeous. I think she'll really love it, but it's a bit pricey."

"That's not important. If you think she'll love it, it's the winner."

"Great, I'll call them to set everything up."

"I can do that, she's *my* wife," Marlon protests, but feebly.

"But she's *my* best friend, and I've got a lot more free time than you do, Mr. Investment Banker Recently Promoted Guy."

Serena, I know you're being your sweet, funny, full-of-personality self when you say things like this, but it reads as *flirting* to men. I'm sorry, it just does. You don't mean it to come off that way, you can't help it; but I know that tone, and I also know it's accompanied by one of your coquettish smiles, a few eyelash flutters, and a sweep of your hair. And all that gift wrapped and given to a man will only make him wonder what your lips would look like wrapped around his penis. You cannot say things like this to a guy; they take it the wrong way. They think it's an invitation, sweetheart. I wish you knew these things like I do. I wish you'd wise up now and then so I am not forced to keep tabs on you morning, noon, and night.

He laughs. Unfortunately it's less of a Steve Urkel snort and more of a sexy, manly-man chuckle. "You're the best."

Yes, she is. And that better not give you any ideas, Marlon.

14

"I'm kind of nervous," Serena admits, fiddling with the hem of her dress as she shifts ceaselessly in the passenger seat of my car. "Is that stupid?"

"No," I tell her, easing into the parking lot of the old folks' home. "It's normal. You don't have anything to be nervous about, though. His memory's not what it was, so he might forget all about it after, if that makes you feel better."

She doesn't look convinced when I turn the car off, so I squeeze her thigh and pull her in for a kiss. "He'll love you."

A fine mist clings to the evening air as we head through the front doors, and suddenly I wonder if Serena will remind my grandfather of my mother. I'm not sure what kind of reaction that will incite either way. He could shed his kindly old-man persona, step out of that skin and into his bitter, brittle, ranting character when he sees her, tell her off for killing herself. Or he could weep with gratitude that she's been sent home to him. Both will be awkward. She could probably use some kind of warning.

Instead of pulling open the door for her, I press my hand against it, looking down at her. "I'm sure I've said this before, but he can be a bit . . . unpredictable."

She bites back her lip, worry creasing her face.

"The nurses confirmed it's a good day, so I'm pretty sure he'll be on his best behavior, but even so . . . he's easily confused, and sometimes that makes him mad, starts him ranting because he doesn't know what's going on. I just want you to know the possibilities rather than throw you in there unaware."

She slides her hand into the crook of my elbow and nods. "Okay. Let's get in there."

The night nurses and aides perform slight double takes when they see I'm not alone, but they don't comment on it as I sign in at the front desk.

I stop in front of my grandfather's door and give it three loud knocks. More for Serena's benefit than mine; I've never knocked before.

"Come in!" my grandfather calls. He's affected a cheery, rich tone tonight, my grandfather. He's lost his hostile edges.

I almost want to laugh when I push the door open and find him sitting on his perfectly made bed, wearing a collared shirt he probably asked an aide to press for him and a pair of pants hiked practically up to his armpits. He's trying to impress my girlfriend. It's equal parts odd and amusing.

He booms out a hello in his new Happy Voice while Serena hovers shyly two feet behind me.

"Hi, Grandpa." I reach behind me, grabbing blindly for Serena's hand. "This is Serena."

"It's nice to meet you," she says, color creeping into her cheeks beneath my grandfather's stare. "I've heard a lot about you."

"I can say the same thing," my grandfather says. "Chris, get her a chair, why are you just standing there like a stuffed dog?"

I only barely refrain from rolling my eyes and drag two chairs beside the bed.

"Thanks." Serena sits, arranging the skirt of her dress artfully around her knees, hands clasped over the purse in her lap.

"It's nice to put a face to the name I've been hearing for months," my grandfather says. "And it's a very beautiful face."

The color in her cheeks isn't so much *creeping* now as *flooding*. "Thank you."

"Dad, don't embarrass her."

"It's a compliment! You're not embarrassed, are you?" He's staring at her like she's a piece of candy he's dying to unwrap, and I almost want to shield her from his gaze.

"Of course not, it's sweet," she lies. She looks so shy and little, sitting across from my grandfather's unabashed stare, so I inch my chair closer to hers and lace our fingers together.

"How was your day?" I ask him.

"The same as all the others!" he shouts, aiming another smile that I'm sure he intends to look roguish, but honestly, it looks more like a leer.

He's showing off. I don't know whether to laugh or call for a doctor.

"Someone had to be resuscitated, they had a guy over to host a bingo hour, and the book club had a meeting. I don't know how they can have a book club at all—none of those ladies can read a blessed thing, even with their glasses. The words are always too small."

"Maybe they can try audiobooks," Serena offers.

"What a great idea," he says, positively quivering with excitement. "I should let them know." For a moment the light behind his eyes flickers like snuffed-out candles when he spares me a glance. "Shouldn't you be in school?"

"Not today," I say, feeling Serena's sympathetic look on my profile.

He nods, and he's got eyes only for Serena again, though his smile slips a little the longer he looks at her. "You remind me of someone." His cloudy eyes run over her.

Don't say it, Dad.

"Oh?"

My grandfather stares at her so raptly that my telepathic *Don't Fucking Say It* can't dent the nostalgic bubble around him. "You look like my Laura."

Great.

"Chris's mother?" She shoots me a questioning look, and I confirm it with a nod.

"She killed herself," he says baldly, boldly, his pupils vacuous black holes of wistful longing.

"That's what Chris told me," she says quietly, her grip on my hand growing tighter.

"She did it after we all went to sleep. Said she was going to take a bath. Chris found her in the morning. He had to get ready for school. Went in to comb his hair and found her dead instead."

Serena's lips move like she's trying to speak, but it takes a while for her voice to catch up. "He told me that. I'm so sorry."

My grandfather pulls open a drawer in his nightstand, takes out a picture frame, and thrusts it into Serena's hands. "That's the last picture that was ever taken of the four of us."

She holds it like it's a creature that's suffered a terrible wound, her tumbling curls hiding her face. I hook a finger through her hair and smooth it out over her back, my arm around her shoulder as she looks down at the strangers I'm related to. They all feel like strangers now, some half-remembered dream. Even when my grandfather's mind is intact, he's never really here. Always in the past.

There they are, my family, the three people who taught me about life and love and heartache, their smiles dull with age. The way they modeled love to me was that you know immediately who your soulmate is. It's either effortless or it isn't, and if it's the latter, you use force to make it work—you jackhammer that square peg into the circle with all your might—or you give up entirely and self-implode.

Serena traces our dusty smiles with her fingertip and hands the photo back to my grandfather. "I'm glad you have it here with you. You should keep it on the bedside table instead of hidden in the drawer."

He would never do that. Then he'd see what happened to his life in sharp relief every morning when he woke up.

I clear my throat loudly, trying to inject some lightness into the proceedings. "We're off to Serena's best friend's surprise birthday party after this, Dad, so we can't stay too long."

"That must be why you look even lovelier than I imagined," my grandfather says. "Women don't wear dresses enough these days. They don't put in as much effort as they used to, back in my day. Some of the nurses here would be knockouts if they bothered with makeup and smiles."

Serena forces out a laugh. "They've got busy jobs. I probably wouldn't bother with makeup if I did what they do."

"You would," he says. "I can tell you would. You're the kind of woman who cares about those things. Chris visited me the day he met you in the grocery store, told me all about you with this look on his face. I knew then that you'd be something special."

And now my heart is dancing a kind of samba in my chest. Of all the ways he could have screwed everything up, this is the worst.

I paste on a patient *your senile is showing again* expression. "No, I told you after she showed me my new house that I realized I'd met her before, at the grocery store."

His face becomes more lined than ever as it twists into a frown. "Really? I thought it was the same day as the grocery store. I remember you telling me about the peanut butter."

Serena's gaze bounces between my grandfather and me. I have never wished I were a mind reader more than I do right this second.

Please don't read too much into this, Serena. He's senile, sweetheart. Demented—I've told you that, haven't I? It's really very sad, the way he gets so mixed up. Just nod and smile and let's be on our way.

"It's okay, Dad, you're just a little confused."

He shrugs, but his forehead is still draped with wrinkles.

I make a show of glancing at the time on my phone and stand up, pulling her to her feet. "We should get going, babe. You can't be late to a surprise party."

She gives me a relieved smile, and it lessens the burning ball of anxiety that has taken up residence in my chest. He's just a confused old man, getting his timeline jumbled. She believes it without question. To quote her, I am the best man she's ever dated.

"It was very nice to meet you, Mr. Fox," she says, bending over to brush a dry kiss against his withered cheek.

"You too, my dear. Make sure he takes good care of you."

◆ ◆ ◆

Serena has outdone herself. The greenhouse she secured as the venue for Rosa's fortieth birthday party has me thinking *A Midsummer Night's Dream*. Twinkle lights everywhere, twisted along the planters bursting with flowers, snaking over the glass walls, crisscrossed against the transparent ceiling, where they echo the stars in a black velvet sky. The greenhouse is dim, bathing everyone's faces in flattering shadows, giving the place a kind of moonlit mystery, like it's coated in fairy dust.

I wish she'd stop for two seconds to admire her handiwork, but she's in business mode. It's odd to see a woman dressed like that being businesslike. Her dress whispers across the petal-strewn ground as she makes her rounds, her unbound hair hiding her exposed back. It's a soft, pink, fluttery fabric that looks like a watercolor painting of ivy and flowers, held high around her neck by skinny straps and nipped in tight at the waist. She's some fairy nymph cut out of an enchanted forest and transplanted here, tonight, to boss everyone around.

"Keep the presents at the back," she says, snagging a waiter by the back of his vest. "I don't want her seeing them when Marlon's walking her over. Can you let everyone know?"

He gives her what he clearly thinks is a winning smile and takes off to do her bidding.

She flings out her hand, stopping a girl in a long pale-green dress. Her hair has been braided into some kind of buttery-blond crown, tendrils escaping in elegant disarray. "You look gorgeous, Emma. Can you do me a favor and tell the other girls we're going to be starting with champagne?"

"Of course."

I trail behind my girlfriend as she orders everyone about in that silver-tongued way, twitching at a long green dress now and then to make the fabric hang correctly, stopping to adjust bow ties. I'm not crazy about that part, obviously, because I know all those boys are looking down at her adoringly as she does so. They don't see it for what it is, her obvious perfectionism; they think she's coming on to them, wants to invent excuses to touch them.

"Babe?" she calls, flinging a backward glance at me as she sends the tenth lucky kid on his way. "Can you find the manager, tell him Marlon will be here with Rosa in ten?"

Those ten minutes fly by, and suddenly the manager is killing the lights, Serena is telling everyone very sweetly to shut up, and the room takes on the dull roar of a bunch of people trying to be quiet at once.

Serena shakes with soft laughter when we hear, quite clearly, Rosa's bitching as she's being herded to the door of the greenhouse.

"Why the fuck didn't you tell me not to wear heels—if I'd known I'd be walking through grass, I'd have gone with wedges or flats or something."

"I didn't think about it," Marlon's calm voice says. He must be used to being constantly harangued. "Sorry."

"Men never think about practical things like that," she grumps. "Why is it always the women who have to remember shit? We have to make lunches and remember snacks and join the football boosters and *oh shit*, Dre needs one of those giant cardboard display things because his science project is due tomorrow, and we have no toilet paper either!"

And then Marlon twists the doorknob, the manager turns the lights back to their flattering, diffused glow, and everyone shouts "Surprise!" to Rosa's beautiful, baffled face.

◆ ◆ ◆

"But it isn't my birthday yet!" Rosa says, once Serena and I have waited for the ebbing crowd around the birthday girl to clear.

"We can't throw a surprise party on the actual day of your birthday, babe," Serena says, kissing her cheek. She stands on her tiptoes as Marlon inclines his head to let her kiss his cheek as well, and I pretend I'm not annoyed by that when he turns his phosphorescent smile on me.

"I've heard so much about you, Chris. Thanks for coming," he says in that plummy, self-impressed voice, his arms snaking out to snare the waists of Serena and his wife.

"Of course, I love Rosa. I wouldn't miss this for the world," I say, even though privately I am thinking, *Can you do me a favor and please stop groping my girlfriend?*

"Are you the real purchaser of this dress?" Rosa asks Serena, plucking at the fabric. It's pretty, one of those off-the-shoulder things, white with wine-colored lace detailing. "Marlon said he bought it for a 'special date' tonight, but this isn't his taste. His taste is low necklines and high hemlines."

"You showed it to me in a text a few months back, remember?"

"Your memory freaks me out."

"I get that a lot." Serena stops a passing waiter, grabs a champagne flute off the fussy little silver tray he's carrying, and wraps Rosa's fingers around the stem.

"Happy—"

"Please don't say *fortieth*—"

"*Birthday*," Serena says, with careful enunciation. "Now go mingle and talk to your friends while I get everyone settled."

15

I realize that as one of the hosts of this thing, Serena's got a certain amount of schmoozing and socializing to get on with. I get it, I do, but I'm pretty tired of following her around or, conversely, loitering at the bar, pretending to have fun, smiling every time she catches my eye from across the room. I'm on my third gin and tonic, and the bartender's put in a bit more gin than tonic.

The ice in my glass rattles as I suck down the watered-down vestiges of my drink, and when I thump the empty lowball down on the bar, someone sidles up to me and requests an old-fashioned.

"Oh. Chris. Hey," Derek says, leaning against the bar, his hair artfully mussed, so imperfect that it's perfect. He hasn't shellacked it into compliance; you can tell he did absolutely nothing to it, but it's still perfect. I can't stand him. "I didn't see you there."

I grunt out a polite hello.

"Where's your girl?" he asks amiably.

"Twelve o'clock," I say, jutting my chin in her direction. She's bending over a table, her hands resting on the backs of two chairs occupied by two men, laughing about something I can't hear, but I'm going to go out on a limb and assume the joke isn't that funny, she's just being polite, but a bit too exuberantly so. The men are related to Rosa somehow, but I don't know their names or why their wives aren't furious with them for their unabashed gawking. Simultaneously, she rubs both their backs as though they're infants she's burping, and then she's off

All Because of You

again, threading through the mob. Someone must have called her name because quite suddenly she whips around, stands on her tiptoes to see over the crowd, spots the waving hand flagging her down, and starts off in the opposite direction. And of course it's a guy flagging her down. She hugs him for far too long and touches his arm repeatedly, and I think I want to kill him.

The twinkle lights all over this stupid greenhouse hit upon the strings of rhinestones she's woven through her hair, and she's beautiful and mine, but it doesn't feel like she's mine at the moment. She doesn't belong to me tonight; she's a crowd commodity. A directionless sort of despair is rising in my chest as I watch her navigate this war zone of merriment, corks popping like cannon fire, laughter like explosions, bombs of cheek kisses. She's choosing all this over me.

"That's a pretty dress she's wearing," Derek offers, taking a dignified sip of his stupid old-fashioned. One of his thick black eyebrows arches after I cut him a look, but he doesn't comment on it. "How long's she been doing the social-butterfly thing?"

"I'm not sure, I haven't kept track," I say, even though I have kept track and it's been thirty-five minutes. "I just got tired of following her around, so I thought I'd hang here instead."

"A wise plan," he says, holding his drink out.

It's a second before I realize he wants to do a cheers clink. I don't especially want to do a cheers clink with a guy who tried to sabotage my relationship, but I do anyway.

"I'm glad I ran into you, actually," he says, his elbow on the bar.

"Are you?" I ask, but it comes out much harsher than I intended.

He presses his annoyingly full lips together, a curious tilt to his brow. "Yeah. Why wouldn't I be?"

I can't seem to stop my persistent glare. I feel it drawing down the corners of my lips, scoring my forehead, the force of it pounding behind my eyeballs.

"I don't know. Why *would* you be?"

Derek gives me a short, humorless snort, and his green eyes have lost their phony friendly glint. "Do you have some sort of problem you want to talk about?"

Yes, but I won't. I'm not supposed to know that you attempted to rat me out to my girlfriend, Derek. She never told me directly that you did what you did. I'm not supposed to know you're the viper in the garden, am I? Well guess what, Serena doesn't believe you, she never believed you. Can't you find some groupie slut to take home? Why do you have to be obsessed with the woman I love?

"I think it might be you with the problem," I say carefully because I think I may be slurring.

Derek is expressionless as he stares back at me, silent for a few seconds. "Go easy on the sauce, Chris. If you ever want to try a direct approach, you come find me," is all he winds up saying before knocking the rest of his old-fashioned down his throat. He slides the empty glass away and winds his way through the crowd without a backward glance.

I turn back to the bartender to order another gin and tonic, and then there's a hand on my back and a body weaving beneath my arm.

Serena stands on her tiptoes to kiss me. "I've made my rounds; it's Marlon's turn. Have you been super bored?"

"Of course not," I lie, though every part of me screams, *Hell yes, I was fucking bored while you were off mingling and flirting; you're supposed to be* my *girlfriend, you're supposed to only have eyes for* me. "I spoke to Derek for a while."

"Oh yeah?" Her cheeks are flushed, prettily pink. "I didn't see him come in."

"I don't get the impression he likes me very much." I avert my gaze, staring into my drink like I'm slightly embarrassed to be admitting such a thing.

"Really?" she says, trying to look surprised. "Why do you say that?"

I shrug. "I don't know. He's kind of adversarial. His tone, the looks he gives me. Did he ever mention me offending him the last time I saw him? I wondered if I could have somehow unintentionally put my foot in my mouth . . ." I trail off, letting my eyes wander as though I'm deep in thought, fighting through thickets of hazy memory to trace back how and when I could have offended that prick.

"No, he never said anything about you." She's trying to spare my feelings. She loves me and doesn't want me to be hurt by Derek's wild accusations. I both love and hate her a little for it. Relationships shouldn't be this way. She shouldn't be hiding stuff from me, mincing around topics. I don't lie to her. Well, not often. Not about anything important.

I shrug again, an *okay, maybe I'm imagining it* shrug.

She slips her bare arm around my waist, her head against my bicep. "I think I'm a little behind on the drinking part. I might need to steal a bottle of champagne."

The bartender's back is turned as he greets another guest, so I snag the nearest bottle of prosecco out of its ice bath and hand it to her.

"My hero," she says, pressing her hand to her heart, and I remember why I love her so much. "Want to sneak outside and open it for me?"

"Of course."

She leads the way, and I'm glad she doesn't see my tipsy (okay, drunken) stumble as I follow her out the side door of the greenhouse.

The clouds curdle around a guttering, incandescent moon, the light from which softens and amplifies the beauty of everything it touches. The cherry blossoms are fragrant; the grass, silver under the glow of the moon, is that perfect balance between "stodgy old man's front lawn" and "charmingly overgrown," and Serena looks like some goddess of flora, the moonlight washing her exposed skin in a luminous sheen, the long hem of her dress twisting around her ankles.

But then I don't think flora goddesses ever drink champagne straight out of the bottle.

"Can you hold this for me?" She hands me the prosecco, using my shoulder to brace herself as she kicks off her heels. "Beauty is pain, babe. You're lucky you don't need much help to look sexy."

She doesn't need much help either. She's sexy first thing in the morning, with mussed hair and violet stains beneath her eyes, before she's even brushed her teeth or made it into the kitchen for her first cup of coffee.

She rolls her foot in a circle, the small, delicate *crack* of her tiny bones sounding like the snap of a twig among the cherry trees. The moon backlights her head like a halo, frosting her hair gold.

She takes another long slug of the champagne after I return it to her and then bends over and twists the bottle into the dirt to stabilize it. "It's pretty out here, isn't it?"

I slip my arms around her waist from behind as she looks up at the stars burning in the sky. Her cheek lifts under the weight of her smile when I nuzzle into her neck, kissing the pressure point where her pulse beats.

Sometimes the way she smells makes me dizzy. It makes me happy and sad and horny and scared, and I don't know what to do with all that pent-up emotional energy; it's too much for one head to contain. I'm ecstatic that she's mine and terrified that I'm going to lose her someday very soon. It makes me want to rip that slinky dress off her and hide her in my closet so nobody else will see her, both at the same time.

Sometimes when I'm this close to her, near enough to slide her zipper down and look beneath the neckline of her top, I get this sudden surge of anger that I'm not the only guy who's done this to her. There was Cole's father, then Tom, and I'm sure I can sprinkle in a half dozen one-night stands even though she's never mentioned having any, but come on. I'm sure she's had drunken nights late at the bar where some slick dickhead managed to take her back to his place.

I haven't consciously chosen to do so, but suddenly my hands are at the zipper above her ass, pulling it down. She's not wearing underwear; I can see so quite clearly through all this beautiful moonlight. It makes me hard but infuriates me at the same time. She *wasn't wearing underwear* as she did her mingling routine. She had her hands on other men and she *wasn't wearing underwear*.

"Chris!" She twists around, laughing, wriggling out of my arms.

"It's been a while," I say, adjusting myself, since my pants have gotten uncomfortably tight in the crotch yet again. Do you see what you do to me, Serena? You're a succubus. You torture me and then you laugh.

"No, it hasn't." She's still laughing. What is funny about the fact that I want her? "Stop, someone might see."

"Who cares?" I pull her back over, peering down her pretty pink dress to get a look at her cleavage.

"Um, me?" She slaps my hand away, and the sting of her denial is an ice pick to the heart. "I'm not going to fuck you in the middle of Rosa's party, Jesus Christ."

"But it's fine for you to have your hands all over a bunch of men back in there?" I fling my hand toward the twinkling greenhouse.

That smile on her face evaporates; it's a black curtain falling on a lit stage. Her mouth falls open, and for a second I think I've stunned her into silent agreement, but she says, in the dangerous, acidic tone I've only ever heard her use on Cole, "What in the fuck are you talking about, Chris?"

"You have a hard time keeping your hands off every single man in there, but *I'm* not allowed to touch you?"

"What the hell are you talking about?"

"Every time I looked up to find you, you were groping a shoulder, squeezing a hand, touching a thigh. Every time. I counted. You did it eighty-seven times."

"You *counted* how many times I touched people?"

Her voice has grown soft, and something dark and fetid in the back of my mind says this is very, very bad for me, but I think it's the gin that goads me onward.

"Only the men," I say, and some distant voice inside me that sounds an awful lot like my grandfather tells me to stop shouting, but I can't. "It was hard to keep track, what with how often you did it, and then

Derek shows up, acting like a fucking asshole while I'm hanging out at the bar, *alone*, and you're over there being Miss Social Butterfly—"

Her beautiful, moonlit face is stony, like she's spontaneously hardened into a life-size statue you'd find in some fancy garden conservatory, but her nostrils are flaring and the breeze is lifting her dark hair and her eyes are simultaneously cold and blazing.

"I think you should order an Uber and go home, Chris." She sweeps her heels back into her arms, grabs the abandoned champagne bottle, and stalks off through the lawn, dew-drenched grass squishing beneath her feet.

My mouth is dry, my heart is hammering, and I call out her name, choking on a sudden upsurge of remorse that tastes like bile, but she doesn't turn around.

"You shouldn't be driving," she says with arctic finality, her voice getting fainter the more space she puts between us. "Just go home."

16

I wake up groggy, my head thick with pain. All I can do is blink and wonder how I managed to get into this state until I remember, and suddenly I am a wasteland.

There was a fight. A bad one. Actually I don't think *bad* quite captures the scope of this fight. We've never had one before. Surely we wouldn't be over after one little fight?

The memories come in scattered showers; they don't hit all at once like a tidal wave.

Me, alone at the bar, watching her cavorting with her friends, an endless supply of leering men enveloping her. Derek and his mocking green eyes. The lawn off the greenhouse where she wouldn't let me touch her. Lots of words, angry words. Most of them from me.

It had to have been the gin.

I roll over. The accusing red numbers on my alarm clock blare 4:47 a.m. as I grope for my phone on the bedside table, but when I blink blearily at the screen, no notifications await me. She's probably erased my number by now, blocked me from sending messages. I can't believe I let this happen.

Jasper creeps over, his whiskers whirling against my bare shoulder. I grab him to my chest, looking up at the ceiling of the master bedroom in the house I only bought because Serena was the one selling it.

My pulse thuds resignedly, in tandem with the throbbing of my head, and I think I might know now why my mother committed suicide.

I pull up the spyware app. No phone activity, not since 8 p.m., when the party began. She hasn't texted anybody about what an asshole I am; that must mean something, I think, until I remember she was in a giant venue full of people she could have bitched to in person.

How did she get home? Fucking Derek probably gave her a ride.

I pull up the app for the recording device, rewinding back to, what, 1 a.m.—when did she finally stumble home?—and I hear nothing. Not for a while. And then at 2:32 a.m., there's the skittering of many nails across the kitchen tile and a rattling I assume is her turning the doorknob.

"Hi, my love," I hear her whisper, and I'm sure she crouched there in the dark, her arms twisted around Sirius's thick black coat. "Did I wake you up, babe?"

And that's it. I fast-forward to the real-time recording, and there's nothing, not even the creak of a distant floorboard or the click of Sirius's nails as he moves from room to room. She must still be in bed, forgetting all about me. I'll wind up being just another name on the list of assholes she's dated, and I'm sure Derek will move in to sweep her off her feet forthwith. He wouldn't miss a prime opportunity like this.

You're the best, babe! Thx for the amazing night. Marlon says you guys planned it together but I know you were the one calling the shots, he couldn't plan his way out of a paper bag, from Rosa at 7:12 a.m., followed very closely by ugh, I shouldn't say the word shots, Jesuchristo I'm hungover, I think I need to update my will.

Serena responds quickly. She's probably in bed, naked beneath her sheer robe, Sirius panting all over her face. At 7:13: Marlon did a lot!

What did he do, apart from wave his checkbook around?

> He fretted about what to buy you, we visited the venue together, and he also waved his checkbook around

Good boy. I should tell him that more often. Am I a bitch? I think I might be a bitch wife

> It's part of your charm, I reckon

Oh hey, tell Chris I said thank you for the Sephora gift card, was his work crisis cleared up?

Ah. I had a work crisis, that's why I had to leave so suddenly.

> It wasn't a work crisis. We had a fight, I told him to leave. I didn't want to ruin your time by telling you last night. Do you think I'm overly touchy or something? That I go around groping unsuspecting men? Am I too handsy with Marlon?

No. WTF?

> That's what we argued about. Mostly. I don't even know, he was pretty drunk.

He SERIOUSLY said you go around groping dudes? What a fucking dumbass

I suppose this means Rosa is no longer Team Chris. That hurts. I loved how much she liked me.

> He was pissed I had to make the rounds talking to everyone but it isn't like I banished him, he could have

> come with me. I HAD to thank everyone for showing up, didn't I? I couldn't just sequester myself in a corner to soothe my boyfriend's tender feelings

Marlon LOVES being banished, then he doesn't have to stand there bored out of his gourd while I'm talking about shoes and the new Dolce lines

> Then he told me Derek was being an asshole

Really? I can't quite picture that. Derek's never been an asshole in front of me

> Apparently. I don't know. I don't know how much to believe, Derek didn't tell me anything and I didn't bring it up because it would have been horrible timing. Then he tried to get me to have sex with him when we were out on the lawn. He just started trying to take off my dress! I told him there's no way I'd fuck him when there's a giant party for my best friend going on, and that's about when he started screaming that I was this mad groper lady who flirts unashamedly with all these poor helpless men

That isn't quite what I said, sweetheart; can you lose the dramatics, please?

It takes Rosa much longer to respond to this, but a few minutes later: that's insane. I literally have no words. How much of it do you think is drunken rambling? FYI I asked Marlon just now if he thought you were a mad groper lady and he said no, but he could use some groping right now, and then he tried to get me to touch his morning wood. Fucking men. Pigs. As if I want a thing to do with penises when I feel like I might yak

Lmao, poor Marlon

Poor ME, I didn't sign up to see his morning wood. So is this the nail in the coffin, you think? Goodbye Chris?

I don't know . . . I'm still really pissed

I don't blame you, I'd have slapped him, probably. So he never texted you after you made him leave?

Nope

Well when he apologizes, and he will because they always do and because the man is crazy about you, you need to make sure he completely owns what he did, no excuses or any of that I'm Sorry But shit. If he pulls out an I'm Sorry But you end the conversation because he's not sorry, he's just trying to twist the argument around to blame you. Don't let him wiggle out of taking the blame like you always did with Tom. If he's really sorry, he'll fall on his sword and own up to everything

We'll see, Serena says ominously.

Well, thanks to Rosa, now I have a script to follow, but I'm still nervous, my pulse humming relentlessly, when I pull up our text thread.
    Do you have a minute? I tap out. I'm sorry about last night.
    She makes me wait, just like I knew she would, and fifteen minutes later, my phone lights up.

You should be. I don't know what the fuck that was, but it's not something I want to be a part of.

Well occasionally you have to deal with things you'd rather not, Serena. It's a part of life. I didn't want to see what I saw last night, but I had to, just the same.

> I'm not sure what it was either. I don't know, maybe it's the stress of my grandfather going even further downhill or work or trying to get this new house in order. I don't know why I snapped. I was drunk, not that that's an excuse.

Surely she's done terrible things when drunk. Hasn't everyone? Can't she just let this one slide if I promise to be a good boy from here on out? She's certainly not the perfect princess I thought she was; she's got a lot of flaws I can sit here and tick off on my fingers, but I never do. I accept them because that's what you're supposed to do when you love someone.

> Look, I've done stupid shit when I was drunk too, but the venom and possessiveness you were spewing was incredibly worrying. You counted how many times I touched people, Chris. That's crazy. You were mad that I had to greet everybody but you had to know that would be part of the itinerary, okay, I was the one throwing the damn party. I don't know what else you expected. You ruined that whole night for me. I had to pretend to be happy for hours after you left when all I wanted to do was go home. I shouldn't have had to put on an act for Rosa's sake. I'm more pissed about that, that I couldn't be genuinely happy to be at my best friend's birthday party.

Now I don't think it would be politic for me to point this out quite yet, but do you really think I should have had to stand there watching my girlfriend get groped left, right, and center? I don't think that's something I should have had to stand for, Serena. You've got a lot to learn about the give-and-take of relationships.

> I'm sorry. The last thing I ever want to do is hurt you.
> I don't know, I guess I have abandonment issues,
> what with my mom and father. It's not an excuse but
> it might be an explanation. Nothing like this has ever
> happened before so I don't know what was going on
> with me. But I can promise you it won't happen again.
> None of this was your fault, you did nothing wrong.
> It's all me. And I'm sorry.

Five minutes slug past, and though the message has been marked seen, she doesn't reply. My throat is getting thick, sealing up, growing tight and hot. I think I'm willing to promise her anything, so long as she doesn't leave me.

I'll have to think about it, she finally responds, and my heart flatlines. It's cold and hollow, a sad empty piggy bank. She's withdrawn all my love coins and never made any deposits. I just need some time to myself, she continues, ruthlessly stomping on my heart. Cole will be back from my mom's place soon and I can't sit here and stew on this.

I understand. I love you, I say, and I really do, because why else would just typing that out make my corneas sting? I've never loved anything as much as I love her. *I know I screwed up, but I love you.*

I love you too, she says, and my heart swells for a second, until it's followed by: but sometimes that's not enough.

17

Serena doesn't appear to be doing much thinking. It's been three days and I've yet to hear anything about our relationship status. Is this technically considered ghosting? She's had no visitors, so I can't hear her expound on what she's really thinking. Her texts have been excessively dull. She said she'd think about it, fine, but isn't three days quite a long time to keep somebody on the hook? I have to troll Instagram to figure out what she's up to.

Here are two martini glasses on a polished, dark wood table. *Pregaming!* Rosa captions it, tagging my likely now ex-girlfriend. *derek_g, mrobbins79, and 27 others like this!*

Two hours later, I am treated to a truly terrible update: *free drinks just taste better, don't they?* It's a selfie, one in which Rosa holds her drink aloft, and I don't think Serena knows how to pose for a selfie because she's looking at Rosa instead of the camera, her head tilted so all that pretty hair swings over one shoulder. That top Serena's got on is making her look like a whore, which I know wasn't her intention, but unfortunately the end result is the same.

I swallow the impulse to show up at the bar because it wouldn't be conducive to mending fences. I know when to leave well enough alone, Serena; you don't need to worry about me smothering you.

I'm bored and restless, sad and scared; and acting on nerves, I scroll backward through Rosa's Instagram timeline until suddenly, luckily, I see an image I missed earlier, probably because Serena wasn't pictured or mentioned.

It's of two boys. One I've met personally. Every time I look at Cole, I find his mother in his face, and when I examine Dre, I realize I see Rosa and Marlon in him as well. He's a nice-looking kid, like Cole; his face has an attractive cast of Black and Latin features. They're not posing for the camera; their attention is on an oversize LED screen, but Rosa's caption (*What is this, like the millionth sleepover of the year?*) gives me a wonderful idea.

Ah, sleepovers. A joy I never experienced as a child. My grandfather was a very particular man and never wanted unknown children with sticky hands traipsing about his home. I've only had adult sleepovers, but I've seen a lot of movies. I'm sure Cole and Dre are gorging on FUNYUNS, playing enough Xbox to give themselves carpal tunnel, looking up internet porn. But thankfully they are doing so at Rosa's house, because Serena does not own that obnoxiously large TV I saw in the picture.

Serena's emergency key is kept out of sight, behind a bush of garish pink hydrangeas and hidden inside an empty peppermint ALTOIDS container, half buried in soil. She's not the key-under-the-mat type. She's too smart for such an obvious hiding space.

I am going to have to trust in the fact that Sirius has seen me plenty of times throughout my months of dating his mother and will hopefully decide not to attack me. I don't think he can be easily bought, but I've got a grocery sack full of stew meat in the laptop bag I've slung over my shoulder to persuade him to let me live, just in case.

He's waiting for me at the side entrance, his terrifying, tiny wolf eyes burning into mine as I ease the door shut behind me.

"Hi, buddy," I say foolishly, remembering how strange I've always found it when other people call him such. I keep my movements slow, methodical, as I twist the laptop bag around and dig for the package of meat stuffed inside it.

His teeth aren't bared, and his head isn't bowed like he's ready to charge, but every sinewy scrap of muscle in his petrifyingly huge, hairy body looks tightly coiled, as though he'd just love for me to give him a reason to pounce.

I manage to poke a hole through the plastic covering the meat and yank out a raw piece. His gaze flickers between me and the beef as though he can't decide which he wants to kill first.

"Sit for me, Sirius," I say, trying to keep my voice light and friendly in the face of this beast. I've become an uptalker, making every statement into a question. I sound like a cheerleader on Zoloft.

He cannot sit, as it so happens. I know he understands that command because he's been able to do so for Serena on countless occasions, but I forgive him his insolence and hold the bit of meat beneath his nose.

The siren scent of blood must be too much to resist; he can't possibly chain himself to the mast. His black lips pull back, his long pink tongue snakes out, and he very carefully bares his teeth to take my offering.

He chews thoughtfully and swallows. His tail isn't wagging, but he no longer has that death look on his face, so I give him another bit of beef and gingerly pat his head.

"Good boy," I tell him, though I know perfectly well he doesn't give a shit either way if I think he's a good boy.

He chaperones me to the living room, where I pull from my laptop bag a pair of gloves and a very expensive camera. I think I understand now why Serena has long one-sided conversations with Sirius, because I find myself wanting to do the same thing. He has such questioning expressions; he gives me looks that demand explanation, and a part of me feels like I ought to keep talking in that breezy tone because hearing me speak might make him forget that he'd really rather kill me than listen to me.

"This is just a camera." I hold it between my thumb and forefinger beneath his nose. He sniffs it without much interest because it isn't oozing blood and looks up at me. "It has a battery life of over four months. Now I'm just going to put this right here, out of the way, and I can see you even when I'm not around. Doesn't that sound nice?"

I dust out the inside of the transparent pink vase, removing the fake flowers furry with months of built-up grime, and place the camera at the bottom. I stick the flowers back inside, arranging them so they don't obstruct the lens, and place it back on the high shelf above the entertainment center.

I take a few steps backward. Sirius does as well, and we tilt our heads back to look at our handiwork. The camera isn't visible and gives off no red light to alert anybody of its presence. I carry on throughout the house, doing the same thing in Serena's bedroom (here I have to unscrew an electrical outlet cover, tape the camera down, and replace the cover) and kitchen (in the smoke alarm). I check the feeds to make sure the lenses are working properly, that the images are crystal clear, and then I sit down with Sirius on the floor and feed him the rest of the meat.

"Thanks for helping me," I say over his snuffling, patting his blocky head. "I'm sure I'll see you soon, okay?"

I suppose it was a bit egotistical to expect a goodbye kiss from him, but I kind of thought we'd bonded. Once he sees I'm meatless, he takes off down the hallway, with rolling shoulders and rippling muscles, and collapses in a heap on the floor of Serena's bedroom.

I lock up behind myself, replace the key, and head back to my car.

I'm not ready to let go. If she breaks up with me, I'll still get to see her, watch her drink her coffee at the kitchen table while she pecks at her laptop. I'll see her watch TV and read her books, curled up on her living room sofa. She looks so beautiful when she's sleeping, and I'll bear witness to that too. It'll be like I'm right there with her.

Who knows? I may be able to find some way to get her back after watching the camera feeds for a while.

The kitchen camera feed plays out in real time, and I'm watching when she gets home. She drops her purse on the table and kicks her heels off as Sirius clicks over the tile to greet her. After ruffling his ears, she peels off her jacket, hangs it on the rack, and heads for her bedroom, Sirius shadowing her down the hallway.

The movement in her bedroom activates the camera. She doesn't flick on the light switch, so her skin is ghostly green, and Sirius's shape is difficult to discern. He's the patch of denser darkness bobbing about her ankles, and when she flops onto the bed, he jumps up beside her.

She pulls out her cell phone, and I follow her lead and do the same, pulling up the spyware app. When she opens our text thread, I think I might vomit.

Sorry for texting so late, but I—

She deletes that, biting her lip, staring down at her phone. *Don't do this,* I want to tell her. *Don't throw us away.* You've been drinking. Now's not the time to break up with your boyfriend. Can't this wait until morning? Did you meet someone in the bar—is that it? I bet whoever he is won't do as much for you as I have.

She's typing again. Each letter blooming across my phone is a dagger in the heart.

Chris, I've—

She deletes that too. I think I'm close to hyperventilating now. This must be how people lined up for a firing squad feel. Waiting is worse than the inevitable gunshot wound. It's the waiting that hurts. It's easy to die, but that cold-blooded walk to your own execution has got to be worse than any killing blow. Why is it so difficult to find the right words, Serena? You're not normally speechless. I suppose I can take comfort in the thought that breaking up with me seems difficult for you.

Are you awake? she finally taps out, and this one she sends.

I'm too desperate to give it a few minutes before responding; I can't bear to put this off any longer. I don't want this lethal injection, but I'd rather not sit around idly waiting for it to be administered.

Yeah

I watch her face, a cold blue from her phone's screen, as she gets my text. She's pressing her lips together and looks resigned and reserved as she taps out, **Can you come over?**

I'm already out the door when I text back, **Of course.**

18

Does she just want to break up with me in person? I wonder on the drive to her place. I can't think of anything more sadistic than that. Someone please remind me why this is a thing, a face-to-face breakup. I don't know what I'll do if she dumps me. I can't predict how I'll react. Will I get angry? Cry? Fall to my knees and beg?

Beg. Definitely beg.

Serena is on her side stoop when I pull up ten minutes later. She's taken off her bar wear, traded in her blouse with the plunging neckline for an oversize T-shirt.

"Hey." She gets to her feet as I shut my car door.

"Hi," I say, nearly retching.

"I'm sorry for asking you to stop by so late."

"No, it's fine. I'm glad you did."

She wraps her arms around herself and blinks up at me. "Thanks for coming."

Just spit it out, Serena. Let's get this over with. But I give her my constant refrain of "Of course" instead.

"It's cold out here," she says, her eyes on her bare toes. "Let's go inside."

So we do, and she slips her arms around my waist, pressing her cheek against my chest, and I'm so surprised, so grateful that she's touching me that I'm shocked I haven't sunk to my knees in relief. I knew she loved me. I think I love her more than she loves me, but I can deal with that. She'll get there eventually.

I hug her back, tighter than I've ever hugged anything in my life. I want to hug her so hard that she sinks through muscle and bone and into my own body.

"Ow," she says delicately, peeling her cheek off my shirt.

She has fragile little bones; I should have known better. "Sorry."

She looks up at me, her fingers scratching the back of my neck the way she knows I like. "I missed you, babe."

"I missed you too," I say, choking on my relief, my regret. How could I ever have yelled at her, for Christ's sake, I'm in love with this woman.

"It wasn't okay, what you did," she says steadily, her features withdrawn and serious, but she's still setting my nerve endings on fire with her nails.

"I know. Of course it wasn't. I'm so sorry."

"But I don't want to say this is over because of some drunken mistake. I mean, I don't want you to think how you acted was acceptable by letting this slide—"

"—it wasn't—"

"—but I love you . . . I don't want to lose us over one stupid argument."

"I love you too," I say, so quickly the words sound glued together in my rush to utter them. I wish her answering smile didn't look so small and sad, but I don't have to look at it for long because she arcs up on her tiptoes and presses a very careful, subdued kiss on my lips.

I don't like subdued little pecks like this, not from her; she's not my grandmother, so I slip my hand around the back of her neck and deepen the kiss until I feel the wet ridge of her tongue. It's doing strange things to my body, this kiss; it's like the bottom has fallen out of my stomach and a hand has snared around my windpipe. I can't breathe, but I don't think I care about that, it's the least of my concerns.

◆ ◆ ◆

I've always wondered what the big deal about makeup sex was, but now I get it. Loving but violent, a silk sheet wrapped in razor wire, soft lips with sharp fangs. I'm torn between treating Serena like she's some fragile antique porcelain doll and ripping that shirt off her.

I'm not sure how many times I mumble that I love her during the thirty minutes (okay, twenty) that I'm able to last, but it's enough to make her whisper a semiamused "I love you too, shut up" as she wraps her legs around my waist.

Part of me thinks I should start little fights every now and then just to have more of this. It's tender and tentative, harsh and urgent, a collection of contradictions that touches some strange, furtive part of me that I don't think has ever been penetrated before. I don't know what to make of it. It's cracked me open, laid me bare, made me more vulnerable than I've ever been, but paradoxically, it's made me feel safe. She loves me again. I'm used to this roller coaster. My mother taught me how to brace myself for impact.

It's lucky timing I placed that camera in her room earlier this evening. I can replay this episode whenever I wish.

"Never again," she whispers, kissing the side of my sweat-slicked throat when it's over and she's curled into the crook of my arm. "Okay?"

"Never again," I agree, a finger tracing the graceful knots of her spine. And I mean it more than I've ever meant anything in my life.

19

Well, we've proven we can navigate some choppy currents, right, Serena? Calm waters don't produce skilled sailors. One fight in nearly nine months isn't that bad. Rosa approved of my apology, though it came with a stern warning via text message: I'm happy it's all better now, babe, and that he said all the right things, but keep an eye out for this kind of shit. Usually that behavior only gets worse with time, and you don't want this to end badly. There's a fine line between cute jealous and scary psycho jealous.

I think we'll be good from here on out, Serena responds. Thanks for looking out for me.

Derek's sentiments are not in the same spirit as Rosa's, however. He doesn't mention me at all until Serena brings it up.

Got a minute? she asks a couple of weeks after our glorious makeup.

Sure, you caught me at a good time

Can you fill me in on your conversation with Chris at Rosa's party?

What did he tell you? Wrong answer, Derek, but your evasiveness works well for me. You sound guilty as shit. Only shrinks and guilty people answer questions with questions.

> He said you were pretty rude and he wondered if he'd ever offended you somehow.

Ha. That's not exactly what happened. Look, I don't want to speak ill of your boyfriend. I know you like the guy, but I can't say I feel the same.

> So you were a dick to him? I just need to know what was said. I don't want either of you to get the wrong impression of each other.

I was the very antithesis of rude. I asked him how he was, general small talk like that, but he wasn't having any of it. Did you tell him I told you about what I saw that night in Destin? Because that would be a damn good explanation as to why he was being such a douche. About all he did was grunt and glare.

> I didn't tell him anything. It's a horrible accusation and you're not even sure it was him.

Well after how he acted at the party, I'm even more sure of it.

> Derek, come on. He didn't have bruises on his knuckles from punching anybody and the guy couldn't even give a description. You saw a tall guy who drove what could have been an Audi—do you know how many guys fit that description?

You didn't see how he acted when you left the bar that night. He was all keyed-up that he couldn't supervise you for an entire thirty seconds. I'd chalk that up to a one-off if he hadn't been staring at you while you were talking to people at Rosa's party

> I don't understand why people think the fact that my boyfriend LOOKS at me is a crime.

Looking and STARING are different. Sure, you're gorgeous, if you were my girlfriend I'd look at you all the time, but he wasn't looking at you and thinking, isn't she lovely or some shit, he was staring at you like you were property. I don't like him

> You've never liked my boyfriends.

With good reason. They've all been fuckheads. It's not like I never kept an open mind, but I'm not going to pretend everything's dandy when I think you're making a mistake

I get the impression Derek thinks any guy who isn't him is a "mistake."

> He's the best guy I've dated. He's not like Tom, some loser asshole with creepy kinks. He takes care of me, he's nice to Cole, he's got a good job. He's crazy about me.

Mary, I think he's just crazy, period.

> You're putting me in a pretty awkward position, you know. I don't want to have to choose between you and Chris.

I'm not the one making you choose. I think that's how you'll realize the difference between Chris and me. I'm not making you choose between the two of us, but I think he will.

I would never make her choose between Derek and me. I think Serena will come to that conclusion all on her own. You can't remain on good terms with someone who heartily disapproves of your significant other; all that does is breed resentment. She won't want to hurt me by continuing a friendship with some guy who actively dislikes me. She cut her relationship with her own mother back to basics after those nasty things Katherine said about me, Derek; do you think you're somehow worth more than her blood?

Serena doesn't respond, and I watch her seething on her couch for a while. She starts and stops three separate messages and then slams her phone onto the cushion beside her, muttering things I cannot hear because those cameras aren't equipped with audio.

A few minutes later, Derek says, **Sometimes faithful service means telling hard truths.**

> You stole that from Ser Davos.

I will never understand this *Game of Thrones* obsession. What is so wonderful about ice zombies and dragons and a bunch of uppity bitches stabbing each other in the back? Maybe I just do not find incest quite as appealing as everybody else. I never found forensics as fascinating as other people seemed to back when *CSI* was in its heyday, either.

> Ser Davos was right. If only Stannis had listened. Do what you want. I just don't want this turning into another Tom fiasco. Cole doesn't deserve to be put through that again.

Serena's eyes bulge and then narrow to icy slits, and I know Derek is walking the tightrope here, dragging her son into this lecture. Bad move, Derek. Have fun climbing out of that hole.

> I'm getting really fucking tired of everyone throwing Tom in my face. That was eight years ago.

All Because of You

All right. White flag. I love you, Serena, I don't want to fight with you. Just promise me you'll be careful.

She doesn't deign that worthy of a response and flings her phone across the couch, where its hard landing wakes Sirius from his doze. I hate to see her this upset, but I might know how to make her feel better.

Can I take you out tonight? I text her. I know it's last minute but I miss you.

The new notification alert makes her scowl even deeper until she retrieves the phone and sees it's me, her boyfriend, the best man she's ever dated.

Yes. I could really use a drink.

Can you wear something slutty for me?

She gives her phone an unwilling smile and sends me a middle finger emoji.

She's had considerably more than "a drink," truth be told, and it's a little adorable.

I watch her slurp down the dregs of her vodka soda, the cocktail stirrer straw crackling, and long after she's drained the glass, she continues sucking.

"I think that one's done for," I tell her. "Do you want me to get you another one?"

I'll have to pour her into my car if her answer is yes, but I don't mind. In fact, I'm quite looking forward to getting her into her pajamas and tucking her into bed. I can be a white knight like Derek; I just need the right in, a good opportunity.

She seems surprised her glass is empty, nothing but rattling, degraded ice cubes, and I take it from her to exchange for a full one up at the bar. She is probably a bit too far past tipsy to notice that I am very deliberately *not* keeping an eye on her as I wait for this slow hipster bartender to mix her up another.

I think this bartender is the one Rosa mentioned way back in October. The one who likes Serena. I don't blame him for that, but I wish he'd focus on his job instead of telling me "I think this should be her last one, okay? She gets hungover pretty easily."

She smiles when I return with what will apparently be her last drink and slips her hand in mine from across the table. She doesn't like to be what she calls "same-siders," the couples who sit on the same booth cushion, but I've made my peace with it. People can still tell we're a couple—she's holding my hand and everything.

"You *do* look at me a lot," she says in that carefully enunciated way of drunk people.

"What do you mean?" I arch an eyebrow so I look politely mystified.

"I mean you look at me a lot."

"Is that bad?"

"No," she says, suddenly irritated. "That's what I mean! What's so bad about that, I want to know."

"I can't help it," I say, kissing her knuckles. "You're gorgeous. Do you want me to try to ignore you?"

"No," she says, for all the world sounding like a spoiled, imperious little girl you can't help but adore. "Why are you laughing?"

"You're funny when you're drunk."

"I'm not drunk." She tries to wave off my words but knocks over the saltshaker in the process, focusing with all her might on the clock behind my head. "What time does that say?"

"It's a little past eleven."

She looks down, blinks at the tipped-over saltshaker, and sets it back upright. "I should get home." She hops down from her stool, slinging her purse over her shoulder with a little too much vigor, so it swings into the back of the man sitting behind her. He turns around, annoyed, but his face promptly shifts gears when he realizes she's not some dried-up barfly, that she's young and hot and standing less than six inches away from him.

"Oops! Sorry," she says, and I can't see her face, but I know she's gracing this guy with her most charming smile. She links her arm through mine. "Let's go."

"I have to pay first."

"Oh." Her brow wrinkles as though paying a tab is a foreign notion. "Do you need my card?"

"No. When have I ever made you pay?"

She shakes her head experimentally. "Okay, I'll just wait for you outside."

I am not the biggest fan of this idea. She's clearly drunk and disturbingly pretty, and I feel like this is the perfect recipe for a pervert to kidnap her, force her into the trunk of his car while she's out there, obliviously vaping, but Jack's is well lit in front. I'm sure she'll be fine. But I keep an eye on her all the same until Brad hands me back my card.

"Make sure she drinks water before she goes to bed," he says, with a smile that's got a slightly forced aura about it and a bit too much familiarity. I don't love that he's giving me instructions on what to do with my own girlfriend, but I overtip him anyway.

◆ ◆ ◆

She's trying to be quiet as I walk her into her house, but she's greeting Sirius in a stage whisper loud enough to wake the coma patients in my grandfather's home.

"Shh," I say, my arm slung around her waist. I'm pretty sure she'll stumble into a wall if I'm not holding her.

"I'm being quiet!" she practically shouts, her breath eighty proof and tinged with peppermint ALTOIDS. "Cole's probably sleeping anyway."

"Let's get you in bed," I suggest, pointing down the hallway.

"I have to take off my makeup first. It's gross if you don't. I heard it makes your eyelashes fall out if you sleep in mascara. I don't want them falling out."

"That does sound like it'd be unpleasant."

She considers this, struggling out of her jacket as we make it inside her bedroom. "You think I'd be ugly without eyelashes?"

"No."

"Are you lying?"

"Let's just get your makeup off so we don't have to find out."

She bangs into her bathroom and opens and shuts drawers so loudly I can't imagine Cole sleeping through it. He'll think the loudest burglar on earth has broken into his house. When she emerges, she's got a blue package between her teeth and is trying and failing to peel off her jeans.

I watch her for a few seconds, trying to figure out if she looks sexy or ridiculous, starting a fight with a pair of pants. "Do you need some help?"

Her reply is muffled by the package of makeup wipes, so I interpret it as an affirmative and undo the button, then push the jeans down her hips. She's actually wearing underwear tonight, hallelujah. A white cotton thong that sets off her tan. She works the jeans off the rest of the way and kicks them aside, flopping onto her mattress.

"Let me get you some water, okay?" I say as she works a wipe out of the package, crossing her legs beneath her. It doesn't seem to be removing the makeup, just smearing heavy black muck beneath her eyes. She looks like a member of KISS.

I stop dead when I make it back into the kitchen. Cole is standing there, shirtless and in a pair of gym shorts Serena's always making him change out of because "they're too ratty and I don't want to listen to Grandma ask me why you always look like a panhandling hobo." He's got his mouth around a bottle of Gatorade, which doesn't entirely hide his smirk, and his hand on Sirius's head.

"Hi," I say. "Sorry, did we wake you up?"

"No, I wasn't sleeping." His Adam's apple bobs as he takes a long blue slug, then he caps the Gatorade, the smirk widening. "How many vodka sodas?"

"Three. One was a double."

"She gets louder when she's been drinking."

"I think that's a universal trait." He moves aside when I take a glass from the cabinet and fill it with water from the fridge. "I'm just going to give her water and some Advil, and I'll be on my way."

He quirks an eyebrow the same way his mother does, and he's got the same dimple in his left cheek. He's not pretty the way she is, but every time I look at him, I find a new feature of hers that's been replicated onto his face. "You're not staying?"

Serena never lets me stay the night when Cole is home; it's the one thing she was firm on from the beginning.

"You've been dating for . . ." He trails off questioningly.

"Almost nine months."

"You've been dating for nine months. I'm not an idiot. I'd just rather not hear anything disgusting, if you know what I mean."

"I have no idea what you mean," I say, trying to look appropriately virtuous, to which he rolls his eyes.

"Right," he says, shaking his head. He heads for the staircase, calling over his shoulder, "Powerade Zero."

"What?"

"In the fridge." Cole hangs off the banister, dark hair flopping into his eyes, the lean muscle in his bicep flexing. "There's Powerade Zero in there. Give that to her when she wakes up. It makes her feel better in the morning. I'll tell you that for free, you can take credit and be the Hangover Hero."

You sound like your mother, Cole. You have her humor. "Got it."

He takes another step up the staircase, pauses, and leans over the banister again. "And a grilled ham, egg, and cheese sandwich. We have the eggs and the ham, but I'm not sure about the cheese." He takes a few more plodding steps before I call for him. "Yeah?"

I follow his voice and find him halfway up the stairs, an arch in his brow. "I just wanted to say thanks."

He doesn't say anything for a few moments, just stares at me with his lips mashed together, the muscles in his arms contracting as he grips the banister tighter.

"I mean it when I say I don't want to hear anything nasty," he finally announces, clomping up the stairs, but I think I can hear the subterranean beginnings of a laugh under his breath. I watch him until the bunched, baggy socks on his feet disappear around the corner and I hear the soft click of his bedroom door closing.

Her face is bare and slightly pink when I make it back into her room. "Where'd you go? I thought you left without saying goodbye."

I set the glass of water on her bedside table and grab her shirt by the hem. "I was getting you water. Get under the sheet now. Let me tuck you in."

Her eyes are already half closed when I tell her I love her and arrange the blankets around her. Sirius watches with interest when I strip off my clothes and turn off the light.

The mattress bounces violently when Sirius hops up, and through the weak moonlight shining through the gap in the curtains, I can see his reproachful yellow eyes are about two inches away from mine.

I pat his head. "Why don't you just lay down. There's a good boy."

He heaves a heavy sigh and makes his camp, his jaw resting on my foot, his front paws stretched out over my legs, pinning me down.

◆ ◆ ◆

I slept like shit. It's hard to get comfortable when there is a dog head, which probably weighs as much as a Buick, lying on your feet all night and your girlfriend's drunken snores rattle the windows.

Exhaustion has my head in a fog, but I couldn't be happier. I stayed the night with Cole's blessing, and now I'm making Serena breakfast to soak up whatever vestiges of vodka remain in her stomach.

Sirius sits by the stove, hoping I'll drop a piece of ham or something. He's already eaten his breakfast. Vacuumed it up, more like. I'd scooped out two cups of the foul-smelling stuff and rinsed the measuring cup under the tap, and when I'd turned back, the dish had been licked clean.

I'm flipping her grilled ham, egg, and cheese sandwich over when she shuffles into the kitchen, cringing at the bright lights, the bottle of Powerade Zero I'd left on her nightstand clutched against her chest like a teddy bear. But despite the fact that I took care of her last night, that I've fed her dog and am currently making her breakfast, she does not look thrilled to see me. More like horrified.

"What are you doing here?" she asks, her voice a mere croak, that hangover she's nursing bleaching her skin a ghastly shade of white.

"I'm making you breakfast."

Her eyes are wild, swiveling about the kitchen. "Did you stay the night?"

You're welcome, Serena. Jesus Christ. "Cole already knows. I was getting you water and Advil before I left last night, and he said I should stay." I'm at the point of telling her *He's fourteen, sweetheart, he's old enough to know that yes, we are having sex, how virginal could he possibly believe you to be when you had him at seventeen?* but I just switch off the burner on the stove and pull her against my chest. "Good morning."

"Chris," she says, but it comes out like a sigh. "I wish you would have asked me."

"But Cole was fine with it."

She unwinds herself from my arms. "It's a pretty clear boundary I've always had. Cole isn't in charge around here."

"You were drunk. I was supposed to ask permission when you were hammered?"

"I wasn't *hammered*," she says, her eyes flashing dangerously. "I would have been capable of understanding a question."

"I just wanted to wake up with you for once."

"I understand that. You should have asked."

I drop the metal spatula into the sink harder than I'd planned to, the clang echoing around the kitchen. "We've been together nine months, and I need permission to stay overnight when your teenager, who knows perfectly well we're having sex, is fine with it? Are you ashamed of me or something?"

She's cold and still, her gaze flitting all over me like I'm someone new, unfamiliar.

"I'm going to take a shower," she finally says, taking one deliberate step backward. "You should probably be gone by the time I get out. I have to get ready for work."

20

My grandfather has been slowly dying for the past year but suddenly he's hurtling toward the grave at breakneck speed, and the worst part is that he knows he won't last much longer. Every time I visit him lately, he's got another bequest. I don't think he remembers I'm going to inherit all his stuff regardless, that he doesn't need to rattle off a list of specifics, but I let him anyway. It seems important to him.

The aides have kept the drapes drawn, the lights dimmed. He's stopped eating and drinking. He hasn't even said anything nasty to the nurses in days. It's called detaching, Nancy told me. He's withdrawing bit by bit from life.

He's propped against some pillows in what will inevitably be his deathbed, his eyelids fluttering blindly. "Will you come visit me?"

"What do you think I'm doing right now?" I ask, but my voice cracks, and for a second I think I might cry.

"Not here. At the cemetery."

I don't want to talk about this. I'd rather stick a finger in my eye and swirl it around a few times, but you can't say something like that to your dying grandfather, so I nod, until I remember he can't see so well these days. "All the time."

He grunts in approval, and I watch the monitor he's plugged into chart his jagged heartbeats as I apply a warm washcloth to his hands. Blankets are piled on him a foot deep, but his skin is still frigid.

"I may be going blind, but I can still hear, you know," he croaks after a while.

I cut him a look that he can't see. "What do you mean?"

"Are you going to tell me how you're really doing?"

"I'm fine."

"Chris."

His voice is arrow sharp, and that's all he needs to trigger an avalanche. I tell him everything. I unspool the film of my relationship with Serena all over the quilt spread across his knees, and his cloudy eyes never leave my face. I tell him how my worries are mutating into a nerve-shredding panic, that I can't get her to choose *me*, to put me first, the way I do for her.

"She's got this overinvolved male friend who keeps butting into everything; she refuses to let me spend the night when Cole's home. Why should she have all these *boundaries* if she loves me like she claims?" I don't get it, I really don't. Boundaries keep people out; why does she want to keep out the man she loves? "You should see the things she wears sometimes—"

He gropes for my hand, pats it until my voice drifts away. "There were a few young men flitting around your grandmother back when we first started dating. Did I ever tell you that?"

The veins springing from his hand roll beneath my grip as I return the squeeze he gives me. "No."

"Yes. Three or four. I noticed them before I'd ever met her. She gave them just enough attention so they couldn't call themselves her boyfriend, but the instant she'd crook her finger, they'd be there. Her own menagerie of Johnny-on-the-spots," he says, smiling fondly, like the memory amuses him.

"It didn't bother you?" He loved my grandmother to distraction; the idea of her, at least. He loved her almost as much as I love Serena. I couldn't turn a corner in the house without finding him adoring her up against a wall, wrapped around her like a python, his lips on her temple.

He tended to her like she was a pet. Always petting and stroking, keeping her within grabbing distance, confining her inside his arms.

"Of course it did. It bothered me before I'd even introduced myself, but I knew I was being unreasonable. She didn't belong to me yet; we'd never even spoken. I didn't let it get too far once we were together."

His words float there, weaving through the air like smoke.

"What do you mean?"

"You can't demand things from a girlfriend, Chris. You have to show them a better way." He tries to struggle up against the pillows piled behind his head, but I keep him pinned with a hand pressed to his chest.

"Don't get up. What's the matter?"

"There's something in my bedside table."

"What do you need?"

"Your mom's ring is in there."

I keep my hand on him as I pull out the drawer, rummaging through it until my fingers hit velvet. "Did you want to . . . take it with you?"

"No," he spits, like I'm being deliberately stupid. "You can't expect Serena to listen to a boyfriend the way she'd listen to a husband," he says. "That's not reasonable."

I flop back against the visitor's chair, turning the box over in my palms. "She's going to think that's way too soon, Dad. We haven't talked about marriage at all." I've always been too nervous to broach the subject, too afraid to scare her off.

His brown eyes are surrounded by translucent lashes, his skin so sallow he looks like a wraith. I can see veins crawling up his neck, as though his skin is so thin and insignificant it can no longer hide his insides properly. "Men take the reins. Don't you love this woman?"

"Of course I do."

He snorts like he doesn't buy it. "Yet you're not willing to take any risks for the sake of your relationship?"

"I'm not willing to risk what we have for a proposal that she could decline. We'd be over for good if she says no." At least that's what happens in movies.

"Then don't let her say no," he says, like it's the simplest thing in the world.

"I don't think that's something I can control."

"Men are the backbones of their relationships, Chris. If men aren't strong, their bonds won't be. What happens to families when the husband isn't strong? They crumble. Wives stray. Daughters turn promiscuous. Sons go soft. I didn't teach you to be soft, did I? Be a man."

I flip open the box. I'd seen this ring on my grandmother's finger my entire life. Sometimes I'd catch her looking at it as though it were a shackle. But she never left, did she? She'd been in it for the long haul.

Three days later, the last of my grandfather's organs give out.

Serena bends over to examine the inscription on my grandfather's tombstone, tracing the decorative filigree. "It's beautiful. You think he'd like it?"

"He'd probably think it was way too girlie."

"That sounds like him," she says, pressing the bouquet of lilies into my hands so I can arrange it against my grandmother's grave. She's wearing white, like part of her knows what's coming.

Humidity prickles the back of my neck and it isn't just the heat making me sweat. I know it will come as something of a surprise, but I hope it's a good surprise, an Ed-McMahon-showing-up-with-a-giant-check surprise.

I guess nobody but us feels like visiting today. The sky looks like a bruise, and Serena and I are alone this muggy July afternoon with only the dead for company. A hot breeze sends ripples through the grass like there's a serpent weaving through the blades, and she kicks off her sandals.

All Because of You

"Thanks for coming with me," I say, watching her flap out a fleece blanket she brought with us. It's my grandparents' anniversary, you see. When I told her it was coming, she insisted we visit their graves to celebrate it for them.

She settles onto the blanket, unpacking plastic flutes from the basket. "They're your family, it's important. Open the champagne. Try not to let the cork hit a tombstone, or some pissed-off ghost will haunt us."

I open it carefully, because I don't want her worrying about being haunted, and pour a fountain of champagne into the two flutes she proffers.

"Happy sixtieth." She toasts my dead grandparents, draining the glass in one go and shooting me a sideways smile. "They were so lucky, being together that long."

You could be lucky, too, sweetheart.

"They never forgot how lucky they were." I toss back my champagne, too, all of it, because my mouth is starting to get dry and I can feel my pulse pounding in my temples. "I love you," I say, the alcohol blistering through my stomach.

"I love you too." She gets to her knees to kiss me and pulls my empty flute from my hand. While her gaze is averted as she pours out two more servings of champagne, I dig through my pockets and pull out the box.

She looks up, holding my flute, and her smile melts into confusion and what looks to be a dash of apprehension. "What are you doing?"

If my grandfather were here, he'd cover his face with his hands and mumble something despairingly about my utter lack of planning, but he'd be wrong. I did plan. I'd planned a little speech, practicing in the mirror, but now that she's looking right at me through wide, slightly scared blue eyes, every word of my monologue escapes me except the most important bit.

"Will you marry me?"

"Are you serious?"

A spike of annoyance hits me behind my left eyeball. No, it's all a clever ruse, Serena. I'm sitting here holding out my dead grandmother's ring as a stupid joke. Jesus Christ.

"Of course I am."

She says absolutely nothing.

"I love you, Serena. I'm pretty sure I've been in love with you from the second we met. My grandfather always told me when you know, you know and there's no point in waiting. I already know what I want. I've known for a long time."

"Chris, I—I don't know . . . you're seriously serious?"

"I am seriously serious as a heart attack." How much longer is she going to make me hold out this ring unclaimed? "I love you. I don't ever want to be without you."

She looks around helplessly at the headstones surrounding us. "I don't want to be without you either. I love you, Chris, I—"

"Is that a yes?"

I've never seen her this scared, not even that one time she stood on top of her kitchen table to avoid that wolf spider skittering across the floor. This is a very bad sign; I can feel it. It tastes like failure in my throat. She can't even look at me; she prefers to look at the inside of her eyelids, squeezing her eyes shut the way she'll eventually squeeze me out of her life.

But then she swallows hard, holds out her left hand, and says yes.

21

OMFG is Rosa's response to the picture Serena texted, a shot of her left hand, her ring finger newly bedazzled. Seriously???

Why the hell is everyone so utterly shocked at the idea of my proposal? Isn't this what women wait for their whole lives? It can't be that bewildering.

Yep. I watch Serena sink onto the edge of her bed through the camera feed. I was surprised too.

Congratulations! Have you set a date yet?

Sirius licks my grandmother's diamond as Serena taps into her phone one handed: It just happened this afternoon, we haven't even talked about that.

What's the matter? You don't sound very excited

I am! It's just, I can't help wondering if it's too soon. She pushes Sirius away and kicks off her heels.

It's almost been a year

Ten months, Serena corrects.

Yes, that's almost a year. I don't think it's too soon, but then what the hell do I know, Marlon and I got married after knowing each other for five minutes. I guess people wait longer than a year to get engaged now, but who cares. All that matters is you're happy. Are you happy?

It takes her much too long, but finally she taps out Yes.

Then be happy and don't worry about it. Want me to come over to celebrate? I know it's late and all but this is a big deal

Serena stares at Sirius as though looking for permission to celebrate her own engagement. He must grant her request, because she looks down at her phone and types Yes, absolutely.

"Wait—he proposed at a *cemetery*?" Rosa sounds equal parts amused and horrified, stopping midpour, champagne fizzling in her flute. "Who the fuck does that?"

"Well, it's his grandparents' anniversary. I was the one who suggested we go there to celebrate. I don't think he'd have done it there if it hadn't been my idea to go."

"A *cemetery*." There's a shudder in Rosa's voice as she fills her flute to the rim. "Of all the places to be proposed to, that might be the weirdest."

Serena gets to her feet, walking out of the camera frame. "I knew someone who got proposed to in a public bathroom."

"Okay, that might be weirder," Rosa concedes, swallowing half the contents of her flute. "Have you told Cole yet?"

"He's at my mom's," her disembodied voice says. "I'll tell him when he gets home."

"What do you think your mom will say?"

"Probably a weak congratulations and a subject change." Serena reappears, a slight grimace on her face. It looks like she's got some kind of toothache as she sinks back into her chair at the kitchen table. "I'm actually dreading telling her and Derek. I may put it off for a while until I come up with a good script."

Maybe it's just my atavistic fear of abandonment elbowing itself front and center, but I can't help feeling wounded that she doesn't want her mother and Derek knowing just yet. I'm an embarrassing dirty little secret she needs to hide until she's found the right words.

Most women would be thrilled to spread the news, Serena. Most women would be snapping a hundred pictures, plastering the internet with their ring, giddy with excitement and drunk on the peppy comments from their followers. But not you. I don't know whether I'm okay with that. Your reaction isn't what I wanted. Your lukewarm acceptance of my proposal, your plans to hide the news—do you really think that's fair to me, or have you not even factored in my feelings? Your selfishness was something I thought I could live with, one of those flaws one has to accept in a relationship, but it's beginning to set my teeth on edge.

Rosa pushes aside her champagne, suddenly sober. "Look, if you're dreading telling people, that's not a good sign. Are you sure this is what you want?"

"I mean, I love him, how could I say no? You know that would break his heart. I don't want to hurt him; I don't want to lose him. I *do* want to marry him eventually. We'll just . . . have a very long engagement."

Rosa is uncharacteristically silent for a while, flicking her thumbnail against her ring finger. "That sounds like a fucking disaster just waiting to happen. I'm all for lying when it comes to how much I actually spent at the hairdresser, but this isn't the way, babe. Tell him it's too fast but you love him and maybe he should try again in six months."

"I *do* want to marry him," Serena says. "He just asked quicker than I expected him to and caught me off guard, that's all."

I sink back into my couch, digesting what I've heard. I live in a state of constant, low-level fear that she'll leave me, and it's spiking higher than ever. We don't need to take our time, Serena—what would be the point? You said you want to marry me; who cares if it happens in six months or a year? The end result is the same. And people don't hide the news of their engagement. They just don't. Not if they have any respect for their soon-to-be life partner. Lack of respect seems to be a trend in this relationship. That'll need to be addressed before the wedding.

We've been engaged for precisely a week, Serena, and you've yet to tell your mother and Derek. You swore your son to secrecy at this very kitchen table I'm sitting at now, let him know in no uncertain terms that he was not to tell anybody, not if he valued that iPhone in his back pocket, and that you'd let him know when he had the green light to mention it.

"How does carne asada strike you?" she asks, her head in her fridge, rummaging through the vegetable crisper. "I hope I've got enough meat. You and Cole both eat like horses."

"It sounds great," I say, trying to bite back my seething resentment. Do you want to know how your total lack of acknowledgment of our engagement strikes me? Not well, sweetheart. Not at all. I am considering making an Instagram account for myself just to shout the news to the internet. They'll find out quicker that way. You're clearly embarrassed of me; it's never been so glaringly obvious.

"Hey," I say, like I've just been struck by the thought, "did you ever tell Derek and your mom that we're getting married? I thought she'd have opinions on when and where and color schemes, but you never mentioned anything."

She turns around, holding a package of steak, her guilty face half hidden behind her hair. "I haven't, not yet. I'm sorry."

"Being sorry doesn't really help the problem, you know."

She looks very surprised by my tone as she throws her hair over her shoulder and secures it with a clip. "I'll tell them soon, I promise. It's just hard to find the words."

"The words are simple. They're *I'm getting married.*"

She yanks out the cutting board, her gaze on the meat. "You're mad."

"Yeah," I say, bobbing my head. "Wouldn't you be?"

"Probably."

"So what's the holdup?"

"I just don't like confrontation, you know that," she says, as though this is an answer I should have expected. "I told you I want us to take our time over the engagement. I didn't think it was that urgent that I let everyone know."

"You think you're going to be confronted about the fact that we're getting married?"

"No, it's just, I don't expect the news to be well received by Derek—you know why even better than I do; I don't know why you two randomly decided to hate each other. And I can't say I've ever been a fan of uncomfortable conversations—"

"So you'd rather make me feel like shit than brave a potentially uncomfortable conversation with your friend?"

She's silent, gazing at me with her lips pressed together, squeezing a lime in her palm like a stress ball. "I hadn't thought of it that way, but you're right. Of course you're right. I never meant to make you feel like shit. I wasn't thinking of your feelings. I'll tell him tomorrow."

I should be gracious. I should thank her for her probably sincere apology and leave it at that, hope she follows through. Trust is supposed to be important in relationships.

"And your mother?"

She slices through the leathery skin of the lime. "I'll tell her tomorrow too."

"No—well, yes, but I meant, What do you think your mother's objection would be?"

"Probably that it's too fast."

"It's been nearly a year. That's not long enough? Plenty of people get engaged fast. Rosa and Marlon got married after knowing each other for five minutes."

Her gaze snaps up, her eyebrows crashing together, and she stares at me for a good long time before she says, "Yeah. They did."

◆ ◆ ◆

Serena has lied to me—outright lied—for the first time tonight.

She's fabricated an emergency involving Rosa and an injured ankle, and somehow she is the only soul alive who can ferry Rosa to an urgent care facility, Marlon and Dre having gone to a basketball game. I had my doubts that it was true but didn't know for sure until just now, as I look down at the screen of my phone, which is mirroring her own.

Rosa's text thread is open, and lo and behold, no crisis has been mentioned; the last thing she'd sent Serena was a GIF of Jack Nicholson. Serena is scrolling up slowly, reading their messages in reverse just like I am, until the never-ending thread freezes and we're at the part where Serena has just informed Rosa of our engagement.

> I don't think it's too soon, but then what the hell do I know, Marlon and I got married after knowing each other for five minutes.

And I realize I may have made a rather large mistake, unintentionally parroting Rosa's words. I close my eyes and slam back against my desk chair, and when I look back at my phone, Serena is changing her security settings from a PIN to her thumbprint.

Cold ripples of panic surge through me. I am probably somewhere at the corner of Shit Creek and Breakup Lane. I wish I could mirror her thoughts, not just the screen of her phone. The best I can do is pull up the camera feed on my desktop, where I find her pacing her kitchen, Sirius tracing her movements with his gaze. She's biting her thumbnail and staring at her phone, ceaselessly moving from one corner of the kitchen to the next.

I don't know what, if anything, I could say to smooth this over. All I can do is sit in my dark office and watch.

She strides about for another few minutes and finally taps out to Rosa, *Can you come over?*

◆ ◆ ◆

And of course Rosa can come over. She clatters through the side door, dumps her purse on the table, and plonks herself down in the chair across from the one Serena occupies.

"What's the matter?" Rosa blinks at the teacups and kettle on the table.

All I can see is the back of Serena's head, dark waves of hair shifting over her shoulder blades. "I think Chris has been going through my phone."

"Seriously?" Rosa looks deeply disgusted as she pours some tea for herself. "Fuck that, that's some next-level creep shit."

"We had a—well, not a fight, exactly—we 'had words,' I guess, tonight. He was mad that I haven't told my mom or Derek about being engaged. He mentioned you and Marlon—quoted something you'd texted me, word for word."

Rosa grimaces after a sip from her steaming teacup. "What did he say?"

"'Rosa and Marlon got married after knowing each other for five minutes.'"

"Hmm."

"What?"

"I don't know." Rosa turns one hand palm up. "It's something I've said before. The 'five minutes' part, anyway. I don't know if I've said those exact words in front of Chris, but it's possible. He's been around me and Marlon plenty of times. He could have heard it then."

"I don't remember you ever saying exactly that in front of him, and I've never discussed your marriage with him."

"Well, I don't remember ever saying it to him, either, but again, it's something I know for sure I've said before, so it's possible that's where he heard it. Have you at least changed your PIN?"

"I did that right away."

"Good. If it's a fluke, there's no harm in being cautious. I think you'll know if it's not. He might start acting funny about your phone if he's been looking through it and can't get in anymore. Did you ever tell him your passcode?"

"No."

"Then how could he get in?"

"I don't know. Maybe he was looking over my shoulder when I entered it at some point." Serena knocks back the rest of her tea, slamming the cup on the table. "If he's been going through my shit, I'll be fucking furious."

"I don't blame you."

"I swear to God, I'll break up with him *immediately* if I ever find out he's been doing that. It's Tom all over again."

Heat rises in my chest, both at the comparison to Tom and the breakup ultimatum. I'm nothing like Tom; I don't try to pimp her out to other men. I do my best to prevent other men from looking her way at every opportunity. She'd go so far as to break up with me over the minor sin of looking through her phone? I realize Tom did a number on her, but why should I suffer these overreactions just because one guy she dated a hundred years ago was a creep?

"This is the first time you've ever been suspicious?"

Serena's quiet for a while, fiddling with her teacup. "Yeah. I mean, we hardly ever even fight. You really think it's all just a coincidence?"

"I think it's *possible* it's a coincidence, but all the same, keep an eye on the situation."

Serena snorts. "Don't worry, I will."

You go ahead and do that, sweetheart. You'll find out your accusations are baseless in due time.

Rosa's eyebrows connect. "You know this isn't a court of law, right? You don't need ironclad proof to end this. You can break up anytime, for any reason. If you don't have trust, you don't have anything." She shrugs one shoulder. "You've been weird about getting engaged, and now this? If you're looking for an excuse or permission to end it, permission granted, call this off. I don't like where all this is headed. You should be happy right now. You shouldn't be sitting here wondering if he's creeping through your shit."

"I don't know. I don't know what to believe," Serena says. "But maybe the engagement was a mistake."

22

Serena guards her phone like a pit bull for the next few days, but I pretend not to notice. I also pretend to be equally disinterested when she lets me know offhand that she's meeting Derek this afternoon, when she plans to drop the *I'm Getting Married* bomb on his head.

"Well, have fun, babe," I say, pecking at my phone for no reason whatsoever. "I've got to go, an unscheduled conference call came up."

She looks somewhere between surprised and curious, watching me collect my shit and push back from her kitchen table. "I will, thanks. Aren't you forgetting something?"

I grope my pockets, feeling all the correct bulges in the right places. "I don't think so."

Rolling her eyes, she closes the distance between us, slipping her arms around my waist. "You forgot to kiss me."

"Sorry. I'm a cad." I tilt her chin back. "I love you," I tell her once we've broken apart. "I'll text you tomorrow."

And I will text her tomorrow, after I've had time to digest the conversation she has with Derek, which I'll be able to hear through the bug I've planted in the depths of her gargantuan purse.

◆ ◆ ◆

From behind the steering wheel of my grandfather's old Cadillac (that I've never felt the need to tell Serena exists), I can see her struggle with the heavy wood door of the bar in which she and Derek are meeting. And through the grimy window, I watch Derek rise from the booth he's snagged and call her name.

As she settles into the space across from him, I access the bug's app on my phone.

"I didn't order for you because you said you were running late," Derek's crystal clear voice says. "Didn't want to stick you with some watered-down vodka."

"That's all right, I'll flag someone down."

"How've you been? I haven't seen you in a while."

"Oh, good. Where's that waitress?" She's twisting her head around, looking about as guilty as Phil Spector. She throws her arm out to stop a passing waitress, says "Vodka-soda-extra-lime-make-it-a-double" as though it's one word, and turns back to Derek, breathless. "How've you been?"

Derek's slightly amused voice matches his expression. "Good. Busy. Gotta go to Atlanta tomorrow."

She grabs a cocktail napkin and twists it through her fingers. "Oh, cool. Bring me back some peaches."

When the waitress thumps the drink in front of Serena, she dives onto it, drains half in one go.

"I don't think I've ever actually seen someone pounce on a drink like that," Derek notes dryly, draping his arm across the top of the booth.

"I actually wanted to talk to you about something. Well, tell you about something."

"Does it have anything to do with that ring on your finger?"

"Oh." She looks down at her left hand. "Yeah."

He's quiet for a long time, gazing at her from across the table. Then he clears his throat, his tone detached. "When did it happen?"

"A week ago."

"Why didn't you tell me?"

"Oh, come on." Serena stabs at the ice in her glass with the straw. "You know why."

Derek shrugs, leaning back in the booth. "Well, it's not like I have to be married to him. It's not my decision. Just would have been nice to hear about it sooner."

"I didn't want an argument."

"Why would I argue with you about that?"

"Uh," Serena says, her voice positively sagging with sarcasm, "because you can't stand Chris."

"And you already know that. So why would I waste my breath?" Derek brings his glass to his lips. "Are you worried about telling your mom? She doesn't like him, does she?"

"She doesn't like anyone. She doesn't even like you. She still calls you my grungy little garage band friend who doesn't know how to brush his hair."

"So where are you gonna live?"

"What?"

"When you get married, where are you gonna live? When *are* you getting married, anyway?"

"We haven't set a date yet."

"Well, what about the living situation? Are you going to move in with him?"

"I—I hadn't thought about it, but probably."

"How do you think Cole will take that? He's never lived with another guy."

"He'll be fine; he doesn't have a problem with Chris."

"How big's the yard?"

"Huh?"

"At Chris's house, how big is the yard?"

"Quarter acre."

"And it's in a neighborhood, right?" He waits for her nod. "Not something Sirius is used to. Hopefully that won't turn into a problem."

"I'm sure it'll be fine," Serena says, but I don't believe her, because she's looking as though Derek is asking her to perform quantum physics.

"You changing your last name?"

"I haven't thought about it."

What have *you thought about?* I want to ask, and it looks as though Derek is silently echoing my question.

"Well, how do you feel about having a different last name than Cole? Think he'll be upset, feel left out?"

"What the fuck is with this inquisition?" She pushes her empty glass to the edge of the table. "I just wanted to tell you because you're my friend and I thought you'd try to be supportive."

"How is asking simple logistical questions not being supportive?" Derek has plastered an innocently curious look on his face, which I don't buy, and it appears Serena doesn't either.

"You're being an asshole, and you know it."

Derek drops the act and the would-be casual tone. "And you haven't thought this shit through. You don't even know if you'll be moving in with him. I mean, Jesus Christ. How have you not considered any of those things?"

Static pulses through the speaker on my phone as Serena riffles around inside her purse. She comes out with a bill and plunks it on the table. "I'm leaving."

"You can't do that when you're married, you know. Just up and leave without discussing shit," he says as she gets to her feet. "Chris wouldn't like that."

For a moment I think she's going to tell him to go perform a sex act on himself, but she just stands there staring at him for a few beats until he leans forward, grabs her hand between both of his.

"I'm sorry, okay, I'm just—"

But even after a few seconds he's unable to articulate what he's just, and she leaves.

I watch her climb into her Land Rover, hear the engine turn over, but she isn't peeling out of the parking space. She's sniffling a little, and I think this could very well be a blessing. Derek nailed his own coffin shut in approximately five minutes. I should buy him another old-fashioned for making my job easier.

I chance a glance through the bar window again, and Derek's still there, nursing his drink, his expression inscrutable. Maybe he can feel the force of my glare, because quite suddenly his eyes cut through the window. Our gazes almost meet, but I'm quicker, get the Cadillac started up as I adjust my baseball hat, and ease out of the parking space.

◆ ◆ ◆

My driveway isn't empty when I turn into my neighborhood after returning the Cadillac to my grandfather's shed. There is a white Land Rover where I normally park. It's a welcome surprise, but when I pull up beside Serena, the look on her face dries my smile right up.

We get out of our cars, meeting in the middle of the driveway.

"What's the matter?" I already know, of course, but I arrange my face into a mask of curiosity, pulling her into a hug.

"Fucking Derek."

Ah. Fucking Derek, indeed. "What happened?"

She shifts away, shaking her head, looking like she'd quite like to hit something. "He's not thrilled we're getting married. Not that I expected him to be, but I at least thought he'd try to muster up some fake enthusiasm or something. We've never really fought before."

"Well, what did he say?" I ask, guiding her up the steps to the front door.

"A bunch of shit. Essentially stuff about how I haven't thought anything through and I'm making some massive mistake."

I hold the door open for her, unsure of what, if anything, to say. Rail against Derek too hard, and when she inevitably forgives him, I'll look like the asshole. If I'm too noncommittal, she'll be mad I'm not on her side.

She stands there staring at me in the foyer, her expression expectant.

"I . . ." I turn my hands palms up. "I really don't know what to say, babe. I think all that matters is if you think it's a mistake."

She looks down at her ring as she twists it around her knuckle. "I don't."

"Then it doesn't matter what he thinks. If you believe him saying you haven't thought anything through has merit, then think it through. We've got time, we can work anything out. Logistics, chore division, whether we get a joint checking account, whatever. All we have to do is talk about it."

"Well . . ." Her eyes dart around the bottom floor of the house. "Are we going to live here?"

"That's what I figured. Unless you want me to move. I remember you telling me how Sirius isn't exactly a neighborhood kind of dog. Not sure if the yard here is big enough."

She gives me a tremulous little smile, following as I sink onto the couch. "He does better with a bigger yard, but I can just take him on long walks for exercise. You've barely moved into this place. Moving again seems like too much to ask."

I pull her onto my lap. "I'd move a dozen times for you."

"Do you want me to take your last name?" She traces the rim of my ear, not meeting my gaze.

"Of course I want you to, but I know that might get complicated, what with Cole having a different last name." I shrug. "I don't care what your last name is, I just want you to be my wife." It's a lie. I do care, but I don't think insisting on anything is going to win me any favors. I've got to be the opposite of Derek. Laid back, calm, someone who "goes with the flow."

"I could, what do you call it—you know that thing some women do, they turn their maiden name into their middle name or something? Does that have an actual term? Not *hyphenating*."

"I don't know."

"Well, Archer is a first name, too, technically. I could make it my middle name. Keep it so Cole won't feel left out."

I lean back against the cushions, and she follows suit, her head on my shoulder. "Not so hard, talking about stuff, is it? We can figure everything out."

She agrees, puffing out a relieved little sigh, working her arms around my waist.

And in the meantime, Derek can go fuck himself.

◆ ◆ ◆

Doubly so when I pull up the spyware app after Serena leaves my place.

Since when has Chris been following you? Is this new or did you know he was there? Derek said at 4:02.

She answered him quickly, within seconds, because at exactly 4:02 she wrote, What in the world are you on about?

> He was outside the bar in an old beige car, maybe a Cadillac, big rust birthmark on the passenger's side. Baseball hat, but I'm pretty sure it was him.

> > He doesn't have a Cadillac or wear baseball hats. You're paranoid and just looking for more reasons to hate him. Every guy in a baseball hat looks the same for fucks sake.

It's not like I don't already have enough reasons to hate him. He was there. I know it was him. Booked it as soon as I looked right at him. You'll ignore me, but when this all goes to hell don't say nobody ever warned you. And when she didn't respond within a couple of minutes: I love you, okay? You're my best friend and I love you and I need you to be safe.

She left him on read, which should soothe my frazzled nerves. She didn't believe him, she's never believed him. I should take comfort in that, but honestly the only thing I could take comfort in right now would be Derek's tragic and untimely death in a structure fire.

23

Is it just me, or have Serena's once-infrequent nights out become a more regular thing?

Every time I turn around, she's out with Rosa while I'm sitting home alone. She turned down my request to see her tonight because she's made other plans that do not involve me, and is it really that wrong for me to think she ought to check with me first? I'm her significant other; that means my ranking is far above Rosa's. Shouldn't I have dibs on seeing my own goddamned fiancée? Why can she make time for Rosa but not me? I've debated stealing her driver's license—she gets carded everywhere; it would make it harder for her to go out until she gets a replacement—but she usually goes to Jack's. They know her there, wouldn't ask for ID.

As usual, Rosa is documenting her night out with my fiancée on Instagram, and I am genuinely mystified as to why Serena would ever think it's okay to go out in public looking that way. Her skirt looks like underwear (is she even *wearing* underwear?) and she isn't wearing a bra beneath that top because it leaves so little to the imagination and the straps would be visible if she were.

Call me old fashioned. I would just prefer my fiancée didn't dress like a prostitute.

My blood pressure spikes higher with each new Instagram photo. There are men in the background, and I can't make out Serena's left hand, which leads me to the obvious conclusion: she isn't wearing her ring. She's out with Rosa, pretending to be single, accepting drinks from strangers, and flirting with them as payment. This is what she'd rather do than spend the night with me?

The Land Rover rolls up to her house a little after midnight, and I know this because I'm parked on the street in front of her house. I get out of my car when she does and meet her at the bottom of the driveway.

"What are you doing here?" she asks, looking remarkably clear eyed for someone guzzling free drinks all night. "I thought we didn't have plans?" I want to breathe a sigh of relief when I see the ring on her left hand.

"We didn't, I just missed you. I thought you'd be home earlier." You should have been home earlier, Serena; you do have a child, after all. You've got a child and a fiancé, and you shouldn't be dressing like a slut.

"Oh," is all she says, but her eyes have a mist of confusion.

"Is that what you wore out?"

"Um." She looks down at her body, then back at me, removing her keys from her purse. "You mean exactly what I'm wearing right now when I got home? Yes." Her confusion has evaporated, overtaken by a dash of defiance and a lot of defensiveness.

"You must be cold."

Her brow furrows as she turns away on her heels, heading up to her side door. "I'm not. Mostly I'm wondering why you even care what I'm wearing. You've never had a problem with my clothes before."

"I guess I didn't think you'd wear something that revealing after we got engaged," I say, trying to keep my voice even, which is very hard to do when you really want to punch something.

She comes to an abrupt stop a few feet in front of the side door and whips around, her bag swinging. "Excuse me?"

"You're dressed like you're single, like you're trying to pick up men. You're not single."

"I really don't think there's a set way to dress based on your fucking marital status, Chris." She stabs her key into the lock and pushes the door open.

"What are you doing in bars, anyway? We're getting married. Married women shouldn't be in bars."

She barks out a laugh, but it doesn't look as though she finds this at all funny as she steps into her kitchen. Sirius pads over, head bowed and eyes locked on me as I plant one foot over the threshold.

She stops me, pressing one firm hand into my chest. "No. You're not coming inside."

"Why not?"

"Because you're being an asshole, and I don't let assholes in my house."

"What, I can't be honest and try to discuss things without you getting offended?" You're seriously barring me from entry, Serena? You have a lot of nerve. I'd never do that to you.

She smiles, but she doesn't look happy. "You be as honest as you want, but if you're going to imply I'm a whore, you're going to be doing it long distance."

And she shuts the door in my face, the locking dead bolt as loud as a gong in the silence.

What's up? Rosa texts Serena the next day. Bumming around in pajamas?

Oh, were you planning on calling on the town whore?

Wtf?

I can see where this is going. Oh goody. Yet another bitch-fest on how poor Serena has the most terrible fiancé in the universe. She hasn't responded to any of my texts, not one. They're not even marked read. I checked on the spyware app, and each time she sees an alert about an incoming message from me, she immediately disregards the notification.

> Oh, you didn't know? I dress like a slut and married women shouldn't be in bars, so I suppose that makes you a slut too.

You really ought to calm down, Serena. Nobody likes a drama queen.

If I'm a slut that's news to me. Wonder if Marlon knows

> Chris was parked outside my house when I got home last night. He said I was dressed way too revealing, like I was "single," and then said women who are married shouldn't be in bars.

Chris can eat a fucking bag of dicks

> Like, does he think I'd jump on the first cock that was presented to me or something? That anyone who even shows me the slightest bit of attention will get himself a BJ? He's never cared what I've worn before but suddenly I'm open for business like the corner whore

You didn't even look slutty, that skirt wasn't that short. If he wants to know what a real slut dresses like I'd be happy to give you a few pointers

> I suppose this means I'm not Virgin Mary anymore but Mary Magdalene. It feels like I'm living inside a Taylor Swift song

Listen, if he thinks it's well within his right to tell you how to dress, he can kindly go fuck himself. Mini skirt days don't last forever, you gotta wear them while you can. Unless you're going out in a bikini that is literally PAINTED ON, he has no say in what you wear. You never dress inappropriately for what the occasion dictates and if he thinks you dress like a slut he can go find himself a fucking nun or something. Jesus Christ I'm pissed for you, let's dress like great big sluts tonight and paint this whole goddamned town red

If you take her up on that offer, we're going to have a problem, Serena.

You know any body painters we can contract?

I figured we'd forgo the clothes completely. I mean, why waste the effort? It takes too long to undress when you're trying to get all the sex with randoms, so why don't we save ourselves the hassle and just go out naked? We ought to optimize our time out, don't you think? Our kids are getting older and we won't be young and hot forever, we should make hay while the sun is shining

Rosa is really beginning to piss me off, but she's given me a pretty genius idea.

24

When Serena swings the door open to me a few days later, she gives the roses I'm carrying an arched eyebrow, but it looks like she'd prefer to give me the finger.

"I don't think whores accept payment in floral arrangements. We only like cash."

"I'm sorry," I say, trying to look appropriately apologetic as I step inside.

"You're sorry," she echoes flatly, the door snapping shut behind her.

"I am."

"What am I supposed to do with an 'I'm sorry'?"

I don't know how I'm expected to respond to that, which she seems to have surmised.

She throws up her hands. "I mean, great, fine, you're sorry. So what? Can I exchange this 'I'm sorry' for something a little more substantial? You're sorry you implied I dress like a whore, but you still implied I dress like a whore. It's not like I can forget that."

"Look." I set the roses on the kitchen table, because she's made no move to take them, and drop the case of my grandfather's tools on the floor. "I never actually said the word *whore*, you know that. You know I don't think you're a whore, for God's sake—you'd been celibate eight years before I came around. It just seems like you'd rather be with Rosa than with me. You're going out a lot more than usual, and I miss you."

She crosses her arms over her chest as Sirius slinks into the kitchen and settles himself by her feet. "Chris, you weren't around all those years when I *couldn't* go out because I had a little kid. We've finally gotten to the age where Cole can hang out at home by himself without constant supervision, so of course I'm going to go out now that I actually can. You're making it sound like I'm always out of the house. It's maybe twice a week, if that. Missing me doesn't have anything to do with you implying I dress like a hooker, anyway."

"I never said *hooker*!" I say, louder than I intended, and it makes Sirius's head snap up and his gold gaze zero in on me. "I never said *hooker* or *slut* or *whore* or any of that, you're twisting my words. Why would I want to marry a whore? That doesn't make sense."

"I said you *implied* all that, not that you actually said it. Which is just as bad."

I really thought she'd let this go after cooling down for a few days. I thought she'd be reasonable, that she wouldn't insist I grovel.

I sink into a chair. "Can you please try to cut me some slack? You know you're beautiful. You know men stare at you everywhere you go."

"I don't know anything of the sort," she says, expressionless. Pitiless.

"Yes, you do. You own a mirror, you know you're gorgeous. It just gets to me sometimes. You don't know how men think. Is it really so bad that I get a little bit jealous knowing other men want you?" Look at me being all vulnerable, Serena. Doesn't that soften something within you? Do you think I like admitting my insecurities? Doesn't any part of you understand my point of view? Don't all women want a man who gets a tiny bit jealous when other guys want their girlfriend? "I mean, would you rather I were like Tom, plastering the internet with your nudes, begging strangers to fuck you?"

"What does it *matter* what other men may or may not want?" Her voice is straining, climbing in pitch. "Why do *their* thoughts even factor into any of this? Because it sounds like you don't trust me, and I've never given you any reason to doubt me."

"Of course I trust you," I say, and I do, kind of. "It's not you I don't trust, it's them."

"And you think they'll come on to me and that I'll fall all over myself trying to hop on their dick. That's what you mean."

I tilt my head back, my eyes pressed shut. "That's not what I mean at all," I tell the ceiling.

"It kind of is. You think they'll have some lascivious thoughts about me and that I'll be helpless to resist their charms because deep down, I'm a whore you can't trust."

"No, I mean you're my fiancée and I love you, and I can't help it if I miss you and don't like the fact that some guys are perverts and think nasty things about you."

She stares down at me, and it's never been hard for me to maintain eye contact with her before right this second. She's furious and cold, and glaring like I've never seen her glare before. Sweat pools beneath my collar, and oh God this might be the end.

"I don't like this, Chris. The jealousy. Pushing boundaries. You act like it's not okay for me to have a life outside of you, and now you're trying to control what I wear. None of this is okay. It's like you think my life should screech to a halt and I should drop everything to fix your problem every time you feel even slightly upset about something. No matter where I go or what I'm doing, you expect me to be focused entirely on you."

We're supposed to be focused on each other, Serena. Our relationship is the most important thing in our lives. You've been my number one priority since the second we met. Is it too much to ask that you put me first?

"I love you." I can't think of anything else to tell her to shut down the argument. "You know I do."

She blinks down at the toolbox. "Why'd you bring that?"

"To fix your dresser. You complained about it the other day."

"Thanks," she says grudgingly, pulling out her phone to check the time. "I've got to pick up Cole and Dre from practice. Lock up after you're done if I'm not back by then."

She makes to brush past, but I catch her wrist and pull her to me. "I'm sorry," I say, my arms locking around her waist. "I think I'm too in love with you and it makes me crazy sometimes."

She doesn't even acknowledge what I've said, just tries to break out of my arms, and my automatic, knee-jerk response is to hold her tighter.

"I have to go, Chris."

I let her go.

◆ ◆ ◆

Sirius follows me into her bedroom after she departs, his watchful eyes never straying far. Her dresser is an easy fix; the glides just need replacing, so I make quick work of it, then unpack my materials.

She gets her birth control in multimonth supplies, so I retrieve them from her underwear drawer, punch out all the pills in the blister pods, and plug the holes with the placebos. I cut out a round of aluminum foil, smooth it out over the plastic disk of pills, and ever so slightly pinch the edges.

The gas torch is the trickiest part, but I've had a lot of practice being light handed, and I let the flame gently lick the foil, fusing it to the disk. I do the same thing with the remaining packs and dump the small mountain of real pills into a Ziploc bag that I then stow in my toolbox.

She's taken about half of the pills this cycle, so I punch out the same ones in the blister pods of one of the fake disks, pop it into the pink case, and nestle it back among her underwear.

You can't really go out and paint the town red if you're pregnant, you see. If you've got a small child at home, nights out aren't a regular occurrence. Babies force you to look at the bigger picture. You can't just up and leave your fiancé if you're expecting.

◆ ◆ ◆

When Serena veers into her driveway an hour later, she tells Cole to get his practice clothes into the washer and stares up at the roof, her hands on her hips as she walks through the overgrown grass of her lawn.

"Trying to kiss my ass?" she calls up. She's not smiling. I must not be out of the woods yet.

"Kind of. But they needed cleaning." I toss a soggy handful of leaves from the rain gutter into a bucket. "I fixed the sink in the half bath too. Can you make me a list of other stuff that might need to be checked for repairs?"

"Why?" *How long is your voice going to be this frosty, Serena? Can you give me a time frame?*

I think I'm overcompensating for her coldness, using the most upbeat tone I can muster. "You're going to need stuff in order when you list this place."

"When I list it?"

We're getting married, Serena; have you forgotten? Yes, you're going to list your house because we'll be living together, and what is the point of having two houses?

I hook the bucket around my wrist and climb down the ladder and onto the lawn. "Aren't you going to be selling it after we get married?" I upend the bucket into her trash can, wiping my sweaty brow with my forearm.

"I was probably going to rent it out."

I don't like this. It smacks of *backup plan*, like she wants her own space to retreat to once she's decided to leave me. *You don't need backup plans in marriage, Serena. You're all in or you're not. You don't get to dip a toe in and then decide it's not your cup of tea.*

"You're going to deal with tenants and all the problems that come with them?"

"A lot of Realtors own multiple houses. It's a safety net, a good source of retirement income."

"Right." I wipe my hands on my jeans. "Hadn't thought about it that way."

She looks at me in that same expressionless, wax-statue fashion she's been doing since our fight and heads inside. I slip through the side door after her and find Cole at the kitchen table, inhaling a Hot Pocket, Sirius curled up at his feet.

"Hey," he says, through a mouthful of scorched cheese and marinara. "How long are you gonna be here? Wanna play *Rust*? The new server I've been on is way better than the other one I told you about."

"You have a test tomorrow," Serena interjects. "It's not going to be a *Rust* night."

She ignores his scowl, and I follow her into her bedroom, where she rounds on me as she rips the ponytail elastic from her hair.

"What are you still doing here?"

The snap in her voice has me falling back a step. "I thought you'd want to be together tonight now that we're not fighting anymore."

"I'm not going to hang out with you like everything's perfectly fine when I'm still pissed."

She cannot seriously be suggesting I leave. This cannot be real. I've just fixed her dresser and her leaky sink and cleaned out her rain gutters, and now she's throwing me out. I feel like I'm in *The Twilight Zone*.

"I've just spent an hour fixing shit around your house," I say. "I want to be with you. Are you saying what I want doesn't matter?"

"You should have thought about that before acting like a dick," she says, herding me to the bedroom door. "I didn't ask you to do any of that. I'd rather be alone tonight."

I'm getting pretty fucking tired of her shutting doors in my face.

A furious look wreathes her face for hours afterward, long after I've left. I watch her stalk the halls and stomp around the kitchen from my laptop at home as night falls fast, filling my office with darkness.

Her scowl grows even more ferocious when her phone chimes as she's brutally scrubbing a pile of dishes, like each has done her a great personal wrong. She slaps her hands dry on a dishcloth, applies her thumbprint, and suddenly she doesn't look pissed anymore.

I pull out my own phone, curious to see what could have turned her mood around.

It's Derek, the first time he's reached out since their text fight after the bar, and he's sent her a picture. A watercolor sunset of red and gold and pink, and it looks like he's sitting on some kind of terrace because I can make out the railing of a patio enclosure, the edge of a shoe braced against it. He must be out of town for a show in some time zone a few hours behind. The Rubenesque curve of a guitar peeks out from the bottom of the photo, and he's captioned it wish you were here.

Me too, she says.

25

The sky is finally beginning to lighten above that doghouse I've been in for nearly a week. Serena no longer looks murderous when she sees my texts, and her replies consist of more than two words. She and Rosa aren't discussing the fight to death anymore, which is a blessing. I'd been wondering how long they planned on beating that dead horse.

It's that time of year again. Football season is beginning, and with it come booster meetings with the blond-bobbed Karens, car washes and bake sales, Friday nights spent at the high school stadium. I am quite surprised that she's signed up for this shit yet again when she couldn't stop complaining about it last time. I've taken to attending the meetings with her because I want to show her I'm devoted to her son, and also because I ought to be present when she's around so many fathers who've got matronly wives and would probably love nothing more than to hit on her. Serena seems to think it's sweet I've chosen to be so involved, and when I sign up to run the car wash, she and Rosa exchange wide-eyed looks of pleasant surprise.

Why wouldn't I volunteer? Serena spends the bulk of football season engaged in these sorts of dreary activities, which eats into my time with her.

Serena and Rosa have been diligently baking for the past week, and it's all come to fruition today, a scorching late-August Saturday, when the school hosts a joint car wash / bake sale extravaganza, all to support the team.

She's set up at a long wooden table laden with cupcakes that have frosting in a riot of colors, truffles that sweat slightly beneath the heat haze, fudge piled high on paper plates, caramels overflowing from buckets. I watch her from across the parking lot, where I'm holding fort for the car wash, and wonder if she's supposed to handle all the customers herself, when a thickset man with graying hair ambles over to her table.

She smiles at him, shakes his hand, and laughs at something unfunny he's probably said, and then they settle into their folding chairs, talking all the while.

They hardly stop talking. Even when customers perforate their conversation, it resumes seamlessly as Serena hands him bills to tuck into the cashbox. Why isn't it a mother she's working with? He probably signed up for the job the second he knew Serena would be manning the table. How can she possibly have this much to say to a man she's never met before?

I've got nobody to talk to over here. All I'm doing is directing traffic, something a monkey could do, so it's easy to catalog every smile Serena gives this guy, every time she leans a bit too close to him. Sometimes I wonder if she can feel me watching, because she's been flicking glances over toward the parking lot.

It's half past three when this nightmare finally concludes. Serena meets me at her Land Rover in the far parking lot, juggling the box of leftover cupcakes, a sheen of sweat on her upper lip.

"How was it?" she asks, dumping the box into the back seat. "Was it all you'd dreamed of?"

"I'm just glad it's only a once-a-year thing."

"You and me both." She buckles herself into the driver's seat, turns the engine over, and thank God we're finally free.

"Who was that guy?" I ask, trying to sound vaguely curious.

She hooks a left out of the parking lot. "Which guy?"

"The guy working the bake sale table with you."

"The father of one of the boys on the team."

"Oh." I stall for a beat, puzzling over what to say next because I can't say what I'd like to, which is *Why, exactly, were you being so friendly with some random football father when you're practically married?* "Was he nice?"

Her voice cracks like a whip, startling me. "Where are we going with this line of questioning, Chris?"

"What do you mean?" Her profile is stony when I look over at her.

"You're working up to something; why don't we just cut to the chase?" Her shoulders have migrated closer to her ears, like she's braced for an argument. "Is that the reason you kept a hawk eye on me the entire time? You thought I was flirting with the fifty-year-old father of fucking Jacob Gladstone, a kid on Cole's team? Why? Because I was *talking* to him? You expected me to sit in silence and sell cupcakes to strangers without even giving the guy helping me out the time of day?"

Yes, that is essentially what I was driving at, but confirming it wouldn't be wise—that much is obvious. She's tense, ready for a fight, expecting to have to defend herself.

"No," I say, forcing out a surprised laugh. "It's just that it would be nice to get to know some of the fathers involved if I'm going to be volunteering for stuff like this. He seemed friendly enough. Maybe like someone I can grab a beer with once in a while. I was hoping you could introduce us sometime."

She applies the brake as we inch toward a red light, looks me full in the face as the Land Rover comes to a complete stop. I can't tell whether she's bought my explanation, because her face is smoothly inscrutable.

"I'm sorry," she eventually says, swallowing a sigh. "I'm sorry for being defensive. Yes, he was nice. I'll make sure to introduce him at the next boosters meeting."

"Thanks."

"But there's no fucking way I'm ever hanging out with his wife, so for God's sake don't suggest a double date if you ever grab that beer with him."

◆ ◆ ◆

Her house has never been in a better condition, thanks to my handyman skills. Over the next week, I work steadily on getting it into prime shape, though she thinks it's for potential tenants. I've still got to convince her that she really ought to list it for sale.

Edging an entire acre lawn with a Weedwacker takes forever. I've been at it for nearly an hour, and Serena has yet to come out and check on me, offer me a lemonade or whatever. My grandmother always made a point to go out and check on my grandfather when he was doing yard work, cold drinks at the ready. I guess Serena isn't the nurturing sort. What is she doing in there that's so important she can't look in on her fiancé, see how he's faring? This isn't even my lawn, but somehow I'm doing all the heavy lifting.

I turn the Weedwacker off, dig my phone out of my pocket, and pull up the camera feed. She's not in the kitchen; all I see is Sirius, sprawled across the tile and gnawing on a rawhide. Nor is she in the living room.

She's in her bedroom, and though I can't clearly make out what she's doing through the bedspread, I've got a pretty good idea. Blood rushes to my head, thrumming at the pressure points in my temples, and before I've consciously chosen to, my phone is back in my pocket and I'm flinging open the side door, stalking past Sirius, and turning the doorknob to her room.

It doesn't budge. She's locked it. Who does she think she is, exactly? Why is she locking herself into rooms?

So I hammer on the door until her bewildered voice answers, "What?"

I don't respond, just keep hammering.

Eventually she opens the door, red patches blooming across her cheeks and her hair a wavy mess. *"What?"* She's actually snapping at me. I don't think the person in the wrong should be allowed to snap.

"What the hell are you doing?" I don't bother trying to keep my voice even. It wouldn't work, and why do I always have to bite my tongue, anyway? She never does.

"Nothing," she says, clinging to the doorknob as though it's a life raft. "What's your problem?"

"You're not doing *nothing*, I heard you from the hallway."

"There is no fucking way you could have heard me from the hallway. You're a nutcase. What, you had your ear pressed against the door or something?"

"Oh, I'm a nutcase? I'm a nutcase for being mad that I'm out there slaving over your lawn while you're in here masturbating? You say you're not in the mood this morning but *now* you are, when I'm outside busting my ass for you?"

"Jesus Christ, what are you, the Gestapo?" She looks at me for a long moment and then shakes her head. "We had sex last night. It's not like I'm starving you sexually in favor of whacking off."

"Why the fuck are you even masturbating when you've got a fiancé?"

Her face morphs from incredulous to furious in the space of a second, disfigured with rage. "This might be news to you, Chris, but you're not actually allowed to dictate what I do with my own body."

"You have zero respect for me, don't you?" It's never been so crystal clear. You snub me constantly, you dismiss my feelings, you flirt with other men, you dress like a whore, you talk shit about me to your friends, and now this. I've been patient with you. Generous. I let you see your friends, I let you do what you want. I shouldn't have to meet with a whole lot of resistance when I need to put my foot down.

"You have some serious anger issues, Chris, if you're going to blow up over something so stupid. Just leave."

I don't have a problem with *my* anger, Serena; I have a problem with yours.

She makes to close the door in my face, as seems to be her custom lately, but stops when I say, "Sure, slam the door on me as usual. I'm sure you'll go out with Rosa and get plastered again, tell her all about how I'm such a dick, poor Serena with her shitty fiancé."

The crack in the door widens, and she stares out at me, her pale-blue narrowed eyes like two chips of ice. "Excuse me?"

"You can't seriously expect me to believe you don't run to Rosa and bitch about me every time we have a disagreement."

She doesn't refute the accusation, but she doesn't address it either. "Go home, Chris. I don't want you in my house." And as usual, she shuts the door in my face, turning the lock for good measure.

Twenty minutes later, when I'm pacing my living room to work out some of my temper and tension, she texts Rosa.

    I seriously need to reevaluate this whole Chris thing.

    God, wtf is he pissed off about now?

And I wait and I wait, but Serena never responds, though the message is marked read at 3:07 p.m. When I pull up the camera feeds and watch her receive the incoming text from Rosa, I see how her index finger trembled over the keypad for damn near thirty seconds before she flung her phone away.

26

The only response I get to my deluge of texts is **Stop texting me. I will let you know when I'm ready to speak to you.**

It's been four days, and she still isn't prepared to give me the time of day, but she finds the time to make pro/con lists on the Notes app in her phone. At least I have this to refer back to next time I'm wondering what my biggest flaws happen to be.

I am "crazy jealous," allegedly. I try to hide it, but she can see it in my eyes whenever Derek is mentioned, whenever she makes plans without me. I'm even jealous of her own hand, if the way I reacted the last time we fought had any bearing. I'm "controlling," presumably because I do not like seeing my fiancée dress like a streetwalker. I've insinuated she is both a whore and a drunk, and *isn't* it a little strange I don't have any friends? I guess I am no better than Jon Snow because I knew nothing about the bulk of this shit. She still has reason to suspect I've gone through her phone (especially after my "tirade" about her bitching to Rosa about me), and then there was that time I had the audacity to count how many people she'd groped at Rosa's party.

She's twisting all those sweet things I do into something sinister, a gremlin fed and watered after midnight. I constantly held your hand when we were out in public because I wanted to be close to you, Serena, not as some sort of proprietary gesture. I wanted to go to all your open houses because you've got a dangerous job; do you know how often

Realtors have been attacked in their empty listings? I hadn't been "trying to supervise" you.

The pros are as follows: *Good job, nice to Cole, not afraid of commitment (clearly),* and *loves me? I think.*

You *think*? When have I ever given you a reason to doubt that? I tell you I love you all the time. I bend over backward to give you what you need, but all the things I need are evidently too much to ask for.

The strange thing is, she hasn't engaged Rosa in any more text bitch-fits about our problems, which makes me feel an odd mixture of mollified and suspicious. She hasn't texted anyone at all, really, other than clients and her boss, the Football Booster mothers, and Cole's coach. Either she suspects I can somehow access her texts, or what I said hit a little too close to home. Maybe she's taking the adult approach and keeping our issues in house. You're not supposed to complain about your significant other to your friends and family anyway; that's called *poisoning the well.* Everyone knows that, Serena.

Now would you please answer your fucking phone?

I haven't yet used the GPS locator built into the spyware app because then her data usage would soar through the roof and alert her that something is afoot, but I don't feel I've got a choice anymore. She isn't home. She isn't at her real estate office; I've checked. She isn't drinking her weight in liquor over at Jack's. I don't see what other options I have but to use the GPS to triangulate her location.

It isn't an address I recognize, but it's definitely not a business or bar; it's in a residential area. I type it into Google, half expecting it to return results about the house being listed for sale, that she's out on a showing, but that isn't the case either.

A few more minutes of poking around online and I've ascertained to whom this house belongs, but the information isn't in any way comforting.

I've periodically checked her location to figure out when she's on the move, and by the time she starts driving home, I've got a forty-minute head start. I'll beat her back to her place and wait. I mentally curse myself for removing that bug from her purse—that was one conversation I'd have killed to be privy to—but I couldn't let it hang out there at the bottom of her bag to get discovered. Eventually she'd find it and spend a few minutes wondering what it was, and then a light bulb would blink on over her head.

It's ten past ten at night when she rounds the corner onto her street. Quite suddenly the Land Rover screeches to a stop, stalls twenty feet away, then rolls into her driveway, gravel crunching.

She flings herself out of her car so quickly I haven't even gotten three steps away from my Audi before she rounds on me.

"What the fuck are you doing here?" She's luminous with rage; it crackles in the air all around her, radiates from her skin like a heat wave, her eyes fever bright. If looks could kill, I'd be dead where I stand.

I assume this is a rhetorical question. I am obviously here because she couldn't be bothered to answer her phone for four days. "Where have you been?"

"I told you I'd let you know when I want to speak to you; you can't just keep showing up at my fucking house, you're acting like a stalker."

"Where have you been?"

"Out!"

"Out where?"

"That's none of your goddamned business."

But it is my business, Serena. It's my business when you decide to go to Derek's house for a long cozy visit and neglect to tell the man you're pledged to marry. It's my business when you make time for him but not me.

"Who were you with?"

"Who says I was with anyone?"

"I'm sure you were, you don't often go 'out' alone. You wouldn't have a problem letting me know who you were with if it was Rosa."

Something about the set of her jaw makes me wonder if she knows that I know. She won't admit it was Derek she'd been with but suspects I've somehow figured it out.

"Where I go, what I do, who I'm with isn't your business. It's just not. You don't get to monitor where I go or what I do."

I wouldn't have to monitor you if you didn't continually hide shit from me, Serena. Stop slinking around behind my back and I'll be able to quit.

"I think you at least owe me some kind of explanation. It's been four days, and I haven't heard a word from you. I'd never leave you hanging and wondering what the hell is happening."

She takes two steps back from me, her eyes averted, her lips pressed together. "I don't want to do this anymore."

"Do what?" I ask, a sense of foreboding descending upon me.

"This." She gestures between the pair of us. "You and me."

I don't answer because I can't; it's like somebody has snipped my vocal cords, clipped the connection from my brain to my voice. I'm motionless where I stand, unable to even blink.

"I don't like who I am with you lately. I don't like being this full-of-resentment woman who can't do anything for fear it will displease you."

"What do you mean, 'displease me'?" I'm not always displeased with her. But what man likes to endure constant rejection? Any guy would be displeased that their fiancée dresses like a whore; any guy wouldn't like being ignored for four days straight. Nobody likes being lied to.

"I mean I'm constantly ready to justify my actions, monitoring what I say and do and what I'm wearing, feeling defensive about getting defensive. I feel constantly surveilled and like I'm going fucking crazy. You're always *watching* me, just staring, like you're looking for something to get angry about. For the past couple weeks I've stood in front of my closet and had to wonder, *What can I wear today that Chris won't have a problem with?* It's exhausting. *You* exhaust me. I can't do anything right in your eyes, you constantly think the worst of me. It doesn't even seem like you *like* me, let alone love me. And I'm not going to do this anymore."

She can't possibly mean what I think she means.

And yet she works my grandmother's engagement ring off her finger and holds it out. After a few seconds have passed and it's clear I won't take it back, she drops it on the gravel in front of my feet, looks at my frozen form for a second, and turns away.

"You can't do this," I'm finally able to choke out to her retreating back. "You can't walk away without even having a real discussion."

"I just did," she says, and closes her side door with a soft *click*.

27

The breakup seems like a fever dream.

She hasn't texted anyone that she's done with me, which gives me a glimmer of hope. Surely if we were really over, she'd let her inner circle know. She'd have definitely asked me to give her back my key to her house.

I text her frequent long paragraphs about how much I love her, to no avail. Well I guess *no avail* isn't quite accurate; she said **stop feelings-bombing me, Chris**, but that's it. I don't know how she expects me to stop. I'm in love with her. If she needs me to grovel, then fine, I can grovel, but obviously I'm not groveling well enough because she still hasn't deigned me worthy of another reply. She hasn't blocked me; all my texts are marked read, but that's the only hint that she's actually seen me pour my heart out, bleed myself dry through iMessage. The unfairness of it all rankles my sense of justice. She ignores me knowing full well I would never do that to her.

Her sharp decline in calls, texts, and data usage continues into the next week. I'm beginning to think she might have a new phone and suspicions of spyware, so I delete the app remotely.

Rosa flits in and out of her house, Derek comes and goes, Dre stays for a weekend; even Marlon makes an appearance under the guise of needing yet more advice on an anniversary gift because he is somehow incapable of choosing something suitable on his own, and is this some sort of tactical strategy? Fill up her house with visitors and maybe she won't have time to think about how much she misses me? Rosa is the only one who even mentions my existence; she has changed my name to That Fucking Asshole and says she hopes I step on a LEGO barefoot every day for the rest of my life.

◆ ◆ ◆

I'm trying and failing to focus on work when there's a knock on my front door around lunchtime. I feel like someone has upended a bucket of relief on my head because I know it'll be Serena, but it's a slap in the face when I realize it's the postman, here with a delivery. It's a package with Serena's handwriting scrawled across the top.

It isn't any sort of olive branch or gift, I find once I slit through the packing tape. It's more like a butcher knife to the heart.

It contains pretty much everything I've left at her house, down to a disposable razor and a travel-size bottle of shaving cream and the coffee thermos I left in her sink. She won't be sleeping in the T-shirts I left in her laundry basket because here they are, neatly laundered and folded. My toothbrush won't rest beside hers in the holder anymore because she's tucked it into a Ziploc bag and sent it back.

She didn't even have the decency to include a note.

◆ ◆ ◆

We obviously need a face-to-face discussion, not a one-sided conversation via text that she can easily ignore. Didn't she agree when I said we can talk through anything? Haven't we proven that we can navigate any problem that crops up?

When I turn the corner onto her street, my weak optimism pops like a soap bubble because she isn't alone. A Mercedes is parked next to her Land Rover. The omnipresent Rosa is here.

Whatever. She can hang out in the kitchen while Serena and I talk this through outside.

The hum of voices abruptly cuts off when I knock on the side door, and I wait and I wait, but nobody answers. Seriously? She's got to know I know she's in there. Are they sitting at the table, heads together, whispering about what to do?

I feel faintly ridiculous, playing into their childish behavior, when I knock again and say, "I know you're in there, I can hear you. I just want to talk."

Still nothing. Who has time for this middle school shit?

So I haul out my key ring, select Serena's, plug it into the lock, and suddenly the kitchen is alive with voices. There's a loud screech of a chair pushing back over tile, and for some reason the lock isn't turning.

The innermost door opens, and Serena materializes behind the frame. She does not look entirely glad to see me.

"You're unbelievable," she says, her voice muffled through glass. I don't think she means this as a compliment. "If someone doesn't answer the door, it means *go the fuck away*."

"I knew you were in there. I just wanted to talk." The key isn't budging. I can't even yank it out.

"I changed the locks." There is an unspoken *you moron* at the end of that sentence. "And I'm glad I did. I had a feeling you wouldn't respect that I didn't want to see you, that I didn't want you coming by. I thought I was just being cautious, but here you are." Her face twitches into something that vaguely resembles a smile but isn't, because her real smiles have never looked tinged with disgust.

"Can't we just talk?" Doesn't she owe me one last discussion? Aren't people always harping on about closure?

"There's nothing to talk about."

"There's everything to talk about! You wouldn't even let me get a word in last time." I'm glad she doesn't have neighbors. We must look ridiculous, arguing over nonsense through a pane of glass. This is what she's reduced us to, a crazy couple having a crazy argument over craziness.

She shrugs one shoulder as she crosses her arms over her chest. "You had the opportunity to say something, but you didn't. You just stood there gaping at me."

"Because I was in shock. I couldn't believe we were arguing about something so stupid—I didn't even do anything wrong."

"The fact that you think you did nothing wrong just makes me more sure I've made the right decision. If you love me as much as you claim, you'd let me go."

I have never understood that saying. It's senseless. Why would I ever let go of something I love? You don't let go of things you love; you hold on tighter.

"What, you're going to crucify me because I was parked at your house after being flat-out ignored for days? Anyone would be pissed about that."

She holds out her hand like she's fending off an attack. "You can give me all the bullshit rationales you want, but they won't make any difference. It's over, I'm not changing my mind. Nothing you say can change that, so why bother?"

"You seriously don't think you owe me a substantial conversation?"

"I don't *owe* you a thing. It's my job to look after me and Cole, and it's your job to look after yourself. If you can't handle being broken up with, that's not my problem."

And now Rosa has edged into the doorway behind Serena, her face creased into an expression of what kind of looks like pity. "You really need to leave, Chris. Just drop it. Go home."

"You really need to mind your own fucking business," I say, stabbing my finger against the glass. "I realize you feel the urge to stick your nose into everyone else's life, but I don't think any of this concerns you."

"Wow." Serena shakes her head, looking at her feet while Rosa reacts much the same from behind her. "You don't get to talk to her that way. If you're not gone in thirty seconds, I'm calling the cops. You've got no reason to be here—I mailed you all your stuff." The door inches toward me until I can only see a sliver of her face. "Thirty seconds, Chris. Leave. Now."

And then I'm staring at yet another closed door as the lock engages from inside the house.

◆ ◆ ◆

"I don't like this." Rosa paces Serena's kitchen as I watch from my laptop back at home. She keeps dragging a hand through her rambunctious curls, reducing them to a frizz of black static. Sirius is going to faint with dizziness if she keeps it up; his head is following her concentric progress from the mat by the door.

Serena's face is in her hands at the table. "I don't either, but hopefully he got the message."

Rosa stops dead center, flinging her hand toward the side door. "He tried to get inside when he knew we were in here, ignoring his knocking. Like, who the fuck does that?" Apparently this isn't rhetorical, because Rosa flaps her arms at Serena's nonresponse. "Seriously, who does that?"

"Chris, it would seem," Serena says in a monotone. She sounds exhausted in a way that goes deeper than her bone marrow—defeated, deflated, like she wants to sleep for three years. It hurts to hear her like that. She'd feel better if we could just work this shit out. We don't need Rosa and her theatrics right now, Serena; we just need each other.

"*Crazy fucks* do that." Rosa smacks the table for emphasis. "What if next time he shows up with a brick and smashes a window in?"

Jesus, Rosa. Have a drink—that always seems to make you calm the fuck down. When have I ever displayed that kind of tendency?

"I told him I'd call the cops if he came back. I don't know what else I can do."

"You can come stay with me. Even just for a few days. The boys would love it—it'd be an extended sleepover. We've got more bedrooms than we can keep up with cleaning, as my mother-in-law loves to remind me."

Serena casts a look down at her dog. "I can't leave Sirius alone for that long."

"So we'll come back for a few hours every day and visit him. Or ask Derek to look in on him. You know he wouldn't mind."

"Derek's always going out of town." Serena exhales long and slow. "I've changed the locks, I've got another phone, I'm going to embarrass myself in front of my boss by giving him a heads-up. I'm doing what I can. There's no reason to go overboard just yet. I'd been ignoring his texts; it's reasonable for him to come by one more time as a last-ditch. I kind of expected it."

"Did you see the way he stabbed the glass?" Rosa shudders, and I cannot believe I am somehow so frightening that I'm inducing women to shudder. This is madness. "I have never in my life been glared at like that." Rosa yanks out a chair, joining Serena at the table. "He looked like a fucking psycho. Like he wanted to rip the door off the hinges."

"It's not you he's angry at. You have nothing to worry about."

I'm not angry, sweetheart; I am heartbroken. Sad and confused. This was not how our story was meant to play out.

"I'm not worried for me!" Rosa all but shouts, ducking her head to meet Serena's eyes. "I'm worried for you. Come home with me for a few days. Just long enough for the dust to settle."

"Marlon wouldn't mind?"

"You really think Marlon's in charge?" Rosa snaps Serena's hand up in hers, gives it one hard squeeze. "Think about it. If you don't want to leave your house, call Derek. Ask him to stay with you while he's in town. You know he would."

Of course he would. He'd love to play white knight again. He'd probably insist on sharing her bed, the better to protect her.

"And lock your bedroom door every night. Keep your gun on your nightstand or something. Not under your pillow—I don't want you shooting your face off in your sleep—just keep it within grabbing distance. Just in case."

What kind of monster do they think I am? How on earth did we get here, protecting her and Cole from the horror that is me? I've never threatened him, I've never hurt Serena, never been violent with them. For God's sake, she's the one who broke *my* heart. I feel like I've entered another dimension where everything is backward and upside down and the woman I love suddenly loathes me without reason. I want to pluck that distorted view of reality out of her head and replace it with mine.

"This is my fault, isn't it?" Serena asks dully. "I keep dating these idiots."

"Of course it's not your fault," Rosa says. "How were you supposed to know he was a controlling asshole? He worked really hard to hide it."

"He used to do this thing where he'd kiss me and put his forehead on mine and stare into my eyes, so it's like you could see but not see much at all at the same time, you know what I mean?"

I know what she means, and suddenly I'm looking down into a set of ice-blue eyes, my hands on the warm pressure points of her throat, my skin on hers, that flesh-on-flesh feeling I can't get enough of. I miss that.

Rosa bobs her head, her eyebrow quirking curiously.

"So I couldn't see much but his eyes, and I always loved his eyes, and his hands would be behind my neck, and he'd tell me how much he loved me." Serena sighs. "Every time he did that, I could feel in my body how much he meant it, I could feel prickles up my spine. I can't even count how many times he did that, but it was a lie every time. I'm such a fucking idiot. I picked another winner."

I think my heart is actually breaking, and I did mean it, Serena. I felt those same spine prickles. I meant it, I still mean it, it was never a lie.

"Babe, you're not destined for a convent just because you dated a couple assholes. You'll find someone else."

Over my dead fucking body.

28

My pulse spikes every time my phone chimes these days. There's always the hope that it'll be Serena, but I'm continually disappointed. It takes a few seconds to ascertain who in the hell this text is from; I haven't saved the number, and the words seem like gibberish until I remember having seen similar messages on Serena's phone.

It's from one of the Football Booster mothers. She's reminding me that I've volunteered to man the ticket booth for the homecoming game tonight, and if I can't make it, can I let her know at my earliest convenience?

I did make a commitment to show up at this thing, and my grandfather always said a man's only as good as his word. A woman with a short blond ponytail is already sitting behind the card table set up outside the gates of the football stadium. She looks way too into this shit, like she's trying to relive her youth, decked out in school colors and a vaguely cheerleader-esque skirt she's about fifteen years too old to be wearing outside of her bedroom. She gives me a great big smile as I approach, wiggling her fingers.

"Chris?"

"Yep." I stick out a hand, surprised at the strength of her grip. She's short but has powerful fingers, like a chimp.

"I'm Carol. Have we met before? Who's your son?"

"My fiancée's son is Cole."

"Cole . . . is he second string?" Her tone is still cheerful, but her eyes have glazed over with boredom. What a bitch.

"Hopefully not for long. He's only fifteen."

"That's the spirit," she chirps, patting the folding chair beside her. "Have a seat. Where's your fiancée? I thought you would have come through the back with the rest of the Boosters."

Shit. I've never been to an actual game; this was supposed to be my first. "We didn't drive together. I had a work meeting."

"Well," she says, her eyes on a stream of people approaching our table, "you can meet up with her at halftime."

Freeport is a small place. High school football is a big deal here; therefore, the entire fucking town has turned out to watch the game. I've ripped so many tickets my fingers are numb, and now, sneaking glances up at the packed bleachers from just before the ten-yard line at halftime, I don't know how the hell I'm going to find her. *If* I should find her. Maybe it would be better to wait for her to find me?

I have a sudden mental image of stadium lights illuminating my form impressively as I stare out at the field, Serena starting when she notices me, her resolve crumbling, her heart softening when she realizes that I kept my word in volunteering for this shit. But in this throng I might run the risk of her never seeing me. This is a living game of *Where's Waldo?*

I stand there for maybe five minutes, playing with my phone for cover, scanning the stands every few seconds, pretending to be busy. I've just opened some work email when a loud voice rings out behind me.

"What the fuck are you doing?" Serena doesn't wait for me to turn around. "I ran into Carol in the bathroom, and she mentioned you were here. What in the *fuck* are you doing?"

My mouth still dries up when I see you, Serena, even after all this time. I'm still ecstatic just to be able to look at you, even though your eyes are like hollow-point bullets, trained on mine.

"I said I'd run the ticket counter. I had no good reason to back out; it's not like I had plans. Our plan for tonight was always going to be this."

"We *broke up*, Chris. That means whatever we'd planned was canceled. There are no 'our' plans anymore. You're not fucking stupid, you know how breakups work. Get out of here."

My own temper spikes. She's not Boss of the Football Stadium; she can't bar me from entry or order me gone. "I have every right to be here, I paid for a ticket."

"You don't pay for tickets when you're volunteering at the game," she says, her tone positively dripping with disdain.

"I paid with my time. I'm allowed to stick around once all the tickets have been ripped."

She takes two steps toward me, and my heart leaps at our closeness. "Am I going to have to take out a restraining order? Wouldn't be the first time you've had one against you."

My heart seems to fail for a second before I can steady myself. You've been checking up on me; at least I've still been on your mind. "The judge ruled against it at the hearing. Anyone can get a temporary restraining order; the permanent ones require some type of legitimate complaint. Scorned women take out TROs all the time. If you know about that order, you'd also know it didn't last."

"Maybe I know a lot more than you think I do."

"Can't we just—"

"*No*," she hisses, her eyes brighter and bluer than I've ever seen them, sparkling with unshed tears in the stadium lights. She's holding back tears, for God's sake; why can't she just admit that she's made a mistake, callously tossing me aside. "You came here to get some kind of reaction out of me at my fucking *son's football game*, Chris; that's beyond the pale. This night isn't about you and your bruised ego, it's about my kid, but here you are, trying to incite some sort of scene."

I will admit I have a strange attachment to my wounds, but the only scene I ever wanted to incite was the one where she realizes she's erred and falls back into my arms.

"*I'm* not the one making a scene," I say with restraint, trying not to sound condescending even though I know I'm right.

"Just get out of my life," is all she says before stomping off up into the bleachers. I watch her thread through the serried rows of people until she drops down beside Derek, and I think my head is going to fucking explode.

His eyes are on mine, and I watch him watching me until the cacophony of the marching band's halftime show detonates behind my back, and I force myself to leave before I do something I may regret.

◆ ◆ ◆

I haven't reached out to Serena in over a week, which feels like a herculean feat, requires a kind of restraint of which I didn't know I was capable.

It's Saturday, 4:32 a.m., and is there anyone more talented at breathing than Serena? I watch her chest rise and fall, the sheets a roiled mess about her ankles, her hair dripping over the pillow and down the side of her bed.

◆ ◆ ◆

Saturday, 7:17. I guess I should get up.

◆ ◆ ◆

Very rarely am I not thinking of her, but at least Monday through Friday I have things to do. Emails to answer, calls to make. Now my weekends are whitewashed without all her living color. I miss her laugh. I miss the way she'd freak out at bugs, how she needed me to eject them from her house. I miss how her hair would fall around my face like a cave when she'd climb on my lap and kiss me. I miss her breath on my shoulder. I miss the way her eyes dazzle in the sun. I miss her toes. *Toes.* God. That's sad.

Do you ever get the feeling that your future is already behind you, Serena, because I do. All the time. All I've got to do is watch you through the camera feeds, carrying on with your routine and your life like I was never in it.

I wander into the bathroom. The burning white lights lacquer me as I run my finger along the neck of the faucet of the Hers sink I've never used.

I catch my own pathetic gaze in the mirror, and I look like a fucking pitfall. On the outside I am normal, solid. Beneath my veneer there's nothing but a yawning hole.

Maybe I'll take up drinking.

◆ ◆ ◆

I still hate grocery stores. They got a brief reprieve when we were together, but I'm lifting that amnesty now that Serena is gone. I wouldn't be here if this wasn't where the beer lives and if the only things in my fridge weren't a bottle of mustard and a primeval box of baking soda.

There is a jungle of wide backs obscuring the fucking beer cooler, so I wander down the aisles instead, throwing shit into my cart at random. I don't realize I've amassed a carbon copy of one of Serena's grocery lists until I find myself in the tampon section, reaching for her brand.

I always felt a little jealous of her tampons. Their constant carnal contact, how close they got to be to her. I once saw one fresh from her insides in her bathroom trash can. She'd wrapped it in toilet paper, and I watched that spot of blood grow steadily larger as I brushed my teeth until she took the trash can outside to empty it.

I throw the tampons into my cart and head back for the beer aisle, where most of the throng has cleared, and I locate a case of Serena's favorite.

It's barely 8 a.m., so only one checkout lane is open, and who should be manning it but fucking Checkout Guy. He watches me unload Serena's peanut butter, her Granny Smiths, those weird expensive protein bars she ate instead of lunch, her fat-free chocolate almond milk, and a case of Shock Top, and now I watch him scanning every item, silently hating him, the fact that he exists. He has a cowlick and fumbly fingers, and if he bruises Serena's apples and mishandles her cucumbers, I will kill him. An electrical storm sizzles in my head, and he asks for my ID as if I look like I'm under twenty-one, and I guess I'm doing an all right job containing all that burning hatred because he smiles brightly as he hands me my receipt.

"Have a good day."

I doubt that's in the cards.

What are you doing, Serena? Are you going on a fucking date?

She's sitting at her vanity, trying to improve upon the perfection of her face with palettes of makeup and complicated-looking implements while I melt into the couch in my living room with a beer, watching on my phone. Clouds brew outside, their fat bellies looming low and black. I check the weather channel: rain forecasted. Good. Let the downpour commence. I hope it fucks up her plans.

The branches of the oak outside scream down the window, and Serena slides off her robe, her fingers slow and sultry, as if she knows I'm watching. It coils around her ankles like smoke as she shakes back her hair, and there's a familiar stirring in my stomach, like I've missed a step going downstairs.

All Because of You

I prop my feet on the coffee table, upsetting the remnants of my dinner spread across it: six drained bottles of beer and the husk of an empty protein-bar wrapper.

A strapless black bra clasps her breasts together, and she steps into a matching thong.

She wriggles into the black dress laid out on her bed. Struggles with the zipper. Her shoulder blades roll and bunch together as she fights with the tab. I bet you're missing me now, Serena. I always helped you with that.

You're definitely not going to Jack's in that getup.

I thought she didn't like fancy places for first dates, that they would make her die of embarrassment. You don't look like you're about to die of embarrassment, Serena; you don't even look nervous. You must not like him very much. You were nervous for me.

You check yourself in the mirror as you plug in a pair of earrings, and yes, you look perfect, and what is this all about? We broke up ten minutes ago, how could you accept a date with some jackass so soon?

Who is this jackass anyway? She hasn't mentioned any new names recently. I need a name. I need another beer. I head for the kitchen, fling open the fridge, and grab a bottle by its throat.

I tilt myself back down on the couch.

The jackass arrives. It's Derek because of course it is. I tip my beer toward him on my phone, tell him to go fuck himself.

She's dressed for a cocktail party, and he looks like he could hardly be bothered to comb his hair. The things you can get away with when you're a guitarist.

He doesn't say anything, just kind of stands there like an idiot, staring at her, his sport coat pushed up to his elbows.

"What?" She inclines her head, looking down at herself. "Do I look stupid?"

Of fucking course not. You're gorgeous. He just doesn't know how to say so without making you uncomfortable since you two are *just friends*, remember?

"No, you look hot. You always look hot."

Hot. What is he, seventeen? Jesus.

I can't see if she's blushing, but she probably is, and I down the rest of the bottle.

Whatever her face is doing makes Derek laugh. "Where is this place?" she asks, jamming a black heel onto her foot.

"Destin. The Henderson." I google it, and you're going to a fucking hotel with this asshole? I'm spluttering on beer-flavored rage, and I almost miss it when he adds, "She's got expensive taste, apparently."

Serena bends forward. On with the other heel. I'm sure Derek's getting quite the view down the front of her dress. "How long an appearance do you think you'll have to put in?"

"Hell if I know. Hopefully just dinner."

"I can't stand Jeremy."

"Erica's no better."

"I feel sorry for the children they'll have," Serena says. "Cole!" She gives it a second, shouts his name at the ceiling again. A muffled voice answers from somewhere upstairs as Derek swings the side door open. "We're leaving! I'll be back tonight! Unless I kill myself first," she says in a normal register to Derek as she slips out into the night.

Cole. Well, if Serena isn't prepared to give me the time of day, maybe Cole will. He's a pale imitation, of course, Pepsi to her Coke, but what are my choices when she remains unreachable?

I know exactly how to find him, and I fire up *Rust*, dust off Discord. My eyes are bleary. Blurry. Am I drunk? I blink a few times, clench one eye shut, focus on the time displayed on my phone. Fuzzy. Yes, drunk.

There he is. There you are, Cole. On Discord you are cerealkilla and you swear even more than your mother.

Start small, I think. Casual. **Hey**

Hi

I can work with that. It's been a while. I just wanted to see how you're doing.

I'm good

Careful. Type slowly. So I don't want to make things awkward, but I just wanted to get something off my chest. I know your mother and I broke up but that doesn't mean you and I did. I'm still here if you need me. I'm still here for you both, okay? I was looking forward to building that base with you.

Did I come on too strong? I think I came on too strong. I receive nothing but radio silence for over a minute, until:

We still have a few weeks until the next wipe. Should be enough time to get building.

I think I'm smiling. I haven't done that in a while, so I can't be positive. Good to start now?

As good a time as any.

There is a weak spot in everything, Serena. That's how the light gets through.

29

It's been nearly a month and a half since you broke my heart, and I think you're experiencing some kind of delayed-onset grief for the death of our relationship. You sit on your couch for literal hours, knuckles mashed against your lips like you're holding back a scream. Sometimes your head suddenly drops into your hands and I can hear a soft groan from the bug in your kitchen. I do wonder for a moment if you're coming down with something, but you don't take any medicine and you're not coughing or hacking or blowing your nose, so I think I can rule out a case of COVID.

You're getting a lot of texts, but you're not answering many of them, and I hate that I can't read them anymore, hate that I don't know precisely what's wrong with you, other than general heartbreak. I'm depressed too, Serena, but we don't have to be. It doesn't need to be this way. I miss being your ritual, your altar, your sun. I miss the way you make me feel when I'm near you.

I don't understand you sometimes. You cry rewatching *The Walking Dead* when Maggie finds Glenn in that tunnel, but you never cry about me. You cry right along with Jon in *Game of Thrones* when Ygritte catches that arrow to the chest, but for me? Fuck all. Jesse makes it out of that tweaker compound in *Breaking Bad*, and there you go again, a combination of laughter and tears while he does the same on the TV screen. I see you experience the entire gamut of human emotion when you watch your fucking television shows, but for me—remember me, the guy you said you loved? For me you give nothing but silence.

◆ ◆ ◆

I miss you so much that it hurts, Serena, and I'm considering drastic measures, but none of these options are right or even passable. I scroll through their pictures and flinch at their vivid flesh, their red smiles. They all have names like Jasmyne and Carmen, and their makeup is thick and heavy, pancaked over pores. The thought of being in such close proximity to it makes me cough.

You are soft and sophisticated; they are hard and simple. Pay them, and that's that. No work involved. I had to unravel you, Serena. You were a love story waiting to be written, waiting on a hero. With them, it's jarringly primitive. You cost nothing but everything I have; they charge an hourly rate. Insert tokens, sex comes out. It sounds easy but I don't want easy, I want you, but you're not here and you're not calling and I need you.

I'm trying to divine something in the pictures I'm flicking through, some indefinable *you*-ness that might tide me over. I don't like perusing this flesh market like some kind of pervert, but I am in a dark place, and you're not coming after me with a flashlight.

I flick through overprocessed blonds, Ronald McDonald redheads, brunettes with yellow streaks, and none of them work because none of them are you.

I'll keep looking.

I've got one eye on the code I'm running and another on my phone. It's Thursday, Serena's day off, and that's probably a good thing because she looks like a sleepwalker as she trudges from room to room, the screen of my phone flickering to catalog every change of scene.

Her quick errand coincides with my conference call, and I'm hanging up by the time she's back home, heading straight for her room, a rattling plastic bag dangling from her wrist.

She swings into her bathroom, so I head for the kitchen to brew another cup of coffee.

I watch her emerge from the bathroom once I'm back at my desk, my brow wrinkling as she putters around her bedroom, picking shit up only to immediately replace it, jiggling from foot to foot. Is she upset or nervous? She tries to stand still, but it lasts only moments before she's in motion again, rolling her neck in a few slow circles and heading back for the bathroom, which I can't see into.

She reappears a few minutes later. Slowly and deliberately, she shuts the bathroom door and leans into it as though she's suffered a sudden gut punch and needs the support to stay upright. Definitely upset. Shit, okay, maybe more than upset, I think, watching her chuck something across the room. Whatever it is arcs through the air and lands on her bed, and I rewind a few seconds and pause the frame, squinting at the screen. It's a very blurry box, I'm pretty sure—the letters bleed together, but I think I can just make out an *E-P*, and oh my God she's pregnant.

30

Why aren't you calling me, Serena? You know I'd be in there in an instant. You don't have to sit there in a daze, alone, staring at the wall.

You're worried, aren't you? You're wondering how you're going to manage. Your lids are purple, and storm clouds lurk beneath your eyes, and you've gone pale, luridly white, ever since you emerged a changed woman from your bathroom three days ago.

You haven't told Cole; I don't think you've told anyone. You want to come to terms with it on your own, which I get. When you're ready to tell me, you'll be so relieved because I've been giving this a great deal of thought. I saw our whole future unfold in my mind's eye the second I knew what you knew, that an entire life we made was budding inside you. The wedding will be back on, of course. It'll probably have to be a rush job because I don't think you want to look obviously pregnant in your dress, but that's fine with me. The sooner the better.

It's lucky that I work from home, isn't it? I can be there with you throughout every sleepless night, every 2 a.m. feeding. You can give notice at the realty office because we both know I make more than enough money for our burgeoning family, and in a few weeks you can put the Hers sink to use when you move in. I think I know what bedroom you'll choose for the nursery—the street-facing one with the sloped ceiling, which gets the most natural light in the house.

I should probably wait to fight about baby names with you, but I can't help it, I've been googling, and I've already got a list of contenders.

You look so sad and scared as you sit there staring at nothing, and I wish you'd snap out of it and admit that you need me right now. I'd make you feel better; you know my presence would soothe you. I'd tell you everything would be fine, and you'd realize what you should have all along, that you're mine.

But you need more time, you're still processing, and I want to reboot you like a machine, but I can be patient and wait for you to come to me.

She's apparently going to go to work like nothing has changed; I watch her robotically get ready while I drum my fingers against my coffee maker the next morning. I haven't felt this close to her in so long. Now we're sharing this secret—this huge life-changing thing that will forever bind us together, and hope burns in my heart. This is exactly what we needed, Serena. I know you're scared right now, but the second you look into our baby's eyes, you'll see everything's worked out exactly as it was meant to.

I've never even held a baby before.

Serena must have a viewing scheduled, because when her side door swings open just after four, it's Rosa who's shepherding Cole into the house, Dre lagging behind them.

The boys shoot off upstairs like missiles, and Rosa parks herself at the kitchen table, one hand on her phone, one on Sirius's massive head. He is staring at her like she's the Holy Grail, and after a while she seems to notice, flailing under his intense spotlight.

"Shit. Are you hungry or something?"

His tail thumps on the word *hungry*, and she stands, sighing, her hands on her hips as she looks down on him. "I really don't want to open that nasty-ass Tupperware."

His tail bangs the tile again. She plucks at her chest. "This is fucking Valentino, buddy. I'll die if it soaks up any of that smell."

Sirius is persistent, and so is his tail. She relents with a groan. "You're lucky you're cute."

Rosa is gagging, gouging Sirius's food out of its container when Serena arrives, and Sirius is so intent on the promise of food that he doesn't even greet her.

"Hey," she says, hanging her purse on the rack. "Thanks for picking Cole up."

"Don't thank me for that; thank me for feeding this shit to your dog," Rosa says, clapping one hand over her mouth and nose as she wrestles the Tupperware lid back on.

Serena laughs, and I'm not the only one who can tell it's forced, because Rosa's carefully groomed eyebrow arches.

You're not a good actress, babe. You can't hold this in forever.

Rosa winds her way around Sirius, who is sprawled at her feet, inhaling his food. "Are you all right?"

I watch Serena try to arrange her features into a smile, but she fails spectacularly. "I'm good. You?"

"What's wrong with you?" Rosa doesn't wait for Serena to respond, her hands finding her hips again. "You need to get out of this fucking house. You haven't left it for weeks except for work. That's bullshit. I'm not going to let you"—it looks like she's casting around for a bad enough word—"*stagnate* any longer than you already have." Rosa stands up straight, suddenly businesslike, with the air of rolling up her sleeves and catapulting into problem-solving mode. "Go change your clothes, let's go somewhere."

"Where?"

"Jack's. We're going to day drink."

Serena shakes her head. "I can't."

"Why not?"

"I'm pregnant."

"Shut up."

Serena doesn't say anything, and now Rosa looks too horrified for words, dropping into a chair, big brown Bambi eyes wide and unblinking. "Serena, you can't have this baby; I'm sorry for pulling rank, but you just can't. You're going to be tied to That Fucking Asshole forever, and he's never going to leave you alone."

You'd better change your tune, Rosa. She's not going to let you talk that way about her husband; she's not going to let you spew your toxic waste bullshit once we're a family.

Serena crosses her arms protectively around her rib cage, staring down at her feet. "It's not Chris's baby."

31

There is some kind of blitzkrieg detonating in my head, a machine gun *bang-bang-banging* out the syllables of *It's not Chris's baby,* and if it's not mine, who the fuck did this to you, because he's going to die. He's just going to. I have principles, Serena, I can't keep ignoring them for you.

"Then whose?"

It seems like Serena can't bear to name the dead man who did this to her. It takes her so long to get a word out that I wonder if she's ignoring the question entirely.

"Derek's."

I can't breathe or move or see anything but my hands around a windpipe, bulging pale-green eyes.

"When the fuck did you sleep with Derek?"

"Will you keep your voice down?" Serena's eyes rake the ceiling. "I'm going to kill myself if Cole heard that."

I'm going to kill someone too.

"When the fuck did you sleep with Derek?" Rosa hisses, slapping the table.

Serena covers her face with her hands and speaks through the gaps in her fingers. "After that stupid engagement party we went to."

There I was, drunk and playing *Rust* with her kid while she was out getting fucked by her *Best Friend Who's Never Liked Her Like That, Chris, Come On.*

"Why didn't you tell me?"

She flings her hands away from her face. "Because it's awful and embarrassing and it shouldn't have happened."

"I told you when I shit my pants in Mexico. That's awful and embarrassing, and it definitely shouldn't have happened. It doesn't mean you shouldn't tell me."

"This is worse than shitting your pants."

"And you're positive it's not Chris's baby? I mean, the timing is right—"

I never thought I'd thank Rosa for words of wisdom. It's not just *possible*, it's probable. We've only been apart for a month and a half. There's no way it's not mine.

"It's not. I had my period right after Chris and I broke up. It's not his." I think you're lying, Serena. I didn't see you bring home a new box of tampons, which you always do before you bleed. You're making shit up because you're still mad at me. "I'd be fucked if it were his. Chris would be too busy obsessing over me to help with an infant. He'd probably be jealous of it, all the attention it would get from me."

Is this why you're saying the baby isn't mine, Serena? You're afraid I wouldn't take proper care of my own child?

"Were you guys drunk? I don't think I've ever seen Derek drunk before."

"No. I mean, there was alcohol, but we weren't even tipsy. It was such an awful party, we were bored . . ."

You were bored, so you let him *fuck you*? Are you fucking serious? That's all it takes for you to spread your legs, being *bored*? You make me wait ten years to have you, but you're *bored* for two seconds and you let *him* inside you?

Is this really happening? I glance around my office as if it will confirm or deny this is actually a nightmare. Something I can wake up from.

Rosa sounds like she's on the verge of incredulous laughter. "The party sucked, so you had sex with him to liven it up?"

"Well, what do you want me to say?" Serena throws her hands into the air. "It's not like I fucking planned any of it—it was a giant mistake that I instantly regretted. I don't know what I was thinking or if all this Chris shit gave me temporary insanity—"

She's blaming me for *her* fuckup. The gall of this woman.

"Have you told him?"

"Nobody. Only you. I haven't talked to him since it happened."

Rosa sounds pissed as she snaps, "He hasn't even tried to contact you?"

"No, he has. I just haven't really responded."

"Why not?"

"Are you serious? What am I supposed to say to him?"

"Derek loves you; you've been friends forever. Even if it was a mistake, you can get past it. He won't want to lose you over something so stupid." Rosa pulls one spiral curl out until it's straight and taut. "You have to at least tell him he knocked you up."

"Yes, thanks, Mom. I know this."

"If it's any consolation, it'll be a really hot baby."

"Enough," Serena says, a wobble in her voice. "This isn't a joke. It's not funny."

She's right, it's not. It's not funny at all.

I can't see her face now, not from this angle, but whatever expression she's wearing seems to be frightening Rosa, who twists out from behind the table and envelops her in her arms, shushing her softly.

"You're right, I'm sorry." She crushes Serena into her ample chest, rocking them both back and forth. "Everything's going to be fine, okay? I promise."

◆ ◆ ◆

Love takes work, Serena. It's not all orgasms and fireworks. It isn't always easy—nothing is—and I'm willing to do that work, but I still have a lot of anger to work through and purge from my system.

I have to go to Crestview to meet her. I'm not thrilled about being away from the camera feeds for as long as this will take, but it has to be done. I foresee no better option. I don't want to live in this red fog of fury indefinitely. I need this. *We* need this.

I gave her very specific instructions through text on the burner phone I've been using throughout our correspondence, and the result isn't perfect, but it's better than nothing.

She says her name is Ivy, but we both know it isn't, and she looks a little curious when we finally meet around the corner from a shabby Waffle House.

"I'm not used to normal-looking guys." She offers her hand. "Ivy."

"Not tonight."

"Right." She laughs, and her smile doesn't look phony. "Of course, sorry."

Serena does a better job curling her hair, but the pale-blue dress rings true, at least. I can picture her wearing it.

"So where are we gonna do this? Do you want to get a room?"

"The car."

"How long has it been since she passed?" Ivy's gaze gets soft and sad, a little misty as we head down the street.

"A year and a half." I told her my wife died, that I couldn't even begin to contemplate dating but I wanted to relive our first time. She agreed to my stipulations and told me how sorry she was for my loss.

It costs $600 because of the special requests, and I used a prepaid debit card to pay a $300 deposit over the phone yesterday. She had to buy the dress and get more piercings in her ears and find some extensions to add length to her hair.

I hand over the money. She tucks it into her purse, links her fingers through mine, and blinks her Serena-blue eyes up at me. "Your first time with your wife was in a car?"

"We were young." I open the passenger's side of the Cadillac for her. "We didn't have many options; we both lived at home."

She's nice, crawls over and unlocks the door so I don't have to do it manually when I get to the driver's side, and I guess she's got a lot of shit to do tonight because I've barely slid behind the wheel and pushed back the seat when she's on me like an animal, straddling my lap.

I try to pretend she's Serena, but I can't. Her lips are rougher, don't meld against mine the right way, and she feels wrong on my lap, ill-fitting like a badly cut T-shirt made by children in China.

Ivy is sweet and isn't irritated that my body isn't responding. She presses her forehead against mine and wraps her arms around my neck and asks me to give her some guidance. She wants to give me what I need, but I have to help her out, okay? *Let's not let my money go to waste.*

"Can you tell me you love me?" I'd feel like a pathetic jerk if I wasn't paying for it.

"I love you, honey," she immediately says, like she knew her line all along but forgot her cue.

"Not *honey*. Babe."

"I love you, babe."

I inhale the perfume I had her buy, and her lips brush my earlobe, and it works, I'm hard.

I let her earn the $600 and try to ignore the porn-star moans, but it all gets to be too much, sensory overload in a bad, loud, annoying Chuck E. Cheese way, so I grab her by the throat to make it stop. She thinks I'm just getting into it at first, being rough, that I like to choke chicks when I come. Her eyes go wide when she realizes she's wrong. She scrabbles at the back of my hand with both of hers, but she's tiny and I'm not, so for all the good it does, she might as well just let me get on with it.

Ivy's done a good job on her makeup, because her eyes look like Serena's even though they're scared and swiveling.

"I have a daughter," she manages to choke out.

No, Serena, you have a son.

"Please," she rasps.

I don't know what she expects me to tell her. Okay, you have a kid, and you don't want to die. Maybe don't be a prostitute then? It's a dangerous job.

I use both hands now so she can't get a word out. Her blue eyes plead because I've robbed her of speech, and a part of me feels sorry for her because I love her, but you can't treat me like this, Serena. You just can't. I can't let you abuse me with impunity.

Her lips frame the word *help*, and I am helping her—she just can't see the forest for the trees. This is going to be a rebirth, Serena. You need one; you're being mean and selfish, and all you see is *you* right now, all you care about is *you* and what *you* want, and I'm going to show you a better way. We all need to learn lessons sometimes, and what do they say about continuing to grow together in relationships? We're going to fucking grow together.

You don't need to look so scared. I'm helping you. I'm the "best guy you've ever dated" and I love you, but we need to do this if we're going to mend this terrible wound you've slashed through our relationship, because that shit isn't on me, Serena. It's not my fault you fucked Derek and wrecked what we have.

It's taking a while for you to die, but I tell you I love you, to trust me, I'll fix it. You're worth it. Your beautiful eyes are bulging and your pretty makeup is ruined, and I'd apologize but what kind of girl fucks her "best friend" right after dumping her fiancé? This is on you.

You're almost gone now, and we're lucky, you know? Some people don't have and never get what we have. Some people sit on the couch by themselves, alone their whole lives. Not everyone finds their someone. I used to think I'd probably die alone, but then we met and you changed me, Serena; you found some way to rewrite my loner DNA. I love you for that.

32

I'm muddy and wistful when I make it back home. It's just after 2 a.m., with a fat moon hanging bright in the sky, and I wish Serena was watching it with me, but she's probably in bed, oblivious that she died in the night and came back to life.

She is in bed when I check, tossing and turning like each position is hurting her bones. It's hard work, dying and rebirthing and personal growth. I wonder if she sat up against the pillows with her hands at her throat when it happened. Could she sense it somehow? I'm feeling symbolic tonight, so I'm wondering.

I plug my phone into the charger on my nightstand and sleep with her the only way I can, with the camera feed shining on me as I crawl into bed, and tell her I love her since nobody else is around to do so.

◆ ◆ ◆

I'm dragging my ass all over the place this morning, Serena, but you're not. You're up at five, my morning girl, and you woke me getting your first cup of coffee going when the camera feed switched from your silent bedroom to your kitchen as you moved between rooms.

She knocks back two cups of coffee before Cole makes his morning appearance, and after she bids him goodbye, she's alone, the way I like her best, until Sirius slinks into the kitchen, silent as a shadow, having sneaked in through the dog door. She murmurs a greeting ("Hey, babe") as he settles down by her feet. They stay like that for a long time, mistress and dog, until Serena closes her laptop with a snap and grabs her phone.

She's making a call now, moving out from behind the table.

You're nervous, Serena, that much is obvious. You look like you want to vomit up that black coffee you drank for breakfast. Not even a second passes before you're speaking, Sirius picking his huge hairy head up from the floor.

"Hi." She shifts her weight from foot to foot, white as a sheet. "Sorry. No, I've just—" She kneads the space between her eyebrows with a trembling fingertip, listening. "Okay, well I'm calling now, aren't I?" She drapes her upper half over the island, propping herself up on her elbows. "Can you stop by tonight?" She consults the clock on the stove. "I don't know, six, I guess?"

◆ ◆ ◆

I've been on tenterhooks all day, and now the time has come—it's "six, I guess"—and I think I'm as nervous as she clearly is. It's a horror movie where you want to shout at the girl, tell her not to go into the cellar because you know what's waiting there for her and it's bad.

Derek doesn't enter immediately after Serena answers his knock, leaning his fist into the doorjamb, his gaze wary.

"Hey."

She's not exactly ushering him in, I notice, taking heart. "Hi."

"You're done ignoring me now?"

She finally gestures him inside, sounding harassed, and turns her back, leaving him to shut the door. "Sorry, I guess I'm just an immature bitch."

"I didn't say that." He sighs and stands there gazing at the back of her neck while she shuffles some shit pointlessly around on her kitchen counters. "Would you look at me?" He whips her around by her elbow. "I can't believe you're this pissed."

"I'm not mad at you."

"Right. You haven't spoken to me in almost a month. I've texted you a million times."

"I'm not mad."

"How are you, then?"

"Pregnant, actually."

Derek doesn't move a muscle, doesn't twitch an eyelid, doesn't do anything at all but look down upon her. Then he snares his foot around the leg of a chair behind him, yanks it out, and drops into it, pulling Serena onto his lap.

He finds his voice after a few moments. "Okay. What do you want to do?"

She's still and silent, her back to the camera, but Derek's eyes get a little round; he looks baffled and scared in equal measure. "Hey—hey, it's okay. No. No, no, no. It's fine, okay? You're fine."

She covers her face with both hands, silently shaking.

Derek engulfs her so successfully in his arms that I can barely see any part of her torso. "It's going to be fine. You're going to be all right." I can't help but think he's being terribly repetitive and that I could think of a million better things to say in a moment like this.

"You've done this before." He rests his chin on her head. "We've both done this before. I was there with you the first time, remember?"

She gives him what sounds like a watery laugh, but it quickly gets lost in a wet, choking gasp. I've seen her cry before, but never like this. It makes me hate him even more. I didn't think it was possible.

I can tell he's casting about for something comforting to say; his gaze is sweeping the corners of the room as if he's hoping inspiration will strike. "Do you want to know what I want?"

She sniffles something that he takes as an affirmative.

"I want you to have the baby." He runs his fingers through her hair, tucking it behind her ears as a shudder rips up her spine and radiates out to her shoulders. She's trembling like a fucking leaf, and it shouldn't be this asshole holding her. "And I want to be there for you and Cole."

Her head lifts, and there are no traces of tears in her voice now; there's a snap in every syllable as she drags the back of her slender wrist across her cheekbone. "What does that mean?"

"It means I want to be there for you guys."

"Be there *how*? In what way?"

"In whatever way you want."

"So, you're putting it all on me."

"No, I—"

She wrenches away from his chest, angrily swiping at her face. "It's your fault this happened in the first place."

"What?" he splutters. "You started it."

"What are you, five?" she sneers. "*'You started it'*?"

"You're allowed to blame me, but I'm not allowed to tell you that's false?"

"Who cares if I started it? You shouldn't have allowed it."

"*Allowed* it." He laughs sarcastically. "Okay."

"Fuck you, Derek."

"Sorry, I'm never going to turn you down if you're offering. I'm not dead or gay. Why would I tell you no if you want to kiss me?"

"Because it would have been the right thing to do," she says loftily, refusing to look his way.

"Okay, so I have to be the better person, but you don't. Yeah, that's fair."

"I was going through a difficult time! Obviously I wish I could take it all back."

"I don't wish that." He cranes his neck to catch her eye. "*I* don't see it as some horrible mistake. It was perfect, right up until you stormed out."

"I'm on birth control!" Serena yells suddenly to the ceiling, sounding as though she's shouting at God. "I don't understand this. I never miss a pill. Never, in fifteen years."

"All birth control fails sometimes."

"And it had to fail *this* time?" She shakes her head. "It's weird."

He lets that hang in the air for a minute, his hand on her knee. "So what do you want to do?"

"I want to hear your answer first."

"I've already told you," Derek says, finally betraying some frustration.

"In the vaguest way possible."

They're facing each other again, so I can't see Serena's expression, only the back of her head, her dark hair swaying down to the curve of her waist.

"You really need me to say it, don't you?" He laughs humorlessly. "I've been telling you for years."

"It had a different meaning entirely. I want the truth; I don't care what it is. I won't know what I want until you're honest with me."

"Serena, we've been friends since we were teenagers. I have *always* loved you, and I've *always* told you that. You're my best friend. Of course I love you."

"But you never meant it in an *in my tender heart, I love you so* type of way." She tilts her precious face up toward him, and I'm sure she looks like some tragic fairy-tale princess, her hair long and wild, her eyes wide and wet. I don't know how he isn't melting into the floor. I'd fetch her the goddamn moon if she looked at me like that.

He averts his gaze, scratches the back of his neck. He won't even look at you, Serena, he's pathetic. "I don't know that that's entirely accurate."

"What does that mean?" she snaps.

He drops his head and sighs. "You are so fucking annoying tonight."

"And you're being a vague asshole. What, you were just sitting there biding your time until I decided to sleep with you?"

"Oh, you got me." He proffers his wrists like he's ready to be clapped into irons. "Yeah, I was biding my time for *sixteen years*, waiting for you to randomly come on to me. You've got me all figured out." But he softens a little when he looks back at her. "It was never the right time for us, okay; was I supposed to ask you to do long distance or something? You're not someone I would have wanted to casually date, and for a long time that's all I could have given you. I didn't live here, I couldn't be here every weekend or even every month. What would have been the point of saying anything?"

I said something. I didn't linger at the edges of your life for sixteen fucking years waiting for my turn; I took some goddamn initiative, and you never had to wonder how I felt about you, Serena. I had the balls to make you mine.

"So you're a coward then. That's what you're admitting."

"Oh my God." He plants one elbow on the kitchen table and digs a fingertip into his temple. "I want to shoot myself."

She shrugs. "Well, why did you never say anything? You had so many chances."

Exactly. If what he's saying is true, that means he's lied to her for years. He's lied to you for years, Serena. He's a liar, and all you've done is fight with him lately, and you always knew damn well that I loved you. I never hid that from you, never.

He closes his eyes, breathes very slowly and deeply like he's trying to control his blood pressure, a muscle working in his jaw.

"What, you're mute now?"

"Can you shut up?" But his thumb strokes the small of her back, so he can't be too angry. "Just, for God's sake, stop talking. You're fucking relentless."

"Asshole."

"Yep. Fine."

She belts her arms across her chest and stares resolutely in the opposite direction, angry bright eyes red rimmed and lips a shocking pink, matching the flush across her cheeks. A heavy sheet of hair swings forward to block Derek from her view, but he pushes it aside and, with one forefinger, turns her chin back toward him.

"Don't touch me," she says, but with no real heat, and she makes no move to swat him away.

Then his hand slides around the back of her neck, and now he's kissing her and she's letting him, and I don't understand any of this shit, how it can

All Because of You

go from fighting to talking to insults to kissing, and I have a lot of time to wonder because he won't *stop* fucking kissing her, his grip on her getting tighter and tighter, her hands in his hair, and I can't watch this, I can't, but I can't make myself stop. The kitchen is full of harsh, heavy breathing and mouth-muffled moans, and it's probably the worst fucking thing I've ever heard in my life. It's disgusting to witness, sixteen years of his badly hidden pent-up molten lust boiling over. This is a scene straight out of my darkest nightmares, but it goes on longer than any nightmare I've ever had.

It seems like she's finally come to her senses because she suddenly yanks away, her hand pressed into his chest. "I'm sorry," she says breathlessly. "I shouldn't have said all that—"

"Stop," he says, pulling her back to him.

"No, I was being a bitch. I don't know what the fuck is wrong with me—"

"Shut up," he says, and he covers her mouth with his so she can't argue.

I watch them have sex. It's over twenty minutes and entirely awful. I try to be detached about it, like I'm viewing some kind of mildly interesting program on the Discovery Channel about animal copulation, but animals don't make out the entire time they have sex, nor do they remain tangled up in each other after the transaction has been completed.

He's propped up on an elbow looking down at her, his hairline glistening, his hand running down her body, reading every sweat-soaked curve like braille, saying things I can't hear and couldn't guess.

His hand is on your belly now, and you slip yours on top of his, and when he leans down to kiss you, you meet him halfway. It's a long, slow kiss, deep as ocean leagues, and when Derek breaks away briefly, it's to say something, his lips still so close they're brushing yours, and I don't need any fucking audio to know that what he said was "I love you."

33

How are you so sure this baby isn't mine, Serena? I mean let's face it: it isn't like you waited a respectable amount of time to jump into bed with somebody else. You and I have had sex far more than you and Derek, and the odds weigh heavily in my favor. I really don't appreciate the thought of Derek's penis constantly being within a few inches of my baby, because you guys can't seem to stop having sex—it's disturbing. How are you not chafed and raw, Serena; I don't think this is healthy for the baby. Aren't you nauseated? I thought pregnant women threw up all the time. I wish that's what you were doing instead of having sex with Derek on your kitchen island. You're completely naked, and the camera is directly on you, and the noises you're making are reverberating in your kitchen and my head, and even though I'm mad at you, you still make me hard.

I climax at the exact same time she does, and I know this isn't a coincidence. We're still connected, even through the hard times, even when apart.

I think I know the reason she's been so quick to jump into a relationship with this asshole. She doesn't want to be a single mother (again) knocked up by a loser (again), so she's deciding to settle for the guy she thinks impregnated her and pretend to be happy.

Are you even happy? How can I tell? People pretend to be happy all the time. Nobody ever says "Not good" when a cashier asks how they are; it's human nature to playact. Everyone smiles and acts like they have their shit together; that's the whole reason Instagram exists.

They say if you truly love someone you'll be happy that they're happy, whether they're with you or not, but I've never heard such a load of bullshit in my life. Why would I be happy the woman I love is happy getting fucked by this second-rate musician? How much sense does that make? I'm not happy to sit here every day watching them have sex, watching them sneak around Cole and pretend they're still Just Friends like they claim they've always been.

How stupid do you think your son is, Serena? Eventually he's going to wonder why Derek won't go the fuck away or why the kitchen smells like sex.

But I have to watch all day, every day, because I need to know when I can publicly "find out" about your pregnancy and confront you—but you haven't told anybody except Rosa.

Derek's at the edge of the island, still connected to her at the hips, his lips on her throat. "I'm gonna be stuck in traffic for hours if I don't get going right this second."

She leans back on her palms. "Can't wait to leave, huh?"

"I'd take you with me if I could." He pulls his jeans back into place and buckles his belt.

Serena makes to hop off the island, but he stops her, collects her clothes strewn about the floor, and helps her down. And isn't he a fucking gentleman, he even slides the dress back over her. He undresses *and* redresses, what a nice guy. I hate this prick.

But not ten seconds after the side door bangs shut behind Derek, it opens again. It's Cole, and he looks pretty irritated for a kid who has a date tonight (JV cheerleader, blond and perky—nice work, Cole).

"Hey, babe," she says, trying to arrange her face into an expression of surprised welcome. "Why are you home so early?"

Serena, you look guilty as shit. Your hair is a mess, your cheeks flush furiously, your lips are red and swollen. You look like you've just been fucked, and Derek has just left; Cole knows this because he literally fucking passed him right now on the way into the house. Your son is going to think you're a slut."

Cole stands there staring at her, both eyebrows raised. "Why was Derek here?"

"He brought by that video game you wanted to borrow before he had to leave for Texas."

He disregards this completely, won't even look in the direction of her pointed finger and the game case. His eyes travel from her (tousled) hair to her (bright-ass red) cheeks to her (twisted) dress with the strap hanging loose off her shoulder, and his expression gets darker and darker.

"Why do you keep fucking lying to me?"

"What are you talking about?"

"Weren't you just fucking *engaged* to someone else?"

Affection for Cole wells up in my core. What kind of role model for Cole is Derek, anyway, Serena? Why do you keep letting him around? He was kicked out of high school; he didn't attend so much as a community college. I'm pretty sure he doesn't even know how to balance a checkbook.

"What does that have to do with anything?" You don't look very innocent and trustworthy as you duck down to hide your crumpled underwear in a cabinet, Serena.

"You are such a fucking *liar*. I don't know why you can't just answer a question."

"If you say any variation of *fuck* one more time, I will throw your *fucking* phone in a swamp," Serena says loudly, swiping the bottle of Clorox by the sink and hosing down the island.

"Oh, because you never do." Cole dumps his backpack onto the floor. "You're perfect; you never say or do anything wrong."

She abandons all pretense, wiping off the Clorox with a wad of paper towels. "I haven't been lying to you, Cole; I just haven't mentioned it yet."

"That's lying."

"It's Derek." She's having difficulty keeping the anger from throbbing in her voice. "You've known him your whole life. You love Derek. Derek loves you."

"And I love both of *you* assholes!" Cole shouts, narrowly avoiding getting his phone tossed into a swamp. "So I don't understand why you need to *lie* about everything."

She crosses her arms over her chest, which is good because she isn't wearing a bra and Cole doesn't need to see that. She looks silently at her son for a while, and he looks back, still angry but confused now, and scared, because he did call her an asshole and she's scary when she's silent for too long.

Serena breaks the spell and looks away; maybe the pregnancy barfing is beginning to kick in because she looks rather nauseated. "I'm pregnant. It's Derek's baby. I found out a couple weeks ago and was still working out how to tell you. None of this is his fault, so I expect you to be polite at the bare minimum the next time you see him. I don't care if you hate me, but you're going to be respectful to him."

Cole is struck dumb in the wake of this bomb. He eyes her stomach suspiciously.

"It *is* his fault you're pregnant," he finally says. "That's how it works."

She shrugs her bare shoulder and readjusts the strap. "He didn't do it by himself. I was a willing participant."

"That is so disgusting," he says, but he doesn't sound as mad. "I don't want to think about that."

Serena turns to leave, but Cole calls after her. "Are you happy?"

"About the baby?" And on his nod: "Mostly freaked out. Babies are a lot of work."

"Do you know what it is yet?"

"It's still too early for that." She lingers in the hallway, offscreen now, so she's nothing more than a disembodied voice. "When do we need to pick up Brianna?"

"Six."

"And her mom is still bringing you home?"

"Yeah."

"Wear your blue flannel," Serena says, her voice getting fainter and fainter the farther she heads down the hallway. "It brings out your eyes."

Derek's right, traffic is going to be murder. I should get going if I'm going to make it in time.

34

I feel for you, Cole. I realize there are limited options for date venues when you're fifteen, but wandering the mall fucking sucks. You don't look like you're having a terrible time, though, and I can only assume it's because Brianna's hand is in yours as you two mosey around.

You make her smile and laugh, and you don't look at all awkward, and I think you must really like this one because you're patient when she stops at every fucking display case you pass, even the stupid ones for crockery stores. What fifteen-year-old girl needs to look at casserole dishes? But she does, so you do, and you lean forward to get a look at what she's indicating, and you act like you're interested even though I'm pretty sure you don't give a fuck.

It's cute, really. It's cute, and you two are cute, but it's getting old, having to stop so often as I lag twenty paces behind.

She pauses at the window for the next store, Kay Jewelers, and I hope she's not hinting at something, Cole—that's a bit soon. There's a hallway beside this shop, thank God—a long and winding one that splits off in two different directions for bathrooms—so at least I can stop just inside the mouth of the hallway and listen in. The last time I had the chance to be close enough to eavesdrop, she'd been on about some nasty thing Jenna had said about her; one of her friends had overheard it in the locker room during gym class. Jenna likes you and hates that Brianna is going out with you, so Jenna is being a massive bitch about it, I guess. I'm glad I'm not fifteen anymore.

Through the branches of the towering potted ficus beside me, I see your arm slide around her waist and her long blond hair shift over your shoulder like she's resting her head against it, and I have to admire your complete lack of clumsiness with girls; I really didn't see it coming. You're slick. I wonder where you learned that; you didn't have a father to teach you.

"Are you excited, at least?" Brianna has a high voice, thin and reedy, peppy, the quintessential cheerleader.

"I guess," you offer. "I'd probably be more excited if they didn't act like I was a dumbass and couldn't tell there was something going on."

"Maybe they thought you'd be mad?" Brianna's hand squeezes your bicep, and I wonder if you're involuntarily flexing. You listened to your mother's wise advice and wore the blue flannel.

"That's still not a good reason to lie about it."

"Well," Brianna says after a few beats, "you're going to be a big brother!"

"A really big brother," you say dryly, and you make me laugh because you're just like your mother. "That'll be a giant age gap."

"You can take him or her for their first beer on their twenty-first birthday!"

You laugh and say you doubt it would be their first beer; you don't want them to be so uncool that they'd never have gone to a party before twenty-one. Brianna concedes this point and gasps so loudly and suddenly that I look around in alarm, expecting to find a gunman taking hostages.

"Let's get something for her!"

"Who?"

"Your mom! For the baby!"

"Jeez," you say. "People are going to think *you're* pregnant if we go in a baby store."

"Oh who cares!" Brianna says, and I can see why you like her, Cole. Her constant enthusiasm is initially annoying, like she's auditioning for *The Price Is Right*, but the longer I hear it, the more endearing it becomes. She's sweet and pretty and she wants to buy something for my baby. "There's a Carter's one floor up. My sister bought all her baby stuff there."

So I guess you're going to Carter's now.

I'm not going to follow you this time. I'm going to assume the two of you will not leave the mall without at least hitting the food court.

◆ ◆ ◆

And you don't disappoint me, because an hour later you show up with Brianna clinging to you and swinging a bright-blue shopping bag, her hair bouncing merrily around her shoulders.

You get in line at Panda Express, and I slide out from behind my table in front of Orange Julius and into the bathroom at the corner of the food court. You're going to be in line for a while.

I let a few minutes pass before heading out of the bathroom hallway, and you're still where I've left you, but now you're holding the Carter's bag in an effort to be gentlemanly, I suppose.

Brianna's still clutching your arm like she's been sewn to it, and I stop ten feet away, pretending to look at my phone, and I hope this will give you enough time to notice me.

You do. When I look up, you're looking at me, and I pretend to be slightly startled before I smile and head over.

"Hey," I say, and you echo me, your smile awkward, edged in nerves. We're friends, Cole, you don't need to be so anxious. How many hours have we spent building our *Rust* base? I'm just a sad guy in love with your ungrateful mother. "How are you?"

"Okay," you say, and Brianna's gazing up at you, so you add, "This is my girlfriend, Brianna. I told you about her, remember?"

She looks thrilled to be introduced as such, and I have to smile because it's adorable and I'm a romantic too. I will get along with Brianna, I know it.

I tell her it's nice to meet her and turn back to you, making a very deliberate point of eyeing the Carter's bag with the gift tag that reads *MOM*, and you notice me noticing because when I look back into your eyes, they're guilty.

And that's it, that's all I need, so I tell you how good it was to see you, and I can finally leave this fucking place.

◆ ◆ ◆

Serena has the real estate office to herself on Mondays from nine to twelve, so I've blocked out those hours on my work calendar to carve out a nice chunk of time for our conversation.

It's the first time I've seen her in person in nearly two months, and the sight of her has my heart hammering in my Adam's apple. She's bent over paperwork at the reception desk, her hair plaited into a thick braid that hangs over her shoulder. Her ice-blue ruffled blouse makes her eyes pop when she looks up. I hope I look impressive silhouetted in the doorway; I hope she wonders for a moment if I'm some kind of apparition because she hasn't seen me in so long.

But I can't even get a word out before she barks, "What are you doing here?"

"I need to talk to you."

"What could you possibly need to talk to me about?"

My voice isn't raised, but hers is, ringing throughout the office, loud as a car alarm, and it draws out the guy apparently sequestered in a back office. She isn't alone.

"Serena?" He sticks his head out the door, and when he sees me, the rest of his body appears. "Is everything okay?"

"Everything's fine," she says, her burning eyes on me. "Chris is leaving."

Chris is not leaving. "I need to talk to you."

She's rooted to the spot, glaring at me, and the guy winds his way around desks to stand beside her. He slips his hand on her shoulder, and even though I am perfectly aware that this is just Gerald, her gayer-than-gay, overly coiffed and overdressed boss, it still pisses me off.

"Fine," she snaps. "Five minutes. It's fine," she repeats to Gerald, whose fingers have contracted on her shoulder. "I'll be right outside."

So she stomps out the door like a third grader, and I follow, but she stops right in front of the bank of windows so Gerald can watch but not hear, like we're putting on some sort of silent film for his entertainment.

"What the fuck do you want?" Her entire clavicle is exposed, blue ruffles framing it, and I swear she's so beautiful it breaks my heart even when she's cussing at me.

"You're pregnant, aren't you?" She looks like I've slapped her, which I would never do, so I say, "I ran into Cole at the mall. He didn't tell me anything, but it was pretty obvious. The gift bag and everything."

"So what if I am?"

"So it's my baby. We need to talk about this."

"You're not the father."

"Well, were you cheating on me?"

"How the fuck could I manage to cheat on you when you rarely ever let me out of your sight and gave me hell whenever I went anywhere?"

"Then it's my baby."

"No it's not. You're not the father, Chris."

"How can you be so sure?"

"Because I can do basic math. I know who I've slept with and when, and it's not your baby."

"Serena." I reach out for her, but she backs away like I'm contagious, and I feel like she's just stabbed me in the heart. I'm not going to give up, Serena. I refuse to let one moment of weakness ruin what we have. "I know it ended badly between us, and I hate that, but I know we could figure things out if we just talked about it. I'm sorry I didn't give you enough space when you needed it, I'm sorry for picking a fight about your masturbation habits—"

"Oh my fucking God!" she yells, throwing her hands up.

"—but I felt neglected and I didn't handle it well, and if I knew how it would turn out, obviously I would have been more zen about everything, but I love you, okay; you mean everything to me. I just needed you, and I couldn't verbalize it properly."

"You need too much," she says, blunt as the thud of a guillotine blade dropping. "You're a black hole of need, and nothing I ever gave you was enough."

"What can I do to prove to you that it'll be different this time?" My voice is getting higher, desperate, but I don't even care that I sound like a high school freshman. "I love you. I've never loved anything like I love you, and all I want to do is take care of you and Cole and the baby—"

"Oh my God, I feel like Maury Povich; you are not the father, Chris!"

"Then who is?"

"That's none of your goddamn business. We're not together anymore; we haven't been for two months. Move on already."

"It's my business if you're fucking someone else when you're pregnant with my baby."

She laughs bitterly, her lips twisting back in some grotesque version of her usual smile. "It's not your business if I'm fucking the entire town, Chris. If I'm throwing orgies and organizing sex parties, it's *still* not your business. *We broke up.* Get a life."

You're my life, I want to tell her. You've been my whole life since the second I saw you by the peanut butter, and can you please stop fucking glaring at me? You have no idea the things I've done for you, for us, and why did you have to listen to Derek's bullshit? Can't you see that he wanted us apart because he wanted you? He kind of made my point, swooping in when you were at your most vulnerable.

"Serena, please, I'm begging you, just give me another chance. I would do anything to make things right."

"The only way you could make things right would be to stay the hell away from me."

She's looking at me like I'm something disgusting she's found after flipping over a rock, like the sight of me turns her stomach and makes bile storm her throat, and did you ever love me at all, Serena?

I want to throw you against the wall and crush your hyoid like a Ping-Pong ball, but I can't because I love you. I want to wrangle you into the trunk of my car and tie you to a chair in my kitchen until you love me again because I *love* you, Serena. I would crawl inside your body and live there forever; I just need you to come to your senses and remember you love me back.

Her glare is framed in a bit of fear now, like she's seen what I've been thinking in a thought bubble above my head. She skirts around me to slip back through the door into the office, where Gerald is watching, waiting.

The lock turns, and the **OPEN** sign morphs to **CLOSED**, and I feel hollow inside.

I wish I could pin you in a glass case like a struggling rare butterfly and observe you. I want to dissect our relationship as if it were some diseased living thing. I want to trap it under a petri dish and watch it writhe and figure out how it went so wrong, and yes, Serena, I am angry at you, but I also still love you.

I was there when Derek called you back on Monday night. He's been busy putting his music before you, which I would never do, and didn't have a chance to speak to you until you were feeding Sirius his disgusting dinner in the kitchen.

You told him I showed up at your work, that I railed about it being my baby. You exaggerated like a teenager and said you had to tell me about a million times that I wasn't the father.

Derek said something that had you backtracking. "No, I'll be okay, you don't need to do that. I was just mad and needed to tell someone. I should have called Rosa instead."

You paused to listen again, twisting one foot on the tip of your sweet little toes that you painted palest pink one hour before. "I'm fine, really, I promise." You bent down to blindly scratch your ankle and didn't realize how close you had gotten to Sirius's water dish, and then you flooded your kitchen. You cursed and put the phone on speaker while you mopped up the mess.

"I don't like it," Derek said, bass pulsing in the background like he was at a rave or something. "I don't like how he just *happened* to run into Cole at the mall, and now he's showing up at your work. How could he possibly know you're pregnant?"

"Carter's is a pretty well-known children's store," you said, wringing out the sodden rag in the sink. "There was a tag on the bag that said *Mom*. I mean, Chris isn't stupid, I'm sure he could add two and two."

"I don't like this. I don't like that it's happening when I'm gone. I'm going to drive back early. This guy is fucking crazy."

You sagged against the island and told him you're fine, it's fine, everything's fine; you don't want him to get pissed off before his set starts, you're sorry for worrying him.

Then he told you he loves you, and you said it back, and I threw my coffee mug across the room.

I'll get past this eventually. You still need time to come to a decision, to your senses. I would never hurt you—I couldn't—but God, Serena, I swear. Sometimes you really deserve it.

35

I'm not feeling very charming this morning. My coffee maker fucks up, brewing me a soup of some kind of caffeinated water with a pile of coffee grounds. Everyone at work is stupid and can't seem to figure anything out for themselves before asking me to "please look into it, Chris." I want to strangle them all, and I kind of want to shake you, Serena, for not being with me, where you belong.

After my morning meetings I get a phone call that probably won't be you because you're still in thrall to Derek, but I answer anyway.

"Yes, hello, I'm looking for Chris Fox?" the woman on the other end says. There are ringing phones and a low tide of voices in the background, and in the attic of my mind, I think I know what this is. I don't have time for it.

Well. Sally forth. "You've got him."

"Hey, Chris, my name is Amanda, and I'm calling from Crestview PD. I was hoping you could stop by in a few and answer some questions."

"About what?" It was the rain, wasn't it? The rain brought her back, but how did it bring her back to me?

"I just need something cleared up. It shouldn't take long. A few questions, that's it."

"I'm in the middle of my workday," I say, curious and concerned. "I'm taking my lunch break right now, though, if you wanted to come to my place?"

◆ ◆ ◆

Why do I compare every woman I see to you, Serena? I judge them all against your qualities. Are they prettier than you? Sexier? Do they wear clothes as well as you? Does something in their eyes make my heart tick faster the way yours do?

Amanda's pretty hot as far as cops go, so I'm assuming she's going to be a total bitch because nobody takes her seriously. Why is this woman a fucking cop when she could have married rich? I'm sure she gets that all the time.

She's not hotter than Serena, but Amanda is made of hearts. Heart-shaped face, scarlet heart-shaped lips, ass shaped like an upside-down heart. Even her hair is spun with hearts; it's a fiery red that burns copper under the lights of my living room and looks even redder against the white of her blouse.

"Thank you for taking the time to speak with me," she says.

"Of course," I answer, as if there was no question I'd make the time. "I only have a few minutes before I've got a conference call. What's all this about?" I direct her to the chair opposite the couch and set the timer on my phone while her back is turned.

"I'm in homicide over at Crestview," she says, and the look on my face makes her laugh. "I'm not here accusing you of a murder or anything. I just need to ask you about a car so I can cross you off my list."

I let my forehead crease. "A car?"

"A woman's body was discovered a few days ago. I don't know whether you'd heard?"

I shake my head. I hadn't heard, but I remember. I remember the sting of rubbing alcohol (the scent does not linger the way bleach does) and freshly dug earth and the wildflowers I laid on her naked chest. It must have been boys who found her, savage little trespassers in that stretch of undeveloped land.

"I've been combing through every security camera I can to look for suspicious activity around the estimated time of death, and I saw a

Cadillac registered to your grandfather that appeared to be in the general area around one a.m. on October fourteenth. I'm guessing it *wasn't* your grandfather because I found his death certificate. It was you?"

"It was."

Swinging one leg over the other, she rests her elbows on her knees and leans forward, red hair dripping over her shoulder like blood spatter down a white wall. "Any reason you were so far from home at that hour in a car that isn't yours?"

"I drive it sometimes when I can't sleep. He didn't pass very long ago, you know, and we were pretty close. There are good days and bad, a lot more good than bad now, actually, but on a particularly bad night about a month ago I did take it out for a drive. We used to do that when I was younger, go for drives. I thought it would make me feel better."

"I get that. I lost my dad about a year ago." She gives me a sympathetic smile. "It gets easier."

"You can take a look at it if you need to," I offer. "I try to keep up with the maintenance, keep it clean. He'd be so mad if I let it slide just because he died. It's in the shed at my grandparents' place."

Now I'm going to have to detail that fucking thing again, just in case.

"I'll let you know if we'll need to see it." She looks up from under her sideswept red bangs. "Thank you for being so cooperative. Not everybody is. Makes my job ten times harder."

The alarm chirps on my phone. I silence it, and Amanda's lips pull back into a smile.

"Gotta get back to it?"

"Yep."

"Thanks for your help."

She pauses in my foyer, her hand drifting through the dust on the long table where I keep my key dish, some of my favorite photos of Serena. The one where she's in a long, breezy white dress like she's having a beach wedding; the candid one Rosa took, where Serena is laughing on my lap. Amanda picks up the one I captured a few minutes after we got engaged, where Serena holds out her left hand, gazing down at the diamond on her finger. We were so happy then. I don't ever want to forget that moment.

"Who's this?" Amanda asks, her hair swinging forward to hide her face.

"My fiancée."

She looks up at me and lifts an eyebrow, interested. "Does she live here?"

"Not yet. We're doing it the old-fashioned way."

"What's her name?"

I don't like the question. I'm not sure if it shows on my face when I wave my phone at her apologetically. "I'm sorry, but I've really got to get back to work now."

Amanda gives me another smile before she sets the photo down and moves her heart ass toward my front door. "Thanks again, Chris. I'll be sure to give you a call if I need anything else from you."

I google it as soon as Amanda leaves. Ivy has been identified, but she isn't Ivy; she's Emily Akers, and the article tells me she had a small daughter and one prior conviction for solicitation. She's smiling, her arms around a little girl in the featured picture, and she looks like a preschool teacher, not a prostitute. I see Serena in her eyes and the delicate curve of her jaw, in the fullness of her lips and the dark hair falling around her shoulders. Not twins but maybe cousins. I feel a little bad, seeing Emily's big smile. I hadn't wanted to kill her; it's not like it was fun for me, but the things we do for love. I'm sorry, Emily, but I loved (love) her, and I needed to purge all those ill feelings somehow. You were such a sweet girl that I think you'd understand.

Thinking about Emily makes me think about you, and it makes me sad, Serena, to remember all I did to try to make things right and how it was all for nothing. Emily gave her life for us, and look how we repaid her?

◆ ◆ ◆

I don't need ears to run code, so I listen to the goings-on in Serena's kitchen the next afternoon. She's at work and Cole's at school, so I hear nothing but the occasional *plink* of water. The faucet I meant to fix is still leaking. It annoys me, things left undone and ignored. I should have fixed the fucking faucet.

Fifteen minutes later there's the scrape of a key and the scurrying of Sirius's numerous nails, and I look up in time to see Derek sliding through the side door. He dumps his shit onto the kitchen table and ruffles Sirius's ears, and what the fuck is he doing there when Serena is gone? They don't live together, and they've only been hooking up (I refuse to call what they're doing a *relationship*) for a month—did she seriously furnish him with a fucking key already?

Derek has just supplied Sirius with a rawhide and opened a bottle of beer when another key slides into the lock. It's Cole, home from practice, and they stare wordlessly, awkwardly at one another as Cole pauses in the threshold of the door. They haven't seen one another since Derek left Serena disheveled and braless a few days ago.

You are the adult, asshole; don't make Cole speak first.

"Hey," Derek says as Cole lets his backpack slide to the floor with a thump.

Oh, nice one. I could come up with about thirteen better openings than "hey" off the top of my head.

"Where's Mom?"

"Still working." Derek brings the beer to his lips and drains it in one. His back is toward the camera, so I can't be certain if he's done it out of nerves or if he's just a goddamn alcoholic. "Should we dispense with the small talk?" He pushes the empty bottle aside, laces his fingers together as he leans over the island. "It's probably not something you've ever registered because that would be weird, but your mom is really hot."

"You guys keep saying the grossest shit."

"Sorry."

Cole takes a few steps farther into the kitchen, arms crossed and eyes narrowed. "And you just suddenly decided this a few weeks ago, huh?"

"She's been hot since high school." Derek shrugs. "It's not like I never noticed before." And when Cole's answer is a curled lip: "It wasn't like we planned this. I know you're upset, but none of it was intentional."

"I'm not *upset*. I just don't like being lied to."

"Nobody outright lied to you."

"You didn't tell me! I expect her to lie about stuff and act like I'm two, but not you."

"You wanted me to tell you I was having sex with your mom? Just like that? You wanted me to call you up and let you know right afterward?"

A gag of disgust catches in Cole's throat. "No, but I'm not an idiot. I could tell something happened. God, you both act like I'm stupid."

"I don't know what else to say. I love her, kid."

"I already knew that." Cole rolls his eyes, and for Christ's sake even Cole knew this, Serena, so why didn't you? "That's always been fucking obvious."

"I'm supposed to throw your phone in a swamp for saying that."

"You won't. You're having sex with my mom; you feel guilty."

Derek laughs, and Cole crouches beside Sirius, his eyes averted and his tone carefully casual. "Do you know what happened with Chris? Mom never told me why they broke up. One day she wasn't wearing the ring, and she said they were over."

The stinging memory of that painful night crashes over me as I grope in the pocket of my jeans for the ring she'd dropped at my feet. I've been carrying it with me everywhere, and I don't know why. Sometimes I'll be stroking the diamond for minutes at a time without realizing it.

He wants Derek to tell him why, I can tell. He wants a good reason why I'm not around anymore, but nobody can give him one because there is no good reason. It was a simple fight, for fuck's sake; we could have gotten past it. My God, Derek and Serena have done nothing but fight (and fuck) for the past few weeks and *I'm* the asshole for having had one stupid argument with her? How much sense does that make?

"Were you the reason?"

"Not at all."

Cole gets to his feet. "Then why?"

"If she didn't tell you, I don't know whether I should."

I watch the back of Derek's head, wishing some portal would open in the middle of it so I can see the inside of his brain and know if he's lying. I find myself hoping he isn't. If Serena hadn't spilled our whole story, it was for a good reason. It means there's a flame in the dark, some hope still alive. She's still holding a piece of us close to her.

The expression Cole is wearing now is easy to decode, so easy that even a moron like Derek can figure it out: *Come on asshole; you're banging my mom, the least you could do is answer a question.*

I hear Derek sigh. "She saw some behaviors she didn't like, some red flags. I'm sure there's a lot she hasn't told me, but that's the gist of it."

"What kind of red flags?"

"Cole, I—" Derek breaks off, shaking his head. "Just stay away from him, okay?"

"He's been messaging me on Discord," Cole says awkwardly, and I flop back against my computer chair, groaning. "He joined the server I play on."

You'd think Cole just told him the house was on fire, how quickly Derek reacts, snatching his keys up from the counter. "Are you fucking kidding me? How did he know what server to find you on?" He throws on his jacket. "He actively sought you out, that's what you're telling me?"

"I told him which server a long time ago," Cole says, falling back a step, looking bewildered. "I guess he remembered."

"What's he been saying?"

"Nothing. Nothing bad. Seriously," Cole adds because it looks like Derek wants to rip someone's head off and piss down their throat.

"Where does your mom keep her files?"

It seems like Cole is experiencing whiplash from the subject change. "Bottom drawer of the desk in the living room." And when Derek makes for the hallway: "Why?"

The screen of my phone splits in two: Cole in the kitchen, completely mystified, Derek storming through the living room toward the desk. He flips through tabs, finds what he's after, and guts the folder on the desk, papers spilling everywhere.

Derek gets out his phone, squares it over the desk as he snaps a picture. Cole creeps up behind him as Derek slides the phone into his back pocket.

"Tell your mom I'll be back soon if she gets home before I do."

I'm halfway through answering the last round of work emails when my doorbell rings. I wonder who that can be. I think the universe has given me a gift, and I feel an odd mixture of controlled and edgy as I head for the door, keeping my pace slow and deliberate.

I let at least a minute pass before I swing open the door, and Derek looks ready to kill, standing there on my stoop, black hair shining blue in the late-afternoon sun.

"You need to stay the fuck away from Cole," he immediately says. "Bumping into him at the mall, joining his servers—that's going to stop. There's no reason for you to engage him at all, he's a fucking kid. Leave him alone."

My heart leaps at his anger, the hard set of his jaw. It's kind of thrilling, knowing I'm capable of inspiring such fury in him. "Coincidences happen sometimes. How should I have known I'd run into him?" I let my gaze drift down his form. "And I'm not sure who you think you are, barking orders at me."

"I've known that kid his whole life," Derek says, as if this gives him license to boss me around. "And I'm telling you to stay the hell away from him."

"Or what?"

"I realize that in your world, *I'm* the asshole, but you need to get a fucking life, Chris. She broke up with you months ago. This is pathetic. You're not going to get her back, and she's not going to give you another chance, so there's zero reason for you to be contacting Cole. It's over. How many times does she need to tell you to leave her alone?"

"I haven't been bothering her."

"You're stalking her son, showing up at her job and claiming her baby is yours—"

"Well, whose is it, if it's not mine?" I ask innocently. "I was stepping up. Just trying to do the right thing."

"It's none of your business whose baby it is. She dumped you almost three fucking months ago. Back off."

"I mean, I guess two months is long enough for her to have met someone else and gotten knocked up, but it doesn't seem very likely," I say, leaning into the doorjamb. "Do you have any idea how long she made me wait to fuck her? It was like she was a born-again Christian or something. Maybe she stopped being so discerning and jumped into bed with some random guy on a whim, but I would never have expected it of her."

He wants to hit me, I can tell, but he swallows the urge, and clearly I'll have to try harder.

"Maybe it was some meaningless rebound thing, who knows, but I don't think it's outrageous for me to assume the baby's mine. And I'm going to be there if it is. I'm in love with her. She's the love of my life."

"Shut the fuck up with that shit," he says, his eyes flashing angrily. "Just stop. Let her go."

"You seem really invested in her love life for some reason."

"I've always been invested in her life."

"Oh, so you've harassed her other exes too?"

He laughs like I've cracked a joke, but his cold green eyes aren't smiling. "They pretty much got the message when she broke up with them."

"You know what I think is amazing," I say, "is that she's only been with three men in her life. I'd never have believed it, the way she knows how to use that mouth."

And that must have worked, but I have no memory of him hitting me. I'd been standing, and now I'm not, and pain is blooming behind my eyeball, the echo of his fist. He hit me hard enough to knock me backward into the foyer, and immediately I can tell I will develop a spectacular bruise within a few hours. He's in his truck by the time I struggle to my feet in the doorway, and he doesn't spare me a second look as he drives off.

Three hours later the bruise is growing purple and edged in blue, surrounding my left eye and bleeding onto my cheekbone. I look like hell, like I've been sucker punched by the Rock. If I were a woman and said I'd run into a door, nobody would buy that shit. I don't apply ice or frozen peas, and my eye swells into a puffy slit.

Serena is in the parking lot of the real estate office when I pull in and park beside her Land Rover. She's fighting with a giant **SOLD** sign and doesn't notice me until I'm right on top of her, helping her push it into her trunk.

She falls back a step when she sees that it's me, her hand flying to her chest. "Chris, what—"

"Can you call off your dog, please?" I try to seem pale and wan, upset but understanding as I look down at her flummoxed face with my one good eye.

"What happened to your face?"

"You don't know?"

She's impatient, roping her arms over her chest. "If I knew, I wouldn't be asking you."

"Derek stopped by my house. I figured he got my address from you. He's never been there before—how else could he find out?"

"Jesus, Chris." She slams her trunk shut. "I didn't send him to your house to hit you. Why would I do that?"

"Then can you please talk to him? He's had it out for me since the moment we met. I don't know why or what his problem is, and now he's sucker punching me at my front door."

She sighs long and loud, closing her eyes as if she's had enough of this day.

"Has he always been violent?" I press. "I don't like the idea of a pregnant woman being alone with someone who could do something like this."

Her eyes snap open, and now she's glaring like I've insulted her. "He's not *violent*, Chris, and you know that."

"How the fuck do I know that? Look at me."

"I'll talk to him," she says, sighing again, and to be honest, I expected a little more horror from her, that Derek could do something like this. I've never shown you any violent tendencies, but you can't say the same for him now, can you? "I'm sorry he did that, but it isn't my fault, and I never asked him to do anything of the sort."

"I know, I believe you," I say, and I try to grasp her hand, but she looks disgusted as she moves farther away. "Serena, I love you; can't we just—?"

"No." She edges around me and hauls herself behind the wheel of the Land Rover, one leg dangling out as she shoves on a pair of sunglasses. "I *will* talk to him; it's not okay for him to hit you, but that doesn't mean I want anything more to do with you."

She tries to shut her door, but my hand is on the other side and she can't slam another door in my face.

"Let go of my door, Chris."

Maybe she can't tell through those giant ridiculous sunglasses, but I love her; I'm standing here with a festering open wound of an eye because of her; Derek couldn't possibly love her like I do, more than I do. Why can't she see that? I've shown her what Derek is capable of, and still she refuses to see it.

"Let go of my door or I'll scream."

Do you even have a heart, Serena? How can you see me in this state and not fucking care? I've killed for you and bled for you and twisted myself in knots for you.

"Chris."

I let go. She doesn't scream, and she doesn't look back when she slams the door and starts the car.

The blue cloud of smoke I'm exhaling shimmers through the air in psychedelic spirals, and I'd really prefer not to smell like cigarettes once this is over, but I doubt it'll make much difference in the long run, and I can't loiter without a prop.

It's dark in this claustrophobic brick alley, lit only by the red neon **EXIT** sign and a single bulb impaled in the back wall of the bar. It's a biker bar. I figured, bikers, right? Better than gang members, probably; bikers I don't think carry guns. I confess I've never actually seen *Sons of Anarchy*. But I guess bikers all stumble out front to smoke their cigarettes and admire their hogs simultaneously, so I've been here for a while, holding up the wall. Nary a burly man has come out to join me.

So I can't go out front and nobody is coming to me. It's certainly an impasse. Maybe I ought to take my business elsewhere. I haven't actually set foot inside the bar, but I did pay the parking meter around the corner over an hour ago.

It's nearing midnight, and it has to be soon, and maybe I should get going. I wouldn't know where—it isn't like I can Yelp this shit—and I'm flicking away the butt when the back door finally opens.

This does not look like a happy woman, Serena. She's forced herself into a pair of leather pants, and her big hair is a rather garish shade of auburn. She looks like every cliché about women from Jersey, so maybe she has a matching temper? It's not like I've got any better option, and are bikers gallant? I've never actually wished I'd seen *Sons of Anarchy* before this second.

I clear my throat and open my mouth, and this lady utters a quiet sigh and says, "Not interested, buddy," before I've even gotten a word out.

I want to laugh but I shouldn't, so I mutter "Cunt" instead in the loudest whisper I can.

"Excuse me?" I've got her full attention now, and I can see her makeup creping around her outrage. "*What* did you say?"

"I called you a cunt," I say, and it comes out a lot more politely than it should, but it doesn't matter, does it? That word does something to women, and it's doing something to her. I hope she won't stomp over and smack me, call it even. That wouldn't work.

"Fucking prick," she sneers, tossing aside her cigarette and heading back into the bar.

I'm steeling myself now, my heart rate picking up, and I'm trying to go to my happy place, but I don't think I've got one except Serena. Does it count if it's not a place?

I throw the pack of cigarettes across the alley; I don't think I'll need them anymore. A deep breath fills my lungs, and I turn my back to the exit of the bar half a second before it bursts open.

"Hey!"

Here we go, Serena. I look over my shoulder and find a man filling the alley—a large man in a leather vest that clings desperately to his chest, seemingly unfit for the task of adequately covering him. His hair is long, his eyes mean, his stance aggressive.

I flick him a glance and keep walking, but he doesn't let me get far. I count only three pounding footsteps until he descends upon me, whirling me around by the shoulder.

The first blow slams me backward into the wall, where my head connects with a crunch. I didn't want that; I don't want to pass out.

Galaxies of white lights twinkle in my peripherals as I slide to the ground, and he isn't done. Pain explodes in my ribs, blisters across my stomach. He's using his boots, and I think they're steel toed, and how many blows does saying *cunt* really net? This frenzy of fists and feet is probably a good thing, but pain is effervescing in my face, radiating from my ribs, and I really can't pass out.

The **EXIT** light whirls like a kaleidoscope.

My lungs shrink as I try dragging shallow breaths within them.

My eye is a corroded garage door that won't open. Is he done? I think he's done. I feel dim light slant over me, a whoosh of air from the door opening and closing.

I should get up. Can I get up? Maybe not. I'm seeing patterns in my one usable eye, and I'll give it another few seconds, but I really should get up.

I can breathe, that's good. Well, I mean it hurts, but I can do it.

Torturously slowly, I climb to my feet. My knees sway, but I brace myself against the wall and stand there until my head stops swimming. My various aches and pains mingle together in a chorus of complaints when I take my first step away from the wall.

Which hospital, again? I feel like an ape stumped over a puzzle that is just a shade beyond him. *The hospital,* I think, dragging out the syllables as I slur it in my head. I know this one.

Oh, right.

I hope I can drive.

36

Freeport's PD isn't exactly a busy one. Mostly petty thefts and meth, the occasional domestic but not typically violent crime, which I suppose is why they showed up at Serena's house at the crack of dawn the morning after I was hospitalized. I don't get to watch until three days later, once the doctors release me. I take my laptop to bed, prop myself up on a mountain of pillows, and settle in.

She's on her deck when they arrive at 6 a.m. She must immediately suspect who they are and why they've come because she throws aside the glass slider and is at the side door to meet them in a matter of seconds.

"Oh God," is all she can say when one of them asks if her name is Serena Archer.

"Is there a Derek Gallagher here, ma'am?"

"He's in the shower." Her gaze bounces between the two of them. "Do you want me to go get him?"

"That would probably be best," the male says.

She's in her bedroom in a heartbeat, opening her bathroom door and disappearing inside. I can't hear their conversation once Derek's back in her room getting dressed, but she looks freaked and all he seems is annoyed.

Back in the kitchen, the cops are suddenly wary. I suspect this has to do with the soft growling I can make out from somewhere offscreen, and suddenly Serena shouts "Sirius!" and the growling abruptly cuts off.

"I'm sorry, he won't hurt you, he just wasn't expecting visitors," Serena says, popping back up in the kitchen, as if worried they'll arrest her dog as well as her fucking boyfriend.

"Mr. Gallagher?" the guy asks, weaving out from behind his partner as Derek appears, buckling a belt, wet hair flopping into his eyes. "I'm going to need to bring you in."

Serena claps a hand to her mouth, and all Derek can say to comfort her is "It'll be all right" as he hugs her from behind and kisses her cheek. To my dismay, the cop does not cuff Derek, despite the handcuffs glittering at his waistband, and they leave with little fanfare. He doesn't even use the fucking siren as he drives off.

Serena doesn't find her voice until long after the side door swings shut behind the pair of them. Eventually she turns to the female officer and croaks, "You're not going with them?"

"Can I ask you a few questions, Ms. Archer?"

"Serena. Yes, of course." She starts, like she's suddenly remembered she has manners, and asks, "Can I get you some coffee?"

"I'm fine, but thank you."

Serena sinks into a seat, and the cop does the same, taking the binder from beneath her arm and setting it beside her on the kitchen table. After turning in a few nomadic circles, Sirius sinks to the floor by Serena's feet.

"Officer Gray," the cop offers along with her hand, which Serena shakes. "You can call me Sam. Do you know what all this is about?"

"Chris."

"Yes. Some allegations have been made, and I'm here to make sure you feel safe at home."

"You've got to be kidding me." I can't see her face, but she doesn't sound angry, just utterly incredulous. "Of course I feel safe at home. The only issue in my life is Chris. Are you charging Derek?"

Officer Gray nods for a moment and slowly says, "Yes. With injuries like Mr. Fox has sustained, charges are brought automatically."

"All this for a black eye?"

"Miss—sorry, Serena—it was significantly more than a black eye."

"No it wasn't. I saw Chris that same day. He came to see me right after it happened. If he had more injuries than that, he would have complained about them to make me feel sorry for him. He wouldn't miss a golden opportunity to make Derek look bad."

Officer Gray's lips twitch from side to side as she studies Serena, then she opens a file from the binder and slips out some enlarged photographs, to which Serena's answer is a horrified, echoing gasp that forces Sirius to his paws.

"The doctors think it was a prolonged beating," the officer says, carefully reading Serena's face, and I wish I could see it for myself. "And that would match up with Mr. Fox's story as well."

I'm sorry you're upset, Serena, but this had to happen; it couldn't be avoided. I tried to show you that Derek isn't a suitable person with whom to build a life, but you didn't go for it; this is kind of on you. He was a rebound, and rebounds are meaningless and never work out. Everyone knows this. Haven't you ever seen a romantic comedy?

Once he's gone and your problems are, too, you'll see that I'm right.

She spends a lot of time in her bedroom, making calls, the door shut, so I can't make out anything she's saying. The light in her house slowly fades and washes everything in gray until she turns on the lights, and she's alone but for Sirius until nearly 8 p.m., when the lock on the side door turns. She leaps from her bed and is at the door in an instant.

"You never called. What happened?" Her eyes are wide and accusing as Derek steps inside. "Why didn't you call me? I would have picked you up."

"I really didn't want my pregnant girlfriend to have to come get me from jail."

She slams the side door, locks it for good measure. "Who even gives a shit about that? I don't."

"Marlon just showed up at the station. I didn't have to call anybody."

"Were you bailed out?"

"It was only five thousand."

"Only?"

He shrugs. "I'll get it back when I show up on the court date."

"You're going to need to get a lawyer, aren't you," she says, her tone a curious combination of flat and shaky. "None of this can be explained without one. You'll sound crazy."

"Marlon contacted someone for me. I'll have to call her later when I get a chance."

"Why are you being so fucking casual about this? You're not worried about your image? How is this going to make you look?"

"Serena," he says, with the air of explaining something simple to an overemotional toddler, "I'm the front man of a fucking band, okay? Nobody's gonna care if I punched some dickhead in the face." He falls back a few steps when she tries to slip her arms around his waist. She rocks back on her heels, looking surprised and a little offended. "I smell like a cell. You don't want to touch me."

But apparently she does want to touch him, because her hands are all over him for the rest of the night.

They're in bed, her nails grazing his scalp for so long he has to have fallen asleep, but her slow-blinking eyes are still open in the dark, a flat pearly white whenever they make contact with the camera. Sometimes she closes them for minutes at a time, but I know she's not sleeping because every so often she shifts or rubs Derek's dead shoulder, kisses his forehead. She's forgoing sleep for this asshole, something she never once did for me—for me she gave nothing but flimsy excuses and lies, and I can't understand what he has that I don't, why for him she gives but with me she took.

Well, I have news for you, Serena: it gets real fucking old, giving and giving and never getting. You're going to *Giving Tree* yourself into a breakdown, and when there's nothing left and you're only a stump, maybe then you'll understand what I went through with you.

I wince at my taped ribs and my sutures and my throbbing eye and fast-forward as light creeps into her bedroom. Derek mercifully leaves, duffel slung over his shoulder. Thank God. A reprieve. I fast-forward at triple speed until Rosa appears.

"—Fucking Asshole, how did he even manage—"

That's enough of that.

Rosa leaves, Serena leaves, Sirius sleeps, Cole arrives, Serena's back. Looks like she's had a dull few days without Derek. I've powered through three days of nothing in as many hours because I need to hurry this along already. It's past midnight, and I need to wake up for work in the morning.

No Zoom calls for me until I'm marginally less horrific. Silver linings, and all.

Being out sick for three days means a shitload of emails are waiting in my inbox, a hundred questions need answering, and I have to schedule about a dozen calls to make up the ones I've missed. I'm almost glad Serena's gone this morning so I don't have any distractions. I work on autopilot as the loud sounds of her quiet house fill my office. Her fridge hums, water crashes around in the belly of her dishwasher, and that goddamn fucking plinking is maddening. I want to break into her house and fix it. It would take all of two seconds. I don't know why nobody has attended to it yet.

My doorbell goes. I hate unannounced visitors unless they're you; is that you, full of good sense and apologies, here to nurse me back to health?

"Hey, buddy," a man I don't even know says when I pull open the door, before rearing back at my monstrosity. "Christ—are you okay?"

"I'm sorry," I say, and I put little effort into sounding very sorry because I'm annoyed it's not her. "Have we met?"

"Oh, right—I'm Dave, at twenty-seven?" I wonder if this is some sort of code until he hooks a thumb over his shoulder. He's my neighbor. He's blond and chubby and looks like a Cub Scout den leader, and now he's gazing at me with distinct apprehension, as if he's deeply regretting coming by at all. I should probably make more of an effort to be pleasant.

"Okay?" I try to smile encouragingly. It hurts my face.

"Noticed your car was gone for a while—are you sure you're okay?"

"I'll live."

"Good, good." He bobs his head. "Anyway, so you were out, but I've noticed a car parked at my curb a few different nights?" He says this as if it's something I should confirm or deny, and I have no idea what this man wants from me.

"Oh?"

"It's a woman," he says. "Watching your house."

My heart skips; were you checking up on me? Did I miss you when I was laid up? "What does she drive?"

"A black Camry."

Not Serena.

"Eventually I asked if I could help her with something, and she wanted to know if I knew where you were, if you'd ever had any female visitors. When I didn't feel comfortable answering, she showed me a badge."

"What did she look like?" I ask, pulling an image of Officer Gray out of the Rolodex of my mind, though I'm not sure why she'd sit on my house those nights I was gone when she knew I was at the hospital.

"Red hair."

What are you doing, Amanda? I thought we'd sorted everything out.

"You know her?" he asks, frowning at the recognition that must be on my face. "I thought it was weird she wouldn't just knock on doors to ask her questions if she were a cop. You obviously weren't home."

Because she doesn't want a helpful Dave letting me know she's been lurking, I assume. "It's a woman I dated. She's been using that badge to make my life difficult." I say it with a brave laugh and a scuff of my shoe. "Thanks for letting me know."

"Is there anything you need?" He looks unwilling to leave me alone in this condition. "I mean, should you be on your own right now?"

No, but what choice do I have?

"I'll be okay," I say. "But I'd be grateful if you could let me know if this woman ever shows up again when I'm out. Can we exchange numbers?"

◆ ◆ ◆

Serena's back home by five and whiles away an hour on her phone, scrolling, tapping, typing out things I can't read anymore and probably wouldn't want to; what if she's sexting Derek or something? She never sexted me, but you never know, do you? She also didn't let me have sex with her straightaway, so her normal rules apparently don't apply to him.

A bit after six, Sirius picks his head up from his paws, and a few seconds after that, Serena twitches the drapes in the living room aside and heads for the kitchen. The side door opens before she makes it there, and oh goody, look who it is. Derek pulls her in for a kiss, and it will never not infuriate me when he kisses her, no matter how many goddamn times I have to witness it.

He sets her on the kitchen island. Her legs go around his waist as his hands creep up her back, and Cole steps inside the kitchen, groans loudly, and immediately stomps back out.

Serena breaks away as Cole shouts "God*damn*" on his way back up the stairs.

Derek is unconcerned that Cole may have witnessed something inappropriate, his eyes half shuttered with desire. "He's going to have to get used to it at some point."

"I'm the worst mother in the world." At least she has the decency to realize she's fucking up. She never would have let Cole walk in on something like that when she was with me.

"I'm pretty sure there's a few out there worse than you. *My* mother, for instance. I missed you." He leans in to kiss her again. "It's pathetic how much I missed you."

Jesus. Shut up.

"You didn't fall in love with some groupie, then?"

He doesn't dignify that with a response, but it's only a matter of time, Serena. "I'm going to start clearing out the extra bedroom in my house for Cole," he says, and he must not like the expression on her face because he adds, "I can't always be around. What if this freak tries something when I'm not here? It'll be harder for him to get to you if you're at my place."

"I don't need you to constantly be around. If he was going to hurt me, he'd have done it already."

"How can you possibly know that?" He sounds angry now, or irritated at least. "You don't live inside his head."

She does, actually. She has her own little bedroom in there, and she hasn't left since the moment I saw her.

"I can't just up and move in with you," she says, and now she's angry, too, her legs thudding against the island as they drop from around his waist. "You're forty minutes away from Cole's school, and there's not enough space for Sirius. We've been dating for ten minutes. It's too soon to shack up."

"You're having my baby. I think that's a pretty compelling reason to 'shack up.' We've known each other for sixteen years, it's not like we're strangers. We can find a brand-new place, somewhere with a big enough yard for Sirius."

She slides off the island. "I don't want to argue about this."

"We're not arguing."

"Feels like we're arguing."

He catches her by the hand as she moves past him. "Don't stomp off and pout."

She makes a noise of indignation and wrenches her hand away, calling over her shoulder as she stalks off down the hallway, "Refusing to have an argument isn't *pouting*."

"It's not far off from it," he calls back, standing there for a few beats before groaning at the ceiling. "Baby."

It's the first time I've ever heard him call her anything other than her name, and I don't like it, don't like how easily it rolled off his tongue, as if he's been using it for a while, as if she's his or something.

My laptop is a split screen, Derek by himself in the kitchen, her in her bedroom, but it switches to a single image when Derek disappears down the hallway and reappears in the doorway of her bedroom.

"You're mad because I worry about you and I love you and want you to live with me?"

"I'm not mad," she says, threatening anger in every syllable. "I just don't want to be pushed into anything. I had enough of that with Chris."

Derek steps farther inside the room and shuts the door, so now I can't hear. I can only see, and I see him sink onto the bed next to her, and I see him turn her so she's facing him, and I see that pissy expression on her face eventually melt away as his sticky words pour over her.

He's kissing you again, and I honestly don't know how your lips aren't chapped and cracked and bleeding, what with all this making out, and do you seriously enjoy the way he's pawing at you, Serena? It's like he's got fifteen hands, and they're everywhere, all over your body. Hot fury scales each vertebra of my spine, and now he's getting up to lock her bedroom door, and you've got to be fucking kidding me.

I really can't understand why you keep letting him inside you, Serena; is there crack in his semen or something? I don't get why you can't ever get enough of it. He's hypnotized you like he's some character in *True Blood*, and that makes a lot of sense, actually; he's always looked vampiric, if you want my opinion. His hair is dark as nightmares, and his smile is made of lies.

Lissa Lovik

It's nearing nine when Derek finally emerges from her bedroom. Serena's taking a shower to rinse him off her; I can see steam billowing into the frame from the direction of the bathroom.

He gets a glass of water from the tap in the kitchen and is completely oblivious to the plinking. Sirius follows Derek into the living room, where he sinks onto the couch and pulls out his phone.

Sirius snuffles around the floor, excavates a tennis ball from beneath the couch, and nudges it into Derek's hand. He isn't careful as he tosses it across the room, and I hear Sirius's nails as he bounds off and a *thud* of the tennis ball crashing into something. Derek's eyebrows join as he looks up, squinting, and the thud must have come from directly across from him because now he's on his feet, using the flashlight on his phone. He sweeps the beam of light from right to left, but suddenly it stops and backtracks sharply, trained on the lens of the camera, so I see nothing but gold halos.

The room is dark again until it isn't. Derek has flipped the light switch, and now I can't see anything but blurs of white and blue and groping fingers, and my heart is drumming madly in the region of my throat because he found it.

37

The screen is pale green now, a color I've come to hate, and I know it's his eye looking into my secret eye, and I close my actual eyes and try to breathe because it's not coming naturally any longer.

"Serena!" I hear him yell in all caps, and the camera in her bedroom blinks to life with her movement as she steps out of the bathroom. She's wrapping a red towel around herself as Derek bursts inside her room.

"What?"

"I found a camera in the living room—you need to get dressed and go."

She shifts the towel higher up her chest. "A *camera*?"

"Yes, hidden in that vase you've got up on that shelf in the living room."

Something catches at the back of her throat. "Are you sure?"

I can't see your face, but I can hear the distress in your voice, and I knew you wouldn't get it, Serena; I could never be honest and explain the depth of my feelings because you wouldn't let yourself accept it. You don't see this for what it is, my obvious love for you, and I can tell there's a cerebral tumble dry taking place in your mind, the words *creepy* and *stalker* and *obsessed* crashing around as you stand there shivering in that towel, not knowing and never understanding how much I love you.

"Yes. I saw the glare with my flashlight app, and I'm pretty goddamn sure you didn't put it there yourself. Get dressed and grab some clothes. You need to leave."

Her voice strains as she clutches the towel tightly around herself. "And you think they're all over the house?"

He moves around, opening drawers, throwing clothes out at random. "He's fucking obsessed with you; I'm sure they're everywhere. I'm sure he's been watching everything you've been doing for months." He wrenches the closet open, yanks out a duffel bag, and presses it into her hands. "You're going to my house."

But she's still frozen, and he stops in front of her, grabbing her shoulders, ducking his head to look her in the eye. "Baby. You need to go."

He brushes past, and now he's shouting for Cole, and I hear his footsteps pounding up the staircase as Serena pulls on clothes robotically and packs the duffel.

She's in the kitchen soon, and her eyes are scared as they dart around the place, staring into corners and combing the walls. She's wondering where the camera is, *if* the camera is. She doesn't know that if she just glanced up and slightly to the right, she'd be looking through the slats of the smoke alarm and right into my eyes.

Cole joins her, and he's in the midst of an argument with Derek, who doesn't seem to care that he's fucked up Cole's *Rust* raid.

"I was flying the plane; you know what happens when I'm flying the plane and suddenly I'm not because you turned off the computer? It means all my friends *die* because the pilot is gone!"

"I don't really give a shit right now," Derek says, shoving Cole's backpack into his arms before turning to Serena. "Did you get everything you need?"

She nods, her throat bobbing as she swallows hard, but she can't seem to summon words.

At least I've never done that, Serena. I've never barked orders and forced you out of your home.

"Mom, what the hell?"

"Get in the car," is all she tells her son, and she and Derek watch him huff out the door.

"You're not coming with us?"

"I'm going to find the rest of them. You know there's no way he only put up one."

"Derek—"

"Just go. Please, I want you to get out of here." He all but throws her out onto the stoop, Sirius bobbing along behind, but before he shuts the door, he grabs her chin and forces a kiss on her. "I love you," he says and then locks her out of her own house.

I can only assume he's standing there with his back pressed against the door because he's waiting to hear her Land Rover roar to life and peel out of her driveway. A flare of yellow creeps through the blinds on the kitchen window, growing fainter and fainter, and now Derek's standing in the center of the room, his gaze moving deliberately, carefully, from right to left.

"I don't know if you can hear me," he says into the emptiness and over the plinking, "but you're a fucking creep, Chris."

And then he slowly and methodically tears the house apart.

He finds them. It takes him all night, and he curses me occasionally, telling me what an insane fucking freak I am and how I wouldn't need to find some way to injure myself this time, that he'd be more than happy to beat the shit out of me. He says I'm lucky Serena ever looked twice at my crazy ass, and have I been watching them have sex? I must be a pervert as well as a stalker. Had I been jerking off with a belt around my throat whenever they got started?

He says I am never going to see her again, not if he can help it, and if I didn't know for a fact I'd be the prime suspect, I would drive over there right now and kill him.

He didn't find the mic in the kitchen though, so I can hear him walking around in there, banging shit on the counters, and now he's speaking aloud again but not to me.

"Sorry, were you sleeping? You're going to be exhausted if you don't even try. Three—the kitchen, the living room, and your bedroom. There was nothing upstairs. I'll call them. You need to go to the courthouse and file for a restraining order the second they're open. You're not coming back here. I realize that. I'm not trying to 'boss you around'; I'm trying to make sure this crazy fucking freak can never get at you again. I'm sorry, would you rather me be completely blasé about it? You're not coming back to this goddamn house. Fine, you can come back for that. He's fifteen, he's going to be pissed no matter what's going on, that's how teenagers are. I don't give a shit if he's mad at me. Well, we're going to have to find something closer to his school eventually. Yes, 'we,' end of story. I don't care how fast it is. I don't want you staying with Rosa, I want you with me." A chair skids over the tile, and there's a muffled sigh, like he's pressed a hand over his mouth to hold back a groan of frustration. "Are you kidding? Are you actually kidding right now? 'I don't care about what you want'—are you fucking serious, you are *all* I care about."

There's the longest pause yet, and I imagine she's ripping him a new one. I never laid down orders, Serena. I never spoke to you this way, like I was your warden.

"Baby, don't cry, okay, I'm sorry. I'm just—Jesus. Fine. Can we fight about this later, I need to call the cops."

How can you prefer Derek over me, Serena? All you do is fight with him, and at least I never made you cry. You and I had issues we needed to work through, but our default was never this kind of argumentative bullshit. He's treating you like you're a child or some sort of simpleton who can't take care of herself; is that really what you want in a man? I'm asking for a friend.

◆ ◆ ◆

Officer Gray finds the cameras Derek's uncovered interesting but states that it's not exactly evidence.

"There's no proof who put these here," she says. "You didn't actually see him plant these, and you're not even a resident of this house, are you? You don't live here full time?"

"I stay here with her most nights unless I'm out of town. Who else could have put these here? Why would she want a *hidden camera* in her bedroom?"

"A defense attorney would say she could have been a camgirl or something similar, live streaming on some voyeur porn website."

"That's bullshit."

"Sure, but still." Officer Gray clears her throat. "How about this—devil's advocate: *you* could have put them up."

"I didn't."

"Can you prove that you didn't?"

"Of course not. I can't prove a negative."

"That's what he'll say too. He's not the only one with access to this house. And he doesn't even have access anymore. You don't know how long these were in place before you found them."

"Can't you, I don't know, dust for prints or something?"

They could, but I wore gloves. They won't find my prints anywhere near the camera locations, let alone on the cameras themselves.

"Will yours be on them?"

"Yes, I'm the one who found them."

"And that would be another hurdle, your prints being present. If this is something the department wants to pursue, then we could get these to a lab, but there's no proof it's Mr. Fox behind it, and we don't have the kind of tech resources here to do much else. Add all this to the assault charge, and it's starting to look like a clusterfuck. He could very easily say you planted these to somehow justify what you did to him; 'I only beat him up because he was spying on my girlfriend' or some such."

"I hit him once. In the eye. Sure, lock me up for that. I didn't do anything else to him."

"Yeah, I know." Derek must have cut her a surprised look, because she says, "The black eye is older than the rest of the injuries. That's what the doctors said. I mean I guess you could have gone back later to beat him up some more, but that isn't what his story was, and it's a huge thing to forget. I pulled CCTV footage from around Serena's work and saw him confront her in the parking lot. Bad angles and grainy images, but it's clear he wasn't nursing any major injuries. Not that my knowing he's lying does any good. His injuries are there; you admitted to hitting him. The rest is for a court to sort out."

Shock and adrenaline can stave off pain for hours after an incident. It isn't so strange that I managed to remain mobile for a while before collapsing. I didn't immediately drag myself to the ER because I'm not a whiny little bitch.

"So basically, there's nothing you can do? This is complete fucking bullshit."

"I don't disagree," Officer Gray says through a sigh. "But that's where we're at right now. Knowing someone has done something and proving it are two completely different things. I'm going to give all this to Stenner and see how he wants to proceed. I'd recommend she get a restraining order in the meantime."

"She's doing that right now. Not that a piece of paper can stop someone who really wants to get you."

"Well." It sounds like she's getting up from the table. "Cold comfort, but if that happens, he'll be arrested."

◆ ◆ ◆

I don't think you applied for a restraining order, Serena, because it's 5 p.m. and I should have been served by now if you got a TRO first thing in the morning; it's not like Freeport PD has anything better to do.

Derek hasn't left the house. I hear him in there all day, walking around, opening cabinets, making phone calls. Just after six, there's the metallic rattling of the doorknob and Derek's voice calling out.

"Serena?"

"Yeah."

"Did you get it?"

"They said they'll have it served tomorrow. It's only temporary until the hearing."

There's no movement, no noise at all, no swishing of material or footsteps or chairs being pulled out. I imagine they're standing there ten feet apart, just staring at one another.

"Are you okay?" Derek finally asks.

"I'll be fine."

Now there are footsteps, and I know they're his because Serena's click with her ubiquitous heels and this is the scuffing of sneakers.

"I know you're not crazy about the thought of living together so soon, and I swear I'm not trying to rush anything, but I'll be too worried about you if you're not with me."

Making it all about himself, his worry, his feelings. Can't you see that, Serena? You were right; he doesn't care what you want.

She's in his arms now, because her voice is slightly muffled as if she's speaking into his chest. "I know."

There's a noise I know by heart and hate more than any other—the sound of him kissing her. "Let's get this over with so we can get out of here."

"Cole wants his computer, hasn't shut up about it. Can you help me get it?"

"I've boxed that and some of his clothes up already. You're weird about your clothes, so I didn't get any of your stuff together."

"How long do you think those cameras were up?"

"I don't know. It seems like they had a built-in battery. I reverse image searched a picture. The information I found says they can hold a charge for four months, so he wouldn't have needed to mess with them that often. They're expensive. He spent good money on them."

"Where exactly were they?"

He tells her, and I imagine her looking up at the smoke alarm, the former home of the kitchen camera.

"You think he was watching us having sex?"

"Yeah."

"Mother*fuck*." Serena makes a noise like an angry cat, clicking off down what sounds like the direction of the hallway.

"What?"

Her voice has grown fainter; she's definitely by her bedroom. "One of the last arguments we had, I was in my room masturbating and my door was locked, and suddenly Chris was banging on it, screaming about how he could hear what I was doing from the hall. I'm not that loud, okay; I knew he was lying. I thought he had his ear pressed against the door, but he didn't, did he? He saw me on his fucking little camera."

"He was mad at you for masturbating?"

She had access to me, I was right there; why would she need to masturbate?

"Furious, it was like he thought I was cheating on him."

"Imagine being jealous of a hand," Derek says in wonder. "How insecure you'd have to be. If I knew you were masturbating, I'd just ask if you needed any help."

More clicking, and it's getting louder, faster, heading back into the kitchen. "And sometimes I'd be planning to cook or whatever and I'd realize I was out of something, and Chris would show up with it when he came over later, like he was just at the store and accidentally bought extra milk or butter or eggs or something. I thought it was sweet because I was always running out of that shit and he remembered."

I only did that twice and you were grateful, Serena; don't act like you weren't. You called me your hero and threw your arms around me, told me I was the best.

"Baby—"

I want to cut his tongue out every time he calls her that.

"This is how he knew I was pregnant, isn't it?" I picture the cords on Serena's neck blue and bulging, an angry flush flaring across her cheeks, eyes like frosty fire. "This is the only reasonable way he could have known; that thing with Cole at the mall—he knew Cole was going there and showed up to stage some kind of chance meeting with him, right? If he hadn't seen that gift bag, he would have found some other way to make Cole let it slip."

"Probably."

Click click click. She's in motion, he's not. I imagine her moving from one side of the kitchen to the other, her arms around herself, Derek following with his eyes.

"All I ever hear from him is how much he loves me, but how, *how* could he claim that and then do something this fucked up and crazy?"

Why are you posing this question to Derek? He doesn't love you, Serena. He wouldn't do what I've done for you; he wouldn't take the risks I've undergone. If you left him tomorrow, he'd find someone new in a heartbeat; he wouldn't mourn you like I have. You think I'm crazy? Well maybe I am, but that's what love is, sweetheart—it's a fucking natural disaster, and you destroyed me a long time ago when you reached for that peanut butter.

"Because he's a nut. He's obsessed with you. I could tell right away there was something wrong with him."

Serena doesn't answer, just wheezes and rasps on all that wrath clawing its way out of her. It's a living, gasping thing, this anger; I imagine it blackish red and smoldering, a dragon with half-furled wings and smoking nostrils, dominating her in its shadow, a ball of flame glowing down its gullet.

"The first time he did that Mr. Hero routine with the groceries, that was maybe, what, ten seven months ago?" She sounds like she's talking to herself, still pacing, garnering speed, *clickclickclickclick*. "So they've been here at least that long; that's seven months of him watching my every move. Watching me get out of the shower, get ready for work, watching me sleep. I'm going to fucking kill him. I'm going to go to his house and rip his throat out with my teeth and let him bleed out on the floor."

I don't know how she can make something so gruesome sound so hot, and I wish she *would* come over; it's been too long since I've seen her.

"You and me, I don't even know how many times we've had sex, but he's seen all of it—every time, he was right there with us." She stops short. "God, Derek, what if he puts it on the internet or something?"

I would never do that. I don't want to share her. Sharing her with Derek is killing me as it is. How could she think it of me? That's appalling. I'm not Tom, plastering her nudes online and asking strangers to fuck her.

"I don't think that's something you need to worry about," Derek says. "Let's just get your stuff, okay? Pack it up, and I'll carry it out to your car. We're just lucky I found out about this shit at all, if you ask me."

"The last thing I feel right now is *lucky*," you snarl, my murderous little pet, and if I were there, I'd slip a muzzle on your face and kiss you because you still feel something for me, Serena. That's better than nothing at all.

38

It's been a week since I've seen her or heard her voice, and she's the biggest earworm I've ever experienced, a song pounding nonstop in my head, poisoning my blood, so loud it's rattling bones. I've been grinding my teeth; I don't notice I'm doing it for hours until a muscle in my jaw starts ticking, but I can't make myself stop. I need a fucking mouth guard or something.

I thought about what my grandfather would have told me last night while I lay in bed, trying to tempt sleep. He'd tell me to get the hell up and do something because I'm never going to get anywhere if I keep my ass planted on the couch. If my grandmother had turned him down that first time, he wouldn't have thrown up his hands in defeat. He'd have tried again, and then again if he had to. I picture him shaking his finger at me, his crazy Albert Einstein hair in a cloud around his head. *No quitting, Chris.*

Love takes work, remember. It doesn't just happen for some people. It's something you've got to work on, build up brick by brick. Sometimes you've got to make it happen. Sometimes you need to use a little force.

I bought a new car a month back, traded in my old one for a Volvo so Serena wouldn't catch sight of my Audi if I ever happened to catch sight of her. Derek's house is across from the bay along a busy highway, and I hear lapping waves mingling with rushing traffic as I look into his windows, my Volvo camouflaged across the street among other cars belonging to early-morning paddleboarders. I'm still getting Google alerts for his band, and after a two-week hiatus he's finally going to be out of town again, leaving her alone in his house.

Someone's thrown the drapes aside to let in the new sun, and I'm thinking it's you, Serena; you've always preferred natural light, and natural light loves you back; it makes your hair shine and your eyes glitter and your skin eerily perfect. I hope you won't force me to use any of the things I packed in my trunk; the idea of hurting something so beautiful doesn't sit well with me, but I will if I have to.

It's Cole's winter break, and he isn't at Derek's (I refuse to call it *home*), so it's just you and your stupid boyfriend right now. You're wearing an unsexy plaid robe over a very sexy bra, and your hair has gotten lighter and longer, shimmering in the sun as you walk barefoot around Derek's kitchen.

What have you done? Are you going blond? I don't like that you're trying to change yourself, like you want to slither out of your real skin and become something else.

You're making coffee, and I know exactly how you take your coffee—does he? Has he ever cared enough to find out?

I watch you for a while and realize there's no way that robe is yours; you're forced to push the sleeves up to the insides of your elbows just to use your hands. It's his; you're in his clothes and his house, and don't you hate being a guest in someone else's place? Aren't you tired of it yet?

Here's Derek, bare chested and dumping a suitcase by the front door. He drags a shirt over his head on his way over, and I guess that coffee isn't for you, because you hand it to him like you're his fucking wife and he's headed off for a business trip.

He lifts you up onto *his* island in *his* kitchen, and you're so little I can't see anything but your arms around his neck and your legs around his waist as the robe that isn't yours flops loose. It makes me ill, but it's over after a few minutes, and Derek walks to the door and you follow, tying the robe's sash at your waist. You kiss him again at the front door before he leaves and again on the porch once he's out of the house and again when he's trying to walk to his truck; you don't let go of his fingers, so he comes back for another.

He's saying something I can't hear, but I can guess what it is, and I watch his hands curl around the back of your neck, and you can't actually *love* him, Serena. You can't, I don't accept that.

He gets into his truck, and you watch him back out of the driveway, waving like he's going off to fight a fucking war.

I lean over to pop the trunk once Derek's truck is a speck in the distance. I will speak to you calmly and slowly, the way a mailman might soothe a growling dog. And I know you're going to be angry, but that's okay; I'm not so happy myself. We can work through it.

Blood pounds in my ears, and my breaths come in ragged spurts, and I don't realize what that vague buzzing is until it becomes a ringtone.

I spend all of two seconds wondering who the hell Dave is and why he's calling me until it clicks.

"Buddy?" he says with a nervous wobble. "She's back."

39

Amanda's not hiding a few doors down in a Camry this time. She's brought her unmarked unit and parked it at my curb, where she leans against it like a languorous Queen of Hearts, dressed in a red trench coat with a badge and a gun.

"Hi, Chris," she says brightly when I climb out of my Volvo, her lips stained red as an open wound. "New car?"

I stop a few casual feet away. "Can I help you with something?"

"Well, I sure hope so," she says, with a feline smile. "I have a few more questions I want to go over back at the station."

I drive myself to the Crestview PD, where Amanda leads me into a windowless mauve room that contains nothing but a table and two chairs.

"It's not much, but it'll do." She's cheerful, dumping some binders onto the table as she folds herself into a chair that looks much more comfortable than the one she indicated for me. "Thanks for coming down." Her hair is haloed in scarlet under the shitty florescent lighting; it's almost painful to look at. "You can call a lawyer if it makes you more comfortable."

All Because of You

"I can't see why I'd need one." I lean back in the chair, legs slightly spread, arms dangling off the armrests. Open body language. The kind that says, *Hey, I'm not hiding anything.*

She crosses her legs, red ponytail bouncing. "I should probably offer my condolences before we get started."

"Excuse me?"

"Your broken engagement?" She smiles at my confusion. "I've done some background work on you. Flagged your name. I saw that you have a restraining order taken out against you by the woman in those pictures you've got in your house."

I feel blood drain from my face and something cold steal through my veins. "What gives you the right to dig through my background?"

"Your name came up in a murder investigation. I can dig through your background as much as I want. Why did your ex get a restraining order against you?"

"What does this have to do with anything?"

She opens the binder to reveal sheaves of paperwork that I don't like the look of. "How about I ask the questions, okay? That's what I get paid for. The restraining order. Why did she get one granted against you?"

"Because she lied."

"Why would she go through the trouble?" Her eyebrows disappear beneath her bangs, and her lips part, so I catch a flash of her tongue before she continues. "Give me a good reason why Ms. Archer lied to a judge and said she was so afraid of you that she needed a court order to keep you away. Spin me a story why this woman would say all these things about you. What, she was just bored or something?"

"I found out she was pregnant, and it's my baby. I tried to talk to her about it a couple times. Her new boyfriend didn't like that and never liked me, so I'm sure he pushed her to file an order to keep me away."

"It's everyone else's fault, then? That's your story? That's not a very good one."

"It's not a story, it's the truth."

She shuffles through the papers on the table and shakes out a few pages. "So all these people are telling lies about you? Is Mrs. Robbins lying? Rosalinda, I believe her name is? How about Gerald Hunt? He's lying when he says you stormed into his realty office and demanded to speak to Serena after she asked you twice to leave?" She only asked me once, but I don't think I should correct her. "They've both attached sworn affidavits. Why would all these people band together just to lie about you?"

"I don't know. I wanted to talk to her, that's it. It's my baby, and we needed to have a discussion about it."

"I met her, you know. Serena."

A lump forms in my throat, but I refuse to swallow and let Amanda see my Adam's apple bob guiltily. "Okay?"

"The stuff she had to say about you, Chris." Amanda shakes her head. "It's some pretty bad shit. Cyberstalking. Actual stalking. Fucking spy cameras hidden around her house. What, are you some kind of voyeur? They have porn sites for that, you know. There's a legal way to satiate that sort of kink."

"I don't have any kinks," I say. "I haven't seen her in weeks. Why haven't I been charged if I've done all these things? She's making it up. This bullshit restraining order has nothing to do with you. It's not even your jurisdiction."

"I'm sorry, are you not having a good time? Did you think this was some kind of social event?"

"I came in to help you, and because you made it seem mandatory. Can I leave?"

"You want to help?" Amanda's heart lips pull up at one corner. "That's great. That would be super." She flips open another binder, pulls out a photograph. "Have you ever seen this woman before?"

I look into Emily's blue eyes and then up at Amanda's brown ones. "No."

She plants a fingertip on the edge of the photo and drags it closer to her. "Remember when we first met and I told you about my murder victim? Well, this is her. Emily Akers. And she reminds me of someone else." Amanda traces Emily's smile. "She kind of looks like Serena. Her hair is shorter here, and she doesn't have all the ear piercings that she had when she died, but I noticed all those holes in Serena's ears when I spoke to her. How long her hair is. It's lighter now; it looks like she's bleaching it out, but in those pictures you've got in your house it's dark brown, just like Emily's."

"I'm not sure what your point is."

"Do you know how Emily died?"

"No. You never said."

"She was strangled."

I grimace, shifting on this uncomfortable, creaky fucking plastic chair with one wobbly leg. "That's terrible."

"I'm glad you feel that way." Amanda stabs her chest with a finger. "I feel that way too. I don't like when shitheads strangle women. It makes me mad."

I say nothing, just blink and let her carry on with what I'm sure is a well-rehearsed performance.

"You know what really pisses me off is that the fucker who did this probably thought, well, *She's a hooker so who cares?* That shit *really* makes me mad. It really infuriates me that someone would contact her for a job, take her out of her home and away from her daughter late at night, have her get extra ear piercings and hair extensions to dress her up as a fantasy, and then fucking kill her. I used to work sex crimes, did I tell you that?"

I shake my head as I sigh, resigned to story time.

"Yeah, for three years. Hardest job I've ever had. I got turfed out after I smashed someone's head against the corner of the table in a room a lot like this one." She almost sounds like she thinks it's a fond memory. "He raped and murdered a couple sex workers too. Anyway, so they threw me out and made me go through anger management, and then they stuck me in homicide."

"Sounds like the anger management didn't take."

Amanda shrugs. "I don't like when men hurt prostitutes. It's not very sporting, going after one of the most vulnerable groups of women. It's like those pathetic assholes who abuse children or old ladies."

"What exactly are you accusing me of?"

"Serena mentioned your Cadillac. That you'd followed her in it before. It doesn't just stay in your grandfather's shed until your grief sends you out on midnight drives." Her gaze is hard, and she's smiling again, so all her teeth show. "You must have been really mad at her. I think you wanted to kill her, but you couldn't, so you went with the next best thing. The CSU team's already towed the Cadillac from your grandfather's shed to our auto yard. You better hope Emily's DNA isn't in there, Chris."

I'm not overly concerned with DNA; I scrubbed that car top to bottom (twice!). Emily made sure to put a condom on me, and I very carefully wiped her body down with rubbing alcohol before I buried her. That, combined with the elements, and I'm pretty confident they'll find nothing at all.

"Do you have a warrant for that?"

"Sure do. Want to see it?"

"I didn't do anything to this girl—"

"Emily Akers."

I push back from the table, my shitty chair squealing over the linoleum. "I've had about enough. If you're going to charge me, then do it, but I'm done talking."

"I'm not charging you yet." Her eyes flick over to the door. "You're free to go for now. If I find out you had anything to do with Emily's death, I will nail your ass to the wall." She stands, stuffing her papers back into the binder. "To the fucking *wall*, Chris."

40

My morning is a haze of coffee that won't take, corkscrew thoughts, tedious coworkers. My boss makes me hang back after everyone else exits the conference call. He's wondering if there's something stressing me out or if I'm having problems at home, because I'm not looking or sounding that great and he's worried. I tell him I think I have COVID and I'm exhausted because my fiancée is driving me crazy with wedding prep.

"Listen," he says uneasily, with the air of someone about to drop a bomb of bad news, "I'm sure I'm not supposed to tell you this, but someone called me earlier today with a few questions about you."

"Who?" I ask, my thumb drumming out a nervous beat on my desk.

"A detective. From some town near yours."

"What sort of questions?" I try to sound confused when what I really am is pissed.

He's quiet for a few awful, spiraling seconds. "She asked about your work schedule. If you called out sick on a specific date back in October. How you get along with coworkers, if we've ever had any complaints about you. I told her no, nothing like that, not for the entire time you've been with us, but she told me you were a person of interest in one of her cases and she's been looking into your background." He pauses, then says in a tumble, "If you've gotten mixed up in anything bad, Chris, I can help. I know some attorneys out your way—"

"No." I try to say it firmly yet flippantly, like this is all some sort of mistake. "I can sort it out, whatever it is."

◆ ◆ ◆

Your faucet leaks in the background as I work. I wonder how much water has been wasted in the plinking after all these weeks. This is so bad for the environment. I'd be doing the earth a favor if I broke in and fixed it.

I make calls and answer emails as the faucet drips all that precious water down the drain, and by 4 p.m. my legs are propped on my desk and my eyes are crossed with boredom and I'm trying to focus on the droning voice of a coworker, when I hear something rattle. My feet hit the floor and I'm up in an instant, but all my doorknobs are motionless, so it's got to be yours. You're home. I don't hear another word while I wait for the conference call to end, and the second it's over, I back up the audio a few minutes to hear you walk through the door. You've got Cole in tow, and he's dragging his feet, grumbling as you tell him, "It's *your* stuff, *you* decide what you're keeping and what you're getting rid of."

"I don't get why it has to be right now; we're not even really moving into the new house for months."

If my heart wasn't already broken, knowing she's secured a new place would shatter it. You're really doing it, really moving on and putting me in the rearview mirror. I knew it was coming—I'm not an idiot—but this is all too fast, blood-pouring-out-of-a-severed-carotid fast; how many more days does this leave me with?

"I want to get it all into storage, Cole. If some prospective renter comes by to see the place, I don't want your shit everywhere. It'll take you all of twenty minutes if you focus."

He plods upstairs, and it sounds like you're doing some work to your cabinets. Why isn't your stupid boyfriend doing all this work for you? Is he too precious for manual labor, can't risk getting paint beneath his nails? He's out of town (again), leaving you alone in his house (again), and you do realize how fucked up this is, don't you, the (alleged) father of your child abandoning you for days at a time to gallivant around with his band? I bet he won't even drive you to the hospital when the time comes, he'll be too busy tuning his guitar. It breaks my fucking heart to picture you rocking a newborn alone in a house that isn't yours. You deserve more than this part-time asshole, Serena.

There's the whine of an electric drill, and I wish it were tunneling into my skull, not your cabinets; I wish it were administering a lobotomy so I'd forget you. I'd rather be a fucking vegetable than lose you; I'd rather we were both dead than apart.

I'm not saying I want us to end like Othello and Desdemona or anything, but you have to admit that would be better than the ending you've written, Serena.

Cole returns, and I listen to their conversation without really hearing, letting her voice soothe me like a balm, but it's a double-edged sword; every word she speaks is priceless, but each feels like a small death.

Your words are numbered for me, just like the days in which I'll have my limited access to them, and if I weren't still in love with you, I'd cut myself off cold turkey instead of waiting around for you to slam the final door in my face.

"Was that your stomach?" Cole asks on a laugh. "You just ate."

"I guess the baby takes after you and its father," she says. "All of you eat like horses."

A memory pokes me from behind, sharp and unexpected. You said that exact same thing to me months ago in your kitchen. That is a goddamn admission if I've ever heard one, Serena. You always marveled at how much food I could pack away, and clearly you *know* it's my baby; you've just admitted it.

She opens and closes a cabinet, and the plinking becomes a gush as she turns the tap on. "I'm coming back Friday to finish the last of the painting; you're going to come with me after school to help."

"I can't," Cole protests. "Brianna planned that whole thing, remember? Her sister's only in town for the weekend. She'll kill me if I cancel."

"Oh shit. I forgot. That's okay, I'm sure I can manage."

"Why do you even have to bother painting? It looks fine in here."

"Because I care," she says simply. "I care about keeping things up, making sure they're nice. Details are important. I don't like overlooking them."

"But isn't it all a bunch of unnecessary work?"

"Everything important takes work," you wisely tell your son, and you're right, Serena. I couldn't agree more.

I don't know how long I sit there listening to the plinking after Serena and Cole leave, but it's long enough that night has fallen and I have to get up to flick on the light.

That's my baby, Serena—we both knew it all along. You're going to have to try to put the past behind us. We need to move forward, together, into our future. I'll forgive you, and you'll forgive me, and we can put all this to bed.

41

I'm in the shower the next morning, letting the water pound out all my tension, when my cell phone rings. I don't recognize the number when I lurch over to the phone, dripping everywhere, and there's an icon for a voicemail. It's the prosecutor wanting to update me on my assault case, and I call him back as soon as I throw on some clothes.

I go through two secretaries guarding the ADA's office line before he picks up.

"Hi, this is Chris Fox, returning your call."

"Of course, Mr. Fox, how are you doing?"

I doubt he cares, and I don't want small talk; I want him to tell me about the case. "Almost as good as new. What's going on?"

"Well," he says, "a few things, really."

I want to yank his tongue out of his mouth and scrape the words off of it. "Okay?"

"The charges against Mr. Gallagher are going to be greatly reduced, from aggravated to simple assault."

I'm not sure if I want to vomit or break something, and it takes a lot of effort to choke out, "Why is that?"

"A few reasons," he says slowly, like he's savoring the words, and did this moron actually pass the bar or just spend all of law school getting drunk in one? "His attorney has made a compelling argument, and I don't think I'd win at trial. Unfortunately, the DA doesn't like prosecuting cases he can't win, and this is beginning to look like one of them."

I'm grinding my teeth again because I never did buy that fucking mouth guard. "How so?"

"There have been some pretty serious accusations."

Focusing on the oxygen shunting in and out of my lungs, I try to control my tone. "Such as?"

That must be his desk chair creaking in the background, as if he's reclining in his seat. Shouldn't he be pissed at this development? Shouldn't he be at least half as angry as I am? The district attorneys on TV would be. "You're aware of the restraining order a Miss Serena Archer has taken out against you?"

"Of course I am. I sent in my response, but I couldn't make the actual hearing because I was still laid up after being beaten by her boyfriend. It's bullshit—she only applied for it after Derek was arrested, and it was probably only granted because I wasn't present in court."

"I can't speak with any certainty on that front, but Mr. Gallagher's attorney has collected statements from the doctors who cared for you in the ER. They allege that the injury to your left eye was older than the rest, that it appeared as though a decent chunk of time had passed between that one and the others."

"That isn't what happened."

"And then there's the matter of the CCTV footage outside Miss Archer's workplace, where she claims you came to see her after the assault took place. You didn't appear to be in dire straits the way you were when you turned up in the ER later that night."

"Shock and adrenaline," I say. "I didn't start to feel the full brunt of it until later."

He's silent for a few seconds but for more creaking, as if he's now sitting up straight at his desk. "Mr. Fox, only you and the defendant know what actually happened, but his story is looking more plausible. His comes with witness statements and persuasive evidence, and yours comes down to what is essentially just your word, which is not looking very reliable at this time."

"So I'm a liar, then? That's what you're saying?"

He doesn't answer that.

"He gets to dance out of a courtroom with hardly a slap on the wrist, and I get to be labeled a liar?"

"Mr. Gallagher admits to causing the injury to your eye and will be taking a plea for simple assault, which will result in six months of unmonitored probation and a five-hundred-dollar fine."

"So he can buy his way out of a charge he completely earned because he's got an expensive attorney?" Embers flicker through my veins, and I'm surprised I'm not breathing smoke. "That's justice, huh?"

"It is." Dead air stretches on between us for a moment that feels like an hour, until he says, "Thank you for returning my call so promptly. Have a good rest of the morning."

I don't have a good rest of the morning.

I can't work; I'm just thinking of you, but then you bleed into my ex's face—angry, pinched, snapping at me. My fingers are tense, and you used to massage my hands sometimes, dig your thumbs into my palms until all the stiffness melted away, but then that always made other kinds of stiffness occur. How long has it been since I've touched you? You wouldn't let me even if you were here; you're still mad about the cameras. Why am I constantly besieged by angry women? Did I kick Buddha's cat in a past life or something? None of you know what you want or what you actually need. Not a single fucking one of you.

Even Lisa, my boss's secretary, snaps at me for having the gall to leave a fucking message, and you all have me surrounded.

I add some sugar to my voice and tell that cunt "Thank you *very* much" and throw my phone across my desk.

I'm supposed to be troubleshooting code, but my mind is a four-way intersection in which every driver wants to be first, and you're gone and my grandfather is dead and what are you doing right now, this second? I hate it but I love you and I might hate you a little, too, and I never knew I could feel so much, Serena; look at what you've done to me. If you were here, I'd kiss you like I used to, deep and slow, harder and harder, until my hands found your throat. I'd stop myself in time, of course, but I think my thumb would sink into that hollow spot where your pulse pounds.

◆ ◆ ◆

Amanda hasn't fucked off.

I step out of my house this afternoon to find a flyer taped to my front door. I snatch it off and shake it out beneath the threatening purple clouds swirling in the sky, and there's Emily gazing up at me beneath the words **DO YOU HAVE ANY INFORMATION ABOUT MY DEATH?** in bold, forty-point font. I hate looking at Emily for long stretches; it makes me feel queasy, like I need to hold on to something to keep myself steady.

I'm not a monster; I'm not proud of what I had to do, but I don't have a time machine, and I can't bring you back, Emily.

There's another on the windshield of my car, held down by the wiper. My gaze wanders down my quiet street, and then my heart falters and lodges itself behind my Adam's apple because Amanda didn't just gift me with these flyers; she posted them on every door on the block, on every car in sight.

I tell myself to relax because they're just a bunch of flyers; flyers never hurt anyone. My name isn't anywhere on these things. Even Amanda wouldn't be that bold. She actually likes her job, wouldn't risk it just to stick it to me one last time. *This is a last-ditch effort,* I tell myself as I collect yesterday's mail and find yet another flyer. When I'm back inside, I throw all three of them away.

Fuck you, Amanda. Get a fucking life, stop wasting all this paper.

I want to tell her how lucky she is, hiding behind that badge, because that is the only reason she's not face down in the dirt. You can't off a cop without making the rest of them extra mad, and I'm not stupid enough to kill one who's got a well-known hard-on for me. You're going to have to do better than that if you want to rattle me, Amanda.

I park myself back at my desk.

I accidentally drink too much coffee, and soon I'm shaking like a withdrawing crack addict, my caffeinated fingers trembling as they fly across my keyboard. I work so quickly that before long I don't even have inane emails to answer, so my thoughts drift to you, Serena, like they're wont to do. You won't be at your house this late, so there's no reason to listen to your faucet leak. Derek's already come and gone within the span of a couple of days, back in Mississippi for another round of shows, so I know you're alone in his house.

I pull up his Instagram just to read the comments his slutty fans have left, but there's no way anybody could comment lewdly on his newest post unless they're a special kind of freak because it's of a fucking fetus. There's a caption—*Coming in July!*—and your name is blacked out at the top of the sonogram like he's ashamed to admit he impregnated you, Serena.

My throat clogs again, and I can't decipher the finer subtleties of my emotions; all I know is that they're dry-drowning me and I can't remember how to breathe.

I'm furious—this is *my* child that asshole is claiming.

I'm bereft—this should be us, Serena, announcing this news as a unit—I'm numb, dazed, like my brain has been anesthetized.

That overcaffeinated tremor has turned into an earthquake; I'm splitting open down my fault lines, and all these *things* are tumbling out, charred and scary angry things I can't name, and this is *wrong*, Serena, all kinds of wrong.

I can't believe you'd let him post something this private; what the fuck were you thinking. What the fuck am *I* thinking: of course *you* weren't thinking because you never think, do you; I've always had to do all that for the both of us.

That is *my* child, not his, and you're *mine*, not his, and I don't care how confused all these pregnancy hormones have made you, this is fucking bullshit.

You need a goddamn wake-up call, and I can be your reckoner.

42

I've been thinking about what our relationship would look like in a physical form, and I think I've finally got it. It's a skeletal resurrected shipwreck, rising up through black water, seaweed clinging to the mast, holes eaten through the sails, the mermaid figurehead gaunt, with dead eyes.

It's a fucking mess, Serena, but it's got good bones. You can see what it used to be if you slap off the barnacles and squint through those algae-crusted portholes. We'll say it used to be a pirate ship; I think you'd appreciate that. It gives us a kind of darkly sexy history.

It's Friday, it's *our* day, and I've been here since Thursday just in case. She changed her locks and added extras to her windows, but she's forgotten that I know her and I know this house, and do you remember who installed that fucking high-tech dog door, Serena? It's massive on account of how large Sirius is and comes equipped with an override password in the event the sensor on the matching dog collar acts up or the PIN is forgotten. She has the numeric code, which I'm sure she's changed since our demise, but I have the overriding password, and I've never felt the need to tell her as much.

Her kitchen faucet isn't plinking anymore, and I've WD-40'd all the hinges on the doors, and it's been boring here, but I've tried to keep myself occupied. I removed the bug I planted outside the kitchen window a hundred years ago; I won't need it anymore and the battery was going to die anyway since I hadn't charged it lately.

I can't watch the sunrise from your deck because it's hidden behind a roiling mess of black and violet, a congealed-blood sky, and this hurricane is supposed to make landfall any day now, but it's wily, keeps changing course and returning to hover over us mischievously. They're calling it Hurricane Chase, and that might be a good name if we have a son; how much did I have to *chase* you, Serena? Our love story was certainly not an easy one. But *everything important takes work*, right?

How long will you make me wait for you? Last time you were here, you told Cole you'd be coming "after school," but that was when you thought he would be coming too, and you're a morning person, Serena—you like to wake up and get things done.

It's another four hours before I hear her Land Rover trundle down the dirt road and into her driveway. She won't see my car; it's parked a half mile down the road and around the corner, where I used to park when I'd watch over her from the brush behind her fence.

My heart picks up now, *beatbeatbeating* in anticipation, and I slide into the hallway closet where she keeps her mops and brooms. It opens and closes noiselessly, thanks to my application of WD-40, and she must be taking so long to come inside because she's brought a ton of supplies.

I wish I could lug them in for her, but this needs to be a surprise so she can't drive off on me. She shouldn't be lifting paint cans and fucking tarps, but I guess I'm the only one who cares about shit like that because here she is, alone, easing through the side door.

I hear the metal clink of a paint can hitting the tile, and my heart isn't so much a beat now as a humming that buzzes in my ears, and how long has it been since I've been this close to you, Serena?

She leaves again, probably to get her second load, and when she returns, she closes the door, turns the lock, sighs heavily. Her boots click. She flicks on the lights.

I see yellow creeping through the gap beneath the door of my closet, and when she takes a few steps past the door, I ease it open silently and step out.

I don't wait for her to whirl around.

My arm is snared around her throat in a (loose, palliative) headlock in a second, my other hand mashed against her lips, and she thrashes against my chest until she hears my voice; it must soothe her the way her voice soothes me, because all the fight drains out of her.

"I need you not to scream, okay?" I'm not worried about anybody hearing you, but I need you calm, I need you to embody the meaning of your name and be serene for me right now, sweetheart.

She nods.

"I want to let you go, but you need to promise you won't scream."

She nods again.

"You promise?" I wait until she nods a third time and release her slowly.

She has nowhere to go; she's backed herself into a corner; her only nearby exit is her empty bedroom, and she can't climb out those windows with their fancy new locks.

"What are you doing, Chris?" you say, and finally I have a good look at you.

Your hair is completely blond now, an icy blond, cold as frost, and it makes your cheekbones knife sharp, your arctic-blue eyes like snowed-in windows. You're you but not you, and is the you that ever loved me still in there somewhere?

You don't look like you're pregnant under that coat you're wearing; it's like your body is rejecting the baby, refusing to acknowledge anything has changed, and there's a ring on your finger that I didn't put there, and what the fuck is going on, Serena?

"I needed to see you. We need to talk about us."

I want to cut off your finger and get rid of that diamond, but I take a deep breath because I need to be calm. One of us has to be.

The red imprint my hand left on your mouth is slowly fading, but I see fear creeping into your eyes, filling you up, and you have no reason to be afraid of me so long as you listen.

"You look different," I offer as an icebreaker. "Your hair."

She stares at me for a moment, chewing the inside of her cheek. "Do you like it?"

"It'll take some getting used to, but you're still beautiful."

She doesn't say thank you, but she never says thank you when I tell her that.

"When did that happen?" I point at the ring.

She twists her arm behind her back like she's trying to hide what I've already seen. "Night before last."

"Is that what you want?"

Her throat bobs and her eyelashes flutter, and she takes a step back as I take a step forward.

You're looking at me like I'm an axe murderer or a meteor falling from the sky, like I'm something you should run from. I'm not a monster, Serena. I haven't brought a gun. I don't *want* to hurt you, and I hope you won't make me.

"I . . . I don't know what I want."

Your pregnancy hormones and mood swings have bamboozled you, Serena. That's not your fault; it's mine. "Let's simplify things, then. We can leave all this shit behind, take off somewhere new and start over, just us."

I don't want to stay here, Serena, trapped in a toxic fog of suspicion from fucking Amanda, choking on all these bad memories. I don't usually love change, but that's all I want now, the new and unfamiliar, somewhere that reminds me of nothing, a blank canvas where we can paint something else entirely.

The only old thing I want to keep is you.

"You want me to leave my life and my son to run off somewhere with you?"

"Cole is almost an adult. He's not going to need you much longer. He won't want to leave his school and his friends. He'd be mad if you made him." I don't mention that Cole is part of the "old" and thus not a part of my plan.

I'm not going to drag a pissy teenager along with us, Serena; it would only slow us down. You'd spend attention that belongs to me on him and ruin what we have.

I picture us in a cabin in the mountains somewhere, no neighbors—you'd like that—nobody for miles. I could still work from home, and you wouldn't have to work at all; there'd be no need, I'd take care of you.

I'd take care of it all.

Everything you'd need would be right there, and you'd never even have to leave the house.

"I never stopped loving you, Serena, not even during the hard times."

"I know." I wait for her to tell me she loves me back—she loves me back, right?—and her eyes flicker between both of mine as she swallows hard. "I love you too."

I back you completely into that corner so you can't squirm away, and kiss you for the first time in I don't know how many months, and it's a different kind of kiss, Serena: it has fangs and talons, and your tongue is so sharp I think you're going to draw blood.

Your new blond hair is twisting through my fingers, and at first I think I'm going to faint with relief, but then I think I'm going to faint with fucking pain because your knee impales my groin and you're screaming like a banshee.

Nobody is going to hear you; you live in the middle of nowhere. The *only* thing I asked was for you not to scream.

I struggle to my feet, with my balls stuffed somewhere in the region of my stomach, and you haven't gotten far, just an arm-snatch away, but you're still screaming like I've stabbed you, like *you're* the one in fucking pain here.

I take a step toward her as a rectangular patch of purple—the dog door—blooms across the tile, and now I can't go anywhere because the hallway is full of growling dog, and Sirius is there between us, huge and hairy and horrifying, head bowed, black lips drawn back and quivering.

"Get the fuck out of here, Chris," she's yelling, and her voice is a shade calmer now but still trimmed in panic. "I won't call him off. I swear to God, I won't call him off."

"Serena, I love you," I say, and I must, because you just kneed me in the fucking balls and still all I want to do is take you in my arms and kiss you.

"You never loved me," she shouts, and the louder she gets, the louder Sirius snarls. "You just wanted to keep me as a pet. You wanted to train and discipline me as necessary, and that's not fucking *love*, Chris."

"If I didn't love you, I wouldn't be here. If I didn't love you, I wouldn't have forgiven you over and over for all the fucked-up things you've done—"

"*I've* done?" You look deranged, Serena. You look like you're about to stomp your feet like a three-year-old. "You're so fucking delusional."

"And you're a fucking liar. How many *I love you*s did you fake the entire time we were together?"

"Chris." Her volume comes down a few notches as she gives me a look that's either pitying or disgusted. "All the love in the *world* couldn't fill your empty spaces."

Sirius is getting closer, and I think he's forgotten that I once fed him an entire two-pound pack of raw stew meat, so I show him my palms as an act of submission and shush him like an infant.

"He's never liked you, Chris. Get the fuck out of here or he'll tear you apart."

I don't want to hurt him and I don't want to hurt you, but you're not giving me much choice. I slip my hand behind my back, groping at the waistband of my jeans, and come back with a knife.

Your eyes are huge, darting from me to the blade, and you call for Sirius, who ignores the fuck out of you.

"Sirius, come!" You're screaming for him, and he's snarling at me, and all I can think is How the hell did we wind up here, Serena?

I want to sit you down and force you to watch a slideshow of how our relationship used to be.

All Because of You

I want to zip-tie your wrists together and walk you through the house, pointing out where our memories were made.

The kitchen island—that's *ours*, Serena. I sat at that table and "helped" your son with his science midterm assignment; remember we laughed about how I earned an A on that project? Your room, where we made a baby and plenty more memories. I'd lay on your bed and watch you unravel after we got home from dates, how you'd ease your heels off your feet, shake the pins from your hair, slide off your dress; that was my favorite erotic ritual, and I never told you that because I didn't want you to think I was creepy.

I'm not creepy, I just love you. Everything you do leaves me spellbound.

"Sirius!"

He doesn't know or care what a knife is; he's not afraid of what it can do the way you are, but he listens this time. Kind of. He inches closer to you backward, but his eyes are still on mine, and his growling still fills the place as you back into the side door and grope for the lock.

Your hands shake, but you manage to open it, and the outside pours inside through the storm door.

"Sirius, come on." She's got the storm door open and one foot on the stoop, and Sirius finally turns tail and follows her out.

The sky is screaming and the wind is whipping, and you're pregnant, Serena; you can't run that fast.

The damp ground is sucking at the heels of your boots and slowing you down. Sirius could easily outstrip you, but he doesn't; he flings his heaving, heavy body in front of you as you stumble and fumble with the handle of the Land Rover's driver's side door.

I'm not pregnant so I'm fast, much faster than you, but you had a head start and you've made it behind the wheel.

You're screaming for Sirius again, but your voice gets blown away by the wind, and he won't listen, he won't stop snarling as your engine turns over, growling just like your dog.

"Sirius, COME!"

I'm a heartbeat away from your door, and Sirius is between us, and I guess he's tired of all this dicking around because he lunges as fast as the flash of lightning I catch in my peripherals.

He knocks me backward into the dirt, and his fangs sink into my abdomen and then my forearm, and his teeth are red when he pulls back to go for my throat.

I feel blood and pain burbling and gushing up from where he's torn into me, and I didn't want to do this, Serena, but I stab him.

Sirius yelps and you yelp, too, and scream for him again, and it's a fucking DOG, Serena; I can't believe you're wailing like an Italian widow over an animal.

He turns and lurches toward the Land Rover, quicker than I thought he'd be but unsteady on his paws, and he leaps over her and into the passenger seat, blood spilling everywhere.

Her face is glazed with tears as she peels out of the driveway and swerves off, one hand on the wheel and the other on her phone.

43

I don't think women like hearing shit like this, but you're so predictable, Serena.

I know what you're going to do before you do it, and here you are at the goddamn vet instead of the police department. It wasn't easy to run that half mile back to my car; it feels like half my guts are hanging out of my body, but the thought of you helped me press forward, and I made it, I'm here, and so is your car.

You won't recognize my Volvo, and I pull it into a space behind an animal trailer and your haphazardly parked Land Rover. You parked like you're a cop or something, diagonally in a clear don't-give-a-fuck angle.

I don't know how long you've been here or whether you've called the police yet, but if Sirius is gravely injured, he's going to need surgery, which could take hours. You're not going to wait in the lobby the whole time, not after our fight, not if you called the cops; they'll be wanting to speak to you.

You'll walk out of the vet any second now, so I tighten the sweater I'm using as a tourniquet around my belly wound and wait.

I'm right but I'm wrong; it's more like five minutes. She sinks to her haunches as soon as she's outside, her face in her hands. Her shoulders shudder, and an ugly flush crawls up her neck, and it would be nice, wouldn't it, if she were as worried about *my* injuries as she is about Sirius's. Here I am with a mangled arm and protruding guts, and all she does is cry over a *dog*.

"Come on, babe," I mutter, feeling my teeth grind together. Go back to your car. You can't stand out here with a storm churning over your head; the sky is going to open up any second now.

Slowly you stop shivering and stand, digging through your pockets, and yes, good girl, it's your keys you're searching for as you head right toward me.

You hit the unlock button on the remote and make to open the door, but I'm right behind you with my arm around your neck and my lips on your ear.

"Remember what I said about the screaming," I caution, but I feel one building in her throat, vibrating against my forearm. I squeeze tighter, dragging her behind the Land Rover, and slam her up against the back windshield.

She's fighting me, kick kick kick, and scrabbling at the backs of my hands, but I'm wearing thick leather gloves so she can't scratch me, and the harder I squeeze her lovely white throat, the bigger her eyes grow, the more desperately they swivel around, but there's nobody out here to save her.

This vet is off the beaten path, located on a literal farm, and sure, I guess the cows and horses are watching, but they don't seem to care.

I'm good at this; I know how much pressure to apply and for how long, and in ten seconds she's out, slumped in my arms. I hold her against me for a bit—I can't help it; I like having her in my arms—and then carry her back to my car.

She has to be awake by now, but she's not banging around and screaming; I'd hear her even over the radio. I'm glad she's docile, that she's realized this is all for the best, but doubt creeps in as the minutes stretch on in silence.

She's not dead, right? I didn't choke her that hard; she should have been out no longer than five minutes, just enough time for me to tape her wrists and ankles together and settle her into the trunk. My breathing accelerates as a cold sweat pearls at my hairline, and my arm fucking kills, and there's a tingling in my gut that feels ominous.

She's not dead and I'm being paranoid, but I drive a little faster all the same. When we're finally here, I enter the gate code the Airbnb host gave me, fly down the winding driveway, enter another code, and ease the Volvo into the garage.

She's not dead and I'm clammy and breathless when I launch myself out of the car, then hit the button by the staircase to lower the garage door.

It takes ten seconds to close completely and seal out the staticky air promising one hell of a storm, and I open the trunk.

She's not dead, I knew it, but I'm flooded with relief as she blinks up at me. I had to tape her mouth shut in the interest of caution, but her eyes aren't wet, there's no snot smeared over her face.

You look pretty calm and snug in there, Serena. You're not going to fight me anymore, I can tell, and I try to remove the silver strip over your lips gently, but I must not succeed, because you flinch and turn away.

There's a mustache of red raised skin above her mouth, and I smooth blond hair off her face, petting her like a cat. "Are you okay?"

"What do you think?"

I cut the binds from her wrists and ankles and ease her out of the trunk, balling the wad of duct tape into my pocket. "I'm sorry if it was uncomfortable. I was just being safe."

"Safe," she echoes dully, and she stands there wearing a bemused expression while I vacuum out the trunk with a Shop-Vac I found in the corner and remove the filter container.

I take her hand and lead her up the short garage staircase and into the house. We make it through a darkened hallway and into the kitchen, and Serena stops dead, her eyes on the counter.

Red roses and baby's breath explode out of a vase beside an ice bucket, and this Sub-Zero kitchen is straight out of *Good Housekeeping*, white marble and glittering subway tile and chrome accents. Once the shock wears off, she'll tell me how perfect it is, how happy she is to be here.

"I can't have champagne," she says, staring at the dripping bottle inside the bucket.

I set the Shop-Vac filter on the counter. "It's not champagne, it's sparkling cider."

A laugh that isn't really a laugh gets stuck in her throat. *Ha.* One sharp syllable, one sharp glance at me. "You think of everything."

I flick on the light switch, igniting the chandelier over our heads, and this is a fancy house—it's an estate on a compound, Serena; it's got a fucking chandelier in the kitchen. Ice-white light shatters from its many bulbs over my grandmother's ring when I take her hand in mine again.

She stiffens as she looks down at her fingers. "Where—"

"I got rid of it."

She doesn't say anything because she knows who she belongs to and it isn't Derek. She's not even curious enough to ask what I've done with his ring.

I press her against me, my face buried in her hair, and it doesn't smell like I remember; she's changed her shampoo, but so what, she's still here, her warm body in my arms, our child reposing in the swell of her stomach.

"What is this place?"

"Our honeymoon," I say, and her shocked eyes make me laugh. "Well, not exactly a *honeymoon*, I'd take us somewhere better for that. It's the honeymoon before the honeymoon. I wanted to celebrate—we're together now."

That fight was a bad one, Serena, but what better place to make up than this fancy fucking house? You're looking at me like you think I'm a fool, but I'm only a fool for you, and you pick up the butter-soft white card resting against the vase.

"Bill?" Her eyebrow arches. "Isn't that your grandfather's name?"

"I booked the reservation under his name." And paid with his account. We need "us" time, Serena; I don't want to be interrupted. You probably called the police in all that confusion, and they're probably looking for you, for us, but they're not going to run any searches under my grandfather's name.

We'll be gone by the time they even think to do so.

You're so calm, Serena—did you take a Klonopin or something? I expected to have to do a bit more soothing, expected you to force me to use zip ties and rope.

You're such a girl, and you ask me where your purse is; you say you need your ChapStick and your vitamins and your cell phone.

"I left your purse in your car."

"Did you turn my phone off?"

What the fuck does that matter? "I didn't touch it. I'm not going back to get it, if that's what you're asking."

"Well, can I use your phone then?"

"I left mine at my house." I have a throwaway cell, but I'm not going to tell you that.

"I need to call the vet. I need to call Cole. Is there a phone here?"

There's no phone here, and you don't need to call anybody; the only person you need to be talking to is me. "No phones. We don't need distractions right now."

"But I *need* to call the vet," you insist, and your voice wobbles. "If you love me so much, why won't you let me check on my dog?"

I don't want you to cry, so I pet your hair some more. "How is Sirius? What did they tell you?"

"Do you even care?"

"Of course I care. I didn't want to hurt him, but I didn't have a choice, he wouldn't lay off."

"He wouldn't have attacked you if you hadn't been trying to hurt me," you say, and sure, that's one way to look at it, but I never would have *hurt* you, Serena, not really; I would not have done anything lethal or permanent.

All you had to do was listen. You could have been calm. You could have sat down and had a conversation. This is on you, really. Sirius would be fine if you hadn't thrown a fucking fit.

I don't want to fight with her, so I grab the bottle of cider and the flutes beside the bucket. She flinches at the popping of the cork but lets me wind her fingers around the stem of the flute after I pour her some cider.

"I love you," I say, clinking the rim of my flute against yours, but it doesn't seem like you believe me, Serena; you're looking at me like I'm the fine print at the bottom of a ten-page legal contract, like you're trying to suss out my loopholes.

"It's over," I say, and I know you hear the finality in my tone, I know you read it in my eyes. No more arguments, no more excuses, no more *I need to call the vet*; that's done, you're going to choose me now, and we're going to be fucking happy. "All that bad stuff is in the past now. We can start over, clean slate. I'm never going to leave you."

Your gaze doesn't waver from mine as you toss that fake champagne down your throat, and you don't look completely convinced, but that's okay, Serena—you've never been easy, and I have the rest of my life to convince you.

◆ ◆ ◆

She keeps trying to get me to leave the house, and it's kind of amusing. First she needs her prenatal vitamins, then she needs purple Powerade Zero because she feels like she's dehydrated and water won't cut it, then she needs heartburn medicine because the baby's giving her acid reflux. She's testing me, trying to see if I'll leave her. She didn't believe me when I told her I'd never leave her again.

"Serena, I'm not going anywhere." I say it like I mean it now, like I'm done with her games. "I need you to relax."

The grounds are huge, sprawling, green, and lush, and there's a firepit set into the stonework on the patio floor, where I burn the contents of the Shop-Vac filter container and the duct tape I'd used on her wrists and ankles.

She shifts restlessly beside me, flames reflected in her eyes, as the duct tape curls and smokes and disappears. The sky is black—midnight in the afternoon—and it rips open, and here's that storm they've been promising us for days, Serena; Chase is finally here, and he's loud—angry-god loud, Zeus throwing a bitch-fit loud.

I lead her back through the French patio doors and start our tour of this expensive house I rented just for her, pointing out the three sitting rooms and six bedrooms we won't use. She doesn't say much until we arrive at the master, and then she doesn't even want to cross its threshold.

I sweep her off her feet like she's a bride, despite the abject fucking agony it causes my belly wound, and carry her in there just to up the romance factor. Standing in the middle of the room, I revolve on the spot so she won't miss a thing. I look like the end of some Shakespearean tragedy when I catch sight of myself in the mirror above the dresser.

"It's massive, isn't it?" I turn my back on our ghosts watching us from the mirror. "I can't imagine getting to live in a house like this."

"It's not like you live in a dump, Chris. Your house is plenty nice."

I figure a little honesty might soften her up. "I only bought that house because you were selling it."

A deep wrinkle appears between her brows, and thoughts churn behind her eyes as she twists the silver chain around her neck. "Your grandfather wasn't wrong about the grocery store, was he?"

"Hmm?"

"It wasn't a coincidence that we met again at the house viewing."

You should be flattered, Serena. Not many women can say they're loved so completely. "I've told you before, it was love at first sight."

I set her on the bed, and my guts sigh with relief. I think that's another gush of blood pulsing against the bandages I wrapped thickly around my stomach. She scuttles back against the embankment of pillows at the headboard, leaving a good five feet between us, and I'm okay with that for now; she can maintain her perimeter if it makes her feel better.

Her gaze scrapes the vaulted ceiling—it's so high above our heads, it's almost like we're stuck at the bottom of a well—dips down to the fireplace, and dashes to the left toward the windows spanning floor to ceiling, giving us a view of the fifteen-acre grounds. It's raining so hard out there, it looks like we're underwater, inside a submarine estate.

"What do you think?" I ask, because she's uncharacteristically quiet.

"It's nice."

"Why don't I believe that?" I know when you're holding back, sweetheart. I know you so well.

She looks like she's debating whether or not she should lie. "It *is* nice," she finally says. "It's objectively nice, but places like this aren't real, they're just a fantasy. You brought me here because you want to sell me on whatever illusion you've built up in your head, and all the fireplaces and stonework and vaulted ceilings in the world wouldn't distract me from that."

I'm starting to get annoyed, my temper smarting like the wounds her savage beast inflicted on me.

We're here because you led me into this dark, lonely place full of fun house mirrors and lies, and you're going to make it up to me, Serena. I'm not blameless, but at least I've tried to rectify my mistakes.

Her eyes keep probing the windows, her fingers at the chain around her throat. "You should get those bites looked at, Chris. They're going to get infected. You might need stitches. Don't they hurt?"

"I'm fine for now," I say, and I hope I'm not lying.

"You're pale, sweaty. Are you sure you're okay?"

"I love you for your concern, but I'm fine."

She thinks I'm lying, but she doesn't press the issue, blinking down at her hands. "How long was I out?"

"Not long. Five, ten minutes."

"Where is this place?"

I feel my nostrils flaring, a smile curving one corner of my lips, and I shake my head.

"Who the fuck am I going to tell? You won't let me use a phone." Her temper flashes red, and she belts her arms across her chest, but the color drains from her cheeks when I move closer.

"It's too warm in here." I try to help her out of her coat, but she's reluctant to remove herself from its folds.

"I'm fine. I'm actually a little cold."

"Then I'll light the fireplace."

She relents, and I toss the jacket across the room, where it lands on the couch by the windows. I was right; her body hasn't changed much despite the pregnancy. Her limbs are still slender, but her breasts strain against that thin clingy sweater, swelling over the neckline, the pendant of her necklace lost in her cleavage.

I pull it out by the spindly silver chain, and it swings back and forth like a hypnotist's clock, but I don't want her getting very, very sleepy, so I let it puddle into the dip in her throat, where it glints up at me, platinum and diamonds wreathed into the shape of a heart.

"Is this new?" I tap her little silver heart and watch it bounce. "It doesn't seem like your style."

"Cole got it for me."

I lean down to kiss her lips, but she jerks away and all I catch is her jaw.

I get it; you're still jumpy, so I stroke your hair to calm you down. Your pulse pounds against my lips on your neck, and you struggle to draw breath, and your body isn't responding to my mouth like it used to. I tell you to relax, but you don't. I say I love you, and you ignore it. I kiss the rim of your ear the way you like, and nothing.

"What's wrong with you?" You flinch at the sharpness of my tone, so I try my best to soften it. "Why are you acting like this?"

"You stab my dog and kidnap me and won't let me call the vet or my kid, and now you're mad I don't want to kiss you? Are you fucking kidding me?"

I did not *kidnap* you; I brought you here to reconnect. I did not stab your fucking dog; I defended myself.

I rented this enormous fucking *estate* to show you how much I love you, and you're beginning to piss me off, Serena; a little goddamn appreciation would be nice.

I grab your chin and force you to look at me, your neck cracking and popping with the strain. I tell you I love you; you tell me I'm sick. I tell you I want you; you tell me you'd rather be celibate for another eight years. I tell you I need you; you tell me I need a fucking caseworker.

I tell you you're making me angry; you say, "So what else is new."

The rain is loud, and the fire crackles, dyeing her red and orange and yellow. I give her one more chance because I love her and I don't want to do this.

"Serena, I—"

"If you tell me you love me one more time, I'm going to jump out that goddamn window."

I don't say anything because that's exactly what I was going to say and you can finish my sentences. This is what chemistry is, Serena. Love has been going out of business for years.

People settle, people choose themselves, people flock to Tinder and OkCupid, get divorces with disturbing rapidity, shed partners like epithelial cells. After all we've been through, all the hurdles, I'm still here, and you're still here, and we are all that matters. You're never going to find someone else who loves you as completely as I do, and I think you know that, because it's as clear as the expensive vodka you used to buy that we were meant for each other.

We don't need words, Serena, we can say entire paragraphs with our glances. We're exchanging tomes right now, and I think it's getting difficult for you to maintain your hard line because your brow is unfurrowing and it looks like you're about to cry.

"I know you're mad," I say gently, "and people say mean things when they're mad. I won't hold any of that against you, but I need you to choose me now. To recommit. I've been patient, I've given you space and time to come around, but I need you to say it. You loved me once; I know you remember. I'm still that guy."

And I *am* still him, perfect, the best guy you've ever dated. That's all you have to say, Serena. Your emotions went temporarily haywire because of the baby, and you didn't mean any of it. We can get back to where we were; it might take some work, but *everything important takes work.*

"Don't you remember why you loved me?"

You say nothing, and I have to prod, let you know I'm not being rhetorical.

"I remember."

You're being difficult again, a stubborn little girl. It makes me smile, which perplexes you, and I finger comb your hair and tell you to list the ways.

"I . . . you were good looking. You treated me well; you were nice to Cole. You made me feel like I was important to you. You made me laugh; you were sweet; it felt like you loved me."

Her words soothe the ragged edges of my anger like a salve. "See? We can get back there, but you need to say you're choosing me so we can put all this behind us."

"But that was all a lie. None of that was you. This is what you are." She flings a hand at my chest, and I catch it by the wrist and press a kiss into her fingers. "I didn't see it at first, but now I do, and there's no unseeing it."

"That's your decision, then?"

She straightens up against the mounds of pillows, gingerly placing a hand on my shoulder. "Chris, I don't know what's wrong with you. I don't know what happened to make you like this. I wish I could fix it, but I can't."

There's nothing fucking wrong with me, and it's your fault anyway; you did all this. I was getting along fine before you came around.

You're on thin ice now, and maybe you realize it; you swallow hard when my hand slides up the side of your throat, massaging it, and you're staring up at me, and I'm staring down at you, and I wish it could be different, Serena, but I gave you a chance.

This will hurt me more than it hurts you. You won't have but a few seconds of pain. Mine will be permanent.

You're crying, but they're not huge shuddering sobs, just one silent tear streaking down your sharp cheekbone, and you say I'm not going to kill you, that I wouldn't kill the baby.

I tell you the baby isn't worth much without you, and you say I can have you, too, then; you'll do whatever I want if it means I won't hurt the baby, but I don't believe you anymore.

I still love you, but you're a proven liar, Serena, so why should I believe you now? You made your choice, and it wasn't me, so thrash all you want. We both know I'm stronger than you.

I squeeze the spot that knocks you out cold in ten seconds because I don't want you to be in pain.

You don't need to suffer; you just need to die.

This isn't my first time, but I feel like an insecure virgin. I keep losing my nerve; my resolve crumbles, and I loosen my grip. I think of my grandfather—*no quitting, Chris*—and I try again, like I really mean it this time.

I squeeze for thirty seconds and then stop because I can't do it. I hate myself, and then I remember what she said, and I squeeze even harder, even longer.

I hate you for making me do such terrible things, but I love you, and I don't think I can do this.

My eyes sting. I can't even remember the last time I cried, but I am now. I never wanted any of this, but I've been out of my mind since we met, off kilter and dizzy in the storm of your changing moods.

You lure me in and throw me out, and I'm trying to remember how chest compressions work as I rip the pillows out from behind your head to lay you flat against the mattress.

The compressions are futile; the rescue breaths I fill your precious lungs with don't take, but I'm not a fucking quitter, Serena, so I go through the routine a few more times.

And yet you remain lifeless and still just to spite me.

I'm panting, propped up on my hands watching her, but there's nothing to see; she's the worst corpse I ever made, and we were supposed to get married, she was going to be having my baby, and now it's dying inside of her, and I want to tear my heart out because I obviously won't need it anymore.

She's dead, and I'm bleeding love all over the place; it's drenching me in cold sweat, and I think I need to throw up, but I can't do that in front of you, can't puke all over your deathbed.

How did I never appreciate what a miracle you were, all smiles and glittering eyes and beating heart?

My face is in my hands when something nudges my knee. Her toes, stirring feebly in their striped fuzzy socks, and now she's gasping and her eyes are opening and she's croaking my name, and it's the most beautiful sound in the world, my name on her tongue.

I scramble back toward her and crush her into my chest.

"I'm sorry," I tell her, and I don't know how many times I repeat it. Both her hands circle my forearm and she's clutching me, breathing like she's nearing the end of a finish line, and I guess it's true what they say—you never really know what you have until it's gone, and I almost lost you, Serena.

Your breathing steadies, and some life creeps back into your cheeks, but your lips are still tinged blue. You're trying to swallow, but I can tell it's hurting you, and I've never hated myself more than I do right now.

I tell you I love you, and you tell me you're cold, and the stupid website said there were complimentary bathrobes, so I fling the master bathroom open and grope for the light switch. I flip all three of them in my haste, so the loud fucking fan whirs to life, and the robes are on a hook on the far wall. They're huge and fleecy, and I help you into yours like your limbs are made of glass. When I prop you up against the pillows, your hands go to your belly.

I kiss her temple and then her cheek and then her lips and she's kissing me back, clinging to me, vulnerable, desperate. It's like our first kiss but better, and her eyelashes are dripping on mine as her tears come in earnest, and I hate myself for doing it, but I have to admit that maybe it was all for the best; maybe it took a near-death experience to change her mind about me.

She breaks away to catch her breath but leaves her damp forehead on mine. I slide my hands around her neck and she balks, but she doesn't have to worry about that anymore; I'll never do it again.

I look down into her eyes so I can see her but not really, and I tell her I love her and hope she remembers all the other times I've done that, when she could feel how much I meant it, just like she told Rosa that one time in her kitchen.

She's wearing a timid glimmer of a smile, and she's so close her mouth brushes mine when she says, "You remembered that?"

"How could I forget?"

Her lips meet mine again, but I don't get a chance to enjoy it because the room explodes with a screaming voice and a pointed gun.

44

Serena looks like she's going to faint right here in my arms.

I shush her, tell it's okay, all she's got to do is tell this harpy there's been some kind of mistake, but for all the good it does, I might not have said anything at all. Amanda screams at me to put my hands up, to move away from Serena, to drop whatever weapon I might be holding, but the only thing I'm holding is her.

Babe, just tell her the truth, I say, my lips against her ear as I hold her fast against me.

Sweetheart, she thinks I've hurt you or something, you need to calm down and tell her you're fine, I say, as Amanda shrieks yet again.

Serena, she's going to arrest me if you don't set her straight, I say, as she tries to jerk away from me.

But you don't hear me, and Amanda is telling me to shut the fuck up for God's sake, and I get that your hormones are all over the place, Serena, but this is putting me in a kind of awkward position. I know sometimes the baby turns your moods into a pendulum and your mind into a trap, but now I'm going to have to spend hours in a police station to get this all ironed out.

I take your chin tenderly into my hand, hoping some of my calm will leach into you. You still take my breath away, Serena, even when there's a gun trained on me.

"Get away from her, Chris. I'm not going to tell you again. Are you okay? Are you hurt?"

And now I'm soundly confused that she cares about my welfare, but when I look up at Amanda, she's looking at Serena, who is doing her best imitation of a slippery bar of soap.

"Does she look hurt?" I ask, as the love of my life tries to kick me in the shins. "I would never hurt her."

Amanda laughs unkindly, like she's just watched me trip and fall. An elbow lands in my gut where I've been savaged by Sirius, and it's all I can do not to double over.

But you don't get very far. You have slender little wrists, Serena—birdlike, childlike, easy to yank, easier to snap—and my hand closes around your delicate bones to tug you back where you belong.

I think it's your wrist breaking, at first, that sound. I worry that I've hurt you. You look so horrified I think I must have, but your hands find your mouth, and now you're staring at my chest.

The room rings and spins, and I stagger backward and sink to the edge of the bed.

The gun smokes as Amanda lowers it, and I am numb and then hot, and I think she had the decency to use the kind of bullets that stay intact once they're fired, because the pain I'm expecting doesn't come, never comes.

"Come here," Amanda's saying, and she sounds almost angry, like she wants to shake you senseless. "By the time Derek called me to say you'd never checked in, the police had already found your car; what the fuck was it doing at the vet?"

"He stabbed Sirius," Serena says helplessly. "They say he'll be fine after a surgery. I told 911 where I was going, what happened; I was about to call you when he found me in the parking lot—"

"Serena," I say thickly, a hand clapped to my chest. "Why—"

"Don't you fucking speak to her," Amanda snaps, grappling for her cell phone.

Serena hooks a shaky finger around the chain and lifts up her little silver heart. "It has a GPS locator in it. I thought I was being paranoid, but here we are."

All Because of You

You preyed on my love, and you know me so well. You knew I wouldn't be able to let you go.

"Is he going to die?" you ask Amanda, but she's busy yapping on the phone now, so you whirl back to face me, your eyes full of tears.

You look so worried I wish I could get up and comfort you, but there's a ringing in my ears and a gathering darkness gnawing at the edges of my vision, and I try to tell you I love you, but all that comes out of my mouth is blood.

We were it from the start through the stop, Serena, and nobody can take that away. You were my beginning and my end, my ruin and my inspiration. There may be bruises and bits of blood clinging to the pages of our story, but the most poignant thing is how vividly I love you.

But you're afraid of my love, and Derek is simpler. He asks for nothing, and I need all of you. The two of you are from two different planets. Your atmospheres don't blend, but he's easy and I'm not, so you're taking the comfortable route.

You need me gone so you can fully commit to this sham, but I can see in your eyes that you wish it were different.

This moment is the only eternity we will ever have. Derek had better take care of you. I can't see my spirit moving on, so I'll have a lot of time to haunt him if need be.

If love is insanity, then throw me into a padded cell in hell, because I'm fucking crazy, I'll admit it. It started in the unreal glitter of that grocery store, and it ended with a bullet. In a just world, she'd probably have to answer for this too. I didn't ask for it. I didn't ask to be pulled apart nerve by nerve, suspended in her incandescent abyss.

I did it all because of her, and I don't regret a second.

AUTHOR'S NOTE

RESOURCES

- NATIONAL DOMESTIC VIOLENCE HOTLINE: 1-800-799-7233
- *Why Does He Do That?* by Lundy Bancroft

I think we all know by now that not all abuse is physical, but I've heard this a lot, and I feel it bears repeating: Once you feel the need to say *I know he'd never hit me or anything*, there's a problem (and someone doesn't have to beat the shit out of you to harm you or make you feel unsafe).

Your Chris might take on a different form than mine, but the root of his problem is control and the fact that he thinks he gets to have it over you.

If he ever touches you in anger, know that he will do it again, and he'll feel less sorry about it each time.

NOBODY IS THAT BEAUTIFUL. He is not über jealous because you're gorgeous (you are); he is possessive and insecure. Those are not things you can fix or love out of him, and it could be a dangerous folly to try. A good man will not make his own insecurity your problem to solve. A good man will not dump his personal baggage at your door and say "Here, sort this out for me while I control your life with ruthless efficiency."

If he says his exes cheated on him and that's why he's such a controlling asshat, he's probably lying. If his parents were mean to him, it's still not an excuse to mistreat, monitor, and control you. (A lot of us had mean parents, but we're still limping along okay.) If his ex-wife is a vicious harpy who made him this way, I'd be wondering what the ex-wife has to say about his general disposition (and surprise! Pretty soon YOU will be cast in the vicious-harpy role to the next unsuspecting woman who comes along).

Call a domestic violence hotline. Speak to a sympathetic, trained professional who can help you make a plan.

ACKNOWLEDGMENTS

Deb, I never thought when I asked a stranger to read a manuscript that she'd be a friend years later. Thank you for your endless patience and encouragement. You're always the first person I turn to when I need a reader or have good news to share.

To my agent, Rachel, thank you for taking a chance on a character as deplorable as Chris and fielding all sorts of strange and random emails from me. Even when it was looking dark and I'd put this novel in the rearview mirror, you never gave up hope.

To Jessica, my editor, for giving Chris (and me!) the time of day. And a big thank-you to my other editor, Angela, for those patient Zoom calls and dealing with my preciousness over such a personal book.

I don't know how any of you put up with me, I really don't.

ABOUT THE AUTHOR

Lissa Lovik lives far away from the hustle and bustle of city life, surrounded by nature and a herd of fluffy malamutes. *All Because of You* is the author's first novel.